OPENING THE
FRONTIER

OPENING THE FRONTIER

SPENCER AND SON

PATRICK LINDSAY

WOLFPACK
PUBLISHING
— EST 2013 —

Opening the Frontier: Spencer and Sons
Paperback Edition
Copyright © 2024 (As Revised) Patrick Lindsay

Wolfpack Publishing
1707 E. Diana Street
Tampa, FL 33610

wolfpackpublishing.com

Paperback ISBN 978-1-63977-541-5
eBook ISBN 978-1-63977-540-8

OPENING THE FRONTIER

SPENCE

PROLOGUE

I sat on my back porch in the early evening, feeling a little chilly as the sun was setting, taking a rare moment to look out at the cattle grazing on my ranch. It had been a long, hard road to get to this place in my life. And, I had to admit, life hadn't turned out exactly as I'd planned. It can be that way when you're on your own at age nineteen. Still, I reminded myself, I'm only thirty-seven years old. I hoped for an easier life going forward.

My name is Clay Spencer, but folks just call me Spence. I started out in Missouri when I was a boy, then moved to Texas with my dad. I wound up in Denver for a while, ran into some trouble and moved out to California and Nevada. I came to Montana with the Alder Gulch gold rush and had some more trouble. It seemed like trouble really followed me around for a while. I had started this ranch about ten years ago with my partner, Buck, and things had gotten better. Well, I told myself, things had settled down. I couldn't say I was exactly where I wanted to be in life.

I got up and moved inside to the kitchen, searching for something to drink. I stopped and stared at my reflection in the window. Once in a while, a pretty lady might flirt with me a little and ask why a handsome man like me never got married. I don't know about the handsome part. I'm about six foot one, one hundred ninety pounds and dark-haired. I have a few scars from some fights I got into when I was younger, and I've been creased by a bullet a couple times. I blush a little when somebody calls me handsome, and I never answer the question about not getting married. That story is way too complicated.

I moved back out to the porch and returned my attention to my herd. I had started with about one hundred head, maybe ten years ago. They were mostly longhorns from Texas when I'd started, but I had mixed them with other breeds as I could—breeds that carried a little more beef. I had sold some along the way, and had lost some to hard winters and predators, and I was thinking I could use a couple good young bulls and some younger cows right now. I just didn't know where to get them. That was the problem.

I heard footsteps coming around the corner of the house and turned to see Buck coming up the steps. He flopped into a chair and stared at me, a sarcastic grin on his face. "You plan on doing any work today?" He chuckled and leaned back, clearly pleased with himself.

I flopped into the other chair and snorted in his direction. "I got more work done by noon today," I informed him, "than your old bones got done all day."

He levered himself out of the chair and went to the door, no doubt planning to search for some food in the kitchen. I wished him luck with that. "I'll agree that my bones are old," he said over his shoulder, "but I ain't gonna agree about how much work you done today." With that, he disappeared inside.

I grinned and shook my head. Buck and I had been partners for almost fifteen years now, and I don't know what I would have done without him. Life hadn't really settled down and taken a turn for the better until I'd met him. I could talk to him about building up the herd another day. We would figure it out.

I stood up and walked over to the railing, thinking back to the time I'd met Buck and the spot he'd pulled me out of. How, I wondered, did life get so messed up sometimes? Can a man ever leave behind all the tough times in his past? My hand strayed down to the Colt .45 I wore on my hip. It seemed like a part of me now, though I'd never needed this new gun to defend myself. I'd owned a couple before this one, though, and I couldn't say that about those guns. I hadn't thought about those days for a while, but as I stared out over my land, my mind wandered, going back almost twenty years...

Chapter 1

Denver City

April 1859

I stood outside the saloon doors, collar pulled up against the wind blowing down off the mountains. I wasn't too sure it was a good idea to go in, but sometimes a man gets thirsty. I wavered for a moment, staring at the sign above the doors. It read: "Mountain Boys Saloon." Smaller letters underneath proclaimed this town to be Denver City.

It was that second sign that threw me a little. I had known this place as Montana City when I'd come last summer. I had drifted in, working my way north and west from Texas by way of Missouri, lured by the news of a gold strike along the South Platte river. It had taken little to convince me to come up here. My pa had come to Texas from Missouri, looking to stake out a ranch for us just south of the Red River after my mom had died. He'd had no luck, and my heart was never in it.

If it wasn't the cows dying, it was grasshoppers eating up all the crops. Pa stayed with it for a couple years, but after a while, I could see he was ready to call it quits. Last spring, he had sold off the two cows we had left, had given me a little money, and headed back for Missouri. I could have gone with him, but at age eighteen, I had decided I could go my own way. I have done some hard living and made a couple decisions that didn't seem to work out too well in the years since. A man has to grow up fast when he's living on his own.

A noise behind me startled me, and my hand dropped to the Colt Navy pistol I had tucked into my waistband. I relaxed only a little when two guys pushed past me and went into the saloon. I removed my hand from the Navy Colt, checked around me for the troublemakers who'd been following me around for the last couple days, then went on into the saloon.

I made my way over to the long wooden bar at the side and slid onto a stool, keeping one foot on the floor after the stool wobbled badly when I sat down. A guy came down along the bar, taking orders. He paused in front of me, one eyebrow in the air, saying nothing.

"Whiskey," I said. I didn't like whiskey yet, but I figured I would get the hang of it if I kept trying.

He nodded and moved along. I cast a glance sideways at the other people along the bar, then swept the room with a glance. None of the people who'd been following me seemed to be in here.

"Here ya go." He slapped the whiskey down on the bar.

I looked up in surprise as that voice had been a lot higher pitched than I'd expected. He half-turned, then stopped, giving me a hard stare. I shrugged and concentrated on my whiskey. I had enough trouble without starting something with the bartender.

I intended to take my time with the whiskey. I didn't have a lot of money, for starters, and I needed to be sober when I left here. I leaned forward and took a sip, feeling the Navy Colt press against my stomach as I did so. I moved it slightly to the side, remembering when my pa had given it to me.

We'd been standing outside the house. Pa had the wagon loaded with the few things he wanted to take back to Missouri. I'd been holding the reins to the best horse we had left, and the two Pa had hitched to the wagon would not take him much farther than back to the old homestead in Missouri. He'd reached into the wagon and lifted the Navy Colt out from under a blanket. He handed the pistol and a box of ammunition to me.

"I don't expect I'll be needing this back home," he'd said. He patted me awkwardly on the shoulder. "I taught you how to use that. Don't never point it at nobody if you don't intend to shoot. Don't shoot 'cept to defend yoreself." He paused, searching for more words, but didn't seem to find any.

It was the last time I had seen him. I'd had about forty dollars to my name, and I knew of a neighbor who planned to drive about fifty cows to market in Sedalia, Missouri. He'd told me I could buy a few cows of my own and drift them with his. He'd said we could get a lot more money for them in Sedalia.

He was right about selling them for more in Sedalia, but we hadn't counted on something called Texas Cattle Fever, and we hadn't known how many folks would hate us for bringing in Texas cows. We'd sold the cows without too much trouble, and I had a hundred dollars in my pocket, which seemed like a fortune to me. Trouble had come shortly after that.

A couple local boys, probably about my age, had stopped me in the street. They had told me they were going to take my money to pay for their cows *after the Texas fever killed them.* One of them pulled a gun, but I shot him before he could get me.

The sheriff had come out of the saloon when the shots were fired. The one I'd shot was lying in the street, and I could see the sheriff had in mind to string me up for it, me being the stranger and all. Luckily, there were four or five people in the street who had seen the whole thing, and the sheriff had no choice but to let me go. He turned me loose and said if he ever saw me again, he would shoot first and ask questions later. It had seemed like a good time to come out to Colorado.

The warmth and the whiskey were making me a little drowsy. It had been a long and tiring day, and I didn't want to go home...I was afraid of what kind of reception I would get at home. On the other hand, I didn't want to stay here too long at the saloon. If I stayed here too long, one of the guys who wanted to rob me might come in and find me here, and I didn't have any friends in this town. I could expect only the worst. I weighed my choices in my head and ordered one more whiskey.

I had come west after the incident in Missouri. They'd found gold here in Colorado. Folks lately had been calling it the Pike's Peak gold rush. I had drifted from Sedalia up to Kansas City, Missouri, and it hadn't taken me long to find some folks coming out to Colorado. I had joined in with them and arrived last summer.

I knew nothing about gold mining, but I had my Navy Colt and got myself an Enfield rifle, and I got a job guarding shipments from the gold mines to the bank here in town. I'd made a few enemies, but I had kept the gold safe. There were usually at least a couple of us guarding the gold. The routes were full of highwaymen looking to rob the shipments, but they were mostly looking for the easy money. Nobody enjoyed looking down the barrel of a couple rifles.

It hadn't taken me long to figure out there was more money in finding gold myself than there was in guarding shipments. After I'd built up a little money, I got myself some equipment and starting panning for gold in spots along Cherry Creek. I'd had a little luck, too. I had some money buried by the trees in back of the place I'd rented. About two hundred dollars in gold coins were out there, and lately, it was looking more and more like it would come in handy.

There were three of them that had been stalking me when I had come back to town from my gold panning. I knew they'd followed me on the last couple trips. I didn't know any names and didn't care to know them. There was a dark-haired, thickly built hulk of a guy that seemed to be the leader. Another one was thin-shouldered and balding and always seemed to have a pistol on him he looked eager to use. The third was a blond kid, maybe my age. He seemed more like a scout. The other two did the dirty work, was my guess.

I had seen them hanging around on the trip before last. I had packed up suddenly and got the jump on them that time. Today, they had been a little more careful, trying to stay out of sight, but I had seen them up in the hills, watching me. They left when they saw me packing up, but I had taken a different route, circling around and coming up behind them where they lay in wait for me.

I had pumped a few shots down there, not trying to hit them, because word along the camps was that these guys were tied in with the county sheriff. I didn't need to get arrested, so I had put a few shots in there uncomfortably close. I wouldn't be surprised if one or two of them had cuts on their faces from the rock chips flying. That had allowed me to get back to town safely, but now they would be after me with a vengeance. And I knew I couldn't expect any help from the sheriff.

As a matter of fact, I would have left town before now if it weren't for Annie. I shifted uncomfortably on my barstool at the memory of meeting her. I hadn't been here for over six weeks when I'd walked into a tent saloon—one of several springing up in Aurora, what with all the folks coming in looking for gold.

I'd walked in and heard what sounded like an angel singing in that saloon. I had to allow for the fact that I'd not seen many women since coming out with the gold rush crowd, but when I'd looked around to see who was singing, I was done for as soon as I saw her. Blond hair, beautiful face, and she could really sing. I decided right then I would marry her.

And I had. Married her, I mean. I hung around that

saloon every night for two months, like a stray dog some-body had fed and couldn't get rid of. I kept coming around, buying her drinks and talking to her. The other guys hung around, too, but maybe I wore her down. I asked her to marry me and she finally said yes.

Things went downhill from there mighty fast. Maybe if my momma had lived, she could have warned me to slow down and get to know this girl better. Anyway, it wasn't long after we'd married that she just seemed unhappy all the time, in particla' unhappy with me. I found an old house—well, maybe more like a shack, but I could pay for it every month and we had it to ourselves. She quit singing in the saloons and I busted my neck trying to make money for us.

Nothing seemed to be enough for her, though. We argued more than we talked, and she kept talking about going to California. Two weeks ago, I found out she'd been singing in the saloons again, and I had a feeling she was saving that money to leave me. This morning, I'd had a funny feeling when I left I wouldn't be seeing her again. Maybe that was why I was still sitting on this barstool. I was afraid to find out.

———

A movement at the edge of my vision caught my attention. I glanced in that direction and froze where I was. Another quick glance told me that my first guess was right—it was the kid that acted as a scout for those other two who'd been following me. I pulled my hat down lower and hunched over the bar, hoping to get out before he could tell the others I was in here. I could feel his eyes on me. I picked up move-ment again from the corner of my eye. When I looked around, he had scuttled out of the room. Reminded me of a beetle. Time to move.

I slipped out the saloon doors and paused by the entrance, looking for them out in the street. I saw nobody. My hand strayed to the Navy Colt in my waistband. I didn't need to check it—I knew I had loaded the powder and ball into all six cylinders. I glanced to my right. My horse Cisco was at the rail. I didn't want to stray too far from him if I could help it.

I stepped out into the street and they came out from a side alley, maybe three buildings down. It was the heavy, dark-haired one and the taller, balding one. They were spreading out, coming at me from both sides of the street. I knew the second one was more dangerous. He would pull a gun on you while the other one was still talking. I couldn't see the blond kid who had scouted for them in the saloon.

"Hey!" It was the heavy, dark-haired one, moving toward me.

There was more movement on my right, and I shifted my gaze in time to see the taller one pulling his gun from his pocket. My reaction was fast, and it was automatic. I pulled the Navy Colt from my waistband, eared back the hammer and fired. He staggered backward and went to his knees, trying to lift his gun. I cocked the hammer, holding the gun up slightly like I'd been taught, and fired again. He dropped the gun and collapsed into the street.

I turned back toward the one on my left. He had frozen when the firing started. He stared at his buddy, laying face down in the street, then turned to look at me. I could see his mouth opening and closing, but he wasn't saying anything now. I lifted the gun in his direction, and he turned and ran back into the alley he had come from.

I could hear them scrambling toward the door, back there in the saloon, and I knew I had to get out of here. If I got arrested, they would hang me, I was sure of that. I jumped toward Cisco and reached out to take the reins when there was the sound of another shot and I felt a burning pain across my side. I stepped into the stirrup and pulled myself aboard, moaning at the sudden surge of pain along my ribs.

I kicked Cisco hard, and he leaped forward. I heard a noise from a side alley as I raced down the street. It was coming from the other side of the street—across from where the dark-haired guy had disappeared. I figured it was the blond kid, shooting from ambush. I fired a shot down the ally as I galloped past and heard a strangled cry. Then I was gone, disappearing down the road as they spilled out of the saloon behind me.

I had to get to the shack before they came looking for me. I would not waste time trying to cover my trail right now. I took the trail straight to the house, feeling the blood seeping through my shirt as I slid off of Cisco. I didn't bother to knock—I burst through the door. If she was home, she should know it was me, anyway.

"Annie!" My shout seemed to echo in my ears as I ran into the room. It didn't take more than a few seconds to know that she had left me. Her clothes, personal items, and travel bag were all gone. There was no note.

None of it surprised me, but it hurt me all the same. I grabbed some rags and tied them around my middle to stop the blood trickling from the wound. I could see he had only grazed me with that shot. Still stung something awful, I thought. I grabbed a little food from the pantry, then trotted outside, grabbed a shovel, and went to the spot in the woods out back where I had buried my money. I dug it up, ignoring the pain in my side.

Only fifteen minutes later, I was back on Cisco. I turned him down into the creek behind the house and splashed through the water for close to an hour, I figured. Finally, I pulled Cisco out into the woods and tied him to a tree limb. I went back and used a tree branch to pull dirt over my tracks, then I kneeled at the creek and splashed water on my wound to clean it. I went back to where I had tied Cisco, laid down beside a fallen log, and pulled a blanket over my head. Despite everything that had happened, I fell asleep quickly.

———

I awoke to the sound of a jay squawking above me and was surprised when I opened my eyes to full sunlight. I lay quietly where I was, listening to the surrounding silence. When I was convinced that I was alone, I rose, led Cisco to the creek to drink, then came back and made a quick breakfast of biscuits and jerky.

I mounted Cisco and guided him back down into the creek. When we had followed the creek for about a half hour, we came back up into the woods and followed along the creek from the cover of the woods for another hour. When we came to a trail that I knew would take us north, we struck the trail and kept moving. There was nothing for me in Colorado anymore.

CHAPTER 2

ALDER GULCH

ALDER GULCH, MONTANA—1866

I walked around the mules carefully, inspecting hooves and mouths, shying away quickly when I spotted a pair of laid back ears here and there. There were ten mules here, and I needed eight for the business I had in mind, but I could only see six I was willing to buy.

I glanced up at the guy who owned the mules. He had followed me around, saying nothing. That included not warning me when any of them looked likely to bite me. I'd heard he had been around for a while, even before the gold strike in Alder Gulch. He looked maybe fifty-something to me, and those eyes had seen a lot, I could tell. I guess he figured I could take care of myself around the mules, and if I didn't know how, I'd better learn soon. I stepped back and looked them over one more time. I looked back at the mule trader.

"What'd you say your name is?" I asked him.

He pushed his hat back on his thinning blond hair and looked at me with some amusement. "Buck," he said simply. He looked away, shifted the piece of straw he had in his mouth and looked back at me. "You're the gunman, ain't ya?"

I whirled around to look at him, sure the surprise was written all over my face. "I'm not a gunman," I said firmly. I held his eyes. "I'm not a gunman," I repeated.

He took a step back and held up a hand is if to back me off. "I didn't mean nuthin' by it, pard," he said soothingly. His eyes dropped to my 1860 Colt, nestled down into my open holster. "That Sonny, he had it comin'. Everybody knew that. He'd been robbin' miners and stealing stuff around here for months. Nobody gonna miss him."

I forced myself to calm down. I had killed four men now and put a bullet into at least two others. Those two might have died, too, for all I knew. I was only twenty-six years old, and I hadn't ever wanted that kind of trouble. From Missouri to Denver to California and the Comstock Lode in Nevada, I had only tried to hold on to what I had rightfully earned. I defended myself with guns as a last resort. I stared at the scars on my knuckles. I'd used my fists a few times, too, I reflected. I'd never figured life would be this tough.

Buck reached out and put a calming hand on my shoulder. "I'm sure you just done what you had to. Nobody gonna miss that Sonny, like I said. Just that nobody around here ever saw a gun come out that fast. Drilled him dead-center through the heart, too." He dropped his hand, saw I didn't like where he was going with this, and changed direction. He pointed out at the mules. "You see some you like?" he asked.

I pulled myself back together. "I like six of them," I said. "I need eight."

It was Buck's turn to look surprised. "Eight mules?" he said, a little incredulous. He seemed about to ask me why I needed that many, then reconsidered. "I've got two more," he drawled. "They're my best ones, though. They ain't never been for sale."

I decided Buck wasn't a bad sort and decided it wouldn't hurt to tell him what I had in mind. "I've done a lot of panning," I said, "Here, and...various places. Made a little money, but I figured maybe I'm in the wrong business. I've done a lot of panning for a little gold, and I've spent a lot of time and trouble keeping robbers and thieves from taking it from me. Done some work for other people protecting gold. Maybe I've had it all wrong. Maybe what I need to do is go into business for myself." I pointed at the mules. "Hauling stuff. Equipment, food, gold, whatever. Everybody and his brother are out there trying to find gold. Maybe I'll make money hauling stuff for them."

He stared at me, then a small grin spread across his face. He nodded. "Smart," was all he said.

I pointed back at the mules. "How much do they cost?" I asked bluntly.

He shifted the straw in his mouth. "That'll depend on which six you like."

I walked around and tapped the six I wanted. "These six," I said. "I can find two more. How much for these six?"

He chuckled. "You shore 'nuff picked the best six" he acknowledged. "They cost the most, though. Those six would cost one hunnert seventy-five apiece."

I did the math in my head and winced. That would take most of the money I had. I still had to buy some supplies and keep food on the table until I got the business started. I shook my head slowly and walked away.

"Hold on," Buck said. He walked around to look me in the eye. "I got another proposal." He paused and thought it over for a second. "How 'bout this? I ain't known you long, but I like what I see. You got sand. You got a good idea, too. An' I think mebbe you could use a partner." He paused to let that sink in. "You buy four mules for one hunnert fifty each, and I supply the other four. An' we'll be partners."

I let that idea roll around in my head for a while. "Partners," I repeated.

Buck nodded his head. "You can save some money and we can help each other. I know all the trails around here. Might help keep you out of trouble, too. Whaddya say?" He extended his hand.

I slowly reached out my hand and shook his. "Partners," I agreed.

———————

I sat outside the little lean-to I called home these days. I'd found a little cave near the Beaverhead River, where I worked my claims. It seemed like a pretty out-of-the-way spot, so I'd built a lean-to outside the cave and moved my few possessions in. Nobody had bothered me here. I wasn't even too sure anybody else knew about it, and that's the way I liked it.

I had a small fire going, and I'd made myself some dinner. Now I huddled by the fire, enjoying the warmth, but not looking into the fire. I kept my gaze focused off into the distance, where I could barely make out the shape of the Bitterroot Mountains. My short, hard life had taught me that a man has to stay ready, and firelight makes it harder to see in the poor light.

I had come north to Montana when I first left Denver City, but my mind couldn't rest easy about Annie and where she had gone. California had been my next stop after a year in Montana. I had gone to San Francisco, where I'd heard Annie saying she wanted to go, but I didn't find her there and didn't find any clues about where else she might have gone. After eight miserable months in San Francisco, I had followed the crowd to the Comstock Lode silver strike in Nevada. Over five years later, I had done okay for myself, but I hadn't really prospered, and my mind wouldn't let go of the idea of finding Annie. I couldn't stop wondering if she might have changed her mind about me.

There were some men who'd gotten rich at the Comstock strike, that was for sure. Mostly, though, it seemed to be the ones who had gotten there first, or the ones who came with money and established a big claim with mining operations. I'd had my choice of panning for myself or swinging a pick in a tunnel in another man's claim. I had chosen the panning, then after a while I had hired out to guard the miners pulling out with their money. I had backed down some robbers and done my job, and put up a little stake with some panning in the streams. I had practiced with my Colt and also learned some prize fighting skills from a man who had done some fighting back east.

After five years, I was ready to move on. I wanted to go back to San Francisco and see if I could find Annie. I didn't think I would be a target for anybody. I didn't think I had enough money to draw any interest on my way out, but I had underestimated what greedy men will do. Plus, I had stopped a few of them from robberies they had planned in the past. I guess greed and revenge are a pretty powerful combination.

I was working my way through the Six Mile Canyon when two guys stepped out into the trail in front of me. They hadn't bothered with bandannas—they knew me, and I knew them. And I knew they didn't plan to leave me alive. They both had a rifle out and generally pointed in my direction, but they were a little too confident I would go down without a fight.

They told me to put my hands up in the air, and I moved like I was going to do that, but after I dropped the reins and lifted my left hand, I pulled the Colt with my right and dropped one of them. I kicked Cisco in the ribs, and he jumped forward, but the second guy got off a shot that hit me in the side. I rode straight into him and knocked him over. When he grabbed his rifle and tried to stand, I put a shot into him. The second man was dead, I was sure. I didn't know about the first, but I didn't hang around to find out.

I was losing blood and feeling weak. I got to the nearest town, where a doc patched me up and told me to stay out of the saddle for several weeks. I found a room in a boarding house where I could stay. Four weeks later, I had dropped the idea of looking for Annie. I threw my things in a duffel bag, took my small stake from my five years of work, and came to Montana.

A slight noise to my left startled me. I reached out, picked up a chunk of wood and threw it on the fire, then grabbed the Colt in one smooth motion.

A voice came out of the darkness. It took me a moment to place it—the tone was familiar. "Easy does it, pard. I'm peaceful. Comin' in with my hands up where you can see 'em."

I relaxed and put the Colt back down by my side. Buck came in slowly, with his hands in the air as he'd promised. He sat down, making a little moaning noise as he did, and glanced wryly at me as he stretched his hands out to the fire. "Pretty slick with that Colt. Remind me not to make no sudden moves around you. I don't need no extra holes in me."

I chuckled and leaned back. I realized I hadn't laughed in a long time. I pointed at a pot sitting near the fire. "There's coffee in there," I said. "It's not very good, but it's coffee."

Buck shook his head slowly, then reached for the pot. "Well," he observed, "honesty is a good thing in a partner." He reached for an old tin cup, filled it up, then tasted it. He grimaced slightly. "Yep, you're honest," he agreed.

A thought struck me suddenly. "How did you know to find me here?" I demanded. "I've seen nobody else around here."

Buck finished the cup of coffee. He scowled with each sip he took, but he finished it, then grinned wryly. "I know most everything that goes on around here," he observed. "Not much I don't know about Alder Gulch. Yore secret spot here is safe with me. Ain't gonna tell nobody."

It wasn't much of an answer, but I let it pass. I found I believed him when he said he wouldn't talk about this place. I wasn't sure why, but I was beginning to trust him.

He switched subjects abruptly. "You been givin' it much thought how you're going to run this here mule train bidness?" he asked. "Cause I got some ideas about it."

I reached for the coffeepot. I was used to this stuff. My

stomach had run up the white flag years ago. I waved my arms in the air. "I'm listening, partner."

Buck belched slightly and leaned back against a rock. "The way I see it," he said, "is we work out of Virginia City." I looked up in surprise. "Virginia City, here in Montana," he clarified. "Folks come there first, gen'rally, looking for the gold fields. We meet 'em and offer to haul their equipment and whatever other stuff they brought, and we take 'em out to Alder Gulch. We don't offer no tips about where to look for gold or nothin' like that. We don't want 'em taking a shot at us later if they don't find no gold. And"—here he waved a finger in the air for emphasis—"We just come back to Virginny City with nothin'. We don't haul nothing back unless we can make a lot of money for that trip."

I looked at him in confusion for a moment, then it dawned on me. "If the mules have nothing on them, they'll know we're not carrying gold. Not likely to get the robbers after us as long as we don't carry gold."

A pleased smile spread across Buck's face. "You catch on quick," he allowed. "I knowed you was smart." He stood slowly and stretched. "How 'bout we start in two days? I can meet you in Virginia City in two days with the mules—the four you bought, and I'll bring four more. Then we look for folks wanting to come to the gold fields."

I started to stand up, but he waved me off. "Two days," I agreed. "Virginia City day after tomorrow." Buck nodded and disappeared into the night.

———

Buck was pretty easy to find two days later in Virginia City. He was the only guy with eight mules braying in the middle of Wallace Street. A few shopkeepers came out and glared, along with hollering a few things in Buck's direction, but he cheerfully ignored them.

I rode up slowly, then dismounted and hitched Cisco to the rail. I circled the mules slowly. I had to admit they were in top shape and looked up to the job. Buck watched me circling, clearly proud of his animals.

"Howdy, pard," he boomed. "Ain't these some fine-lookin' mules?"

"They are," I agreed. I looked around at the irritated faces of the merchants, glaring out the shop doors. "Maybe..." I started. Buck shifted impatiently on his feet. "Maybe," I continued, "we don't need all eight for each trip. I'd figured on taking four on each trip and resting the other four each time."

Buck considered that one, then slowly nodded his head in agreement. "Yeah, mebbe that's a good plan," he allowed. He inclined his head toward the far end of the street. "There's a livery stable down at the end of the street where I can board four of 'em". He gathered the ropes and led four of them away. "Back in a second," he said.

I waited for about fifteen minutes, then looked up to see Buck coming back with two men. I observed them as they got closer. Both wore sunburns, I assumed they had gotten recently on the way out here. They wore thin, patched coats —far too thin for the weather they would deal with here. Both also wore excited grins.

Buck steered them over to me. "This here is Jeff," he said, pointing at one of them. "And this one here is Al. They just come here from Illinois. They're wantin' to go to the gold fields with their stuff." He pointed vaguely at a sizable pile of clothes, small pieces of furniture, and various digging tools stacked at the side of the street, about a hundred yards away. He turned back to Jeff and Al. "Ready to go get some gold?" he boomed.

Jeff and Al agreed they were ready to get some gold, and Buck motioned back toward their pile of belongings. "Be right with you boys," he told them cheerfully. He led the mules in that direction, leaning over to mumble in my ear on the way past. "I give 'em two weeks out there," he said.

After much urging from me, Jeff and Al stayed in town

long enough to buy some heavier coats, and we headed for the gold fields.

———

Six months later, business was booming, and we were doing better than we could have imagined. News of the gold strike had traveled widely, and there seemed to be a never-ending supply of newcomers eager to try their luck in Alder Gulch.

Our problem came when a man named Roy approached us in a tent saloon after a long trip, hauling five men and their supplies to the gold fields. A man approached our table and took a seat without being invited. I barely glanced up, which was more than Buck did. When the stranger didn't leave, I just stared at him, waiting.

"My name is Roy," he began nervously, glancing around him. "I have a proposition for you. It's worth twenty-five dollars apiece to you, and you won't have to go out of your way."

Buck stopped eating and looked up at him for the first time. "Go on," he said.

Roy, appearing encouraged, leaned forward. "I've had some luck," he said. "I want to get out of here, but I think I'm being watched by robbers, or road agents, or whatever you call them." Getting no response, he pressed on. "I want to go back to Virginia City. You don't need to take me any farther. I have several bags of gold, but your mules can handle them easily. That's all. Just get me back to Virginia City, and I'll pay you twenty-five apiece."

I exchanged glances with Buck. "Give us a minute," I told him. Roy got up and walked to the corner of the tent, watching us.

"Fifty bucks is a lot," Buck said without preamble. "I could use that money. Maybe we can get a little more out of him." I stared at him doubtfully. "We can leave before it's light in the morning, and I know a route we haven't used," he said. "We said we would do this only if it looks like a great price. Let me work him up to thirty-five apiece."

I didn't have a good feeling, but eventually, Buck persuaded me. He went over to talk to Roy again, then came back to the table. "We've got thirty-five apiece," he said. "We can leave at six in the morning."

I nodded reluctantly, then watched Buck as he walked back over to agree to the deal. A little voice in the back of my head was telling me this was a bad idea. I should have listened to the little voice.

CHAPTER 3

VIRGINIA CITY

There was only a trace of dawn in the sky when we set out at six o'clock the next morning on horseback, with the gold on pack mules. I rode with the reins in one hand and my right hand resting near my holster. I also had my Springfield 1861 rifle in the scabbard, within easy reach. I had trained myself to load and fire it three times in a minute, but I had a feeling I would only get one shot if I needed it. As light spread slowly across the sky, I relaxed just a little.

We moved along a distinct path that followed the banks of the Ruby River. At this hour, we saw no other travelers. I knew this to be about an eleven-mile trip, and by the time the sun climbed in the east, we had put a couple of those miles behind us. Not only had I seen no one else, I had heard nothing besides a couple of bird calls and the creak of saddle leather. I noticed that our customer, Roy, was mopping sweat from his brow despite the chilly morning breezes.

I had taken the lead, with Roy between us and Buck bringing up the rear. I so focused on scanning both sides of the river that it took me by surprise when Buck pulled up on my right. I reined in Cisco and looked at Buck for explanation. He, in turn, motioned Roy to come alongside, then motioned toward a sharp bend in the path ahead.

"Here's the first spot we need to be worried about," he informed me. He pointed again at the bend in the path for emphasis.

I stared at him. "I wasn't aware," I informed him dryly, "that there were any places we needed to be worried about."

Buck stared at his shoes and harrumphed a couple times. "Well," he said eventually, "we are carrying quite a bit of gold." I heard a faint moan from Roy's direction.

"Maybe," I mumbled, "you have a plan for this place we need to be worried about."

Buck brightened noticeably. "Sure do," he said breezily. "Roy and I are going to take to the woods over there." He pointed to the dense trees and brush to our right. "I have ol' Betsy here," he said, lifting a shotgun. "And," he added, "I happen to know that Roy, there, has one too, just in case we need it."

I pulled the Colt from my holster and checked to be sure it was loaded. I did likewise with the rifle. "I guess," I said, "that leaves me out here on the path."

Buck tied the rope from one of the two-pack mules on to my saddle. "Well," he said, "they say you can pull that pistol out of the holster faster'n anything I've ever seen. And we're gonna have you covered all the way."

With that, he pulled his horse and the other mule into the woods and brush at the side of the path. Roy followed. I called Buck's name softly, and he turned at the edge of the trees. "If there's trouble," I told him, "you take out the one on the right first." He nodded and disappeared.

I nudged Cisco forward, my eyes traveling from one side of the path to the other as we approached the bend. As we rounded the corner, three men emerged on foot and spread out to block the path. All three had rifles trained on me. They eyed the pack mule, then looked back at me.

I halted Cisco in the middle of the path and looked them over. They were no-nonsense, hard-bitten characters, all of them. Your typical road agent, in other words. Dressed in buckskins, each of them had a pistol tucked into his belt, besides the rifles. And those rifles were squarely on me. I waited for them to say something.

The one on the right stepped forward. He was the oldest, it looked like. His dark hair was streaked with gray, and he was missing at least a couple teeth. He waved his rifle briefly at the pack mule, then back at me. "We'll be takin' the mule," he snapped. "And yore saddlebags. We don't need no trouble with you."

I held his gaze, my mind racing. "Your trouble isn't with me," I assured him. "Your trouble is over there." I inclined my head toward the trees to my right. I could only hope Buck was in position and ready.

They hesitated a moment, but those rifles didn't waver, at least not at first. Then came the roar of a shotgun from the woods, and it threw the man on the right backward onto the path. His rifle clattered to the ground, and the other two ducked instinctively with the sound of the blast. I had only a moment to react. I kicked my feet out of the stirrups and threw myself sideways off the horse.

My movement got them both going—they swung the rifles and fired at the same moment. I felt a burn across my left shoulder. When I hit the ground, I rolled and came up on my knees. With both rifles empty, they had dropped the rifles and grabbed for their pistols. I fired at the one on my left—a minie ball to the chest is devastating at such close range. He staggered backward and didn't move when he hit the ground.

My heart sunk when I looked to the one in the center— his gun was coming level, and I didn't have time to get off another shot. A slow smile was spreading across his face when a shotgun boomed from the woods again. His rifle discharged harmlessly in the air as he pitched over, and now, all three of them lay dead on the path.

I checked my left shoulder where I could feel the burn from a rifle bullet. There was a slow seep of blood from the wound. I walked several yards to pull a rag from my saddlebag and to calm Cisco. I tore the rag into strips and tied it around my arm to stop the blood.

There was a rustle in the brush, then Buck stepped out onto the path. He was holding a shotgun in each hand. Roy followed a few moments later. Buck glanced at me, then walked over to look at the dead highwaymen. After a moment, he came over to check on me.

"Sorry," he said shortly. "I didn't expect three of them coming after just the three of us. Somebody must have tipped them off." He waited while I finished tying the rag. "Sorry to cut it so close on that third one. Roy wouldn't fire, and I had to pull his shotgun away to shoot the third one."

I let that sink in and cut off the angry words I was starting to say. "OK," I told him. "Next time we need a better plan." I waved at the three corpses in the trail and walked over to look at them. "Except," I said, "maybe there doesn't need to be a next time. Maybe nobody else will come after us."

Buck nodded absently, staring at the face of the first man he had shot. "I'm afraid," he said slowly, "that this isn't the end of our troubles. Actually, we have a bigger problem now."

I looked at the first robber he'd shot, then back at Buck. He said nothing at first, so I just waited him out.

Finally, Buck prodded the robber with his foot. "This one," he said, "works for Henry Plummer." When he saw the blank look on my face, he kicked at a clod of dirt on the path, then looked back over at me. "Henry Plummer," he explained, "is the sheriff over in Bannack. Folks have been speculatin' for a while now that he runs a gang of these highwaymen."

Bannack, I knew, was about a day's ride west of us. I flashed back to the nasty spot I was in back in Denver City and wondered how I'd wound up in the same nasty situation twice. I blew out a miserable breath, then helped Buck drag the dead bodies off the path. If these guys had horses around here somewhere, we would not look for them.

Roy didn't say a word the rest of the way to Virginia City. For that matter, neither Buck nor I had much to say, either. Finally, as we rode into town, Buck leaned over and told me: "I have a plan."

After this morning's plan, I didn't feel any better that Buck had another one.

———

We left Roy outside a tent saloon there in Virginia City. He had paid us fifty dollars apiece instead of thirty-five after the shootout his morning. It didn't make up for what had happened, but I knew we never should have agreed to bring him to town.

Buck and I moved down to the next tent saloon, which wasn't hard to do. There was a different one just about every block in town. Buck bought us a couple beers, and we found a place to sit down. He could tell I didn't want to talk much, so he said nothing until we were working on a second beer apiece.

Finally, I looked up at him. "I don't think we can do what we've been doing anymore," I started. I put down a couple more swallows. "The mules, I mean..." I stared off into the distance. "I'm done fighting a stacked deck, with a sheriff backing the bad guys. I've done that before." I plunked the glass down on the table and said nothing else, just shaking my head.

To my surprise, Buck didn't argue with me. "Yeah." He traced a circle on the table with the tip of his finger. "Henry Plummer is pretty powerful around here. We're probably done for if we stick around here."

I looked up at him glumly. "Thanks for cheering me up, pard. I thought maybe you had some good news for me." I slumped back down in my seat.

"I'm gettin' around to that he said," sounding a little

wounded. "I'm gettin' to it." He looked around for a minute, then leaned in. "Have you heard of Nelson Story?" he asked.

I furrowed my brow for a minute, then remembered where I'd heard the name. "Yes, I've heard of him," I said. "He's one who got rich around here, didn't he? Struck it rich with a claim. Is he still around town?"

"He's still around," Buck agreed. "And yeah, he made a lot of money mining. He heard of a place along Alder Gulch, kinda out of the way, and he worked at that. Like you set out to do, 'ceptin' he struck it rich."

I snorted into my beer, set it down and wiped my mouth off. "I see you haven't got around to cheering me up yet."

Buck waved a hand in the air. "I'm getting' to it," he said again. "The reason I wanted to come here is because Story comes here a lot. An' he's in here tonight. I been watching him over there." He waved a beer glass at the corner of the tent. "I'm gonna' see if he'll come over here and talk to us."

Buck got up and moved to the corner, then came back after a while with a man I assumed to be Nelson Story. I glanced at him sideways as he came to the table. He didn't look to be much older than me—maybe just a couple years older. He had a long beard and looked like somebody who knew how to take care of himself.

Buck introduced us and waved Story into a chair at the table. "Nelson," Buck said, "can you tell Spence here what you're thinkin' about doing. What you told me the other night, I mean."

Story picked up the beer that Buck shoved in front of him and took a couple pulls while he sized me up. He shrugged, put the beer down, and got right to it. "I'm planning to go to Texas and buy some longhorn cattle. A lot of them. I mean, maybe one thousand, maybe even two thousand head. Then I'm going to drive them north and sell them for a lot of money."

This sounded pretty familiar to me. "You going to drive them to Sedalia, Missouri?" I asked.

Story looked a little surprised. "What do you know about driving cows to Sedalia?"

"I've done it," I told him. I went on with the story about driving cows from Texas to Sedalia, and I finished up with the Texas Cattle Fever story.

"Hmmm..." Story stared at the back of the tent for a minute, then gave his beer some attention. "Well," he said, "I'm not for sure I'll sell them in Sedalia. I might go over to Kansas. And if I can't get my price in Kansas, I might drive them clear up here to Montana."

Buck had been leaning back in his chair, and when Story said he might drive the cows to Montana, the chair came back down with a thump. "You never said that the other night," Buck sputtered. "How crazy do you have to be to drive cows from Texas to Montana?"

Story looked at us with a thin smile on his face. "I'm crazy enough to do what it takes to make a lot of money," he assured us. "The question is, are you boys interested? If you've got a little money of your own, you can buy cows cheap in Texas. You could sell 'em for a lot of money up here, or maybe even keep 'em and start a ranch." He looked at me. "You interested?"

I smiled, probably for the first time that day. "Maybe," I said. "I might be just as crazy as you are."

Story looked me over again, then looked at Buck. "What about you?" he asked Buck. "Are you crazy too?"

Buck shook his head, then laughed. "I'm prob'ly too old for this, but yeah, I can be as crazy as you boys. okay."

Story nodded and thought for a second. "I've got to ask you one more question," he said. "Why? You've got a little business going. Why would you sell your mules and come with me?"

Buck and I looked at each other, and he gave me a nod. So, I told the story of what had happened that morning, leaving out nothing. Story listened to all of it, then nodded and stood up. "I just need some people with some backbone, some sand, people who can deal with tough times. I think you boys have it. If you want to come with me, let me know within a week. You can find me in this place most nights." With that, he walked away.

A week later, Buck and I had sold the mules, gathered up our money and our belongings, and rode to Texas with Nelson Story.

———

LIVINGSTON, MONTANA—1877

I stretched out my legs on the back porch, slowly bringing my mind back to the present. Behind me, I could hear Buck mumbling to himself and slamming doors in the kitchen. I grinned a little as I listened to him talking to nobody in particular, wondering why he couldn't find any food in the kitchen. In a minute, I knew he would suggest going to the café in town. That's what we usually wound up doing for dinner.

I could hear some mooing out in the pasture, some of it coming from cows I had brought up from Texas eleven years ago on the drive with Nelson Story. We'd had no luck selling the cows in Missouri or Kansas, and had come on through to Montana, against all odds.

We had taken a long route toward Fort Leavenworth, Kansas, to avoid the Jayhawkers who wanted two dollars per head to cross into Kansas. But first, we had paid ten cents per head to the Indians to drive the cattle through the Nation. The army had told us to stop when we reached Nebraska, on account of Sioux warriors causing trouble. We had evaded the army and come on anyway, fighting the Sioux along the way. I shook my head at the memory. How had we ever gotten through?

Back there in the kitchen, Buck gave out a bellow of disgust about not finding enough food. I knew what was coming next. "Do ya wanna go to the café to get some supper?" came his shout from the kitchen.

I chuckled and walked back into the house, picking up a jacket on the way through. "Let's go," I said.

We saddled up, rode into town, and went into the café, where we got the same food we got most nights. We were just happy to get something we didn't have to cook. While we waited for the food to come, I told Buck what I'd been thinking about for a while.

"I've been thinking," I said, "about how to get some good young cows and a young bull or two for the herd."

Buck nodded absent-mindedly, looking around him for the food. "We've been talking about that for a while," he reminded. "We haven't had a good idea on how to do it yet, though."

"That's what I wanted to tell you," I said. "I think I know how to get some good young stock."

Buck turned around and gave me his attention. "OK, tell me. How you gonna' get some great young stock in here? Nobody around here wants to sell, and the stock we've been seein' ain't that great."

I leaned my elbows on the table and looked him in the eye. "What we do," I said, "is to go down to Denver and buy some there. They come in by rail from Kansas now. Or maybe we have to go to Kansas, bring 'em to Denver by rail, then drive them up here."

Buck's mouth dropped open, and he stared at me absently. "You want to go on another cattle drive," he said flatly. He slumped down on the table and cradled his head in his hands. "I'm too old for this," he mumbled.

CHAPTER 4

SHERRY LEE

S herry set the last batch of rolls for the morning in the oven and leaned back, wiping her brow with a towel. Owning a bakery and café had its advantages, but you had to prepare for the early morning hours and heat that came from working in front of an oven all morning. Still, she had few complaints. Life had started out hard, and she had made the best of it.

She took a few minutes for herself before the customers started coming in. It was still pretty dark outside. Her bakery sat at the corner of Olive Street and Santa Fe Road in Denver. Her one window looked out on Olive Street. She stood and looked out the window, wiping her hands on an apron. A few people were moving up and down the street despite the darkness, their faces reflected in the light from an occasional flickering gas street lamp.

The door opened and closed in the back storeroom, and Sherry turned to look as her assistant, Bess, hustled in, coat still buttoned up against the morning chill. Bess called out her usual cheerful hello as she checked the rolls in the oven.

"Looks good!" she announced.

Sherry smiled as she walked behind the counter and they began preparing sweet rolls, and her specialty, donuts, for the morning crowd. Cowboys and miners couldn't get enough of them.

They chatted as they worked, and Sherry knew she had taken Bess in because she reminded Sherry of herself a few years ago. Sherry had come west with her parents, arriving in Cheyenne, Wyoming, at age eighteen. Her parents, like so many others, lost their lives to typhoid fever on the trail. They had brought Sherry to a family in Cheyenne who cared for her, and she found occasional work over the next three years.

When the railroad line was completed to Denver three years later, in 1871, she had taken all the money she'd been able to save and had come to Denver. Cold and hungry, she had shown up at the door of this bakery at closing time and asked for work. After five years of working and saving, she'd had enough money to buy the business when the owner moved to California. At age twenty-eight now, she felt happy and settled in Denver. It was, she reminded herself, just a little lonely at times.

She smelled the food before Bess set it on the table: unasked, Bess brought her breakfast every morning. She looked down at the table to see eggs and a biscuit on a plate in front of her. Bess placed a steaming cup of coffee beside them, then sat down in the chair across from her. It had become their morning routine.

Bess sipped her coffee and watched as Sherry ate. Sherry knew the oil for the donuts was heating, and they would soon be busy with the morning rush. They kept their conversation light and cheery, focusing on upcoming events in the town and plans for the bakery. Sherry knew they were both a little worried about con men and criminals who had arrived in town. So far, they hadn't troubled her or her bakery.

Chief among the criminals and con men was a recent arrival who went by the name of Soapy Smith. He'd had a con game that involved placing money inside a few bars of soap, then raffling the soap bars off in a bar or on a street corner. Only Smith's confederates could buy the bars with money in them. When the confederates loudly announced there was money in the soap, they sold many other bars at inflated prices to unwary customers.

Still, Sherry reflected, Colorado had been admitted to the union as a state just two years ago, and Denver hoped to become the capital. With those changes, she hoped there would be laws enforced in the town, and that it would be a safe place to continue her business.

A brief burst of wind accompanied the opening and closing of the door, and Bess rose to serve the customer. "It's your reclamation project," she whispered as she passed by.

Sherry knew instantly what Bess was talking about. She turned part-way to watch a young man pass by and walk to the corner. She knew him only as "Luke"—she hadn't been able to get a last name from him. She estimated he was about eighteen years old. He was thin, with old, poorly fitting clothes, and she guessed he was thin because he had little money for food. He reminded Sherry of herself, about seven or eight years ago.

She knew what his order would be, as it was the same every morning. He would have a cup of coffee and a single biscuit. He would linger over it at a table closest to the stove. She suspected he slept in the livery stable down the street. She wondered what he was doing to earn money for the small breakfast he managed to buy in here every day.

Bess served him his usual order, and he retreated to his usual table. Sherry made a decision, then rose and walked around behind the counter. She whispered to Bess to make him a plate of eggs and bacon, along with two more biscuits and another cup of coffee. When they were ready, she walked over and placed them on the table.

Luke's head came up sharply. "I didn't ask for those," he said, staring at Sherry suspiciously.

"I know," Sherry said simply. "I brought them for you because you look hungry."

The suspicion in Luke's eyes deepened. "I don't need your charity," he said gruffly. "I pay for what I eat."

Sherry pulled out a chair and sat down across the table from him. "It doesn't need to be charity," she informed him. "There's a pile of logs and an axe outside that back door over there. You could chop those logs and bring in some firewood for me. You could just put it over there by the stove."

She watched as he fought a mental battle between his pride and his hunger. Finally, the hunger won out.

He reached for the plate she had brought. "Okay, I'll take it if I can work for it." The words were almost drowned out as he shoveled down the food.

Sherry was curious about where he slept. She was hesitant about prying into his situation, but she was a little worried about whether he was at least able to sleep inside a building somewhere. "Do you have a place to stay?" she asked eventually.

There was a defensive edge to his voice, but he jerked his head and pointed to the south. "I sleep in the livery stable. I muck out the stalls," he added quickly. "I do work for him and he lets me stay in there. It's plenty warm," he added, anticipating her next words.

She let that one go, but she wanted to make one more try at learning a little more about him. She waited for him to finish his food, then pushed the second cup of coffee across the table to him. "Do your parents live here in Denver?" she asked as casually as possible.

Luke shook his head, looked past her at the back wall, then finally said, "My mom, she's gone. Last year," he added eventually. He looked down at the table, offering nothing further.

"I'm sorry," Sherry said instantly. She hesitated. "Did she live here in Denver?"

Luke shook his head again. "No, we were from...out west," he said evasively.

Sherry, expecting him to drop the conversation and leave, tried one more question. "And your dad, is he..."

Luke shook his head again and stood up from the table this time. "I don't know my dad," he said, the defensive edge coming back into his voice. "Never met him. I'll...get that wood now," he said, pulling on his coat and walking out the back door.

Sherry walked around behind the counter and joined Bess. They kneaded dough for another batch of rolls.

"What did you find out?" Bess asked.

Sherry shook her head and glanced involuntarily over her shoulder toward the back door. "Well," she said, "it sounds like he's an orphan. His mother died last year, and he doesn't know who his father is. There's something more he doesn't want to tell me about that, I think." She watched as two regular customers approached the front door. "He sleeps in the livery, just like I thought."

Bess nodded and wiped her hands on a rag, moving to serve the customers who had just come in. Sherry shook her head and continued to knead the dough. She would let Luke know before he left. He could earn breakfast every morning by chopping wood if he wanted to. It seemed like a small thing, but it was all she could do for now.

———

Luke stopped outside the bakery door, pulling his collar up against the chilly morning breeze. It was April, but his coat was old and didn't provide the protection he needed in the early mornings and at night. He knew how lucky he was that he hadn't arrived in Denver in the middle of winter without a place to stay.

He walked toward the livery stable where he had an hour or two of work ahead of him, cleaning out the stalls. He was hoping for a better life here, but he knew he had to work for it. His mother had at least taught him that.

As he walked, Luke reflected on the surprise conversation and breakfast back at the bakery. The woman made him nervous, asking the questions she'd asked, and he was by nature on his guard. Still, she seemed to want to help him, and he wasn't going to turn that down, so long as she let him work for it. He would not take a gift because nothing in his life had taught him to accept gifts. His experience was that gifts came with strings attached.

He reached the livery stable, walked past the owner with a nod, and grabbed a shovel. He began to shovel out the stalls. The morning work at the bakery would make three jobs for him every day, but none of them took a lot of time. The livery stable job gave him a place to sleep, and the bakery job would give him breakfast and a warm place to go every morning.

The third job made him a little nervous, but it provided some money. He needed the money in order to rent a room somewhere. Then, he could figure out his next steps. The third job mostly involved working in a saloon in the evenings. He cleaned up and ran a few errands and did some odd-jobs. He knew that the guy who ran the saloon didn't own it, but that was the guy who paid him. His name was Al —that's all Luke knew. Sometimes, he would watch them raffle things off in the saloon. Bars of soap with money in them usually. Luke had a feeling it was crooked, but he minded his own business.

Al had told him there was more money in it for him if Luke did his job well. That was the part that kept him coming back to work at the saloon. If he could earn enough trust doing his job, maybe it was the start of something good for him. Meanwhile, he kept his mouth shut and went about his business.

After about two hours of shoveling and throwing hay in the livery stable, Luke was finished for the morning. A glance at the sun overhead told him it was a little early to report for work at the saloon, but he had nothing else to do. Maybe there was extra work for him today. He left the livery stable, turned left on Olive Street and walked over to the Mother Lode Saloon.

I sat with Buck in the kitchen, looking at the maps. We had to decide the route for a trip to Denver. We agreed that we would go down to buy around fifty to sixty head, including two young bulls. It seemed about the right time of year to go. Late spring would work for the trip down if we chose the right route. That would give us plenty of time to get them home in the warm weather.

Word had just reached us concerning a Nez Percé Chief Joseph, who now led a band of his tribe after leaving the reservation in the Idaho Territory. They had eluded the army so far, and we didn't want to run into them. In any case, the territory south of us through the new Yellowstone National Park was probably too mountainous for us, especially in the springtime. The Nez Percé were south of us, probably trying to get to Canada.

Our best route, we decided, was to go east for almost one hundred miles, then turn south before reaching the Crow Nation. Then, we could proceed on south through the high plains of the Wyoming Territory, east of the Rocky Mountains. We hoped to make a stop at Fort Phil Kearny for any provisions we needed, then move on down to Denver. We could return the same way with the cattle.

We had a minor concern about running into bands of Sioux or Lakota warriors on the way. The Black Hills War with those tribes was still going on, though most of it was east of us. They had killed General Custer, along with all his command, last summer at the Little Big Horn. We'd heard in just the last week of a battle at Powder River, here in Montana, between the army and some Cheyenne warriors. Again, that was east of us, and we thought we could avoid trouble.

We sat back and looked at the map we had drawn for ourselves, ending up in Denver. "What do you think?" I asked Buck. "Maybe three weeks to get there?"

Buck studied the map, then slowly nodded his head. "Maybe three, three and a half weeks, assumin' we don't hit no trouble."

Before turning in, I got out my guns and ammunition and laid them on the table. My revolver was brand new. It was the Colt Frontier model. Some folks called it the Frontier Six-Shooter. I'd had time to practice with it for just a few weeks. I considered briefly taking my old Navy Colt because I was so used to it, but finally decided I might need the extra firepower from the Frontier.

My 1861 Springfield rifle was gone, replaced by a Winchester 73. I'd had that for a few years now, and I knew how accurate it was. A bonus was that the Colt and the Winchester could use the same ammunition. That helped a lot on a trip like this. I made sure I had plenty.

Buck watched approvingly while I set up my weapons. After a while, he picked up his Sharps rifle and set it by the door. "I still got my buff'ler gun" he mumbled as he trailed off to bed.

Morning found us on the trail, headed east. The mornings were still cold in early April, so we had our collars buttoned up against the chilly winds. Each of us brought two horses, knowing the second horse would be useful when we drove our new cattle north on the return trip. We made good time, stopping before the sun went down to set up for the night and to gather firewood where we could find it.

We rarely had long conversations, but Buck surprised me that evening, as I was enjoying the warmth of the fire after eating. Buck tossed another chunk of wood on the fire, keeping it small.

"Are you still married to Annie? Legal, I mean. Are you still legally married to her?"

Buck knew my history—no surprise there, but the question came out of nowhere. I leaned up on one elbow and stared at him across the fire. "Why?"

Buck shrugged and avoided making direct eye contact with me. "I dunno. It just seems like it was a long time ago, and you was married down there in Denver. I guess…I guess I figgered maybe you could find a judge down there and get yoreself unmarried. Just in case there was somebody else that came along. There wouldn't be no complications."

I laid back down and stared at the stars. "I guess I could," I said finally. "Wouldn't hurt. Never really thought about it."

"I think you should," came Buck's voice across the fire. There was a long pause. "I was married one time."

I was back up on one elbow. In all the time I'd known Buck, he had never mentioned it. I wasn't sure I'd heard him right. "What?" was all I managed to say.

"Yep, I was married once. She was a wonderful woman. Died of cholera. Long time ago…" His voice trailed off.

I laid back down again. "I'm sorry," I offered after a while. "I didn't know." There was another long silence. "I'll look into it when we get down there."

"Good. I think you should. Ya never know what can happen." He fell silent again, and finally, I heard light snoring.

We turned south on the fourth morning, and we were making good time, but after several hours on the trail south, I had the uncomfortable feeling we were being followed. I couldn't quite put my finger on why I felt that way, but I had learned to trust my instincts over the years.

After a while, I pulled up to a stop and just sat in the saddle quietly, listening to the sounds and checking the back trail. Buck pulled up alongside me and did the same. We were following a faint trail, strewn with boulders on both sides. The countryside we were traveling, had some rolling hills. I knew the terrain in front would level out and open up a little more.

"You think so too?" Buck asked abruptly.

I nodded, still searching the path in front and behind. "Not sure why," I added. "Maybe a few bird calls, I'm not too sure, are really birds. Can't see anything, but I think there may be a few of 'em out there."

Buck nodded silent agreement. After a while, we moved the horses forward. There was nothing to do but keep going.

CHAPTER 5

RENEGADES

As we approached the Wyoming Territory, we were still moving to the east and south. The Rocky Mountain range stretched off to our right as we rode, and the high plains greeted us. We were glad for any increased warmth we could find. Each day was proving to be a long, bitter day in the saddle.

My brain told me we were moving away from trouble with every mile we rode farther south, but I found I couldn't relax. I couldn't shake the feeling we were being watched. Every bird call made me tense up, and I scanned both the horizon and the back trail constantly. I rode with my right hand resting on my thigh near the Colt. Behind me, Buck had the Sharps buffalo gun resting across his lap. He was at least as tense as me.

It was the afternoon of the second day after we turned south that they struck. We were following a faint trail, mainly to the south now, and there were a couple large boulders to either side of the trail in front of us. Although I was mainly worried about an attack from the rear, I still had a wary eye on the boulders as we approached. I was never sure how the warriors got around in front of us undetected.

Motion on my right made me duck instinctively, and I palmed the Colt as I spurred Cisco forward. I felt the burn of an arrow across my back, and I fired at the warrior as he dropped the bow and pulled a tomahawk. The shot was at nearly point-blank range, and he had only a moment to clutch at his chest as the shot bowled him over backward.

The Sharps rifle boomed behind me as the second man sprinted from behind the other boulder and launched himself at me, knife in hand. I didn't have time to bring the Colt to bear before he hit me low and hard, knocking me backward out of the saddle. The Colt slipped from my grip as I fell to the ground.

The second warrior hit the ground and rolled, tripping for an instant over the one I had shot as he regained his feet. I glanced behind me only for a second, as the Colt lay on the ground about two feet behind me and a little to my right. I didn't have time to go for it, as he was gathering himself to rush me with the knife.

He let out a blood-curdling scream and rushed me, knife high in the air, pointing downward and clutched in his right fist. He launched himself at me again, and he was a big, muscular man. I fell backward, partly intentionally, and partly because I couldn't hope to keep my balance when he hit me. I heard a cry of triumph as he knocked me to the ground. I lifted an arm and blocked the downward thrust of the knife, but only for a moment.

He lifted his arm to strike at me again, but I had fallen with my legs bunched under me, feet pushing against his chest and stomach. As he drove down with the second blow, I shoved upward with all my strength and launched him up and over me. I rolled over and grabbed the Colt, then lunged to the side as he came at me again. As he flew through the air beside me, I fired twice. The first shot hit him in the shoulder and knocked him to the side and the second went between his eyes.

The Sharps rifle boomed again, and I looked back to see that Buck had barricaded himself behind his horse, which was lying on the ground in front of him. There was a little blood on the ground beside Buck. I could see he may have been hit. There were arrows in the surrounding ground—they seemed to have tried raining a few down on him. Now, they were behind cover and were bracketing him with arrows from both sides. They had taken little notice of me. Cisco had trotted off several yards to my left. I sprinted to reach him and lifted the Winchester from the saddle. An arrow whistled by uncomfortably close as I did.

I could see where one brave had risen from behind a rock to take the shot at me. I laid the Winchester across the saddle and fired as he notched another arrow. His shot went harmlessly in the air as the rifle bullet lifted him up to his toes before knocking him down behind the rock. I moved the Winchester and sighted a buckskin-clad leg sticking out from behind a rock on the other side of Buck.

I fired and heard a scream of pain as the bullet hit home. He rose from behind the rock, and Buck's buffalo gun sounded one more time, lifting him in the air and dropping him limply to the ground. I stayed behind Cisco and swung the Winchester back and forth, looking for targets.

Finally, Buck rose from the ground and urged his horse back to its feet. "That's all of 'em, Spence," he called hoarsely. "Assumin' you taken care of those ones back there."

I walked back over to check the two I had shot. They wouldn't be going anywhere. I led Cisco over to Buck, watching as Buck sat back down and examined an arrow wound on his right calf. He yanked an arrow from the ground and threw it away in disgust. "One of those they shot in the air sliced me on the way down," he explained.

Buck looked around at the horses. We still had all four, and they looked unharmed. "Lucky they didn't shoot the horses. That woulda been next." He looked over at the brave he'd shot with his Sharps. "Sioux?"

I shrugged. "I think so. Not really sure. Could be Lakota."

I pulled a rag from my saddlebag, splashed water on it from my canteen, and cleaned the wound as best I could, then tied the rag around his calf to stem the bleeding. I looked up at Buck questioningly. He pulled a bottle of whiskey from his saddlebag, pulled the cork with his teeth, and downed what was left in the bottle.

"We're about a day and a half from Fort Phil Kearny," I told him. "Can you make it there?"

Buck never really answered the question. He grabbed the saddle horn, stepped into the stirrup with his good leg and pulled himself into the saddle. "Let's get started," he rasped. "We're wasting time."

We had reached Fort Phil Kearny the evening before, and I had bunked in the soldier's barracks. I was in the same room with ten soldiers, and I had awakened early and walked outside the barracks, stretching and soaking in some sunshine. I had thought I would sleep later, but I'd never heard so much snoring in my life. Now, I was rooting for Buck to recover even more than before.

The day and a half's travel to the fort that I was estimating after the Indian attack had stretched closer to two days, and I had begun to question myself about finding the fort. Buck had slept fitfully at night, calling out in his sleep sometimes, and he had grown more and more pale from the loss of blood and lack of sleep. I had begun halting every fifteen minutes, sweeping the land in front of me with my binoculars, and it was during one of those halts I had spotted a patrol of five men returning to the fort. They had escorted me in, and we had taken Buck to the sick bay in the fort.

The doc had checked him right away and seemed optimistic that Buck would recover soon. The wound hadn't festered or turned color, other than showing a bit of bruising. He had told Buck to get some sleep and had given him some medicine. I planned to check on him after breakfast.

I ducked into a long, low-ceilinged room where I'd been

told I could get some breakfast. I fell in line behind a couple soldiers and was given a plate with a few strips of bacon, some gravy, and what appeared to be a couple of biscuits. I sat down at a long table, eyeing the food with mistrust. I prodded at the biscuits with the old spoon they'd given me, but hunger won out eventually.

"Mind if I join?"

I looked up to see the colonel commanding the fort standing across the table from me. I motioned at him to sit down, and we both ate in silence for a while. When I had finished, I glanced at him curiously and waited to see what he wanted.

Mostly, he wanted to find out what he could about the attack. I told him what I could, describing how far we had traveled to get here since the attack, recounting the battle and answering the few questions he asked.

He nodded absently after I had answered his questions and stared at the back wall. "They were probably Sioux warriors, leaving the Black Hills area. Quite a few of 'em didn't want to move south to a different reservation. Can't say as I blame 'em. It was their bad luck, having gold on that land." He fell silent for a moment, then rose. "I'll send a patrol up to where you were, see if there were others. That's about all I can do. Let me know if you're going back through there on your way home."

I nodded as he walked away, then went over to stand in line for a cup of coffee. It didn't taste any worse than what Buck had been making on the trail, I had to give it that.

Speaking of Buck, I decided it was time to check on him. I took the coffee with me over to the doc's office. As I arrived, the doctor was leaving, shaking his head and muttering to himself. I kinda felt sorry for him. I knew Buck wouldn't make an obedient patient.

As I entered the room, I heard a spitting noise. Buck had been leaning over the side of the bed and he straightened up as I came in. He relaxed when he saw it was me. I walked over to the bed, one eyebrow raised. "What did you just spit out?" I asked.

Buck pointed at a bottle sitting on the table beside his cot. "Tastes even worse than it smells," he told me.

I picked up the bottle and read the label. "Foley's Pain Relief," I drawled. I set the bottle back down. "Maybe you shouldn't have spit it out," I advised. "It says it relieves pain." I sniffed the air and wrinkled my nose in disgust. "What is that smell?"

Buck snorted and pointed at a bottle beside the bed. "Only thing that smells worse than the pain relief stuff," he assured me. "Doc rubbed it on my leg. I tole him I didn't appreciate it none." He heaved a long sigh and laid back down.

I picked up the second bottle and read the label on that one. "Kickapoo Oil." I set it back down in a hurry. I had to agree with him about the smell. "Maybe it will help," I said lamely.

Buck snorted loudly and reached under his pillow, producing another bottle. "This is the only thing gonna help," he assured me. He popped the cork and took a long swig, sighed deeply, replaced the cork and hid the bottle under his pillow again.

"Whiskey," I said. It wasn't a question. I shook my head slowly. "Where did you get that? I don't the think the doctor gave it you."

Buck gave me a smug grin. "Let's just say there's a Private Jones that's got him a twenty-dollar gold piece he didn't have before. Best money I ever spent. He's gonna get me another when I'm done with that 'un. For the same twenny dollars, I mean. I ain't stupid."

I laughed despite my concerns and glanced at the leg. It was bandaged, and the doc had said he could probably travel in two days if it kept healing well. "Two days," I told him, "we can move on in two days if your leg is okay."

"Okay," Buck promised. "I'll stay off it and rest. Two

days. I'll even save a nip or two for you from the second
bottle."

I shook my head and left.

———————

I stood outside the doctor's office in Denver, laughing at the
noise going on inside as the doctor attended to Buck's leg.
Buck had done well. I hadn't heard him complain about his
wound at all until the doctor's office came in sight here in
Denver.

The wound hadn't festered, and the doctor here had said it
would heal in a few more days. He was in there changing out
the bandage now. Buck had let me leave him to the doctor's care
under two conditions. The first was there wouldn't be any more
Kickapoo Oil used on his leg. The doctor had promised that he
didn't even have any Kickapoo Oil and had never used it.

That had solved the first problem. The second condition
Buck laid down was that I would go to see a judge here in
Denver about my marriage to Annie. For such a tough old
coot, Buck had a soft side to him, and I think he felt I wasn't
moving on with my life because I'd done nothing about that
marriage so long ago. I had to admit he might be right, so I
had promised him I would find a judge.

The doctor had advised me how to find the courthouse,
just a few blocks away, and said there was a Judge Sampson
with offices there who could probably help me. I turned left
onto Olive Street at the corner and found my way to the
office of Judge Sampson. A deep voice told me to enter
when I knocked, and I found myself sitting across the desk
from a tall, stern-looking man. I told him my story.

The judge's features seemed to soften a little as I
completed my story. He folded his hands behind his head
and leaned back, listening. Then he leaned forward and
placed his hands on his desk, watching my face as he asked
a few questions.

"You say you married here in Denver?" he began. After I nodded, he continued: "And you say you haven't seen... Annie...since 1859?" I nodded again, and he made a few notes on some paper in front of him.

"What you're describing is called abandonment," he rumbled. "Usually, it's the other way around—the husband abandons the wife. In any case, divorce is a little easier out here in the west than it is back east." He tapped his knuckles on the desk for a few moments, then threw a searching look across the desk.

"Are you willing to write down what you've told me and sign it? The facts about your wife leaving you eighteen years ago, you made reasonable effort to find her, and could not?"

I told him I was certainly willing to do that. He reached into a drawer and produced some paper and a pen. It took me about ten or fifteen minutes to write out the fundamental facts I had described to him. When I finished, I signed it at the bottom and pushed the paper back across the desk.

The judge briefly read what I had written, then nodded and placed the papers in a basket on his desk. He reached over and grabbed some other papers on the desk, adjusted the spectacles on the end of his nose, and spoke without looking up: "Come back and see me in three days, Mr. Spencer. I'll take care of it by then."

It took me a minute to realize I had been dismissed. I stood, thanked the judge, and found my way out. I found myself back outside on Olive Street, processing in my head what had just happened. It seemed that my story was no longer so complicated.

I jammed my hands into my pocket and began walking down Olive Street, not really sure where I was going. It was too soon to go back and deal with Buck at the doctor's office. I grinned when I thought about that. Better to let the doctor deal with all that whining and moaning.

I had proceeded maybe two blocks when the smell of muffins or some kind of baked goods stopped me in my tracks. I realized I was hungry and had eaten nothing but trail food and army food for a couple weeks now. Looking up, I saw a bakery to my left. People were coming out with all kinds of things that looked good and smelled delicious.

I walked in after holding the door for two ladies coming out. I stepped in, and two things caught my attention immediately. One, the baked goods smelled even better now that I was inside the shop. And two, there was a beautiful, dark-haired woman behind the counter. We locked eyes, and I immediately felt like a schoolboy. I looked down and shuffled my feet a few times, then looked back up. She was still watching me, a faint smile on her mouth this time.

"Spence, old boy," I told myself, "you've been on the trail a long time, but not that long. That's one pretty lady over there." I reached up self-consciously and rubbed my hand over my whiskery jaw. Too late to do anything about that. She was still watching me out of the corner of her eye. I grinned a little sheepishly and headed over to the counter.

CHAPTER 6

LUKE

Sherry watched as her newest customer turned and moved down along the counter to place an order with Bess. She'd gotten that his name was Spence—that's all he had said, and she wasn't sure if it was a first or last name. She had told him her name, and she gathered he was just visiting in town for a few days. She heard Bess tell him to take a seat, and that Bess would bring his breakfast to him.

Sherry hadn't seen all that many customers come through here that were really interesting, but this one was. She had promised herself that she wouldn't be shy if somebody like this came along. He was tall, dark-haired and handsome in a rugged way. He had clearly been self-conscious about being unshaved and having his hair uncombed, but that just meant he was accustomed to being more presentable when he met a woman.

Sherry moved over to where Bess was scrambling a couple eggs, and spoke to her in a low tone: "When you have his order ready, let me know. I'll take it to him."

Bess turned, looking surprised. She opened her mouth to speak, then reconsidered. She glanced over at the man who'd just ordered, and a smile spread slowly across her face. "You're the boss," she said. The smile, Sherry noticed, stayed in place.

When Bess had loaded a plate with scrambled eggs, bacon, and two muffins, Sherry carried them, along with a cup of coffee, and put them on the man's table. "Here you go, Mr. Spence," she said.

The man looked up, an expression of surprise crossing his face when he saw who had brought the food. "Just Spence," he said, "no mister, just Spence."

Sherry smiled and lingered near the table. Spence looked at her, then half-rose, pointing at the chair across from him. "Please join me if you'd like," he blurted suddenly.

Sherry slid into the chair. There was an awkward silence for a moment. "Please," she said. "Eat your food." She spoke for a few minutes, telling him a little about herself and how she came to be in Denver. He listened attentively, and she thought it struck a chord with him she had come to Denver alone and made a life after the loss of her parents.

He finished his food, pushed the plate back, and explained that he had come with his partner to look into purchasing cattle and driving them north to his ranch in Montana. He talked a bit about living here in Denver many years ago, then talked a bit about mining jobs in California and Nevada. Sherry nodded and asked a few questions as he talked. The time seemed to pass quickly, and she wasn't sure how to ask the one thing she most wondered about. Finally, she decided on the direct approach.

"Did your wife come with you on this trip?" she asked, the words coming out awkwardly.

Spence's head came up. "It's a little..." His voice trailed off, and he looked away, then turned and faced her again. "I don't...uh...I don't have one of those," he said, reddening a bit when Sherry chuckled at the answer.

"That's okay, Spence," she told him. "I don't...uh...have one of those either. Husband, I mean." The awkward moment passed, and he told her about his partner, over at the doctor's office, and his hatred of Kickapoo Oil.

"That reminds me," he said, glancing at the clock in the

corner. "I should take him some food and get him out of there. The doctor has probably had all he can take by now."

Sherry turned and waved at Bess. "Let me have a plate made for him," she suggested. "Same thing you had?"

While they waited for the plate, she told him what she knew of ranchers in the area, and suggested a couple places where he might inquire about cattle. At length, he took the plate from Bess and walked to the door with Sherry, promising to return the next morning with Buck, even though he said it was *"against his better judgment"* to bring the partner in, on account of his *"not having a lot of manners. Barely even housebroke,"* was his summary of the situation.

Sherry closed the door behind him and turned to see Bess watching her with knowing eyes, and the same smile was on her face she'd had when Sherry had come over an hour earlier to take Spence's plate from her. Sherry held up her hand to forestall any questions, then went over and busied herself with washing a few dishes.

———

Luke stood outside the door on the second floor of the saloon where he'd been working for a couple weeks now. He knew there was something else going on up here on the second floor, but he hadn't been in a hurry to find out more about it. Whatever it was, it seemed like a secret, and his gut told him it could be trouble.

This morning though, Al, the guy he'd been working for downstairs in the saloon, told him they needed help upstairs. When he'd dragged his feet, Al seemed to tell him he could go upstairs and help out, or else he didn't need to bother coming in for work at all. Now he was staring at the door on the second floor, hearing laughing and some yelling inside, and wondering if this was a good idea.

The doors swung open downstairs, and he looked over the railing to see a couple hard-faced characters walking into the saloon. He had seen them before, and he knew they always came upstairs. He couldn't just stand here—he had to knock on the door, or he had to leave. He reached out and knocked on the door.

Luke shifted nervously from one foot to the other as he heard footsteps approaching the door. When the door swung open, he was looking at a very young man, maybe only two or three years older than himself. A pair of cold, cunning eyes looked him over. Then the door swung open farther, and he stepped inside. The door stayed open while the two men he'd seen come in downstairs walked past him into the room. Then the door swung shut.

The kid who had let him in walked away, and Luke watched as a large, very heavy man in a red shirt and greasy vest came toward him, trailing an enormous cloud of cigar smoke. He stopped in front of Luke, removed the cigar and puffed out another cloud of smoke. "You the kid Al sent up?" he asked.

Luke nodded and rubbed his hand on the side of his pants before offering his hand. "I'm Luke," he offered.

The man stared at him and shook his head. "Don't care," he rumbled. "Your name is Kid as far as I'm concerned. Come over here."

As they walked, Luke's eyes surveyed the room. It was maybe half the size of the saloon downstairs, and it was covered with about eight to ten tables. There were card games going on at each table. He saw a dealer standing at each table, with maybe three or four card players either sitting or standing as they played. A dense cloud of smoke hung in the air.

The big man he was following reached a bar running down nearly the entire length of one side of the room. He ducked around behind the bar and slapped a tray down on the counter. He then put four glasses on the tray and filled each glass with a foul-smelling brown liquid Luke assumed was whiskey.

The man waved his hand over the tray and pointed at the

room. "Anybody wants whiskey, you give it to 'em. Costs two bits. You take their money. They need change, bring it to me. Anybody asks for Burt, that's me. You tell me when they ask for me." Luke took the tray and turned to go. "Oh, and Kid," Burt said, "anybody gives you tips, you split 'em with me at the end of the day. If'n you keep any money that don't belong to you, we're gonna have some trouble."

Luke served the tables from early evening until Burt told him his shift was over several hours later. He produced two dollars in tips from his pocket before he left, giving one dollar to Burt and keeping the other. He stumbled down the stairs, eyes stinging and clothes smelling of the smoke, but the dollar he had been given by the gamblers plus the fifty cents he was paid for the shift was far more than he had ever made in a day before.

Luke had instinctively avoided the other kid serving whiskey named Jed. More than once, he'd had the impression the other kid resented him and tried to trip or push him on the way past. He had avoided trouble, and thankfully, Jed had left several minutes before him. Luke also had a feeling they rigged the games, and the gamblers were getting cheated, but he had seen that kind of thing before. It was why he didn't gamble. He planned to mind his own business about that.

Luke moved out through the saloon doors and turned down the street toward the livery stables. The night wind was a cold surprise after the hot, crowded conditions in the upstairs room. He jammed his hands in his pockets and hurried along, remembering the looks on the faces of some gamblers as they had left. He knew they had been cheated, and he felt sure the secret upstairs location was to keep the sheriff out of the picture.

He brushed aside the temporary feelings of guilt when he thought about those faces. He'd had some hard times, too. His thoughts were so occupied with the evening's activities that he jumped in surprise when a shadow came out of the alley. He turned, lifting an arm to defend himself, then recognized the face. It was Jed, the kid from the gambling hall. He held a club in one hand, half-raised.

"You'll be splitting your money with me," Jed announced. He brandished the club threateningly to back up his statement, and he held out his other hand.

Luke wasted no time. The other guy was armed, but he wasn't expecting an attack. Luke took a quick step forward and lifted a hard, sweeping right fist to Jed's midsection. He could hear air whooshing out of Jed's mouth as he stumbled backward, swinging the club down almost as a reflex.

The club connected with the side of Luke's head and it had enough impact to stagger him. He steadied himself and charged inside the next downward sweep from the club. He swung a hard right, then a sweeping left to Jed's face. The club clattered to the ground, and Luke kicked it away. Jed staggered back against the wall behind him as Luke connected another swing to his stomach, then lifted an uppercut to the chin as Jed sagged forward.

Jed fell to the ground, and Luke stayed only long enough to see that he was down and not getting up. Then he left quickly, trotting to the livery stable and climbing into the same haystack where he slept every night. After a few minutes, the scare of the moment had faded and his racing pulse had calmed, and he dropped off to sleep. His final thought was that he had made an enemy tonight. He would have to watch out for Jed now.

——————

Luke awoke to a throbbing headache, and his left eye was sore and sensitive to the touch. He suspected there was the beginning of a nasty black eye and bruise there, probably extending to the hairline. The club had connected with the side of his head there. His suspicions were confirmed when the old man came into his livery stable and stared at Luke while he cleaned out stalls.

"Had yourself a little set-to last night, did ya?" His gaze lingered on Luke's left eye.

Luke shrugged, then finally spoke when the old man continued to stare at him. "I guess so," he mumbled, avoiding the old man's gaze.

"Just remember what I told ya to start with—don't bring no trouble to the stable, an' do your job an' you're welcome to stay here." He walked away, muttering over his shoulder.

Luke walked down toward the bakery when he had finished at the stables. He really didn't want to run into Sherry and have to explain the eye, but he was hungry, and he couldn't beat the breakfast they gave him at the bakery.

When he reached the bakery door, he trotted inside, waving quickly at the two ladies behind the counter while he bounced to the back door and chopped and stacked the wood. When he could put it off no longer, he went inside and walked over to the counter to get his usual breakfast.

There was a quick intake of breath from Sherry when she saw his eye, and she came out from behind the counter quickly. She reached toward his face, but he backed away and raised an arm to keep her from getting too close.

"I'm okay," he blurted. "It looks worse than it is. I tripped. I'm okay."

Sherry stopped and looked at him skeptically. "That must have been quite a fall," she said, her eyes telling him she wasn't buying his story.

Luke avoided a direct answer to any other questions she had, assuring her he was fine. When his breakfast was ready, he grabbed it and headed out the door instead of staying in the bakery to eat. Sherry's eyes followed him out, but she refrained from more questions.

Relieved at reaching the door, Luke yanked it open and hurried out, brushing by a tall, dark-haired man he had never seen and an older man just behind him. They stepped back to avoid a collision, then continued into the bakery.

———

I jumped back a bit to avoid a collision at the bakery door. It took me by surprise. I had just a brief impression of a young man in old, worn-out clothes, head down and hurrying by me. Buck turned to glance at him as he brushed past.

"Had him a bit of a dust-up with somebody, that one has," Buck observed. He watched as the boy hurried away.

I hadn't gotten that much of a look at him, and I turned a questioning eye on Buck as we walked through the door.

Buck pointed at his eye. "Turnin' colors, I'd say. Got him a nice shade of purple goin' around that eye."

I nodded understanding and turned back around to see Sherry hurrying over. She seemed a bit distracted, glancing out the door as it closed behind us, but she gave us a warm welcome.

"Spence," she said, patting my shoulder with her left hand as she reached out her right toward Buck. "You must be Buck," she said. "Welcome."

To my astonishment, Buck took off his hat, took her hand in both of his, bent over it and kissed it. My mouth dropped open in astonishment, and I stared at him. "Well," I said, "in fifteen years, I've never..." My voice trailed off.

Sherry's laugh filled the small room, and I could hear her assistant laughing as well, over behind the counter. Sherry took my arm and steered me toward the same table where I had sat the day before. "Clearly, Spence," she said, "you don't know Buck as well as you thought you did. You boys sit down, and I'm going to bring you some breakfast."

As she bustled away, I kept staring at Buck. "Where in the world did you come up with that?" I demanded. "I thought we were in a king's palace somewhere. All you forgot was to bow, or drop to your knee, or something."

Buck chortled heartily, and a sly grin stayed on his face after he was done laughing. "I was wonderin'," he said, "why you was so keen to bring me over here. I mean, the muffins was good yesterday, and everythin', but now I see you wasn't so much concerned with the food."

I was saved from having to answer that when Sherry

returned, pulled a chair over next to mine, and sat down. "I have eggs and bacon coming for you," she said, "and then I have a treat. We have donuts."

Buck made a small moaning noise, which made me afraid his old manners were returning. I was glad to see he didn't lick his chops.

"Are you going to look for cattle today?" she asked. She laid her hand on my arm as she talked, and the grin on Buck's face widened.

"We are," I said. "There are two ranches west of town—you gave me those names yesterday—that we are going out to see. I'm a little particular, though, especially about the bulls. We'll keep looking until we have exactly what we want."

We made small talk until the food arrived, and it didn't last long on the table. When we were done, Buck entertained Sherry with greatly exaggerated tales about our trip down from Montana and our encounter with the Sioux. We were in no hurry, and many people came and went from the shop while we talked.

I was shocked when I looked over at the clock in the corner. It was ten o'clock already. We stood and moved toward the door. I blurted out the thought that had come into my mind. "Would you like to come with us?" I asked Sherry. "We could have a pleasant ride, and maybe you'd like to..."

"I'd love to do that," she said. "Give me about twenty minutes? I could pack some food for us, and we could stop and eat a picnic somewhere."

We agreed to come back in twenty minutes. As we left the shop, I looked over at Buck. "If we stop for a picnic somewhere, maybe you could..."

"Yeah, I'll get lost. No problem." He chortled loudly and was still snickering after we'd walked about a block.

"Oh, shut up," I told him.

CHAPTER 7

GAMBLING HALL

Buford "Burt" Morton considered himself to be a practical man. He didn't care to work for a living if he could make good money with little or no work. On the other hand, he didn't think much of going to prison. Two years in the Yuma Territorial Prison had taught him he didn't really get along with prison. He had also learned that sheriffs and marshals tended to go after criminals who ran big operations and had big names for themselves when they were looking for people to put in prison.

So, it had worked out really well for Burt—so far, anyway—when he had met Soapy Smith at the Robber's Roost hideout several months ago. Burt had been staying out of sight while the heat died down on an ill-advised stage robbery, and Soapy...well, Burt was never sure why Soapy was there, but nobody really spent much time at the Roost unless he was hiding from somebody.

Soapy was making a lot of noise about how he was getting ready to set up a big operation in Denver. Burt had never been to Denver, but that was a plus. Nobody knew him in Denver. Soapy had also been bragging about how the deputy marshal in Denver was making a little money on the side, looking the other way, while Soapy made money raffling off bars of soap.

The idea of paying off a deputy marshal made sense to Burt. Why spend all your time hiding and running if you didn't have to? The other part, about raffling off bars of soap, made no sense to him at all. Who in their right mind would spend good money buying raffle tickets for a bar of soap?

Soapy, who had apparently gotten his nickname from these soap bar raffles, explained that he hid money inside a few bars of soap and raffled them to people in his gang, who made a lot of noise about the money they found in the soap. Then some other chumps bought the rest of the soap, which, of course, had no money in it. Burt shrugged and agreed to tag along to buy a few bars of soap. He was really more interested, though, in the saloon and gambling operation that Soapy planned to set up. Burt knew how much money there was in rigged gambling.

So far, Burt judged that things were going very well. The deputy marshal was a greedy man, so that worked out great. He wasn't terribly smart either, so that helped. His name was Oscar Camp, and he didn't seem to do a lot around town, but the people liked him. He took his regular payoff when Burt had it sent over, and once in a while he came up and swilled a little free whiskey upstairs.

Oscar's boss, the marshal, had been in office a long time and seemed like he was getting ready to retire, meaning he didn't want trouble. He wasn't crooked, as far as Burt could tell, but he didn't look too hard for outlaws and crooks, either. If he had any suspicions about the soap raffles or the saloon and gambling den, he wasn't doing much about them.

That just left the county sheriff, a man named Hal Peters. Burt frowned, took out his cigar, and tapped it on the edge of the tin can he kept on the bar. Hal Peters was an honest lawman, and he took his job seriously. Burt didn't much like guys like that. When Peters came into the saloon, Al would send a runner upstairs to alert them. They would stay quiet in the gambling hall until they got word Peters had left. So far, that had worked. And luckily, Peters spent a fair amount of time out of town checking on the rest of the county. Denver was more the marshal's territory, but Burt didn't really trust Peters to stay out of it. Word had it that Peters had the governor's ear.

The door to the gambling hall opened, and the kid named Jed came in. Burt blew a cloud of smoke and looked at Jed through narrowed eyes. Jed's face was bruised, he was walking with a bit of a limp, and when he turned or bent over suddenly, he stopped and grabbed at his stomach. Burt eyed him speculatively. Jed was a greedy, smart-mouthed kid. Maybe somebody had taught him a lesson.

The door opened again, and the new kid came in. Burt knew his name was Luke, but he would not call him anything but Kid. He knew he was putting the kid in harm's way, letting him work up here, and he kinda liked this kid. Nothing he could really do about the getting in trouble thing. The kid was broke, obviously, and he could make a little money up here.

Burt narrowed his eyes, staring through the cigar smoke, and watched the two of them. The new kid, Luke, was looking a little beat up, too. Not as bad as Jed, but he had a nasty black eye and a big bruise forming on the side of his head. Burt glanced back and forth between the two of them. They had nothing to say to each other. As a matter of fact, they barely looked at each other. When they did, Jed looked at the ground, and Luke had a defiant look on his face.

Burt turned around so neither of them could see the grin on his face. Maybe the new kid had taught Jed a lesson last night. Maybe Jed had tried to take his money. Well, the new kid was younger and smaller, but it looked like he'd gotten the best of it, anyway. No wonder he kinda liked the new kid.

Well, he would separate them for a couple of days and maybe this thing would work itself out. Burt ground out his cigar in the tin can, pointed at Jed, and waved toward the door. "Kid—Jed—we don't have that much going on up here today. I only need one of you. Go back down and tell Al I don't need you today. You can work down there."

Burt observed the look of pure venom Jed shot toward Luke on the way out. Burt lit a new cigar, walked over and handed a broom to Luke. "Sweep the place out, kid," he said, then turned and took a few steps toward the bar. He halted and turned back. "Watch your back, kid," he advised. He motioned toward the door. "That one hates you."

———

Luke had an easier time of it on this second night in the gambling hall. For one thing, Jed wasn't around, trying to push him or trip him. That made it easier, plus he was getting the hang of carrying that tray around and keeping it level. He'd already figured out that he needed to pay the most attention to the ones that gave him good tips.

As the evening wore on, there were two things he was increasingly aware of. First, a few of the customers were getting pretty drunk. They'd gotten a little drunk last night, too, but last night they'd all been cooperative. He knew they lost money a lot faster when they were drunk, but they had taken it pretty quietly last night. Tonight, there were one or two who were loud, angry, and threatening.

That's probably what had called his attention to the second thing he was very aware of this evening. There was a man leaning against the far wall, arms folded, just watching. He wasn't drinking, and he definitely wasn't dealing or playing cards. He just watched. He wore two tied-down guns, and he seemed to straighten up and move a step or two toward anybody who got loud.

There was one player in particular who was drunk and angry. On one of his trips to the bar, Burt pointed at the player and told Luke to serve him only one more drink. After that, Burt said, they would tell him it was time to leave. As he said that, Burt took a bat out from under the bar and laid it on the counter.

The man waved for another whiskey, and Luke brought it to him. He stood by the chair, waiting for the man to pay. Instead, the man ignored him and continued to play.

Luke glanced over at Burt, who stood watching them from behind the bar. Luke swallowed nervously. "That's two bits, sir," he said, keeping his voice as even as possible.

The man lurched to his feet, his face reddening. "TWO BITS!" he shouted. "That whiskey ain't worth two bits." He turned to face Luke, swaying on his feet.

The room grew quiet. Then Luke could see men moving to clear a path behind the drunk man. Luke was also aware of the man with the tied-down guns moving toward them. Luke realized he was in the line of fire and moved to the side.

The drunk turned to face the man with the tied-down guns, and the fight seemed to drain out of him. "It's bad whiskey, that's all I'm sayin'," he mumbled. "A man shouldn't have to pay for that whiskey." He belched and fell silent.

The man with the guns spoke quietly, but there was a chilling edge to his words. He hitched a thumb over his gun belt. "Your choice, bud," he said. "You can try me, or you can put your two bits and your gun on that table and leave."

The man swayed indecisively on his feet for a moment longer, as Luke moved a little farther to the side. Finally, the man fumbled in his pocket for a coin, which he tossed on the table. He stared around him sullenly for a moment, then slowly and carefully pulled his gun from his holster. He laid it on the table and left.

The room seemed to heave a collective sigh of relief. Luke stepped to the table to pick up the coin. The stranger with the two guns stepped over to pick up the gun from the table, and Luke noticed that he also picked up the gambling money left on the table. Nobody said a word as he stuffed the money in his pocket, then carried the gun over and left it on the bar.

The rest of the evening passed without trouble, and at

the end of his shift, Luke had two dollars in his pocket after splitting with Burt. He heard Burt call the man with two guns "Dunn." He learned nothing else about the man, and he was smart enough not to ask questions around the gambling hall.

Coming back to the livery stable, he took a different route, going a few blocks out of his way, just in case Jed was carrying a grudge and lying in wait. He arrived at the livery stable without seeing anyone. To his surprise, the old man had stayed later than usual, and was just on his way out when Luke came in.

Luke nodded to the old man, who only grunted in response. Curiosity got the better of him, and Luke asked about the man he'd seen that night.

"Do you know anything about a man named Dunn? Came to town maybe a week ago? Wears two guns…"

The old man wheeled around in his tracks. Luke had never seen him move that fast. "Dunn, the gunfighter? Where you been hanging around, kid?" The old man pointed a finger at him. "You stay way clear of him, you hear? That's the best advice you'll ever get." After shaking his finger a few times for emphasis, he turned and left.

Luke stared at the back of the old man as he left, then climbed into the haystack where he slept every night. A little voice at the back of his brain kept telling him he might be getting in over his head.

———

Arriving at the bakery late the next morning, Luke was disappointed to watch Sherry mounting a horse outside the bakery, along with two men. Then she moved off down the street with them. She saw Luke approaching the building on foot, but just waved as they moved down the street. He continued on down to the bakery. He still had a job to do, and he was hungry.

Bess nodded at him as she waited on a couple of

customers. He continued on to the back and split the wood, then carried it inside and stacked it near the oven. Bess served his breakfast and made some small talk, but he really wasn't in the mood for it. It occurred to him that Sherry was the one person he considered a friend. He had wanted to ask about the gunman, Dunn.

He finished breakfast and was leaving when Bess waved to him as he opened the door. "Bye, Luke," she called, then stopped him with a question: "What's your last name, anyway?"

He paused, started to answer, then stopped. "Collier," he said. Then he stepped out into the street. Collier was his mother's last name, and it was the name he had always used. Why, he wondered, had he started to give his father's last name? He'd never met the man. He reached up to the chain around his neck and pulled up the locket with the small picture inside. It was the last thing his mother had given him before she died. He stared at the picture of his parents, then put the locket away.

———

The morning had been a disappointment in terms of finding cattle, but the rest of it had been enjoyable. We had covered two ranches, but the stock they had for sale hadn't been what I was looking for. The breeding stock wasn't even as good as what I had on my ranch. The cows weren't bad, but nothing measured up to what I needed for my two additional bulls. By early afternoon, we had seen what was being offered and had called it quits for the day.

Buck, good to his promise, said he needed to see the doctor about getting a bandage changed, waved and rode off. Sherry and I continued until we found a meadow alongside a babbling stream, and we laid out a picnic lunch.

When we had finished eating, Sherry offered another suggestion for getting my cattle. It involved getting them from Kansas by railroad, which was something I had discussed with Buck.

"The Kansas Pacific railroad runs out to Denver," she told me. "It runs clear east to Kansas City. The cattle drives from Texas have brought a lot of cattle to Kansas, and there have been ranches out there for several years now. They ship cattle to Denver, but mostly those cows are just going to be slaughtered for meat. But maybe you could take the railroad out to Leavenworth, Ellis—somewhere along the line—and find the breeding stock you want."

The more I thought about it, the more sense it made to me. We could ship the stock to Denver, then drive it north just like I'd always planned. I resolved to check with the railroad the next day.

"You know," she said, "I feel a little funny still not knowing your full name. Is Spence a first name or a last name?"

"Lots of people don't know more than that." I chuckled. "I never go by anything besides Spence, but my full name is Clay Spencer. Somewhere along the way, back when I lived in Denver before, it just became Spence." I told her, for some reason, about my earlier life in Denver, including my brief marriage. I hadn't told that story before to anyone other than Buck. "Tomorrow," I concluded, "there's a judge over on Olive Street who is going to give me a paper telling me I'm divorced."

She reached over to put her hand on mine. "Thanks for telling me that," she said. "I had a tough time for a while, too. I lost my parents on the Oregon Trail and had to fend for myself at the same age you did. I know what it's like to struggle to find work and barely have enough to eat. I'm a little protective about young kids trying to make a life for themselves. My assistant Bess is one of those. There's another young guy I'm worried about. He comes into the bakery every morning and does a little work for me in exchange for breakfast. Maybe you can meet him."

"Sure," I said. "How old do you think he is?"

"No older than eighteen, I'd say. He doesn't really tell me much." She shook her head in frustration. "He came in yesterday with a black eye and an enormous bruise on the side of his head. I think he was in a fight, and I think he might be working for a man that runs gambling, shell games, robberies, and who knows what else. I don't know how to steer this kid away from it."

It reminded me a lot of the start I'd gotten in life. "What else do you know? I guess he might work at a saloon or run some errands to make a little money. Lots of ways to get in trouble doing those things." I shook my head. I had done those kinds of things at that age. "I'd be glad to talk to him, if he'll listen to me," I said. "I know how that kind of thing turns out."

Clouds gathered suddenly above us, and a spring thunderstorm seemed to blow in out of nowhere. We gathered up the food and blankets and made a run for a large aspen tree near the bank of the stream. It didn't shelter us completely, but we huddled together under the blankets while we waited for the rain to pass over. I'll have to say I was pretty disappointed when it did. I could have stayed huddled together under that tree for a long time.

CHAPTER 8

PAYOFF

L uke had a few hours to kill before he needed to report to the Mother Lode Saloon for work. He hung around down the street from the bakery, watching to see if the woman returned. He wanted to talk to somebody about how much trouble he might get into with his work at the saloon, and the woman Sherry was the only one he could think of. He supposed it might have something to do with his mother.

Not that Sherry reminded him of his mother. They weren't very much alike at all. It had to do with somebody who might care about him and try to help him out. He had known little of that in his life.

Most of his memories had to do with his mother, and with one or both of them working in a saloon. He had faint memories of her singing at saloons in San Francisco, down by the docks. They had actually done a little better in those days, as far as he could remember. He remembered a room they had lived in there in San Francisco. The room wasn't very big, but it was warm, and it seemed like they always had food.

By the time he was about ten, though, his mother wasn't well a lot of the time. She seemed to cough a lot, and before long, she wasn't able to sing anymore. She kept working at saloons, but she was serving drinks or mopping the floor and cleaning the place up after closing. They left San Francisco and worked wherever she could find something, often at mining towns. Sometimes, they slept in a back room at a saloon, or sometimes, they stayed in a tent at the edge of town.

Luke started working, too, so they would have enough food. He did a lot of mopping and cleaning at saloons, and as he got older, he would help carry boxes, wash glasses, and run errands. He would also look for other work, helping at livery stables, helping blacksmiths, whatever he could find. His mother could work less and less, but he kept a roof over their heads.

He had always asked about his father, and for many years, she wouldn't talk about it at all. Finally, there toward the end, she had told him that Luke's father didn't know about him. She wouldn't say more than that, but she told him his father's name, where she had met him, and she had given Luke that locket.

When she died, Luke had left California for good. He had come to Denver, and things hadn't worked out the way he'd hoped so far, but he was determined to stay with it. He wanted to stay here—he had drifted a lot with his mother over the last several years, and he wanted to stay somewhere. Denver seemed to be a busy town, so he might as well be here.

Luke had one more reason for choosing Denver, but he had said nothing about it to anybody. He'd kept his eyes and ears open, but he was leery about asking questions of anyone. Maybe he would start with the lady at the bakery. He had come to Denver hoping to find his father. His mother had said that's where his dad had lived when she knew him.

A couple hours passed without the woman returning to the bakery, and it was time to report to the saloon for work. Luke got up and walked around the corner. When he entered, he wasn't sure now whether to report to Al downstairs, or go upstairs to the gambling room. He was both relieved and disappointed when Al told him to stay down-stairs to help in the saloon today. He felt safer down here in the saloon, but he couldn't make much money.

A few minutes after Luke started work, he saw Jed come in and climb the stairs to the gambling hall, smirking at Luke as he went. He ignored Jed and started his work. About halfway through his shift, Al pulled him aside and pointed upstairs.

"Go see Burt upstairs," he snapped. "Keep your mouth shut and your eyes open, kid. You can make some money and get out of that stable where you're sleepin'." He hung on to Luke's collar a moment longer. "Don't get too curious. Do what you're told." He started to say something else, then changed his mind and waved Luke away.

When he entered the gambling hall, he could feel Jed's eyes boring into him. He looked away and walked over to Burt, who was serving drinks behind the bar. Luke stopped and waited. His eyes swept the room, and he saw the gunman, Dunn, leaning against the wall with his arms crossed. He looked back at Burt, who shoved a fresh cigar into his mouth and beckoned Luke to come around behind the bar.

Burt put an arm around his shoulders, surprising Luke. "You like to make a little extra money, don't ya kid?" Burt's eyes narrowed against the cigar smoke as he studied Luke's face.

"Sure," Luke responded. He felt a lurch of anxiety in his stomach, but he held his eyes, unblinking, on Burt's face.

Burt held him in a searching gaze for a moment longer, then nodded in satisfaction. "You come in here tomorrow afternoon, around two o'clock," Burt told him. "I have an important letter for you to deliver. You get three dollars for delivering the letter."

Luke choked back his obvious questions about who the letter was for and what was so important about the letter. He also wondered how far he would have to go with the letter. He didn't even have a horse. He only nodded, saying nothing. His gut told him Al had given expert advice about keeping his mouth shut. When Burt turned away, he left.

He was keenly aware that Jed's eyes followed him all the way out of the room.

————

Sherry found Luke seemed to be in a more talkative mood than she had seen lately. He took his usual breakfast to his usual table after stacking the wood. She joined him there, noticing that the bruise and black eye on the side of his face were healing. At least, she thought, there weren't any fresh injuries. None that she could see, anyway.

Small talk didn't last long, but that didn't surprise her. Luke had never joined in much if he didn't have something of substance to stay. Still, he lingered a bit after he finished eating, and Sherry was guessing he had something on his mind. She went for the direct approach.

"Tell me what you do for your job. The other one, I mean, over at the saloon."

He began to talk about it, telling her about working for a man named Al, cleaning up in the saloon, sometimes serving drinks, carrying boxes. He became a little animated, saying that he was saving money to get himself a boarding room. He was tired of sleeping in the hay at the livery stable. He wanted a regular place he could pay for.

Luke glanced up at her as he talked. "I can make enough money in another month, I think, to get myself a room. Especially..." His voice trailed off, and he looked away.

Sherry waited for him to go on, but he seemed to need a nudge. "Especially...what?" she asked.

Luke said the next words in a rush. "Especially when I work in the room upstairs." He seemed relieved to have said the words, and he looked at Sherry for a response.

She was pretty sure what the upstairs room was for, but she needed to know for sure. "Are they gambling in the upstairs room?" she asked.

Luke only nodded, so she pressed him a little farther. "Is it legal?"

He shrugged. "I'm not really sure," he mumbled.

Sherry let the silence settle for just a moment. "Do you ever see the marshal up there? Or the deputy marshal? Or the county sheriff?"

Luke only shook his head, but she could tell by the look in his eyes he knew it wasn't legal. She waited for him to elaborate, if he chose to.

"I can make so much more money up there," he finally explained. "I can make twice what I do downstairs. It won't take long to have some money saved up. I can get a boarding room for myself, and maybe even a horse after that." He shifted uncomfortably in his chair. "After that, I can quit working upstairs."

Sherry let the silence settle in. "Why did you tell me about this?" she asked.

Luke stared down at the table and heaved a sigh. "I'm not sure if I'll get in trouble," he murmured. "Not sure if I might get hurt."

"Have there been any shootings up there?" she asked.

He shook his head. "There's a gunman up there, though. If anybody causes any trouble, I guess he might shoot them."

She reached up and touched the bruise on his face. "Did he give you this?"

Luke shook his head again. "Nope, that was a fight with another kid my age that works up there. He tried to take my money one night. I don't think he'll try that again."

Sherry waited until she could see he had told her all he was going to about the saloon and the gambling room. She tried another subject.

"Do you have any family around here, Luke? Anybody you can tell?"

A tear formed at the corners of his eyes, and she was instantly reminded of how young he was. "My mom ain't around no more," he whispered. "She died almost a year ago. I buried her back in California. They said it was consumption. She was real sick there at the end."

Sherry reached out to cover his arm with her hand. "I'm so sorry," she said, feeling how inadequate the words were. She paused. "What about your dad? Is he around here somewhere?"

Luke waited for a very long time, seeming to choose carefully what he wanted to say. He shook his head. "I don't know my dad," he mumbled. "My dad don't know about me at all. That's what Mom said, anyway. I..." He got up and left without finishing the sentence.

Luke left the bakery and hurried down the street. He'd wanted to ask about the errand today and why somebody would pay him so much money for a simple errand. He thought he knew, though. It probably wasn't legal. He resolved in his mind to quit his job at the saloon just as soon as he had enough money to pay for a boarding room for a few weeks. The horse would have to wait.

———————

Jed leaned against the wall of the general store just down the street, his hat pulled low over his eyes. He was determined to get even with that other kid that was taking his money. That's the way he saw it. He didn't beat the kid in a straight-up fight, but that just meant he had to get smarter. He'd been following Luke for a day now, and this was the second time he'd watched him go into the bakery.

When Luke left the bakery, Jed watched him go down the street, then resisted the impulse to follow him. Maybe he would keep an eye on the bakery lady for a couple days. Following Luke hadn't helped. What he needed was some information that would get Luke in trouble with the guys at the saloon. Something that would get him fired. Maybe, he thought, he could learn something good enough to take to Dunn, the gun hand. That would really be something. A slow smile spread across his face, and he settled back to watch the bakery. He had a couple hours before work.

——————

Sherry paced back and forth in the bakery, convinced she needed to do something to help the boy, but she felt powerless when it came to finding just what she could do. After Bess had watched her make three trips around the small room, she came over and guided Sherry to a chair.

Bess settled into a chair across the table and leaned forward on her elbows, arms crossed. They had worked together long enough that she said nothing. She raised a questioning eyebrow and waited.

"It's the boy, Luke," Sherry blurted out. "He's in trouble, I'm sure, working at that saloon, but I don't know how to help him. I'm afraid that if I go to the marshal, they'll connect it back to him, and he'll be in real trouble. I'm not sure I really trust the marshal's office, anyway." She drummed her fingers on the tabletop.

"Maybe if I helped him get a different job." She stared out the window. "I don't know where, though. The only work he's ever done is doing what he's doing, helping in a saloon. I guess I could ask around, maybe at the blacksmith or the newspaper office." She shook her head. "I don't know if I could get him to take a different job, anyway. Maybe he just needs to get out of Denver."

Bess traced a pattern on the table with a forefinger. "You went around to a couple of ranches yesterday with Spence, right?"

"Yes." Sherry frowned, staring at Bess. Then she realized what Bess was suggesting. "You're saying maybe he could get a job at one of the ranches." Her face showed hope. "He would be out of town, sort of, and learning something besides working in a saloon." She got up and paced again. "He doesn't have any experience with cattle, but maybe somebody needs help and will give him a chance."

She dropped into her chair and beamed a smile in Bess's direction. "Great idea, Bess," she enthused. "I'll get Spence to come with me to those ranches tomorrow. He can help me." She got up and began pacing again.

Bess smiled knowingly at the mention of Spence's name and went back behind the counter. She watched as Sherry stopped pacing abruptly, went over to the corner and picked up her coat.

As she opened the door, she looked back at Bess. "I might go over and see Sheriff Peters, too," she said. "I trust him." The door closed behind her.

———

Sherry hurried out the door, intent on getting over to the sheriff's office, and hoping she could find him there. She didn't want to mention Luke by name. Head down, she began half-walking, half-trotting the six blocks to the sheriff's office. In her preoccupation with her own thoughts, she'd didn't notice when a young, scruffy-looking boy in his late teens, or maybe about twenty, came away from the wall where he had been lounging outside the general store. He followed her.

The closer she came to Sheriff Peters's office, the more uncertain Sherry became. For one thing, she didn't really want to mention Luke's name yet. But, she reasoned, if she came in with some vague story about a boy who might be in trouble, the sheriff would need to know a name, and he would need to know where to look for the boy. She felt sure Luke would deeply resent that, and might cut off all contact with her. Maybe it wouldn't really do any good.

When she reached the sheriff's office, Sherry kept going. She glanced over and could see Sheriff Peters inside, sitting at his desk. She reached the end of the block and turned around, then walked past the office again. She stopped in indecision, then shook her head and retraced her steps to the bakery. She would wait a little while before involving the sheriff.

———

Jed watched, puzzled, as the bakery lady paced back and forth outside a building across the street. He ducked into an alley and peeked around the corner when she doubled back in his direction. Finally, she walked away. He watched her go, feeling sure she was returning to the bakery.

When she was out of sight, Jed crossed the street and read the sign on the door she had walked past. It read: "Hal Peters, County Sheriff." Jed whistled under his breath and began walking back to the saloon. He needed to start work pretty soon, but this morning had been worth the time he'd spent watching the bakery lady. She hadn't actually gone into the sheriff's office after talking to Luke, but he could leave that part out.

He reached the saloon just in time to see Luke walking out. Luke was tucking an envelope into his pocket, and Jed's eyes widened in rage. He knew what that envelope was. Luke was moving in on the best-paying job Jed did for Burt. He looked at the saloon doors and decided he would just have to be a little late for work today. He turned and began running, intent on reaching Luke's destination before Luke got there. Jed would take things into his own hands. He could settle this himself.

———

Luke entered the saloon, still thinking about his conversation with Sherry. He felt more uncertain than ever about working at the saloon, at least in the gambling hall, but he could really use the money. He glanced at the clock in the corner and saw that it was two o'clock exactly. He hurried up the stairs and down to the gambling room. It was empty.

As he stood and looked around, Burt straightened up from behind the bar. He waved at Luke, then struck a match under his cigar. Burt stood and wheeled nervously when he heard a door open and close on the far side. It was Dunn. He didn't like the man, but Soapy insisted on having him here.

Burt reached under the counter and produced an envelope. He reached out, pulled Luke's coat open and tucked the envelope into an inside pocket. "This is...uh, a letter. You take it to Deputy Marshal Camp. Nobody else, you hear. Give it to him personally. Shouldn't be nobody else in the marshal's office this time of day. Anybody else there, you wait to give it to him. Got it?"

Luke nodded. "Nobody else. Got it." He glanced involuntarily over at Dunn, who was sitting in a chair at the side of the hall. He nodded again.

Burt reached back under the counter and produced something else. It was wrapped in a kerchief and looked bulky. Burt pulled the kerchief off, and Luke saw it was a gun. Burt handed it to him. "You put this in your waistband and pull your coat over it. Anybody tries to take the...letter, you discourage with that gun. Got it?"

Luke could only nod again. He saw no way out of this. He would have to make the delivery, but he knew it was money. Luke could feel how thick and bulky that envelope was, resting in his coat pocket. He turned and left the gambling hall. He glanced behind him, relieved to see that Dunn hadn't left his chair.

Luke trotted down the stairs and paused at the saloon entrance, his back to the empty room. He pulled the envelope out of his pocket and stared at it, then hefted it up and down in his hand. It was a lot of money. He wanted to get it delivered and be done with it. He yanked open the saloon door, putting the envelope back in his pocket. He turned south and began hurrying along to the marshal's office. The sooner he finished this job, the better.

CHAPTER 9

ANDERSON RANCH

T he gun in his waistband felt heavy and extremely uncomfortable as Luke set out for the marshal's office. It was a cool, breezy morning, but it wasn't long before the sweat rolled down the back of his neck. He found that he badly wanted to open the coat so he could cool himself down a little, but he didn't dare. He experimented with shifting the gun more to the side. That enabled him to unbutton the coat. He felt confident it didn't show, but still found himself holding his right arm stiffly against his side to keep the coat from opening too far.

As he came closer to the marshal's office, Luke's nervousness actually increased, and the sweat broke out on his forehead. The office and jail stood apart from other buildings, and he knew he would need to cut through an alleyway to get there unless he chose to walk several blocks out of his way. When he reached the alley in question, he stopped and looked. He saw no one. Reproaching himself for running from shadows, Luke started through the alley. It seemed safe enough. He wanted to put this behind him, deliver the money and get out.

When he was about halfway down the alley, Luke broke into a trot. He skidded to a stop when he saw a shadow fall across the exit at the end of the alley. A moment later, Jed stepped into the alley, wearing an evil grin and holding a Bowie knife in front of him, blade up. He moved the blade back and forth, and Luke watched as the curved blade swung from side to side.

"Not feelin' so high and mighty now, are ya?" Jed's mouth curved into an even wider, wicked smile. Luke's mind seemed to freeze for a moment. He absently fixated on the gap in Jed's teeth, making no move as Jed advanced. When Jed held out the blade and gathered himself to rush forward, Luke pulled the pistol from his waistband, lifted the gun and fired.

Jed's eyes grew large as saucers when he saw the gun. He skidded to a stop, then turned and tried to lunge away as the gun came level. He grabbed at his ear, dropped the knife, and fell after Luke pulled the trigger. He clawed at his ear and screamed as the shot echoed in the empty alleyway.

Luke stood stock-still, gun still extended, trying to process what had just happened. He had drawn and fired as a reflex, and his mind scrambled to catch up. He saw Jed rolling to his side, then sitting up against the wall of the alley. He held his left ear with his hand, and Luke could see blood on Jed's hand. Jed moaned softly and made no move to get up. The knife lay in the dirt in front of Luke.

Luke stuffed the gun back into his waistband and pulled the coat over it. He turned and ran back to the entrance of the alley, then darted onto the street, slowing to a walk as he put some distance between himself and Jed. He walked for several hundred yards along the street which was, to his relief, almost empty. No one seemed to take notice of him.

He finally reached the corner of the next street. He turned left and began walking, circling back around to the marshal's office. At the end of the side street, he stopped and looked around the corner. The marshal's office stood by itself and apart from any other buildings. Deputy Marshal Camp stood in front of the building, holding his gun out and swinging his head from side to side. Luke knew it was Camp, even from this distance. He stood facing to Luke's left, and there was no mistaking that vast belly. Eventually, Camp shrugged and re-holstered his gun, then went back inside.

Acting on instinct, Luke took the gun out of his waistband and stuffed it under a bin in back of one building along the side street. He double-checked his pocket to make sure the envelope was still in there, then crossed to the marshal's office. He knocked lightly, then opened the door and let himself in.

Camp looked up from a plate of food in front of him at his desk. "Whaddya want?" he mumbled, spraying bits of food in Luke's direction. He pushed the chair back, gathered himself and stood.

Luke stepped forward, slowly reaching up to pull the envelope from his pocket. He held it out to Camp. "Burt from the Mother Lode Saloon told me to bring this to you." He stood silently while Camp opened the envelope and rifled through the contents.

Camp stuffed the envelope in his pocket and stared at Luke through narrowed eyes. "Didja look in the envelope, kid?"

Luke shook his head and remained silent.

Camp grunted briefly, then changed subjects. "There was a gunshot out there a few minutes ago. You know anything about that?" Camp's suspicion was clear.

"I heard it. Sounded like it was off to my left as I was coming down the street over there. I kept coming to bring you the envelope. Didn't see what it was about." Luke shuffled his feet briefly, but held Camp's gaze.

Camp reached out, grabbed Luke's shoulder roughly and spun him against the wall. "Put your hands up here on the wall, kid, and don't move till I tell you." His hands searched Luke roughly and thoroughly. Finding nothing, he moved back over to the desk and lowered himself slowly into the chair. He took a huge mouthful of food and gestured at the door. "Get outta here, kid."

Luke let himself out and crossed the street. After looking

in both directions, he retrieved the gun from under the bin and stuffed it back into his waistband. Twenty minutes of brisk walking brought him back to the saloon, where he climbed the stairs and entered the gambling hall. He spotted Burt behind the bar. He crossed the room, walked behind the bar, then kneeled, wrapped the gun, and placed it on the shelf.

Burt watched, nodding briefly. He pointed at a tray loaded with whiskey. "Serve some drinks, kid," he said gruffly. As Luke grabbed the tray, Burt put a hand on his shoulder to stop him. "You seen Jed? He hasn't shown up, and I expected him more'n an hour ago."

Luke shook his head and left with the tray. Burt bent down below the bar, picked up the gun and sniffed it. He spun the cylinder and saw there was a bullet missing. He re-wrapped the gun and replaced it on the shelf, then stood to watch Luke as he moved among the customers with the whiskey.

Burt grunted softly and shook his head. "That," he thought to himself, "is one nervy kid." About twenty minutes later, Jed entered the hall, his ear covered with a large bandage. He steered well clear of Luke as he came over to the bar. Burt stood, staring at the ear, waiting for an explanation.

Jed shrugged and grabbed a tray, avoiding eye contact. "Just an accident," he mumbled.

Burt watched Jed moving away. His gut told him the missing bullet and the ear bandage were connected. His gut also told him he couldn't keep these two working together. He would have to figure out what to do about that. They both knew things that could cause him trouble.

———

Buck and I were walking over to the bakery for breakfast, and we had come to the conclusion we were better off going to Kansas to get the cows I needed. The only real problem I was having came when I had to convince Buck to ride the train over there and back. You would have thought I had asked him to walk back to Montana.

"You wanna ride them steam cars, huh?" There was an injured tone to his voice. "Why can't we just ride our horses out there and drive the cows back?"

"That would take weeks instead of days," I explained patiently. "Plus, I would have to hire some more guys. We'll have to drive 'em to Montana from Denver, anyway. You'll be sick of driving cows before we're done. The train can save us a lot of trouble on the first leg of this."

Even Buck could see the logic of it. He huffed along, grumbling under his breath for another block or two. "What if them sparks catch us on fire? What if the train breaks down, out there in the middle of nowhere?"

"The trains don't catch on fire from sparks," I said. "And, we'll have our horses on the train. If it breaks down, we can ride." I searched my brain for something to clinch the deal. "I'll buy the drinks when we get to Kansas."

Buck brightened up. "The whole time we're in Kansas?" he asked hopefully.

"I don't have that much money," I said. "I'll buy 'em the first day we're there. I know how much you can put away in one day."

He didn't answer, but he stopped complaining, which I knew meant he would take the ride with me. As a last resort, I could go by myself, but I much preferred to have him come along.

Sherry greeted us at the door of the bakery and gave me a hug. She turned to Buck and patted him on the arm. "Buck," she said, "we have fresh donuts this morning." Buck was already halfway to the counter, following his nose. Sherry guided me to the same table we'd been using the last two mornings.

"I've been waiting to talk to you about something," she said quickly. "It's about the boy I told you about who comes in here and stacks wood for me in the mornings. His name is Luke, by the way."

I nodded. "I said I would do what I could to help. What can I do?"

"He's working at a saloon down the street," she explained. "It's called the Mother Lode Saloon, and he told me yesterday he has been working in a gambling hall they are running upstairs. He said they shut things down if the marshal comes in the saloon downstairs, so I'm sure there are illegal things going on up there. He wouldn't tell me much more about it, but I'm sure he's headed for trouble if he's working in a gambling hall."

Sherry paused, and I waited. We could hear Bess laughing over at the counter. No doubt Buck was entertaining her with a bunch of tall tales about his exploits over the years.

"I thought about going to the town marshal," she continued, "but he is about to retire, and I doubt he'll get involved in anything. The deputy marshal...well, I don't trust him at all. Just my instincts, but I've learned to trust my instincts over the years. That leaves the sheriff for the county. I walked over to his office, but changed my mind before I went in. I guess I'm not really sure what he could do at this point."

"It gets worse," she told me after a brief pause. "The rumors around town are that the Mother Lode Saloon is owned and run by a man named Soapy Smith and his enforcers. Have you heard anything about Soapy Smith?"

I shook my head. "Strange name," I offered.

She nodded, then explained how he had gotten his name with the soap bar raffles. "He's into other things, though," she added quickly. "Gambling, robberies, you name it. They say he brags about having marshals and judges on his payroll." She paused and shook her head. "I've really got to get Luke away from these guys."

I puzzled over the problem for a minute and gathered my

breath to speak, but she laid a hand on my arm to stop me. "I thought of one other thing, and maybe you could help me with it. Well, actually, it was Bess's idea, but I really liked it. What if we could get him a job out of town at one of those ranches we visited yesterday? He could learn how to run a ranch, he would have a place to stay, food to eat, and make a little money!"

It sounded like a good idea to me, and I told her so. I noticed her hand was still on my arm, and I liked that a lot. I looked up to see Buck returning to our table, along with Bess. They were carrying a lot of food. I noticed Buck's jaw chewing vigorously, and I shook my head slowly. "That's the only man I ever knew could eat his own weight in donuts," I observed.

We explained the idea to Buck. He pointed out that we would need a few hands to drive the cows to Montana after we brought them here, and maybe we could also ask, while we were out at the ranches, where to find hands. "Ya know," he said after a moment's thought, "mebbe we could hire the kid to help us drive the cows if we can't find him a job here. I could show him what he needs to know."

I shot a quick glance at Sherry, who was wearing mixed emotions. "We'll bring him back to Denver if he wants to come back," I told her.

"Good, I'm getting attached to him, like he's my brother or something," she said. She gave my arm a squeeze. "Make sure you come with him for a nice long visit in Denver."

We decided to try a ranch named the Rolling R, located several miles east of town. There was an older couple named Anderson there, with one son helping them run several hundred head of cattle. They sounded like maybe they could use a hand. We adjourned after breakfast, with the three of us riding out to the Anderson ranch.

———

Luke stayed out of the bakery when he saw Sherry talking to the two men he had seen in there before. He had decided he needed to tell her about the money delivery, but he didn't want to do that with other people hanging around. He didn't even know who they were.

When she left with the other two men again, he put aside his disappointment, went inside to chop and stack the wood, then grabbed his breakfast from Bess and left. He carried the food to a bench down the street from the saloon and started eating. He was still chewing the first bite when he noticed two men standing in an alley across the street. He stopped chewing, leaned over and stared.

He took another long stare, then got up and moved out of sight. He found another bench and sat down to finish his food. There was no mistaking it. Jed was in that alley talking to Dunn, the gunfighter. Luke remained sitting on the bench long after he finished the food. Of course, Jed could have been talking to Dunn about anything, but he'd never seen them talk before, and Jed seemed determined to cause Luke as much trouble as he could. Luke had a bad feeling about this one.

Luke circled back around to the bakery, but Sherry didn't come back before it was time to report to the saloon for work. He would have to come back and talk to her tomorrow. He sighed, got up and walked back over to the saloon. At least, he thought, he would only work downstairs in the saloon tonight. He felt safer when he stayed down there.

———

Things went better out at the Anderson ranch than I had expected. They were, in fact, short on help and struggling to keep up. They balked a little when we told them the boy had never worked on a ranch before, but I pointed out that he wouldn't be expecting much in the way of money. Sherry assured them that Luke worked for her every morning, came without fail, worked hard, and did his job well. She explained he was an orphan. I glanced at the Andersons' expressions, and I could tell she had scored a point there.

The Andersons looked at each other, and then the wife nodded at him and patted his arm. "It's the least we can do, and he can help us." The husband nodded and took us out to what had been a bunkhouse in the past. It was a little worse for wear, but he promised he could fix it up in no time.

"The boy can sleep out here and have his meals with us," he said. "I can pay him only about fifty cents a day, but he should have everything he needs here. I can teach him about cattle, and even show him a little blacksmithin', if that's something he decides he would like to do."

Sherry promised she would tell Luke about it, and would do everything she could to persuade him to take this job and leave the saloon. We shook hands all around, and I could almost feel Sherry's relief. She was, I thought, an exceptionally kind-hearted woman.

We reached town, put our horses in the livery stable, and walked Sherry back to the bakery. I told her we would leave on the train for Kansas in the morning, but I would come to see her as soon as we got back. She promised to let me know about Luke's decision just as soon as I returned. She gave me a long, lingering hug. I seemed to have trouble letting go of her.

As we walked back to our boarding room, I kept hearing snorts and chuckles from Buck, though he was careful not to look in my direction. "Oh, shut up," I told him.

CHAPTER 10

LOCKET

Buck had volunteered to hang around the train station the next morning to see what he could find out about cows in Kansas. Mostly, we needed to know where to get off the train and start looking. The Andersons had advised me I could stop somewhere in central Kansas and find a lot of cows that had been driven up the Chisholm Trail from Texas. That was mostly good with me—the longhorn was a good, tough breed that could survive in Montana. I was hoping maybe I could find some that had been mixed with some other breeds to carry a little more weight, though.

The other thing the Andersons told me about stopping in central Kansas had to do with the Texas Cattle Fever line. Cattle from Texas had been infecting local cattle with a fever, and more and more towns in Kansas were refusing entry to Texas cattle or requiring quarantine. That was pushing the drive destinations farther and farther west. That suited me, as I wouldn't have to travel as far to find good herds. I needed to be careful about the cattle fever, though. I remembered the problems it had caused when I was a boy. That could destroy a herd.

I stopped off at the judge's office first thing in the morning, and he had a paper for me, saying they considered me to be divorced in the state of Colorado. I paid him, stepped outside and read it over. I supposed it had been about time to get through this. I hadn't seen or heard from Annie in almost twenty years. I folded the paper and tucked it into a pocket, then headed over to find Buck at the station.

I found him right outside the train depot, talking to a wizened old man who only identified himself as Skeeter. A broom rested against the side of the bench where they were talking, and I gathered Skeeter had taken a break to talk to Buck.

"Skeeter here," Buck told me, "has made the drive from Texas to Kansas eight times. Knows all about Kansas, too."

"Rode that Chisholm Trail, I did," Skeeter added proudly. "Rode it till these old bones were too old to make the trip. Then I worked on ranches over there in Kansas till I got too old to rope and ride much. Now they give me a bit o' money to clean up around here. Don't know nuthin' about ridin' these here steam cars, but I can tell ya where to look for cows."

"Do you know," I asked, "if any of the ranches have something besides longhorns? Maybe a mixed breed?"

Skeeter scratched his chin thoughtfully. "Yeah, you can probably find some. Got some ranchers over there and brought some bulls from back east. Yeah, you can find some. Might cost a little more." He looked at me speculatively, pausing and waiting.

I flipped him a dollar coin. He caught it expertly and slid it into his pocket in one fluid motion.

"Ellis," Sheeter said, nodding his head for emphasis. "If'n I was you, I'd go to Ellis. Ain't no more than halfway across Kansas, got a bunch of ranches around there. Got them a post office, a school, an' even a ho-tel where you can stay. Mebbe you can get cows over there for twenny dollars a head, mebbe a little more if you want breedin' stock." He stopped and scratched his chin again. "If you cain't find what you want there, maybe just ride down the line one or two stops. Don't know the names of them towns, but there's ranches all along the way."

A man came out of the depot building, looked at Skeeter sitting on the bench, and cleared his throat loudly. Skeeter showed a surprising turn of speed as he jumped up, grabbed the broom, and put it to use.

I stepped over to the ticket window and asked when the next train ran, and when it would reach Ellis. The young man consulted a schedule, then glanced at the clock on the wall. "Next train in two hours, sir, at twelve o'clock. Time it takes can be a little different every trip, what with needing to stop for passengers and load up wood and water. You should be there first thing tomorrow, though."

I paid for the tickets. He advised me to be here at eleven thirty to get our horses loaded up so we could leave on time. I sent Buck to get the horses, then took a trip over to the bakery.

Sherry looked surprised to see me, but her face lit up in a smile. I suppose my face looked about the same. I told her we'd be leaving at noon, and I planned to stop at Ellis to look for cattle. "They tell me there's a hotel there, so we'll probably stay there two or three nights and look for what we want. If you hear anything about the boy Luke, or need to reach me for any reason, you can send a telegram to that hotel. I'm sure it's the only one in town."

"Hold on." She stepped behind the counter and put together two thick sandwiches, wrapped them, and put them in a bag. "For the trip," she told me. "Come see me as soon as you get back."

"Count on it," I said. "We should be back in a few days. Depends on how fast we can find what we want." The door swung shut softly behind me, and I found I was already looking forward to getting back to Denver.

Sherry had given up, for the second day in a row, on seeing Luke when the back door opened, and she soon heard the axe chopping wood. Sherry glanced involuntarily at the front door, and Spence had left not five minutes ago. Maybe she could introduce them next time.

When Luke had seated himself with his breakfast, she moved over to join him, eager to explain about the opportunity to work at the Anderson Ranch. He surprised her by telling her, for the first time, that he needed to talk about something. Mildly disappointed, she nodded and waited.

Luke pushed his food around the plate for a moment. "I shot a guy yesterday," he blurted. He raised a hand when he heard Sherry's sharp intake of breath. "I only grazed him. Nicked his ear. He came to work afterward."

Luke didn't seem inclined to say anything else. He avoided Sherry's gaze and began nibbling at his food. Finally, she had waited for as long as she could stand to wait. "He works at the saloon, too? How did you wind up shooting him?"

Luke glanced up at her unhappily, then told his story. "Burt, the guy that runs the gambling hall, told me to take an envelope to the deputy marshal. His name is Camp. I...I looked in the envelope. It had money in it. A lot of money. Burt paid me three dollars to take it over there. That's a lot for me." He fell silent again, refusing to meet Sherry's eyes.

She wasn't sure which question to ask first. "Who did you shoot? Did you get the money over to Camp?"

He answered the second question first. "Yeah, I got the money over to him. Gave it to Camp. I guess they're payin' him to stay out of the gambling hall, huh?"

Sherry nodded. "That and maybe ignore some other criminal things they're doing. I doubt the gambling hall is the only shady thing they have going on." She paused. "So, this guy Burt knows you got the money delivered, and he's not looking for you? You're okay with him?" She relaxed when Luke nodded.

She remembered her other question. "Who did you shoot? And why?"

Luke pushed his plate away, leaving most of the food untouched. "That was Jed, the guy I got in a fight with when he tried to take my money. He was waiting in an alley I cut through to get to the marshal's office. He had a knife out. He rushed me with that knife, and I think he would have killed me with it. Burt gave me a gun. It was in my waistband. I just pulled it out and shot—didn't really think about it. I was afraid he would kill me."

He was hunched over the table now, and the usual tough front he put up was gone. He rocked gently back and forth in his chair.

Sherry reached over, took his chin in her hand, and gently raised his head to look him in the eye. "We'll figure this out," she said. "We'll get through this. I think I have some good news." She waited while he mustered a small smile. "You say you just grazed this guy, Jed?"

Luke nodded. "He came to work later. He had a big bandage on his ear. I don't think he'll tell anybody I got the better of him twice. He hates me, though..." His voice trailed away. "I saw him talking to the gunman Dunn outside the saloon yesterday."

Sherry's alarm level went up again while she prompted him for the story of Jed and Dunn talking outside the saloon. She couldn't figure out what that might have been about, but like Luke, she had a bad feeling about it. Another thought struck her.

"You said Jed was waiting for you in an alley over there. How did he know you would be there? And how would he know you were carrying money? Do you think he heard Burt talking to you about delivering that money to the deputy marshal?"

Luke's forehead furrowed, and he stared across the table at her. Clearly, he hadn't thought about this. "No, there's no way he heard Burt talking to me. He wasn't even in the gambling hall when Burt told me. That guy Dunn was in there, but he wasn't payin' much attention." He shook his head in confusion. "I don't know how he knew. He was late comin' to work on account of this..." He lapsed back into silence.

Sherry's mind raced, turning the problem over in her mind. This was more serious than she had realized. The possibility of the boy Jed working with the gunman scared her the most. The gunman might have Soapy Smith's ear, and Smith was said to be ruthless.

"He must have followed you," she concluded. "Maybe he started following you and figured out where you were going, then ran to get there first...maybe he used to make those deliveries." That last idea made more sense to her, the more she thought about it. "If he did, then he would have known you were carrying a lot of money. He could have taken the money, but you'd have been blamed for losing it."

Sherry looked at the door. "Could he have followed you here?" she asked. "Does he know where you sleep at night? He could still try to get even with you."

For the first time, she saw fear creeping into Luke's eyes. She reached out to cover his hand with hers.

"Never mind," she said. "I think I have a way for you to move on and stop working for these guys." She told him about the visit to the Anderson ranch and their offer to hire Luke. He was nodding his head yes before she even finished.

"So, you'll do it?" she asked. "You'll take the job?" He nodded again, hope showing in his eyes.

Sherry got up and walked to the bakery window. She scanned up and down the street, then walked back to the table. "You need to get over to the livery stable and get your things," she told him. "But we need to make sure this boy Jed doesn't know where you've gone." She sat down and drummed her fingers on the tabletop.

"If he's watching, he's watching the front door," she concluded. "Go out the back door and circle around to the stable. I'll walk around out front and see if I see him. Get your things and come through the back door. We'll wait until you and Jed are both expected to be at work, then I'll borrow the buggy at the general store and take you to the Anderson Ranch. You can stay out of sight over there. They'll forget about you after a while."

They reached the Anderson Ranch just four hours later. Sherry felt a minor disappointment for him when she saw the condition of the bunkhouse, but it didn't seem to bother Luke. It was, she realized, a step up from the livery stable. The Andersons left them to talk and returned to the house. Sherry promised to visit him once a week or then turned to leave. Luke stopped her with a hand on her arm.

"There's something else I wanted to tell you," he said. "I got a little sidetracked, what with the shooting and all that, but there's one thing maybe you could still help me with."

"Name it." She sat down on a bunk.

"It's about my dad." He chewed on his lower lip, then plowed ahead: "I came to Denver mostly because it's the last place my mom saw my dad. Long time ago, but I thought maybe he could still be here. I kinda been looking for him." He reached up and pulled up a locket hanging on a chain around his neck. He opened the locket and held it out to her. "This is what he looked like."

Sherry felt a sharp jolt of surprise. It was an old, faded picture, but the similarity was remarkable. She looked up at Luke. "What is your dad's name?" she asked, knowing what the answer would be.

"Spencer is his last name. Don't really know the first. Mom said folks called him Spence."

Sherry took one more look before she closed the locket and returned it to him. "I know your dad," she said simply.

———

A couple hours later, as she returned the buggy and strolled home, she found she was still in complete surprise, maybe even shock. She could only imagine how Spence would feel when he found out he had a son. Luke had been so excited, peppering her with questions about his father. She'd answered them as best she could and promised to bring Spence to the ranch when he returned.

She passed the telegraph office and toyed with the

thought of sending Spence a telegram, then immediately rejected the idea. She would tell him in person. Luke was out of harm's way for now. It would be better to tell him face-to-face. A small smile crossed her face. What an unbelievable day. She couldn't wait for Spence to return.

Sherry reached the boarding house where she kept a small room, then turned in through the front door. It was her plan to make a place at the bakery, maybe by adding a second floor. Then, she could move in and live right above the bakery. She closed the door behind her and went to see what the landlady was serving for dinner. She had no idea that a young man with a large bandage on his ear had followed her from the general store.

———

Jed watched the bakery woman disappear into the boardinghouse. The disappointed expression on his face matched what he felt inside. He had followed Luke over to the bakery this morning, then watched the front door from across the street until it was time to go to work. He was certain Luke had never left the building. The woman had come out and walked up and down the street a little, but then she had gone back inside.

The night had been so slow over at the saloon and gambling hall he'd been sent home. They didn't have enough work to do—sometimes that happened. He had decided to come back over to the bakery, even though it was closed. Maybe, he thought, he would see Luke sneak out of there after dark. Instead, he had stumbled across the woman driving up in a buggy, then walking to a boarding house.

What did any of this mean? He still hadn't seen Luke, but he had been sure the woman had still been inside. Clearly, she had slipped out of there without him knowing it. Luke could have done the same. He ground his teeth in frustration. Dunn had shown some interest when Jed told him about the woman walking past the sheriff's office. He'd said he "might mention it to Soapy." He said to keep an eye on Luke. This, Jed thought, is what he needed. He needed Soapy Smith to take an interest in him. Now, he couldn't find Luke.

Jed took up watch outside the bakery for another hour before giving up. There was nobody inside—it was completely dark in there. No one came or went. He went over to the livery stable to see what he could find over there. The old man was there when he first arrived, taking a horse from a stranger, and putting it in one stall. Then the old man left, and it was dark and quiet at the livery stable. No sign of Luke.

The night wind set in, and Jed shivered inside his thin flannel shirt. A drunk stumbled out of an alley behind him and gave him a scare. He didn't want to admit it, but he was a little jumpier since he'd been taken down twice by Luke. He wanted to get even, and he was determined to get his chance.

Finally, the cold and darkness got to him, and he started for home, cursing under his breath. He'd watch the bakery again in the morning. Luke always went over there. Maybe he would have more news to report to Dunn when he got to work in the afternoon.

CHAPTER 11

SMITH'S ORDERS

Luke stumbled along behind Tom Anderson in the near dark of the early morning. The man had said he would be out to get Luke first thing in the morning to start chores, but Luke had no idea the morning would start this early. The part of his brain that was working had heard his new boss say they would milk cows before breakfast. He was still trying to translate that one in his head. The barn loomed in front of them. Luke ducked just in time to avoid the boards nailed across the top of the entrance door.

Tom pulled a small stool alongside a cow in the first stall and sat down to give Luke a demonstration. "Nothing to it," he told Luke confidently. "Just grab the teat, wrap your fingers around it and squeeze. Give it just a little pull. Not too fast." He demonstrated and was rewarded with a squirt of milk in the pail. Tom stood and gestured at the stool. "Your turn."

Feeling a little more awake, Luke sat down on the stool to take his turn. Two stalls over, he could hear Tom's son Zeb milking. It was a steady splashing sound. Luke took hold and squeezed. Firmly, not too fast, he told himself. His first three squeezes were rewarded with...nothing. He heard a chuckle behind him.

"You'll get it," Tom said. "Wrap, squeeze, pull, you'll get a rhythm going."

Luke muttered under his breath and did as he was told. After a couple more tries, he drew a small stream of milk into the pail.

"That's it." Tom chortled. "You're getting it. Now, jus' keep squeezin' till there ain't no more milk." He moved to the stall next to Luke and began milking. "Three cows, three of us," he called. "After this, we'll go in and get some breakfast."

After a few minutes, Luke decided he had gotten a little rhythm going, but the sound of the milk hitting the pail in the next two stalls told him he was far slower than the other two. He leaned his head against the cow's flank and kept squeezing, aware that his hands were already feeling a little tired and cramped.

After several more minutes, Tom quit milking in the next stall. He carried his bucket past Luke and poured the milk into a large container near the barn wall. He walked back, untied the cow he'd been milking, and turned her out of the barn. He returned, leaned in, and looked into Luke's pail.

"Pretty near halfway done, I'd say," he observed. "Told ya' you'd get the hang of it in no time. Pour the milk in that big container over there when you're done and come to the house for breakfast." He left the barn, whistling under his breath.

Luke resumed muttering to himself and kept milking. He paused to give his hands a rest, then heard footsteps coming from the third stall over. Zeb leaned in, then tapped Luke on the shoulder. "I'll finish up," he said. "You can go in for breakfast. It won't take me more'n a few minutes."

Luke mumbled his thanks and trudged to the house. Breakfast improved his mood. Tom's wife, Arlene, heaped his plate high with eggs, biscuits, and gravy, then set a steaming cup of coffee in front of him. When he emptied his plate, she filled it up again. Luke pushed back after the second plate and mumbled his thanks.

"We ain't payin' you much, so we got to feed you proper," Tom boomed. "Come on, time to learn somethin' about shoeing horses. I told that nice lady Sherry I could teach you some blacksmithin' skills."

The rest of the morning was more to Luke's liking than the milking episode had been. He worked with Tom and Zeb, first shoeing Tom's horse, then an old mare Tom said they used to pull the buggy to town once every two weeks or so. "Ol' Lucy," he said, patting the mare's rump, "ain't as young as she used to be. We take her to town every couple weeks. You can borrow her and ride her in if you need to go to town."

Sherry had cautioned him strongly to avoid town for several weeks, but he nodded his thanks, glad to know he had a way to make the trip if he needed to. The rest of the day passed quickly. A quick tour of the ranch followed lunch. Tom showed him the herd and the wheat fields, promising that he would let Luke work mainly with the cattle.

Evening found Luke in his bunk, knowing how early Tom would show up in the morning. He stretched out on the mattress. It had a few lumps, but it beat sleeping in the stable. Luke clasped his hands behind his head, wondering when he would meet his father. Sherry hadn't told him much, only that he was a rancher from Montana, and was at present buying cattle in Kansas. She promised to bring him to meet Luke when he came back to Denver.

Luke reached over and pulled his duffel bag out from under the bed, reaching into it and searching for his diary. Next to the locket with the picture of his parents, he prized his diary the most. He had been pretty much alone for most of this life, with only his mother for company, and now she was gone. Writing in the diary allowed him to feel a bit like he was talking to a friend.

He searched through the bag for several seconds, then pulled it up on the bed and held the lantern over it with one hand while he searched with the other. When it became obvious the diary wasn't in there, he set the lantern down and slumped on the bed. He must have left the diary in the stable in his rush to get out of town.

Luke pushed open the door to the bunkhouse and walked outside, standing in the dark and thinking things over. He had to get the diary back. Maybe tomorrow or the next day, Tom would let him borrow the old mare and ride into town. The longer he waited, the less likely he could find the diary in the stable.

———

Sherry was still in a good mood the next morning. She had two things that were making her feel upbeat: she had moved Luke out of harm's way, and Spence would come back in maybe another day or two. She had much to tell him.

As the morning rush thinned out, she reconsidered whether she wanted to tell Sheriff Peters about Luke's experiences at the Mother Lode Saloon. She had held back from doing it before, in part, because she worried that, in some way, it might endanger Luke. She no longer felt that way. Luke was safely tucked away at the Anderson Ranch.

Another hour passed, and Sherry ran out of things to do. The pans were all washed, and the tables and countertops had been scrubbed twice. When she went over to stare out the window for the third time, Bess spoke up.

"Whatever it is you want to do, I think you should just do it," she advised. "You're going to wear the tops of the tables off if you keep scrubbing. Do you want to go out and see Luke already?"

Sherry was already shrugging into her coat. She paused at the door. "I'm going to Sheriff Peters's office," she called over her shoulder. "I'll be back in about an hour."

There was no hesitancy today when she reached the office—she knocked on the way in. A middle-aged man wearing a badge looked up from some papers on his desk when she came in. He rose and escorted her to a chair beside his desk.

"Sherry Lee," she told him, extending her hand.

"I know," he said with a slightly sheepish smile on his face. "I come to the bakery sometimes. Love the donuts."

"I thought you looked familiar," she mused. "Well, next time, the donuts will be on me. I have a problem. Actually, a very young man who does some work for me has the problem. He's been working at the Mother Lode Saloon, and they've had him doing illegal things."

The sheriff studied her face. "What kind of illegal things?"

"Things like working in a secret, probably illegal gambling hall. Making payoffs to city officials. That sort of thing."

Peters frowned. "Have you talked to the marshal's office? This sounds like something they should get involved with."

"I would have," Sherry agreed. "But he's making the payoffs to Deputy Marshal Camp. The payoffs are coming directly from the gambling hall," she added.

Peters rubbed his hands over his eyes, then reached for a pencil and a few sheets of paper. "Okay," he said. "Sounds like I need to look into it. Tell me what you know, from the beginning."

Fifteen minutes later, the sheriff sat back and tapped the pencil point absent-mindedly against his teeth. "Good job getting the kid out of there," he said. "That makes it less urgent. Definitely a delicate situation," he mused. "I don't know how far the payoffs go. I need to check around quietly for a while. Keep the kid out of sight."

Sherry rose to go, then paused at the door as Peters added one more thought. "Do you think they know your connection with..." He scanned the paper in front of him. "Your connection with Luke?"

"No," she said immediately. "Well," she continued after a moment's thought. "I don't think so. He does some work for me in the mornings, but he's said nothing about me over there. I don't think they know he works for me."

Peters nodded, unconvinced. "Okay," he drawled. "But just to be safe, assume they do. Soapy Smith has an ugly reputation."

Sherry left, feeling less upbeat than she had before. She resolved to be careful when she went to visit Luke. She hoped Spence would be back soon.

Jed ducked behind the corner of a building as she emerged from the sheriff's office. His morning wasn't a total waste, after all. There had been no sign of Luke this morning, and he hadn't come in to work yesterday. That frustrated and angered Jed. But things were looking up a little now. Dunn had told him to let him know right away if the bakery woman went back to the sheriff's office. At least he could report on that.

———

Dunn walked along Larimer Street until he reached 16th. He found the Broadwell House easily enough. He didn't bother to stop at the desk. He knew where Soapy Smith's room was, on the second floor. He climbed the stairs, grudgingly admiring Smith for being able to stay in nicer places than the boarding houses and shacks where he usually stayed.

That was part of the reason he was here today. The kid Jed had tipped him off on Luke's friend, going to see the sheriff. Dunn didn't really care what Jed's reasons were for spying on Luke, but if Dunn could impress Soapy Smith with the information, there might be money in it for him. Watching for cheaters at the gambling hall was okay, but he could make more money from holdups or "cleaning up problems," as Smith liked to say. This might qualify as a problem to be cleaned up. Maybe even two.

He entered when he heard "come in" after knocking. Smith's voice was surprisingly high and maybe even a little girlish, he thought, but he made sure not to mention that. Smith had plenty of money to hire other guns.

Smith was shaving in front of a mirror. He waved at a chair, and Dunn took a seat until Smith had finished shaving. He wiped his face with a towel as he crossed to another chair opposite Dunn.

"Whatcha got?" he asked without preamble.

Dunn told the story of how Jed had followed the other kid to the bakery, then trailed the girl from the bakery to the sheriff's office. He added that the two had apparently gotten into a couple fights, with the new kid Luke, coming out on top. He also mentioned that Luke had apparently taken over Jed's job of taking the payoff money to Deputy Marshal Camp.

Soapy Smith continued to wipe his face with the towel while he thought about the things Dunn had told him. He scowled and tossed the towel into the corner. "So," he intoned, "what we've got is the kid who knows I'm paying off Camp is friends with the bakery owner, who has gone to see the marshal. And this other kid is trying to get even with him, so he comes to you."

"That's pretty much it," Dunn agreed. "Burt might have trusted the wrong kid. You want me to do something about this?"

Smith nodded and stared out the window, scratching his chin absently. "Yeah, we'll have to do something about it. Can't do it here, though, with that sheriff maybe sniffing around. You'll have to take 'em out of town. Take 'em to the Roost."

Dunn's expression changed for the first time. He sat up in the chair, staring at Smith. "The Roost? That's mebbe... four hundred miles from here."

Smith's scowl deepened. "I wanna operate in Denver for a long time. This can't get back to me, and I can't have a problem here. Take 'em to the Roost. Take the kid Luke first. Find out if he told the woman about the gambling hall. If he won't talk, assume he did. Take him first. If you have to take care of the woman, have somebody else take her. They won't let her in the Roost. Have somebody else do it, far away from here. Have the Blount twins do it." He lapsed into silence, then went looking for his whiskey. He poured a shot and downed it.

Dunn eyed the whiskey bottle, and he could see why Smith wanted things done far away from here. "Okay, if we have to take the woman, I'll make sure they get her out of Colorado. Maybe somewhere close to Robber's Roost. Maybe make it look like Indians got her." He could see the meeting was over, but there was the little matter of payment.

Smith stuck his hand in his pocket, came out with two twenty-dollar gold pieces, and flipped them to Dunn. He caught them expertly, then met Smith's *why-are-you-still-here* stare. "I gotta pay the Blount twins, too," he pointed out.

Smith made a growling noise and fished in his pocket again. He flipped two more gold pieces to Dunn, who left without further questions.

Dunn paused outside the hotel, tossing the gold pieces in the air before catching them and stuffing them in his pocket. He would make the Blount twins split one twenty-dollar piece. They were small-time operators, anyway, robbing miners on their way to town. They fancied themselves gunfighters, but they weren't all that much. Good enough to get the woman and do some dirty work.

Dunn walked toward the saloon, turning things over in his mind. He would find the Blount twins and get that set up. He hadn't told Smith that Luke had disappeared. He would have to put some heat on Jed to find him. Smith wasn't a patient man. Neither was Dunn, for that matter.

———

I had to hand it to old Skeeter, as he knew where to go for cattle in Kansas. The first ranch we stopped at didn't quite have what we were looking for. The cows had some bloodlines besides the longhorn blood and looked pretty good, but the bulls he had weren't quite what I was looking for. One was too young, the other too old. The owner suggested we try an outfit called the Box M, located just a little to the east.

The fences and barn looked a little ramshackle when we first rode up early in the afternoon. I changed my mind when I saw the cattle, though. They were well cared for, fattened up on the spring grass, and he had two mixed breed bulls that were just what I was looking for. I pretended not to show too much interest. Buck rolled his eyes and walked away while I started bargaining with the rancher.

After much haggling and moaning, what we settled on was twenty dollars per head, including the bulls, and he would supply two hands—both his sons—to help Buck and me drive them back to Ellis and put them in the holding pens for tomorrow's train. I paid him in cash, and by four o'clock in the afternoon, we had them in the holding pens. I paid the boys an extra two dollars apiece for the help, and they rode out.

The agent at the station told me there was a train leaving at six o'clock sharp in the morning, scheduled to arrive in Denver and seven o'clock tomorrow night. I promised to be there at five in the morning to load them on. Buck did a lot of whining about that, but I ignored him. That didn't entirely work, so I promised to buy him a round.

On a whim, I decided to send Sherry a telegram. I started and stopped a message several times, then finally sent one:

SHERRY, FOUND THE COWS I WANTED. STOP. SHOULD BE BACK IN DENVER TOMORROW NIGHT SEVEN O'CLOCK. STOP.
    SPENCE.

There wasn't a lot to see in Ellis, so we strolled up and down the street a few times, then stopped at the saloon so I could pay off on the round of whiskey I promised Buck. We moved on to the café next door, then decided to turn in early so we could load those cows the next morning.

I stopped off at the station to see if I might have a return telegram. To my surprise, there was one waiting for me. I paused to read it after I stepped away from the window.

SPENCE, COME TO THE BAKERY WHEN YOU GET HERE.
   S.

I stuffed the note in my pocket and whistled a little on my way back to the hotel.

CHAPTER 12

FOLLOWED

Luke decided morning didn't seem to come quite so early today, and his hands didn't feel so cramped after milking the cow. Maybe he could get used to this, after all. He walked to the house for breakfast with a little more spring in his step today. Tom's wife, Maude, hovered over him as she brought breakfast, then settled across the table from him as he dug in.

"Did you sleep okay out there, Luke?" she asked. "Did you have everything you need? Another blanket? Anything?"

Luke nodded yes to the first question about sleeping well, but hesitated a little over the second one about having everything he needed. He opened his mouth to say something, then changed his mind. She picked up on the hesitation immediately.

"What? What is it? I put a pillow out there, didn't I?"

"You did. And I have enough blankets." He nodded his head to emphasize his answers. He felt hesitant to ask for time off so soon, but he could feel the three sets of eyes watching him. "I...I just left something behind at the livery stable, that's all. Maybe I can get it when you don't need for me a couple hours. It can wait."

Tom looked up from his eggs and weighed in. "What is

it? If it's important, you can borrow the old mare and just ride in and get it."

Luke was starting to feel embarrassed. "It's not that important, I guess. It's a...well, it's a diary that I've been keeping. I've been writing in it most nights for a few years..." His words sounded foolish in his own ears.

Maude jumped in right away. "Well, it sounds like it's important to you. Tom, you can spare him for a few hours this morning, can't you?" It was more of a statement than a question. Luke glanced over at Tom, hopefully.

Tom chuckled as he rose from the table. "Sure, we can spare him. Luke, you're probably a little sore from your first day's work, anyway. Take the old mare and get your book. Zeb and I will mend fences today. Join us when you get back, and we'll show you a few things about the fences."

Luke walked to the corral after breakfast, saddled the old mare, and turned her toward town. Things were getting better for him, he thought—the move to the Anderson's ranch for a while could turn out pretty well. He had Sherry to thank for that. As the mare trotted toward town, Luke considered stopping by the bakery, but rejected the idea immediately. Sherry would be very unhappy with him for coming back to town so soon. Besides, he reflected, she probably didn't have any more news yet about his dad.

The livery stable was empty when he arrived. Probably, the old man was just a little late today. Luke hitched the mare to a rail and hurried over to the straw pile he had used for a bed these last few months. He felt a stab of disappointment when the diary wasn't in the niche in the wall where he normally put it. He threw a few handfuls of hay in the air, then grabbed a pitchfork and began raking the hay, but without success.

A sound behind Luke startled him, and he whirled around, holding the pitchfork out in front of him. The old man was standing there, eyebrows raised.

"Kinda jumpy, ain't ya?" He held out the diary. "Yer

prob'ly lookin' for this. I saw you left it yestiddy, so I saved it for ya."

Luke dropped the pitchfork and grabbed the diary, babbling a quick thank you. "It's a...special book for me," he offered, feeling some explanation might be necessary. He hoped the old man hadn't been reading it.

"Makes no never-mind to me." The old man shrugged. He picked up the pitchfork and began forking some hay into a stall. "You need to sleep here again, you can," he said over his shoulder.

"Thanks, gotta go," Luke said hurriedly. He unhitched the mare, climbed aboard, and turned her out of the stables. He still had time to do most of a day's work back at the ranch. He picked up the trail to the ranch a few minutes later and moved the mare along at the best speed she could manage.

Jed slouched on a bench down the street from the livery stable, hat pulled low, pretending to read a book. He couldn't read, but nobody else needed to know that. He had divided his morning between the stable and the bakery. He was watching the stable at sunup, then switched over to watch the bakery. When Luke didn't show up at his usual time at the bakery, he moved back to the stable.

Dunn had let him know in no uncertain terms that he needed to find out where Luke was. Jed didn't like to admit it, but Dunn scared him. He regretted that he'd ever talked to the man. If Luke didn't show up in a couple days, Jed was thinking he needed to hop a train and go somewhere to get away from Dunn.

"Do you like that book?"

Startled, Jed looked up to see a woman, probably about the age of his grandmother, beaming at him while also blocking his view of the stable. "It's okay," he mumbled, dropping his head and pointedly ignoring her. He squirmed a foot to the side so he could see the stable again.

"I used to teach school," she gushed. "I'm so happy when I see a young man like you reading." She moved a little closer to get a look at the book.

"Gotta go, lady," Jed snapped. He slammed the book shut, dodged around her and crossed the street. He looked back to see her staring at him, hands on her hips. Jed shrugged and swiveled back around to look at the stables. He could see activity now, with a little hay flying up above the tops of the walls.

His vantage point on this side of the street wasn't as good, so he crossed back to the bench as soon as the woman moved on. Now, as he watched, the old man came into the stable and moved inside, toward where the hay was flying. Jed sat down on the bench and opened the book, but he riveted his eyes on the stable. A couple minutes later, Luke came out, riding an old mare. Jed left the book on the bench and sprinted across the street to where his horse was hitched.

There was little travel on the trail Luke was taking, and Jed had to stay back quite a way to keep from making Luke suspicious. The old mare was moving slowly to start with. Jed stopped and let his horse graze a few times to keep from catching up. They wound around a few turns in the road, but each time, Luke was still there on the trail in front of him when Jed rounded the bend. The road was totally unfamiliar to him. Jed grew impatient and urged his horse forward, closing the distance a little. Luke was riding straight ahead, never pausing to look back.

The trail took another turn, and Jed slowed his horse, not wanting to come around the bend too suddenly and find Luke stopped in the trail. He reached the bend and moved slowly around it, then stopped and cursed under his breath. The road ahead of him was empty. He urged his horse forward, noticing a small, little-used trail branching off to his left. There was a small sign there with some letters crudely etched on the weathered boards.

Jed stared at the sign, moving his mouth as he tried to make out the words. After a moment, he moved his horse down the main trail at a trot, looking to see if Luke might still be out there ahead of him. After a few minutes, he was satisfied that Luke had turned off the main trail. Jed returned to the faint trail with the sign by the road. He could make out a Rolling R brand burned into the boards, and he could recognize the word Ranch. The first word started with an A. He was sure it was the family name, but he couldn't read it.

He gathered up the reins and urged his horse into a spanking trot back to town. Now he had something to report to Dunn. Luke was staying at a place called the Rolling R Ranch. Jed could take Dunn to check it out.

———

Dunn looked around the room at the Broadwell House Hotel sourly. He counted five of them in here, along with Soapy Smith, who was in a foul mood. Dunn had never known things to turn out well when Smith was in a foul mood. He had reported the kid's news about Luke and the Rolling R Ranch just two hours ago. Now, there were four besides himself. Burt, the Blount twins, and Clem Haskins were all here.

He knew why the Blount twins were here. He had recruited them at Smith's insistence. That meant Smith wanted to take care of the girl, too. Dunn wasn't sure why Burt was here, and he was completely surprised to see the fifth man. Haskins was another gunslinger used by Smith from time to time. Dunn could see no reason Smith needed another gun to handle this wet-behind-the-ears kid.

Smith paced the room, growling to himself as he threw his clothes into a bag which he had opened on the bed.

Clearly, he was checking out of the room. When the bag was full, he snapped it shut, then threw his cigar out the window.

"I'm clearing out of Denver for a while," he announced abruptly. "When a lawman I'm not paying starts checking into what I'm doing, I clear out. Now, you all," he said as his arm swung from side to side, "need to clean up the mess you've made here." He lit another cigar and jammed it into his mouth, turning to face the Blount twins. Their names were Horace and Len, but he couldn't tell them apart, so he just pointed, or called them Twin One and Twin Two.

"You two get rid of the girl. You gotta get her out of the state." He jabbed his cigar at them for emphasis. "Fastest way to get hung is to mess with a woman. Get way out of Colorado. Anybody connects this to me and you'll be sorry you were born. Got me?"

The twins nodded in unison, not sure if they should answer.

Smith stood, not moving, glaring at them. "Get out!" he shouted.

Both men grabbed their hats and darted out of the room, glad to escape.

Smith swung around to face the remaining three men. He chewed on the end of the cigar and spit into the spittoon at the foot of the bed. "You three," he said, his voice quieter but still menacing, "get rid of this Luke kid. Do it tonight. Take him out of here and get him to the Roost. Take care of it out there. I want to work in Denver again. I like this town. Make sure nothing happens anywhere around here. Get rid of him quiet, after you get there."

His gaze swung to Burt. "I'm gonna have to close the gambling hall for a while. That's why you're going. I'll tell you when you can come back." He looked at Dunn next. "You been seen around here too. You clear out to the Roost for a while. We wait until this blows over and the sheriff ain't so curious about me. Clear?"

They all nodded and stood to go. Smith turned his back, facing the window, as they filed out. He turned when another thought struck him. "Take the kid Jed with you, too. Get him out of here." He looked at Haskins. "I don't like a kid that tells tales about folks he works with." Haskins nodded and stepped out into the hallway.

Dunn pulled the door shut behind him. It occurred to him that Smith had said nothing directly to Haskins, but he wanted Haskins to do something about Jed. That could mean only one thing. Haskins was here to clean things up. He would also take care of Burt and himself if Smith decided they knew too much. It was something to keep in mind.

———

The gas street lamps were flickering, and the streets themselves were quiet and empty as Sherry walked down the street to the bakery. She could hear noise from the saloons, but they were all a few blocks away. It was one thing she liked about where the bakery was located. She would feel completely safe when she was able to add a second floor and live above her shop.

As she reached the door and slipped the key into the lock, she thought she heard a rustling noise behind her. She reached into her coat pocket, her hand closing around the small revolver she had there. She pulled the gun from her pocket and glanced up and down the street. Seeing nothing, she relaxed after a moment. Maybe she was just a little jumpy after hearing Luke's story and talking to the sheriff. She turned back to the door, opened it and went inside.

Once inside, she prepared a batch of dough, kneaded it, then shaped a dozen rolls. With that in the oven, she began preparing dinner for Spence. She hoped he hadn't eaten something on the train. This was going to be a special evening for him.

Hidden in the shadows of a doorway, two shops down

from the bakery, the Blount twins glanced at each other. Both had seen the gun come out of her pocket, and they were in no hurry to rush the bakery. They had trailed the girl from her boarding house, and she seemed to be settling down to stay a while in the bakery. Each slid down to a sitting position in the doorway, content to take their time. They had all night. They could afford to wait a while.

———

Dunn struck a match and studied the sign at the edge of the trail. The half-moon they had tonight didn't give enough light to read it, and he would not take Jed's word for it. Jed pouted and pointed down the trail.

"House and barns over there," he said. When Dunn ignored him, he resumed pouting.

Dunn glanced around him. Jed was pouting because he hadn't been invited to the meeting with Soapy Smith. That would be the least of Jed's problems, but he would find that out soon enough. Burt was there, his face an absolutely unreadable mask. Haskins had remained on his horse, hanging back on the main trail. He was letting Dunn take the lead, but Dunn knew he was a dangerous man.

"Rolling R," Dunn confirmed in a low tone. He looked down the faint trail toward the ranch, then turned to Jed. "They got a bunkhouse? Where does the kid sleep?" When he got only a shrug for an answer, he fought down his anger, remounted, and led the way slowly down the trail. Mainly, he was worried about a dog. If they had a dog at this ranch, the barking would probably wind up causing some shooting, and Smith wouldn't like that.

They fanned out and slowly rode down the trail, hearing only the creak of saddle leather and feeling a soft breeze on their faces. After they had advanced about two hundred yards, the dim shapes of a house and barn outlined themselves in the distance. Dunn gave the signal to dismount.

They hitched their horses to tree limbs and continued on foot.

When the house and barn had clearly taken shape in front of them, Dunn halted, irresolute. There had been no dogs barking, and he felt relief about that. How to proceed—that was the problem. Luke could be anywhere in that house. Dunn jumped when he felt a tap on his arm. He whirled to see Burt standing next to him, pointing at a dim shape in the trees, off to their left.

"Could be a bunkhouse," he whispered.

Dunn nodded, relieved at seeing the third building. He motioned to the others, and they crept toward the building in the trees. They circled it, and Dunn began advancing silently toward the door.

Zeb Anderson, meanwhile, was swinging on the porch of the farmhouse. He often had trouble falling asleep, and he liked to rock in the swing when the weather was nice. He found that the motion of the swing usually made him sleepy. Sometimes, he fell asleep out there on the porch, but most times, he just got up and went to bed after fifteen or twenty minutes in the swing.

Tonight, he was feeling sleepy and decided it was time to go to bed. As he rose from the swing, he thought he heard a faint noise and saw a little motion out by the bunkhouse. Puzzled, he looked around for a lantern, but none was handy. He stepped down off the porch and walked to the bunkhouse, peering into the darkness.

"Luke?" he called softly.

Hearing the noise, all four intruders melted back into the shadows of the trees surrounding the bunkhouse. Zeb continued forward, seeing no movement now, but he still called softly. As he neared the building, Haskins reversed his gun and stepped forward. He swung the gun once and struck Zeb soundly on the forehead. Zeb collapsed silently to the ground.

The four intruders stood without moving for a moment. The man on the ground wasn't moving, but they took some time to listen for sounds from the house. Then, they heard a creaking noise coming from inside the bunkhouse. Realizing that Luke might have heard his name being called, Dunn drew his gun and walked to the bunkhouse door. As he reached for the door handle, the door swung open suddenly, and Luke stood framed in the lantern light from inside.

CHAPTER 13

KIDNAPPED!

Luke settled on the cot in the bunkhouse and dug a pencil out of his duffel bag. He jotted down the events of the last two days, concentrating on what he was learning. It had always seemed to him that his mother had drifted from one thing to another without a plan. The diary was his way of mapping out his life. He didn't want to just follow along with whatever happened next. He could plan things and think things through a little better. He knew he could have avoided the problem at the saloon if he had thought that one through a little better.

Luke thought he heard his name being called. He paused, pencil in the air, listening for the sound he'd just heard. There it was again—he was pretty sure it was Zeb calling his name. Luke put down the diary book and crossed to the door. When he pulled the door open, he was shocked to see Dunn standing there, gun in hand. Dunn froze where he was for a moment, looking surprised to see Luke in the doorway.

Moving first on pure instinct, Luke shoved at Dunn to get him out of the doorway, then tried to swing the door shut. He wasn't quite strong enough or fast enough. Dunn got a foot in the doorway, then shoved the door open, spinning Luke to the side. As he staggered to regain his balance,

Luke felt a sharp blow on the back of his head. His vision seemed to spin around, then blackness closed in, and he felt himself falling...

Voices seemed to come from far away and then gradually grew louder. He had the presence of mind to keep his eyes closed and remain motionless. He could feel the gag in his mouth and the rope that tied his hands together in front of him. He seemed to be sitting upright on the cot, propped up against the bunkhouse wall.

He heard two voices in the bunkhouse. One was Dunn's voice, the other he didn't recognize. After a moment, he also recognized Jed's voice. The voice he didn't recognize sounded angry and quarrelsome: "How hard did ya hit him, anyway? We can't carry him all the way to the Roost."

Dunn responded, also sounding angry, but more controlled. "He'll come to in a minute. I didn't hit him that hard. How 'bout the one you hit? He come around yet?"

The voices grew fainter, and Luke risked opening his eyes. He was alone in the bunkhouse for the moment. He swung his arms to the side and grabbed the diary and the pencil. Opening the diary to the first blank page, he held the book open with his left hand. He grasped the pencil with his right hand and scrawled the word ROOST in the book. As the voices and footsteps returned, he closed the book, tossed it on the floor and shoved it under the bunk with his feet. He leaned back and closed his eyes as the voices came through the door.

He heard footsteps on the bunkhouse floor again. They sounded like short, shuffling steps. A soft thump followed those sounds. Luke was struggling to make sense of the noises when he suddenly received a sharp slap across the face. He jerked in surprise and inhaled sharply but opened his eyes slowly and feigned coming to his senses for the first time.

Luke's eyes swept the room quickly. Dunn was there, and Jed was leering at him from the corner of the room. Next to Jed was a man he didn't recognize. That man wore tied-down guns and a harsh expression. Burt was also there, standing in the doorway. When Luke looked at the floor, he saw Zeb tied up much the same as he was, with a large bloody knot in the middle of his forehead.

There was a throbbing pain at the back of his head. When Dunn grabbed his arm and told him to stand, Luke moved to do so, but the room spun when he stood. He stumbled and sank to his knees. Dunn yanked him to his feet and Jed grabbed the other arm. They hustled him out of the room. Someone doused the lantern in the bunkhouse as they left, and they manhandled Luke down the trail until they reached some horses. They tied his hands to the saddle horn and moved out.

Luke grasped the saddle horn grimly and hung on. The jolting trot of the horse magnified the pounding in his head. The other riders surrounded him and increased the pace. He knew that by morning they would be out of Denver and well down the road toward the Roost, whatever that was. He could only hope that someone would find the clue he had left and would know what it meant.

——————

Sherry glanced at the clock in the corner. It was after seven o'clock. There would be some unloading and herding cattle into the pens at the station, but Spence should be along pretty soon if the train had arrived on time. She pulled the rolls out of the oven and set them down on the counter. She lifted the lid on the stew, stirred it, and replaced the lid. Maybe, she thought, she could make a special place setting.

There were some flowers in a vase on the windowsill, so she carried those over and placed them on the table where they'd had breakfast each morning. She was reaching for some plates in the pantry when she heard a noise at the front door.

Sherry turned from the pantry and looked over at the door. Two men had come into the bakery. The first was walking toward her. The second was closing the front door behind him. They were clearly identical twins. Both had long blond hair, dirty and stringy. Both wore guns and a smirk as they advanced on her.

She knew it would be a mistake to show fear. "Can I help you?" she asked, striving to maintain a steady tone in her voice.

They looked at each other with matching sarcastic laughs. "Well now, ain't that polite, Len?" said the first one. "She wants to know if she can help us."

The second one, apparently named Len, guffawed as he pulled a roll from the pan on the countertop. He burned his hand on the pan and cursed, dropping the roll on the counter. He sucked at his thumb briefly, then picked up the roll and popped it in his mouth. He pulled another roll out of the pan and tossed it to his brother.

"I don't think you can help us that much, lady." It was the first one talking again. "We're going to go for a little ride. Maybe we'll take these rolls with us."

Sherry looked from one to the other, trying to think of a way to stall them until Spence came. "There's food, too," she offered. "Are you hungry?"

They seemed to consider it briefly, then shook their heads in unison. "Time to go, lady," said the first one, advancing toward her.

Sherry pointed toward her coat, hanging on a rack in the corner. "Can I get my coat?" she asked. "It's cold outside at night."

The one named Len moved toward the door as the other one walked over, picked up her coat, and removed the gun from the pocket. "Okay, lady, here's yer coat." He tossed it to her.

Sherry caught the coat and draped it over her arm. As she walked toward the door, she palmed a paring knife and tried to slip it under her coat, but she hadn't moved fast enough. The twin leaped across the room, grabbed her arm and banged her wrist against the counter. The knife dropped to the floor.

"That's the last time you try somethin' like that, you got me?" He twisted her wrist until she gasped with pain, then slowly eased his grip. He started to say something else, but a scuffle at the front door drowned his words out.

The door swung open suddenly, and Sherry heard the solid *thunk* of a punch being landed. Without looking at the door, she grabbed a towel, picked up the pan of rolls and pressed it against the intruder's arm. He yelped with pain, then cursed and shoved her to the floor. She heard two gunshots, followed by a third.

———————

The train rolled into Denver five minutes early. I had arranged for the use of some holding pens near the station, and I was hoping we could offload the cattle quickly. I had paid Skeeter to find one other man to help with the cows, and I was glad to see both of them walk over to join us. I paced back and forth as the few passengers unloaded.

Buck watched me pace back and forth, and seemed to guess why I was in a hurry. "I can handle the cows for ya. Me and Skeeter and that other kid. You can get outta here if you want to."

I was thinking that Buck was getting too good at guessing what was going on in my head. Sometimes it can come in handy, though. I shoved my hands into my pockets and set a brisk pace over to the bakery. I was eager to see Sherry and hear about the boy we were trying to help, and any other news she might have. I found myself thinking there were trains from Denver to Utah and stagecoach lines from Utah up to Montana if I wanted to make trips in the future.

I saw lights on in the bakery and smiled to myself as I picked up the pace for the last couple blocks. As I got closer, though, I could see there was somebody else inside the bakery. I looked through the window as I crossed the street and saw two men inside with Sherry. One was headed for the front door. The other looked like he had just given her a shove.

I broke into a run, crossing the street and arriving at the bakery door about the time I figured one of them was arriving there. I eased up just slightly as I reached for the door handle. As it swung open, I gave it a shove and jumped into the doorway. There was a man just in front of me, reeling backward. When he reached down for his gun, I stepped in and swung a left hook that connected solidly with his jaw.

The one I'd just punched went down in front of me. Toward the back of the shop, the second one was cursing and lifting his gun from the holster. From the corner of my eye, I could see Sherry diving to the floor. I palmed my gun and fired as his gun came level. A bullet struck the door-frame, and I could feel the sting of wood splinters hitting my cheek.

He staggered back against the wall, but he wasn't down. I steadied and fired the second shot from a crouching position. His gun clattered loudly to the floor, then he slowly slid down the wall. One look told me he was finished. The first one still wasn't moving. I took his gun and dashed across the floor to check on Sherry.

"It's over," I told her, and pulled her to her feet. We stood and hugged for a very long time.

"I was just trying to stall them, hoping you were almost here," she murmured. "They took my gun, and he caught me trying to hide a knife in my coat..." She stared at the one I'd shot, then looked over at the other one. "Is he dead, too?" she asked finally.

I turned and crossed over to the one I had punched. "No, he'll just have a sore jaw and a headache," I told her. I flipped him over onto this stomach and pulled his hands behind his back. "Do you have any rope, or rawhide strips, or anything I can use to tie his hands?"

She hurried to the pantry. "I have some rope you can use," she said as she rummaged around on a back shelf. She came out with a short length of rope. I tied his hands and stood back.

The door burst open again, and Bess rushed through the door. "I heard shots!" she began, then stared at the two men on the floor. She hurried over to check on Sherry, then collapsed into a chair. "I live over a shop just a couple doors down," she told me, then lapsed into silence, staring again at the men on the floor.

Sherry came over and helped her from the chair. "Bess," she said, "there's something I need you to do. Right now, if you can." Bess nodded silently. "Get Sheriff Peters," Sherry said. "He lives close to his office and the county jail over there. Please find him and get him over here. We could have trouble if the deputy marshal shows up first."

Bess hurried out the door. There seemed to be nothing to do at the moment but wait for the sheriff. I pulled out a chair and sat down. Sherry wandered over to me, sat in my lap and put an arm around my shoulder. We sat in companionable silence for about fifteen minutes.

Suddenly, the door banged open, and a short, very rotund man barged into the room. A badge hung from his shirt pocket. "Oscar Camp, deputy marshal," he announced loudly. "I heard there was some shooting down here." His eyes grew round when he saw the dead man on the floor. The other one struggled against his ropes on the ground at Camp's feet.

"Marshal, these men broke in and attacked me," Sherry informed him. "They were getting ready to kidnap me."

"Mmphh..." was Camp's only comment. He walked over to inspect the dead man. "Did you do this?" he asked me.

I nodded. "I defended myself, yes."

The one on the floor spoke for the first time. "We was in here for some food, marshal. He killed my brother and attacked me." The words were very muffled, and there was a large knot forming on his jaw.

"You'll have to come with me," Camp announced. He produced a rawhide strip from his pocket and walked across the floor, motioning for me to hold my hands behind me.

Two more people entered the front door. It was Bess, with the sheriff, much to my relief.

Sheriff Anderson sized up the situation quickly. "Movin' kinda quick, ain't you, Camp?" He didn't wait for an answer, but walked across the room to look at the dead man. He turned to Sherry. "This is your shop, ma'am. Tell me what happened here."

Sherry recounted what had happened, ending with how I had entered and fired after one of them had fired on me.

Peters looked across the room at Camp, who was still holding the rawhide string, shuffling from one foot to the other. "Did you bother getting her story, Camp?"

Camp spoke for the first time since the sheriff had entered. He nodded his head vigorously. "Sure did. But this man"—here he pointed at the man on the floor—"he says they was attacked by this man I'm taking in as my prisoner. I'll sort it all out." He cleared his throat and turned around to tie my hands.

"Not so fast." Peters walked across the floor and took a closer look at the man I had tied up. "Camp, you don't recognize Horace and Len Blount? They've got a little history around here, I'd say." He moved closer to Camp. "Have you come into an extra money lately, Camp? Maybe I should look into that."

Camp blanched and put the rawhide string back into his pocket. He backed slowly toward the door. "I guess you've got it taken care of, sheriff," he mumbled. A moment later, he was gone.

Peters walked over and held out his hand. "Hal Peters."

"Clay Spencer. Folks call me Spence," I added.

Peters nodded absently. "I'll take this one over to the jail," he said, prodding Len Blount with his foot. "I'll need another horse."

Bess got up and moved to the door. "I'll get a couple horses," she said, and disappeared.

Peters moved over to the dead man, kneeled down and studied him for a moment. Then he stood and looked around at me. "I'll get the undertaker over here for ol' Horace, here, as soon as I can. Meanwhile, Spence, can you give me a hand carryin' him out back? I don't think he'll be much good for Sherry's business the way he is now."

I moved over and helped Peters carry the corpse out to the alley. We put him down, and Peters took one more look at him by the light coming from inside the bakery. I waited for him in the doorway. Sherry had brought out a mop and was cleaning up when we came in.

We stood waiting for Bess to come with the horses. Peters pulled Len Blount to his feet, then looked over at Sherry and me. "I'll need you two to come over to the office with me," he said. "I'll put Len here in the jail, and you two can both tell me what happened."

We both nodded, and he fell silent for a moment. "Two shots," he said, almost to himself. "One in the chest, shot on the move, and the other right through the heart. T'other man was handy with a gun and had the drop on you."

I said nothing.

"They say there was a young man here, maybe twenty years ago," he went on. "Name was Spencer. They say he was as fast and deadly with a gun as anybody had ever seen. Got into trouble with a crooked sheriff and took off. Nobody ever saw him around here again." He glanced at me sideways.

"Twenty years sounds like a long time ago," I said.

CHAPTER 14

BLOOD TIES

S herry sat outside the sheriff's office, listening to Spence recount what had happened in the bakery. She suspected the sheriff just wanted to hear that his version matched hers. She had briefly told the sheriff what had happened. It was really no different from what she had said in the bakery, but this time, the sheriff took notes. Spence finished talking, came out of the office and sat next to her on the bench. She took his hand while the sheriff went around the corner to the cells. She could hear him talking to the prisoner, but couldn't hear what they were saying.

She hadn't forgotten that she planned to tell Spence about his son this evening, but nothing had gone the way she expected. She wanted him to know, but sitting in the sheriff's office after the attack at the bakery didn't seem like the time or the place for it.

Spence seemed to stare blankly at the opposite wall. He had just killed a man, and she knew that was probably what was bothering him, but she didn't know how to talk about it. She reached over to take his hand in both of hers. "Are you okay?" she asked. "I know it must be hard, the things that happened at the bakery. Is it bothering you that you..."

"That I killed a man tonight?" Spence interrupted. He

paused and shifted uncomfortably on the bench. "I've killed men before," he admitted slowly. "The sheriff hinted at that a while ago. It's true I've used my gun before. This time... this time will probably bother me less. They were going to take you away and maybe kill you. I can live with this."

Sheriff Peters came out and stood in front of them. His hands were in his pockets, and he rocked slightly on his heels. "You folks can go," he told them. "They might ask both of you to say something in court when the judge gets around to this." They nodded and stood to go.

"What will happen to him?" Sherry asked, nodding her head toward the cells in the back.

Anderson shook his head. "He attacked a woman, along with his brother, and probably intended to get you out of town and kill you. He'll wind up in the same condition in his brother, most likely, but this one will be at the end of a noose."

Sherry nodded grimly, and they turned for the door. Before they reached it, the door burst open and Tom Anderson rushed into the office. His breath seemed to come in rugged gasps. "Sheriff," he blurted, "you've got to come to the ranch. Luke's been taken, and Zeb's been hurt!"

Sherry gasped as Sheriff Peters grabbed his gun belt, strapped it back on and dashed out the door. Spence turned to follow him, but Sherry grabbed his arm to hold him back. "Spence," she said, "before we go, there's something you need to know."

I was intent on following the sheriff. I stopped when she grabbed my arm, but I had one eye on the door as the sheriff left.

She reached for my hand and gave it a squeeze. "Spence! I don't know how to say this. Luke, he is...your son."

The words hung in the air. The door swung shut, but Sherry had all my attention now. My mouth worked open and closed a few times, but no words came out. I stared at her.

"My son? You're sure?"

"I'm sure. He knew your name, and he had a locket his mother had given him with a picture of you and her. He came here hoping to find you."

My mind reeled with so many questions I couldn't narrow it down enough to ask one. I stared at Sherry, wondering if Annie had known about this when she left me. If she didn't know, why didn't she come back to find me after she found out? It was no good asking Sherry any of those questions.

"When did you find out?" I finally asked.

"Right after you left for Kansas," she said. "I've been trying to figure out how to tell you. I know it's a shock."

Peters stuck his head back inside the door. "You folks comin' or not?" he asked.

I nodded my head slowly. Sherry put her arm around me as we came out of the office. I felt numb.

———————

We pounded along at full gallop behind Tom Anderson and the sheriff, and my head seemed to spin faster than the horse's hooves. In all the scenarios that had played out in my head during those many years after Annie left me, it had never occurred to me we might have a child. When we turned down the lane to the Anderson ranch, I wasn't that much closer to coming to grips with it.

Anderson's wife came running out with a couple of lanterns as we rode into the yard and dismounted. As we dismounted, a question came to my mind, and I turned to Sherry. She leaned forward to hear the question I murmured into her ear:

"What about his mother? What about Annie? Where is she?"

Sherry put an arm around my waist and leaned in to whisper the answer. I knew from her expression it wouldn't be good news. "She died, I think, in the last year or two. Luke said it was consumption."

My mind reeled again. I hadn't heard from or seen Annie in almost twenty years, but a wave of sadness washed over me at thinking she had died at such an early age.

Sheriff Peters glimpsed my expression and lifted the lantern to get a better look at me. "You okay, Spencer? You look pretty pale over there."

I flinched at the light in my eyes. Peters lowered the lantern, but he was still looking for an answer. "I'm okay," I reassured him. "There's just a lot that's happened tonight." He nodded sympathetically, no doubt thinking I was talking about the shooting. He had no way of knowing, of course, about the news I'd been trying to absorb in the last half hour.

Zeb Anderson was sitting in a chair on the front porch, and a doctor was checking him over. The sheriff climbed the steps to the porch and waited for the doctor to finish. Eventually, the doctor wrapped a bandage around Zeb's head and told him to avoid sudden movements or heavy lifting for several days.

The sheriff sat down next to Zeb and asked if he was up to answering a few questions. He tried to nod in response and winced with the pain. Peters waited while Zeb leaned back and drew a few deep breaths.

"Ain't much I can tell ya," he mumbled. "Wish there was more. I was out here in the swing, an' I thought I heard a few noises and saw somethin' moving out there at the bunkhouse. I figgered it was Luke, so I went out there. Didn't have a lantern, so I couldn't really see nuthin'. I got almost to the bunkhouse, called out his name a couple times, then got clobbered on the head. Woke up a while later and there was nobody out there. Door of the bunkhouse was open, but Luke wasn't in there. I stumbled over to the house and woke up Pa."

The sheriff stood and started down off the porch. He

stopped and looked over at Tom Anderson. "Do you have a dog?"

Anderson shook his head. "Not no more. We had a dog, but he died a few weeks ago. Haven't got around to gettin' another."

Peters tapped a pencil on the little book he'd been writing in, then put both of them in his pocket. He mumbled something, then started walking away. "Can you bring a lantern and show me the bunkhouse?" he called over his shoulder. The rest of us followed.

The door to the bunkhouse was standing open. There was a cot against the corner that was pulled away from the wall a little. An old chair in the other corner was lying on its side. There was nothing else I could see, other than a lantern sitting on the floor. There were no clothes, books, or anything that looked like somebody had been living here.

Peters prowled around, looking in the corners, pulling the chair upright and putting it back in the corner. There was no bedroll on the cot—just the mattress. Peters pulled the cot completely away from the wall and mumbled something to himself. He reached down and lifted a small book from the floor.

The rest of us crowded around to see what he had found. Tom Anderson lifted the lantern to give a little light as Peters paged through the book. "Looks like a diary," he observed. He finished paging through the entries in the book and stopped at the last page. He mouthed a word, then held the book out so the rest of us could see the last page. I leaned in and read only one word: ROOST.

It looked like he had scrawled that last word in a hurry. The words on the opposite page, by contrast, were written neatly and clearly. I puzzled over what it might mean, then backed up and sat down in the chair when I realized what Luke was trying to tell us.

Sherry kneeled in front of me. "Spence? What does it mean?"

I stared at Peters. I felt pretty sure he had come to the

same conclusion as me. "I think," I said slowly, "it means Robber's Roost. It's an outlaw hideout in Utah."

Sherry stood and turned around to face Peters. "Sheriff?" she asked. "What do you think?"

Peters had been watching me, but he looked back at Sherry and nodded. "Sorry," he said, "but I think Spencer is right. Soapy Smith has spent some time out there, from what I hear." He looked at me closely. "You've gone pale again," he observed. "How do you know this kid, Luke?"

Sherry answered for me. "Luke is his son," she said. "He only found out about it tonight." She held out a hand. "Can you give us the book? I think Spence should have the book."

Peters gave her the book, then shuffled his feet and cleared his throat. "I'll look for him around town," he said. "They might not have left." He moved toward the door, then looked back at me. "If you're gonna leave town, check with me first. I'll fill you in on anything I've been able to find out around here."

They had set a relentless pace out of Denver, pushing for several hours. Luke was shivering against the morning chill. His back was rapidly stiffening from being bent over and tied to the saddle horn. He knew better than to complain, so he hung on in silence, wondering when they might finally make a stop.

When they had put Denver well behind them, they did finally stop. The sun was just beginning to rise behind them. Luke had already known they were traveling west—he could see mountains ahead of them, and they were climbing steadily. The others began watering their horses. Luke decided it was time to risk asking if he could ease his position. When Burt came over, untied his ropes, and threw his jacket over his shoulders, Luke made his request.

The man they called Haskins seemed to be clearly in charge. He watched as Burt untied Luke, but said nothing.

Burt handed him a canteen and murmured softly that he could climb down and stretch for a minute. Haskins started in his direction as soon as he moved. Luke froze where he was, but Burt held up a hand.

"I've got an eye on him," Burt assured the others. "He's not goin' anywhere." Haskins stopped but kept a wary eye on Luke. Dunn barely glanced in his direction. Jed drifted in his direction, but Burt cut him off and muttered something. Luke surmised that if he had a friend here, it was Burt. Dunn seemed indifferent, as though his job had been finished after they took Luke out of the bunkhouse. Jed still hated him, but Haskins was the cold-blooded, dangerous one.

They pushed on through the day, clearly eager to leave Denver behind them. They stopped every few hours to rest and water the horses, and each time, Burt untied his hands and allowed him to get down and stretch. Even so, his back had stiffened to the point it was becoming unbearable. At the third stop in the mid-afternoon, a small groan escaped him as he dismounted.

When Haskins gave the command to mount up, Luke pulled himself into the saddle and laid his hands on the saddle horn. This time, though, instead of tying him up, Burt mounted and moved his horse alongside Luke's.

"I ain't tying you this time, kid, but I'm gonna be right behind you. You try to break away, you'll get one through the back of your head." He spoke loudly and pulled his gun for emphasis.

Luke said nothing but nodded vigorously and mounted up. Haskins watched, narrowing his eyes at Luke, then staring suspiciously at Burt. After a moment, he shrugged and led the way. Dunn still looked uninterested. Luke knew he had no chance to break away. He was simply grateful to have his hands untied. He instinctively knew it would be a mistake to thank Burt, so he rode in complete silence.

For two more days, they climbed, with mountain peaks showing on both sides of them. It grew colder, especially during the nights and early mornings. Luke started wearing both his shirts every day, as his coat was threadbare and didn't provide enough warmth. On the fourth day, they descended to lower levels, and the air was warmer.

That same day, they broke for camp a little earlier. The sun was just beginning to decline in front of them when Haskins called a halt. There was a thick stand of spruce trees to their left. Luke noticed a few deer feeding near the tree line. They faded into the spruce trees when the party dismounted.

Haskins stood, staring out at the trees, then grabbed his rifle from the saddle. "Hey, kid," he barked. "Grab your rifle. We could use a little meat. We'll go get a deer." Hearing the word "kid," Luke turned, then saw that Haskins was looking at Jed. Burt told Luke to come with him to gather some firewood. Luke trailed behind Burt, wondering if the early stop meant they were slowing their pace.

Several minutes later, as he was returning with an armful of firewood, Luke heard one gunshot, then a second. He began arranging the wood for a fire. Dunn stared off into the distance, offering no help with the wood. Burt returned with more firewood, glancing out at the spruce trees from time to time.

When he had the fire going, Luke looked up to see Haskins returning. He was riding on his horse and leading Jed's horse. Luke stared, not understanding. There was a deerskin on the second horse with several cuts of venison loaded onto it. He looked away as Haskins grabbed the deerskin and threw it down next to the fire.

"Cook that, kid," was his only comment. Dunn stared off into the distance. Luke swung his head around to look at Burt, who only shook his head and stared at the ground. Luke moved to pick up the venison and hung several pieces over the fire.

Now he knew what the second gunshot was for. He moved around mechanically, feeding the fire when necessary. Jed was his enemy, but Jed was gone. But now he knew.

Haskins wasn't just dangerous, he was capable of murder. Later that night, rolled up in his blankets, Luke shivered, but it wasn't from the cold. He stared up at the sky and wondered why Jed was dead and he was still alive.

———

We were scattered around a table in the bakery with the few maps we'd been able to round up laying on the table in front of us. I had lost a brief argument with Sherry this morning about whether she was coming with us. Now, I was trying to explain how dangerous the Robber's Roost would be. Buck had wisely sat it out, downing several donuts and making no comments. I finally turned to Buck and asked him to weigh in on it.

Buck stirred his coffee for a few seconds, then turned to Sherry. "You know I like to make jokes," he started. "But I'm deadly serious about this one. The Roost has never, to my knowledge, ever allowed a woman in there. There are some who maybe ain't so violent, and maybe some stage robbers and highway agents and such who would leave you alone. But there's also some violent, deadly people in there. I don't know what they would do to you if they caught you in the Roost."

Sherry sat back and studied both our faces for a while. "We can't bring the law in there with us? What about the army?"

We both shook our heads. "They picked it because it's too hard for a force of any size to get in there," I said. "You try to bring a posse or the army in there, they'd be targets in a shooting gallery. We'll have to sneak in, probably at night."

"Okay." She reached across the table and took my hand. "I appreciate that you are looking out for me. I'll come to the edge of the canyon with you, but I'll stay out of the canyon and out of sight. Deal?"

We agreed on that all around, and I relaxed. She looked

over at Buck again. "What do they do in there all day, anyway? So far away from anyplace."

Buck shrugged, but a small smile returned to his face. "Lots of drinkin' and gamblin', that's what I hear. Word is they gamble with twenty-dollar gold pieces." He sipped his coffee and shook his head. "Only thing is, you win too much money, I'm none too sure if'n you'd get out with it alive."

A somber mood was settling in, so I redirected our attention to the map I had gotten from Skeeter yesterday. It showed the major towns, mountains, and rivers. I traced a line I had drawn through Northern Colorado to Utah, then south to Robber's Roost. "It's about four hundred miles," I told them.

It completely surprised me to hear a voice directly behind me. "That's how I'd go."

I wheeled around to see Sheriff Peters standing behind me, looking at the map. He nodded his head for emphasis, then joined us when I pointed at an empty chair. Sherry waved at Bess, who dished up some breakfast for the sheriff.

Peters sat down and updated us on his morning's activities. Clearly, he had been busy. "I went over to the Mother Lode Saloon this morning and padlocked the gambling hall upstairs. I'll check on it every few days to make sure it stays that way. Word is, Soapy Smith has checked out of his hotel and left town."

Bess came with his breakfast, and Peters reached into his pocket. Sherry tried to wave him off, but he shook his head firmly. "I always pay," he insisted. He dropped a coin on the table and kept talking around a mouthful of food.

"I paid a visit to the marshal this morning and advised him to check into what his deputy has been up to. I don't think Oscar Camp will be a deputy much longer. He might pack up and leave town pretty soon."

When Peters had finished eating, he leaned back and looked at Sherry and me. "I expect the judge will get around to Len Baker's trial in two or three weeks," he said. "Can you both be here?"

Sherry nodded, and he looked at me. "I'm keeping my cows over at the Anderson ranch for a while," I said. "I expect I can be back from the Roost and here when you need me."

Peters nodded in satisfaction and stood. He took one more look at the map on the table. "That's how I'd go," he said again. "You'll be watching out for the Utes, of course."

CHAPTER 15

ON THE TRAIL

Silence descended around the table. We'd been feeling pretty happy about the sheriff's news, but that was swept away now. Sherry, Buck, and I exchanged confused glances. Peters saw our empty looks and took a seat again to do a little explaining.

"The Utes are a little unhappy out west of here. Not a full-scale uprising, mind you, but they're not happy. There's a new Indian Agent out in that area." He pointed vaguely at Western Colorado on the map. "Agent's name is Nathan Meeker. He's got it in his mind to make farmers out of the Utes. They ain't taking it none too kindly. Can't say I blame them."

Peters paused and looked at our discouraged expressions. He seemed to reconsider talking about this, but I waved at him to continue. "We need to know about it," I told him.

"Well…" He looked around at the other two, who asked him to go on. "Word is, lately, that Meeker plowed a race track under and made a field out of it for farming. That has them riled. Not on the warpath, but pretty unhappy. I don't think they've gone for the war paint yet, but you might run into one or two renegades. Just be careful."

Peters left, and I glanced at Sherry and Buck. It was no use offering to let them change their minds if they wanted to. Those were two determined faces. I glanced at the clock in the corner. It was nine exactly. "Buck and I told Tom Anderson and Skeeter we'd meet them at the pens near the railroad to drive our cows out to the Anderson ranch at nine thirty. Sherry, meet you back here at three?"

She agreed, and we all stood. Buck left, and I was prepared to follow when a thought struck me. I hadn't asked about the bakery and whether Bess could keep that going. I stopped and asked if she needed any help making arrangements.

She flashed a quick smile and said it was all taken care of. There was a young girl in town who they had brought in to help from time to time when things were busy. Bess would have her help as long as needed.

"I guess I should have known you'd have it taken care of," I said. "See you at three?"

She leaned in impulsively and gave me a lingering kiss on the cheek. I'll be ready to go at three," she told me. She hurried out the back door.

I touched my cheek in surprise and watched her leave the shop. I turned to go and caught Bess grinning at me from ear to ear. I left the bakery, but I felt that kiss all the way out to the Anderson ranch.

Buck, Skeeter, and I gathered the cows and reached the ranch with no trouble. We herded the cattle into a pasture east of the ranch house. Skeeter volunteered to help for a couple weeks if the extra cattle and Zeb's recovery time left Tom Anderson overloaded. Anderson agreed, and I slipped a gold piece to Skeeter. He beamed.

"Thanks, guvnor." He grinned. "There's still some life in these old bones, ya know."

That just left the matter of paying Anderson for watching the cattle and letting them graze on his pasture. At first, he refused payment, but then he looked speculatively at the cows I'd bought. "You know," he said, "those are a couple of fine-looking young bulls you've got there." He looked across at his herd in the neighboring pasture. "If you let me find work for those bulls around here for a couple weeks, we could call it even."

I chuckled and extended my hand. We shook on it. I had a feeling one of those bulls would be in the pasture with his cows by nightfall.

Sherry was as good as her word, and we were-assembled at the bakery a little before three. We hadn't talked about how many horses to take. Buck and I discussed it back and forth. Sherry simply said she would trust our decision. In the end, we decided to take just one extra horse, in case of injury or lameness. We didn't want to be a target for horse thieves, be they Indians or white men, and we might be a little short on grazing and water. If we needed another, there might be a town or fort along the way to buy one.

I went down to the livery stable and struck a deal with the old man down there for a mouse-colored mustang with two white stockings. He wasn't a lot to look at, but I was betting he had stamina and maybe even a little speed to him. He would do as an extra mount.

We rode out of Denver just a half hour past our three o'clock target. We were traveling light and would need to find water and maybe a deer along the way, but we didn't expect that to be a problem. We rode west and stopped to make camp at dusk. I was estimating they had less than a one day lead on us. I was hoping, since they didn't know we'd found the book and knew about Robber's Roost, that they would ease up on the pace once they got away from Denver.

———

Burt sat on a stone near the campfire, whittling. He only whittled when he was troubled. Luckily, none of the other people around this campfire knew that. He had a fairly thick cedar branch, and he had whittled it just about in half already.

Burt had done a lot of things he wasn't proud of in his

life, but the killing of Jed a couple hours ago had crossed the line for him. He had cheated a lot of people in gambling halls, robbed a few people on stagecoaches, and had even helped with a bank robbery. He wasn't proud of those things, but they didn't keep him awake at night, either. He supposed he still had a conscience, and it was hurting him.

He really didn't even like Jed, but Jed was just a kid. He didn't deserve to be taken out and shot. He had heard the remark Soapy Smith made to Haskins, and he had known the kid might be killed. He'd just assumed it would happen later on, after Burt had found a way to leave the Roost and get away from these people. It hadn't happened that way. He could still hear that second gunshot in his head, and he had known right away what it meant.

He turned the stick a little and resumed whittling. Shavings flew on all sides. Dunn looked over at him, and he slowed the pace on the whittling so as not to call attention to himself. The thing was, he liked this kid Luke, and he knew Luke was likely to be next, after they got to the Roost. He might even be called on to assist in some way. He couldn't do that.

Murder was a line he hadn't crossed in all his fifty-seven years, and many of those had been outlaw years. He certainly couldn't live with the shooting of Luke on his conscience. He just didn't know what to do about it. If he stood up to Haskins, or even Dunn, he knew he was a dead man. He had handled a gun a few times and done okay, but he wasn't in the same class with those two.

The cedar branch broke in half after a few more strokes and he tossed it aside, then put the knife back in its sheaf. He had a few days to figure out what he could do about this situation. He went over to his bedroll and rolled up in the extra blankets. He hoped he could sleep tonight. He wasn't optimistic about that.

———

We moved along a faint trail to the west, keeping a brisk pace. Our best chance lay in overtaking the kidnappers before they could reach Robber's Roost. We wove through stands of cottonwood and quaking aspen trees, and we could have enjoyed the late spring breezes and sunshine on our faces if not for the fear we all felt about Luke's fate. We paused only to rest and water the horses. Other than that, we ate in the saddle and pushed ahead.

I had taken the point, with Sherry in between and Buck bringing up the rear. We were mindful of Peters's warning about hostile Utes and slowed our pace a bit when the terrain rose and showed folds in the hills. Those places could hide warriors.

We came to a more level, open space, and I could see the foothills rising in front of me. I heard hoofbeats moving up and turned to see Sherry pulling up beside me. We rode in silence for a minute, then she asked me a question I'd been expecting since the sheriff's comment to me at the bakery.

"Peters said something just before we left the bakery," she began. She glanced at me sideways, trying to determine if this was a sensitive subject.

I returned her glance and nodded. "It's okay to ask me," I said.

"So," she said hesitantly. "Was that you, the really young Spence who got into trouble with a corrupt sheriff and was...very handy with a gun?"

"That was me," I admitted. "I don't know about the handy with a gun part. They tell me I am. I just know I've been fast enough and accurate enough when I've needed to be."

We rode along in silence for several hundred yards. "How many men have you killed, Spence. Does it bother you still?"

I answered the first question after thinking it over, going back in my mind over the last eighteen years. "That last one was number seven," I said, feeling neither regret nor pride. "Yes, it has bothered me each time, including the one at the bakery. But each time, my life has been on the line. If I can avoid killing a man, I do."

We fell silent again, riding until the ground rose into a stand of blue spruce trees. She reached over and patted my arm. "I think you're an honorable man," she said. Then she fell back into a single file line.

We rode until the sun had almost set. I knew we needed some time to set up a small camp, and I knew Sherry must be saddle-sore from the full day. I looked ahead and saw we would soon climb up and follow some narrow trails along the shoulder of some smaller peaks. There would be patches of snow up there ahead of us. It was time to stop for the day.

We would have only a cold supper tonight, but we would need a small fire for the warmth. Maybe tomorrow I could shoot an elk or a deer for some meat. In the meantime, Sherry and I collected firewood while Buck built a crude shelter against a hollow log, using two large spruce trees to protect us against the north wind. We built a small fire and talked quietly about the likelihood that we could overtake the kidnappers before they reached the Roost. We knew the chances were small.

As the evening wind grew stiff and cold, the bedrolls and blankets started to sound good. We banked the fire and let the hot coals burn for warmth. I volunteered to feed the fire through the night. I rolled up in my blankets and stared at the sky, still wrapping my mind around the fact that I had a son. If I could find him and free him, what then? Would he want to be a part of my life? Sherry had said he was looking for me in Denver, so maybe he wanted to know me.

A slight rustling noise caught my attention, then Sherry was whispering in my ear. "I'm cold," she told me.

I started to hand her one of my blankets, but she pushed my arm away. Then there was more rustling, and she was under the blankets with me.

"Shared warmth works the best," she whispered. "Don't you think?" She snuggled up next to me and pulled both sets of blankets over us.

Come to think of it, this shared warmth thing really worked. I thought maybe I could hear Buck snickering over there, but I decided to ignore him.

———

Luke felt a quiet desperation setting in. Every day was going to bring them closer to Robber's Roost. He hadn't known what that was until he had asked Burt yesterday evening while they were gathering firewood. Burt had explained it was an outlaw hideout. When he had asked what they were going to do with him there, Burt had gone silent. Between that and the death of Jed, Luke felt hope slipping away.

When it came time to gather firewood that evening, Luke remained silent and kept a little distance from Burt, who had been distant and gruff all day. It caught Luke by surprise when he heard a low murmur coming from Burt after they had moved about fifty yards away from the camp.

"Just keep gathering wood and don't look in my direction," Burt hissed.

It surprised Luke, and he nearly looked at Burt in his astonishment. He recovered his wits at the last moment and kept gathering wood without looking.

"I'm gonna try to help you get away when we get to the Roost," came the indistinct murmur. "Not before then—they won't let their guard down before we get there. After we're there, if they start drinkin' and gamblin', well, maybe there'll be a chance to get away." There was a pause. "You hearing me?"

"I'm listening." Luke had been afraid to say anything, but he felt a little hope rising inside him for the first time since they had left. "What will I do if I get away from them at Robber's Roost?"

"I dunno, kid, but if you get away, you've got a chance. It's a pretty deserted area around there, but mebbe you can steal a horse and get away. Just get out of the Roost if I get you free of them. I'll help if I can."

Burt drifted away, and Luke knew the conversation was over. They finished gathering wood and moved back to the campfire. Luke started building the fire and avoided looking in Burt's direction. Burt grabbed a big stick and started whittling again.

Luke tossed in his blankets for quite a while before falling asleep, just as he had done since leaving Denver. This time, though, he had a ray of hope. He would look for a chance to get away after they got there. As he fell asleep, he wondered if anyone had found the clue he had left in the bunkhouse. If anybody had, maybe there was a little more help coming.

———

The trail had been steadily rising all morning, and we were seeing patches of snow on the ground to either side. We were skirting a peak on our left now, and the trail became rocky and narrow. I was watchful of the trail ahead, looking for sudden outcroppings or treacherous patches of shale. We paused to give the horses a breather, and Buck rode up alongside. He seemed preoccupied.

We had traveled a lot of trails together, and I could tell when Buck was uneasy. "Thinkin' about those Utes?" I asked.

Buck nodded grimly. "I been havin' a bad feeling for the last thirty minutes. I'm hearing bird calls that might not be real bird calls." He gestured at the trail in front of us. "They could come up right out of the ground on some of these sudden turns. Can't get but one of us on the trail at a time. Don't like bein' strung out up here..." He lapsed into silence.

I'd been having some of those same feelings myself, but I knew it didn't necessarily mean anything. Sometimes, I'd been attacked when I had no idea they were coming. "Nothing to do but keep moving," I pointed out. Buck shrugged and moved back behind Sherry. We kept pushing ahead.

We moved around a bend and topped out on a small mesa. I could hear water moving, so I dismounted and led my horse over to the edge of the mesa, away from the cliff on my right. There was a small drop-off there with a stream of clear water running down to form a pool at the bottom of the drop-off. The side of the mountain rose on the other side.

Buck and Sherry had both dismounted, and I could tell they had the same idea I did. We could rest and water the horses here, and fill our canteens. There was a small grouping of boulders at the far end of the mesa. I drew my gun and walked slowly over, glancing behind the boulders. I saw nothing.

When I turned and re-holstered my gun, they took the horses' reins and began walking them down to the pool of water below. I stretched and breathed in deeply, relaxing for the first time in the last hour. I turned and watched as they worked their way down the hillside, reaching the pool after a few minutes. They turned the horses loose to drink and began filling the canteens.

I turned my back to the boulders and took a few steps toward the cliffs in front of me. We had climbed farther than I had thought this morning. The drop to the valley below must have been several hundred feet. When I heard the whisper of moccasins on the rocky ledge behind me, it came as a complete shock.

CHAPTER 16

AMBUSH

I spun, leaning away from the boulders. I knew I had somehow missed seeing them back there. As I came full circle, drawing my Colt as I spun, I saw two warriors coming at me. The one closest to me was only a few feet away, tomahawk upraised and already beginning a downward descent. I shot him point-blank in the chest as he prepared to leap. The shot knocked him backward and aside. He landed heavily on his shoulder and flopped onto his chest.

I turned to meet the second one, but it was already too late to get off a shot. He sprung into me, knocking the gun aside and out of my hand. It clattered away, sliding to the edge of the mesa. He had a knife in his left hand, slashing downward toward my throat. I blocked the blow with my arm, but his weight and momentum knocked me down, and I fell heavily onto my back.

I shoved at him with all my strength and twisted away from him, getting to my feet and backing away in time to avoid his next lunge with the knife. We circled on the mesa, me without a weapon, and him holding that knife out, weaving back and forth. I wanted to get my jacket off and wrap it around my right hand and forearm, but there wasn't time for that.

He leaped and slashed twice. I avoided both attacks, but

gave ground both times. He circled around me so that the edge of the cliff was to my back, then pressed forward, edging me closer to the cliff. I knew what he had in mind, but how could I not give ground when he led with a nasty-looking blade on every attack? I looked left and right but saw nothing to use as a weapon. I could hear Buck calling, and I knew he was climbing back up the incline to help me. At the least, I had to buy some time.

He gathered himself to rush me, and suddenly, I knew what to do. I just hoped I had calculated how far it was to the edge of the cliff. There wasn't time to look, and my life depended on it. As he launched himself on me, I went with the lunge, falling backward onto my back. I gathered my legs under as I hit the ground, bracing my feet against his torso. The knife came down, and I blocked his arm with mine again, then shoved upward with my feet as hard as I could.

We were a little farther from the cliff edge than I'd thought, but I had shoved hard, with desperation giving me strength. He flew over my head and bounced to the edge of the mesa, teetering and hovering over the canyon below. His knife fell from his hand, and I could faintly hear the clatter as it bounced off the rocks on the way down.

He tipped over the edge, unable to stop himself, and grasped at the rocky ledge with his left hand as he swung back and forth. He locked eyes with me and reached up with his right hand, trying to get a grip on the edge. I backed away slightly and moved slowly toward my gun, which I could see at the edge of my vision. Suddenly, his hands slipped away from the edge, and he was gone.

I picked up my gun and glanced around, making sure there was nobody else on that mesa. I saw Buck burst up from the trail on the other side and jump forward onto the mesa, rifle at the ready. He relaxed when he saw I was alone. I edged cautiously to the edge of the cliff and peeked over. I had heard nothing when he fell—no shouting or screaming. I scanned the rocks below and saw him lying at an odd angle, three or four hundred feet below me.

I sat down on the mesa and drew deep breaths, waiting for the rush of energy and nerves to subside. Buck went over and inspected the first warrior, the one I had shot.

"This one's done for, too," he announced.

There was noise and activity again on the valley side of the mesa, and Sherry burst over the rim, holding a pistol, sweeping it from side to side. Buck held his hands in the air. "All done up here," he announced. "Spence didn't leave nobody for us to deal with."

She let out a loud sigh of relief and hurried over to kneel beside me. She took both my hands, looking me over for injuries.

"I'm fine," I said. "They didn't hurt me."

She sat down, facing me, and wrapped her arms around me. After a moment, she drew back and picked up my hands in hers again. "You're shaking," she told me.

"I know," I agreed. "I just need a few minutes for things to calm down. I'll sit here for a little while longer."

In the meantime, Buck had walked over and looked down into the valley and pond where they had gone to water the horses. "Good job, you tethered 'em," he told her. "I'll go down, finish watering, and bring 'em back up." He swept a glance around the mesa, then moved out of sight.

In another few minutes, Sherry went down to help Buck with the horses. I kept my Colt in my hand, but went over and propped myself up against boulders until the other two had brought the horses back up. We stood and discussed what to do next. None of us felt we could change our plan, other than maybe to move a little faster to get out of Ute country.

We agreed we would feel a little safer when we reached Utah and started south, hoping nothing had agitated the tribes over there. We would travel a little faster and go an extra hour every day until we were out of this area. With that in mind, we mounted again and headed on through the mountain pass.

They had come down out of the mountains a couple days ago. Burt knew they should have turned south by now. He had been to Robber's Roost before, and he was certain they had passed the turning point several hours ago. They continued until nightfall, and he was sure he could see a peak or two directly west of them now. He made no comment, but gathered firewood with the kid and said nothing. He didn't need any suspicion directed his way. He had an idea they were heading for the silver mining camps east of here. Whiskey and gambling could be found there, and Burt had a pretty good idea that's what Haskins had his mind set on. Probably Dunn as well.

They were up at sunup with a cold breakfast of beef jerky, washed down with coffee. Haskins took Dunn aside before they mounted up. The two of them walked off several paces, and a loud discussion ensued, followed by a heated argument. When Haskins backed away a few paces and hooked a thumb over his gun belt, Dunn stopped talking and stalked off. Dunn's face, Burt noted, was beet red with anger as he walked to his horse and mounted. Haskins stayed where he was, thumb in his gun belt, until Dunn rested both hands on the saddle horn.

They pushed hard to the west all day. There was no conversation between any of them. Luke's eyes went from Haskins to Dunn, with an occasional glance flicked in Burt's direction. Burt knew the kid was dying to ask what was going on, but he was smart enough to keep his mouth shut.

The trail they were following grew wider and more distinct, and Burt was sure now they were heading for a silver camp, probably Parley's Park City. He got another surprise when Haskins led the way off the trail with about two hours left until sundown. He took them south of the trail for half an hour, finally stopping near a small stream with some scattered trees and vegetation around.

Haskins dismounted and spoke for the first time since

his argument with Dunn that morning. "Camp," was all he said. He watched as Burt and Luke unsaddled their horses, then he walked over and tossed a loop over the neck of each horse. He tied the ropes to his saddle and climbed back up.

"You boys are going to camp here tonight," he informed them. "I'm going over to Parley's Park City to, uh, get some supplies and such. Can't have nobody leaving here, so I'm taking two horses and leaving Dunn's horse. See you in the mornin'." With that, he kicked his horse in the ribs and set a brisk pace toward the mining camp.

They built a small fire and cooked some venison and beans. Dunn kept to himself and no one spoke. Burt knew that although Haskins didn't trust anyone here, he had at least shown a little trust in Dunn by leaving his horse. He would watch for a chance to get both himself and the kid out of there. With a decent head start, they might get to the railroad and catch a train to California or somewhere.

Burt's hopes for getting away were dashed about an hour later, when Dunn got up and started saddling his horse. "I'm goin' to town, too," he announced. "Don't care what Haskins wants," he mumbled under the breath. He looked at Burt and Luke and snickered. "Don't you two go nowhere." In another minute, they could hear the hoofbeats as he rode away.

Luke glanced in Burt's direction, deciding whether it was safe to ask a question. Finally, the curiosity was too much for him. "What's happening?" he asked.

Burt shrugged. "They're going drinking and gambling, is all, kid. They'll be back tomorrow and we'll probably go on down to the Roost. Just get some sleep if you can."

Burt felt sharp disappointment at losing any chance to get to the railroad. They wouldn't see any travelers out here after dark. By tomorrow, they would head down toward Robber's Roost. There would be maybe a two-day delay by going out of their way and staying over a day at the mining camps. He rolled up in his blankets and fell asleep.

Burt came suddenly awake when he heard a horse

approaching. He squinted at the sky, and it was around sunup. He stared at the approaching figure on horseback and saw it was Dunn. He quickly unsaddled and rubbed down his horse, then rolled in his blankets. Thirty seconds later, he was snoring.

After a half hour passed, Burt got up, built a small fire and put some coffee on to boil. He unwrapped a few pieces of bacon and set them in a pan on the fire. Luke got up and joined him, saying nothing. After breakfast, Burt kicked dirt over the fire, and the two of them saddled their horses. Burt sat down on a rock and started whittling.

Haskins rode up an hour later, eyes red-rimmed and bloodshot. His saddlebags looked fuller than they had last night and Burt wasn't sure if it contained food or money. Or whiskey. Haskins stumbled over to the sleeping, snoring form of Dunn and kicked him. Dunn came out of his blankets with a start, his hand reaching under the blankets for a gun. He eased away from the blankets when he saw it was Haskins.

They moved out as soon as Dunn had saddled his horse. This time they moved south and a little east. Burt had no doubt they would travel directly to Robber's Roost now. Haskins slumped over his saddle most of the day, appearing to doze from time to time. Burt estimated they would reach Robber's Roost in two days. He did not know what would happen after that.

———

We had come through in pretty good shape since the run-in with the Utes a few days ago. We had come through the mountain passes in Colorado and now turned south in Utah. The vegetation was thinning out, the air was warmer, and we were seeing some rocky formations the more we came south.

The truth was, the biggest problem I could see now was in making sure we found Robber's Roost. Neither Buck nor I had been there, and it wasn't easy to ask directions to a place like that. There were a few cattle ranches along our way, and we had traded for some supplies there—mainly swapping venison for canned beans and jerky. We didn't expect to have a lot of campfires for a while.

About half a day after turning south, we pulled over and talked about what path we would take from here. We were following a faint trail, but it wasn't much more than a game trail. We thought we were on the right track, based on Skeeter's recollections and hand-drawn map, but we needed a little more confidence in our direction.

We finally came up with a plan we wanted to try. Riding south for another hour, we reached a rocky draw big enough to hide Sherry. We unsaddled her horse and the mustang I'd bought at the livery stable in Denver and tied one horse each to my saddle and Buck's. Sherry hid herself down in that draw, and Buck and I waited for somebody to come down the trail. We also tossed a coat over the brand on both the spare horses.

After half an hour, our patience was rewarded. We saw a guy coming down the trail, leading two horses. "Good sign," Buck mumbled. "He might be a buyer, not a seller. More likely to talk to us if he bought instead of stealin' them horses."

We made a show of watering our horses, waiting for the traveler to reach us. He glanced at us, tipped his hat and made to pass us. My gut instinct told me he was a small rancher, not doing too well, judging by his worn clothes and run-down boots. He looked at the horses, his glance lingering for a moment on the fact that we had covered the brands on two of them.

Buck turned away from watering his horse and lifted a hand in the air. "Give us a little help with directions, bud?" he drawled.

The man looked us over suspiciously, but he pulled up and waited. He looked us over and tugged nervously at the brim of his hat. "Whar you wantin' to go?" he asked, eventually. He leaned over and spit, but his gaze stayed on the mouse-colored mustang for a few seconds.

"Roost," Buck said, gambling on a direct answer. "We got some bidness to conduct down there. Never been there." He wiped his forehead with his sleeve and waited.

The man waited, seeming to weigh a couple answers in his head. He looked at the mustang again. "You buyin' or sellin'?"

"Sellin'," Buck answered promptly.

The man leaned over and spit in the dirt again. He pointed at the mustang. "How much you want for that one with the two white socks? I might be interested in him."

Buck shook his head. "Sorry, they're both promised. Got to git 'em down to the Roost in the next two days, if'n we're that close."

Showing mild disappointment, the man pointed in the direction we'd been going. "Foller that trail you're on," he said. "You kin make it in two days if you keep up a right smart pace. The Roost is near on to twenty miles long, but full of draws and gullies, some rocky faces and such. You'll know it when you see it. When you git to the Dirty Devil River, you'll be close." He clucked to his horses and moved on.

I led Sherry's horse over to the draw where she had been hiding, re-saddled for her, and rode back to meet Buck. He was watching the man who'd given us directions moving away, several hundred yards down the trail now. "Did you see those brands?" He chuckled. I shook my head.

"They'd been worked over pretty good. I think he'd come from the Roost, alright."

We held to a fast pace for the next two days, stopping at twilight and moving out at dusk, and just as the man had told us, we reached Robber's Roost near sundown two days later. The traffic on the trail had picked up, some of them appearing to be small-time ranchers leading horses, others looking more like hard-case outlaws.

Sherry pulled her hair up under her hat, threw on a

jacket despite the warm weather, and rode with her head down. We could see the main canyon now, with a few tents and ramshackle buildings on either side. There were rocky crevices and draws here and there on both sides, some showing water running through the bottom of the draws.

We made plans quickly. We had arrived at the best time of day. Darkness was falling, but we still had time to make camp, if we could find a place where we could hide away. We inspected a few of the draws running out of the canyon and found one to our liking. There was enough footing to get the horses down into the narrow gorge and out of sight. There was vegetation, though sparse, on a narrow mesa. It was enough to last them for a couple days.

We descended a little farther into the draw and found a hollowed-out area under an overhang where we could set up camp and have a small fire without drawing attention. The way in here from the canyon required wading through waist-high water, which would discourage visitors. We could wade out through the water for several hundred yards and climb to a vantage point, which allowed us, with binoculars, to view the canyon for maybe a mile in either direction.

We had the horses staked out, and camp set up in no time. After a quick dinner, we huddled around the campfire and talked about what to do next.

I had focused my attention on getting here. Now that we'd arrived, I was scrambling to think of a way to find out if Luke was here. I searched my mind, came up blank, and looked at Buck and Sherry for help.

Buck leaned back on his elbows and looked through the draw toward the main canyon. "A man can learn a lot, just playing cards in a saloon," he observed. He looked in my direction. "I can play a pretty mean game of poker, but I'd need a stake to play down there." He nodded toward Robber's Roost. "Those boys mean bidness."

I realized, with a sinking feeling, what he was asking me for. "How much of a stake are you talking about?" I asked resignedly.

"One hunnert dollars oughta do it," he said emphatically. "Don't worry, your money is safe with me." He stroked his chin reflectively. "Well," he amended. "I might have to lose a little of it to git out with my hide still on me."

"Uh-huh," I said. "Are you sure you're that good at poker?"

Buck's face assumed an injured expression. "I always beat you, don't I?"

I handed over five twenty-dollar gold pieces and reached for a refill on the coffee.

CHAPTER 17

AT THE ROOST

Buck had been eager to get down into the Roost and look for saloons last evening, but in the end, we had convinced him it was too dangerous to go in there alone in the dark. This crowd was too anxious to shoot first and ask who you were later on. He had left us a few hours after breakfast this morning to look for an entrance to the canyon he could access on horseback. There would be little activity at the saloon this early, but he would have time to look things over. He wouldn't need to explain why he was here, as nobody came to this place unless they were hiding from the law.

While Buck was trying to get some information at a saloon, Sherry and I decided to wade through the draw below us and watch the canyon below with binoculars in hope of seeing Luke. I didn't know what he looked like, and neither of us knew the men who had taken him or what they looked like. Sherry couldn't walk through the Roost looking for Luke, so this seemed like the only thing we could do for now.

The water in the draw was surprisingly cool as we splashed through it. I held my gun belt out of the water, and Sherry held the binoculars. The rocks were slippery in spots and we held hands for balance as we progressed down toward the canyon. After fifteen or twenty minutes of wading, we emerged from the draw and climbed up a sloping rock face to a flat surface above. We laid down on the warm rock, pulled a rag over the binoculars to avoid any glare, and took turns surveying any activity we could see below.

There was little movement down there. We saw Buck after a couple hours had gone by. We could see him framed in the early afternoon sun as he went into a flimsy-looking wooden frame building covered by canvas. It seemed like a safe bet he had found a saloon. After several minutes, he emerged and walked down the canyon until we lost him from view. I assumed he was looking for another saloon.

I passed the binoculars to Sherry so she could take a turn watching. I stretched out beside her on the rock, feeling like I wanted to explain how much I had enjoyed meeting her, and how I wanted to see her in the future. That was a lot to explain—I felt myself getting tongue-tied before I even got started.

Time to give it a try, I told myself. "I feel like I found something I was missing when I came to Denver," I said. I glanced sideways and had her attention. That was a start, anyway.

She rolled over to her side and held my eyes. "What do you mean?" she asked.

Here came that tongue-tied problem again. I hemmed and hawed a few times. "I mean, I have a good life in Montana—got a nice cattle ranch. I'd love for you to see it sometime. Buck is a good partner. I've done a lot of things I wanted to do with my life, but I've just recently realized how it is still kind of...empty. I've been missing..." My voice trailed off, and I twisted my hands in frustration.

"Family?" she asked.

She had hit the nail on the head. "Yes. I guess that's what had been missing. Having the ranch is nice. I love it there. It doesn't, uh, doesn't keep me company." My words sounded foolish to me. I stared down at the rocks below, trying to think of a better way to explain it.

She moved closer, took my hand in one of hers and lifted my chin with her other hand to look me right in the eye. "That is exactly how I'm feeling," she said. "Between meeting you and feeling like Luke is my little brother, it has filled a big empty spot inside me. If you mean it about me coming to see your ranch, just tell me when."

I leaned in and we kissed. Several times. "We'll see each other," I promised. "A lot. I'm going to make that happen. I know you're in Denver and you've got the bakery, with me in Montana with the ranch..."

She reached up and patted my cheek. "We'll both work to make this happen," she promised. "It will work out. You'll see."

My head was spinning with the possibilities. I looked back down into the canyon, excited that she felt the same way. I saw a small party walking past and looked away, then my head snapped back. I grabbed for the binoculars and focused on the group below. There were three men and a boy.

I handed the binoculars to Sherry and pointed down below. "There's a group walking by," I blurted. "Three men and a boy."

She rolled back over onto her elbows and looked, swinging the binoculars back and forth, looking for them. The glasses stopped moving, and she locked in on them, watching intently. She let out a small gasp. "It's Luke! That's Luke!"

I reached for the binoculars again and watched for a few more seconds, trying my best to memorize the faces I was seeing. Then I gave her the binoculars and began crawling away from the edge of the rock, moving on hands and knees. "Stay here," I told her. "They don't know me. I'm going to get down there and follow them." I scrambled down the rock face and started working my way down to the canyon.

The water level dropped as I got closer until it was only

ankle-deep. I splashed through, but the slippery rocks just below the surface slowed my progress. A jutting rock formation cut off my view, so I couldn't see the party of four I had seen from above.

As the draw leveled off and met the canyon floor, three men came into view from my left. I knew it would look a little strange to come wading out of the draw, so I moved over behind a boulder and waited for them to pass. I chafed at the delay.

Finally, I moved out to the canyon floor and looked down the passage. I couldn't see them. I picked up the pace until I broke into a trot, but they were nowhere to be seen. As I moved farther down the canyon, I passed a few passages cutting into the rock face. Some were narrow and seemed unlikely destinations, others were fairly wide and dry. I paused in each of those and looked, but I saw no one.

Half an hour later, I stopped. They must have turned off, but I didn't know where. I bent down and put my hands on my knees, shaking my head in frustration. I would retrace my steps and keep looking, but I had the sinking feeling they had gotten away from me.

Burt hung slightly behind the others as they trudged through Robber's Roost. They had found what passed for a livery stable and left their horses there, after paying a ridiculous amount of money for feed. At least they wouldn't have to find forage for the animals while they were here.

Burt had stayed here for a couple weeks before coming to Denver. That had been...he searched his brain, trying to remember. Maybe four or five months ago, he guessed. He had found a narrow notch in the canyon wall and followed it back to a beat-up old lean-to propped up against a small recessed area in the rock. If he could spot that place, it would be a decent place for the kid to hide until he could get out. That was assuming he could get away from Haskins and Dunn at all.

They passed the saloon. Burt remembered the saloon clearly. Dunn turned and began moving in that direction. He mumbled "saloon" before turning off abruptly.

"Hold it!" Haskins barked. He seemed in an even more surly mood than usual since arriving at the Roost, Burt thought. Maybe the thought of killing the kid bothered even Haskins.

"Where you goin'?" he demanded.

Dunn pointed at the ramshackle saloon.

Haskins stared at the saloon, then looked at the kid. He shook his head emphatically. "We get to the cave first," he announced.

They walked another half mile, Burt estimated. In doing so, they passed the niche that led to the lean-to he had used. He flicked a quick glance in that direction and he was sure that was it. In another two hundred yards, Haskins turned off into a wide arroyo. Following the gash between the canyon walls for a short distance, he turned and climbed the rock into the wide mouth of a cave.

"We're here," he announced. He pointed at Burt. "Go back and get us a bottle of whiskey. The two of you can stay busy with that. I'll go back to the saloon myself after a while." He tossed his bedroll on the floor of the cave, laid down, and folded his hands behind his head.

Burt hurried back to the saloon, buying two bottles of whiskey and brushing by an old man in buckskins as he hurried out the door. He kept a brisk pace on the way back until he reached the niche in the rock walls they had passed just a short while ago. He checked in both directions, then squeezed through the niche. Splashing through ankle-deep water for a few minutes, he reached the old lean-to he remembered. He climbed out of the narrow creek bed and peeked cautiously into the structure. It was empty.

He retraced his steps to the main canyon and trotted the

last two hundred yards to the arróyo. He hurried up the arroyo to the cave. When he walked in, he handed a bottle to Dunn. Haskins got up without a word, strapped on his gun belt and left, no doubt headed to the saloon for some gambling and whiskey. Burt found a discarded mattress in the cave's corner and made a point of ignoring Luke as he slid down onto the mattress and stretched out. It was still early evening, but he was tired.

Buck dodged the man coming out with two bottles of whiskey and stepped into the saloon, pausing to let his eyes adjust to the dim light. He glanced around, taking stock of the people inside. He had the disadvantage of not knowing what the people holding Luke looked like. All he had were names: Dunn and Burt. That was all Luke had told Sherry.

There were a few tables that were somehow still standing, though one had been propped up with an old log. A long splintered board placed on top of three old whiskey barrels served as a bar. There were four men inside, plus somebody standing behind the bar. He wore a tattered pair of pants, suspenders that looked like they would pop any minute, and a torn shirt. He had the bleariest pair of eyes Buck had ever seen. This, apparently, was the bartender. Two men were standing at the bar, and the other two had a card game going in the corner.

Buck stepped over to the bar and ordered whiskey. The bartender stared at him owlishly, his mouth opening and closing twice before any sound escaped. He cleared his throat and tried a third time. "Glass or bottle?"

"Glass," Buck told him. He would need to keep his wits in here. He received dollar coins in change after handing over one of Spence's twenty-dollar gold pieces. One man playing cards, seeing the money Buck was tucking into his pocket, waved and invited Buck to join the game.

He sat down and began playing, although his gut told

him these were a couple of small-time horse thieves and definitely not the men he was looking for. This gave him a way to stay in the saloon and keep looking for the kidnappers without raising suspicions. He purposely discarded some good cards in order not to win too much. After fifteen minutes, he was up by two dollars, though he could have easily taken another five dollars of their money. He needed them to keep playing.

Buck's back was to the door, but he felt a cool evening breeze as the door opened and shut behind him. He glanced to his left and saw the newcomer step past him and over to the bar. He wore a pair of tied-down guns, and the bartender showed unexpected speed in moving over to give him a bottle of whiskey and a glass.

The newcomer thumped his bottle down on the table and sat down uninvited. The two horse thieves glanced at each other uneasily, but stayed at the table. An hour later, the stakes were up to five dollars, and the horse thieves were gone, replaced by two new gamblers. The man who'd joined uninvited an hour earlier was still there. The bottle was half-gone, he had about twenty dollars of the horse thieves' money, and Buck had heard the name Haskins. It meant nothing to Buck, but he kept playing.

Five hours later, several players had come and gone, but Buck was still there, along with the man Haskins. Haskins had grown a little more reckless with his betting, and Buck had forty dollars of his money. He was thinking that could be dangerous.

The door opened and shut again, and another hard-case with double tied-down guns came in. Haskins glanced over, swore, and threw down his cards. "Play this hand without me," he muttered, then went over and exchanged some heated words in the corner with the man who'd just come in. The tone grew angrier and the words louder. Men close to them at the bar began to back away uneasily. Finally, it was quiet, as the two of them stared at each other. Haskins backed away several paces. "Get back up there with the kid," he snarled.

Haskins got only a shrug in response. The other man reached out slowly, picked up a glass of whiskey and downed it. He thumped the glass back down on the bar and shouldered past Haskins on his way out. Haskins glared at the man's departing back, but returned to the table.

Buck wanted to follow the one who'd just left. "The kid" had to be Luke, and the guy who'd just left could lead him there. Buck had an uneasy feeling about leaving with Haskin's forty dollars, though. Nobody would raise an eyebrow around here if Haskins shot him and took the money back. Buck settled down and waited for the next hand to be dealt.

The cards came and Buck looked at his hand in dismay. He had two pair, nines and sevens, plus a jack. He sensed Haskins studying his face. Buck glanced up, and Haskins returned his gaze to his own hand. Buck realized his own look of dismay had been misinterpreted, and Haskins thought it was a bad hand. In fact, Buck needed to lose some money if he wanted to leave.

Taking his time, Buck discarded one of the nines and the jack. He was dealt a deuce and a queen, giving him just the pair of sevens. Across the table, Haskins couldn't quite cover his own satisfaction at seeing two pair, kings over fives. He looked around the table and raised twenty dollars. The other three players folded. Buck hesitated, thinking things over, and again Haskins misinterpreted. Buck tossed in his twenty dollars and waited. Haskins raised another twenty. Buck matched his twenty and called. When Haskins laid his cards down, Buck mumbled in disgust, took his remaining money, and left the saloon.

Standing outside with only a half-moon for light, Buck swept a glance in both directions. He saw nothing to his right, but there appeared to be one man moving down the canyon to his left. He turned and followed. In a few minutes, the figure he was following seemed to turn to his right and disappear. Buck hurried to catch up, but he stopped in his tracks when he heard a gunshot.

———

Burt came awake with a start. He rose and moved to the edge of the cave. It was dark outside. He must have been asleep for several hours. He moved back into the cave and looked around. Luke was asleep on a bedroll against the far side of the cave. Burt moved around silently, looking for the others. When he realized he was alone in the cave with Luke, he hurried over and shook the boy awake.

Burt covered the boy's mouth before he could say anything. "Just listen," Burt hissed. "You can get of here now, and you gotta move fast. Take the bedroll, blankets, and a canteen. Follow me."

Luke jumped up, stuffed the blanket into the bedroll, and grabbed his canteen. He followed Burt silently out of the cave and down the draw to the main canyon floor. Burt pointed to his left. "Down there about two hundred yards, keep your eyes open, and you'll see a little niche in the canyon wall. Squeeze through there, move down the creek bed, and keep your eyes open for an old lean-to up against the rock face. Get in there and hide. I'll come down there in a few minutes. Now move!"

Burt watched as Luke ran down the canyon, then stopped, then disappeared into the niche. Always was a smart kid, Burt thought to himself approvingly. He turned and went back to the cave, taking a few minutes to gather up his own bedroll and blankets. He grabbed his knapsack and checked to make sure his pistol was inside. He knew he was low on ammunition and searched in the cave until he found a box of cartridges. He stuffed those into the knapsack, picked it up along with the bedroll, then turned to see Dunn standing in the entrance to the cave.

"What're you doing?" Dunn's speech sounded a little slurred. He stared at Burt suspiciously, then looked around the cave. "Where's the kid?" He turned back to see Burt clawing inside the knapsack.

Burt's hand found the pistol inside the knapsack, but he was too late. In the dim light, he saw Dunn's hand drop to his gun, then he felt a blow to his chest. He stumbled back, hearing the gunshot echoing in the cave. The darkness closed in. He didn't feel it when he fell to the cave floor.

CHAPTER 18

TIGHTENING NET

Luke found the niche in the canyon wall. The moonlight had helped a little, and he had kept count of his strides as he ran. Once he slipped through the niche, things became a lot harder to see. The walls of the draw rose above him, and there were gnarled and scraggly trees at the top, partially blocking the moonlight. He panicked a little at the thought of Dunn or Haskins following him in here, then forced himself to calm down and keep moving.

Luke reached out with his left hand and put it on the rocky wall of the draw, then worked slowly forward. As his eyes adjusted, he was able to move a little faster. Minutes crawled past, and he began to worry that he had passed the lean-to. He stopped and moved to the middle of the draw, craning his neck to see above the rocky walls. He stood there indecisively, wondering whether he needed to turn and retrace his steps. He went forward, moving over to the left side and reaching for the wall with his hand. As his hand touched the wall, he heard a gunshot.

He froze and listened for another shot. There was none. He was unsure which direction it had come from. It had been loud enough to be close by, though. The thought that Burt may have been shot while trying to escape brought back the feelings of panic he had wrestled with earlier. He might be completely on his own out here, and the thought was terrifying.

The idea that Dunn or Haskins might be right behind him got him moving again. After another five minutes, there was a slight bend in the path, and the embankment on his left seemed to fall away and possibly be flattening out up above. Luke put down the bedroll and duffle bag to free his hands, then climbed up the embankment. At the top, he found a small table-like flat surface, with a weathered wooden structure nailed together, leaning up against the rocky wall behind it.

There wasn't a door on the lean-to, just an opening cut into the boards on one side. Luke sucked in a short, deep breath and stuck his head inside. He relaxed a bit when he saw it was empty. He moved into the structure and saw there was a small recessed area in the rock surface at the back of the structure that gave the place more depth than he'd seen from outside.

He scrambled back down the embankment to retrieve the bedroll and bag, then returned to the lean-to. He spread out the bedroll and sat down, propping himself up against the back wall of the cave. It was so silent in here, he could hear himself breathing. He could feel his heart thumping and tried to calm himself down by making some plans. There was no question of moving out before daybreak—it was too dark out there. Even after morning light came, he asked himself whether he should try to escape. He didn't believe Burt would come now, and he didn't feel like sitting in here until they found him or he ran out of food and water. He would try to get away.

Luke slowly slid down the wall of the cave and stretched out on the bedroll. Sleep was out of the question. He could only wait for morning. Then he would take his chance to get out.

Buck had reached the spot where he had last seen the man from the saloon before he disappeared. Buck slowed his pace, checking over his shoulder from time to time. He didn't need that other gun hand, Haskins, slipping up behind him. Burt moved forward until he saw an arroyo opening up on his right. He moved into the shadow of one wall and stared down the passageway.

He had the best chance of finding Luke if he could follow this guy down the arroyo. The big problem was that Buck wasn't armed. Never terribly comfortable with his six-gun, he usually just carried his Sharps rifle. He had decided against carrying that into the saloon, figuring he had the best chance of coming out in one piece if he came in unarmed and didn't walk out with too much of anybody else's money. Now, he felt naked as he stared down the arroyo.

When he heard the gunshot, he jumped straight up in the air. There was no question it came from out there in front of him. There was no chance he was going down that arroyo without a gun in the dark. Not when shots were being fired down there. He also didn't want to come back to Spence and Sherry without more information than he had now. Buck looked around him and spotted a large boulder near the wall of the arroyo. He moved over to it and found that he had room to squeeze behind it. He settled in to wait and watch. He needed to know where the boy was.

Buck didn't know what time it was or how many hours had passed. He came to and realized he had been dozing, despite the uncomfortable, cramped position behind the boulder. He heard the scrape of boots on rock and risked a glance around the boulder. It was Haskins, dimly visible in the faint gray light of dawn. Buck pulled back and waited behind the boulder until Haskins had passed him, moving down the arroyo. Buck waited until Haskins was almost out of sight, then followed him.

Haskins never stopped to look behind him, but Buck stayed cautious, remaining just close enough to see his quarry. A bend in the arroyo's bed gave him pause, and he leaned back against the embankment wall and waited for a few minutes before easing around the bend. He was just in time to see Haskins climbing up a short, sloping grade. Buck eased forward, straining to see where Haskins had gone. He could hear voices now, and they sounded like angry voices. Buck took a few more steps forward, then tripped over something soft that lay at his feet.

Buck turned to see what had tripped him, then shrank back in disgust. It was a corpse, lying face down at the edge of the embankment. There was no part of him that wanted to touch that corpse, but he had to know if it was the boy. He nudged the body with his foot, then shoved the body to flip it over. He strained to see the face. It wasn't Luke, it was a much older man.

The angry voices up above had risen to the level of shouting. The voices echoed in the enclosed spaces around him. Through the confusing sounds of the voices shouting back and forth, reverberating off the arroyo walls, Buck clearly heard one of them yell, "Find the kid!" That was all he needed to know.

Some gray light was filtering into the arroyo now, and Buck took advantage of it to hurry back down the path toward the main canyon. He rarely looked behind him, as he was counting on speed to get him out of there. Once on the main canyon floor, he could get back to the camp and tell Spence what he knew.

Buck reached the mouth of the arroyo and took a sharp left turn, moving out of sight from anyone behind him. He was several hundred yards away before he looked back and saw someone else coming out. It wasn't Haskins, it was the other man, who stood for a moment before turning and coming in Buck's direction. He wasn't hurrying, though, and he seemed more interested in looking from side to side, surveying the canyon walls as he moved.

After a half hour or more, Buck had reached the turnoff to their camp. He looked behind—the outlaw was still in sight, but just barely. He didn't seem to look this way. Buck ducked around some boulders and began splashing through the creek bed, not worried about noise now. He needed to get back to Spence as fast as he could.

Now the creek bed took a turn, and the water was waist deep. He could see the place where he needed to leave the creek bed and climb up. He called out in a low voice, splashed out of the water and climbed. In a moment, he was rewarded by the sight of Spence's face, peering over the edge. As Buck reached the top, Spence reached down, grasped Buck's extended arm and boosted him over the top.

Buck bent over, hands on knees, catching his breath. At length, he moved over to the small fire they had going there and sat down beside it. Spence and Sherry took a seat, waiting for Buck to tell them what he knew.

"Found them," he said. "Played poker for several hours with somebody named Haskins. He seems to be in charge. Somebody else came in the saloon—another gunhand like Haskins, I'd say. They got into an argument. Haskins told the other guy to go back and watch the kid, so I followed."

Buck looked up and saw frustration and impatience on both faces. He shortened the story. "Luke's got away from them. They had him in a cave over there. He got away, and the two gunhands are lookin' for him. Somebody else is dead. Older guy."

Spence buckled on his gun belt and checked to see that it was loaded. He moved back over to Buck. "Which direction do I need to go?" He nodded when Buck pointed. "Could anybody have followed you up here?" Spence asked.

Buck thought that one over, then shrugged. "It's possible one of them saw me coming this way. I don't think so, but it's possible."

Spence considered that, then stared down at the creek bed below. "Stay here for a while," he said. "Stay with Sherry, just in case someone followed you here. Then you can go back down the creek and check the canyon between here and there. See if you can find where he might have gone. I'm going this way—he pointed up toward the rim of Robber's Roost. I'll work along the top and see what I find in the draws and arroyos along the way." He leaned over, picked up his Winchester, and handed it to Sherry. "Don't hesitate to use this if you have to."

Spence climbed a short way to reach the mesa where the horses were tethered, then moved out of sight.

———

The farther Dunn walked, the better he liked the idea of walking down to that dump that passed for a livery stable, saddling up, and riding to California. He hated Haskins but didn't feel like testing the man's skills with those pistols. Dunn could just ride out of here and never see Haskins or Soapy Smith again. He had nothing against the kid. Dunn decided that's what he would do. He stopped looking for the kid and moved down toward the livery stable.

After he passed the saloon, Dunn paused at the entrance to a canyon draw. A creek emptied into the canyon floor from above. Dunn had seen the old man go up in this direction. He stopped, remembering the old man in the saloon, playing poker with a lot of money on him. He stared up the canyon draw. It wouldn't hurt to have a little extra money to take with him to California.

Dunn waded into the stream. It was ankle-deep at first, but he reached a point where the creek bed widened, and most of the water spilled off to the right. It would be deeper from here. He took off his gun belt and held it over his head as he continued upstream. He knew he would be a sitting duck out in the middle of the stream, so he waded over to the bank and worked along the edge. He came to a place where he found wet boot-prints and looked up. Somebody had climbed this embankment recently. He pulled his gun from the holster and climbed up silently.

Dunn reached the top of the embankment and peered cautiously over the edge. The old man had his back to Dunn, and he seemed to be putting out a small campfire. Dunn waited until the old man finished with the fire, then reached down to pick up a battered coffeepot. The old man looked around, put down his rifle and poured himself a cup of coffee.

Dunn stepped up onto the mesa and cocked his pistol. The old man turned slowly, looking at Dunn's gun, then glancing over at his rifle, leaned against the rock wall. "You'll never make it in time, old man," Dunn advised. "You need to just empty them pockets and toss your money on the ground." He cocked the revolver. "Then it'll be time to say your prayers, old timer."

Someone stepped out from a recess in the rock on Dunn's right and he turned his head, eyes widening in shock. It was a woman! She held a Winchester rifle on him. "Maybe you should say your prayers, mister," she said.

Dunn held his pistol on the old man, studying the girl with the rifle. "D'you even know how to use that thing, missy?"

She only nodded.

"I don't think you got the guts, missy, even if you know how to use it."

She said nothing. The old man didn't move.

Dunn wheeled and swung his gun toward the girl. He would shoot her first, then get the old man before he could get to his gun. Dunn's finger tightened on the trigger as he turned. Almost there...

The roar of the Winchester rifle was the last thing Dunn heard. The force of the shot tipped him over the edge and he tumbled down the slope, landing at the edge of the embankment. His eyes stared upward, sightless.

———

Haskins came out of the arroyo and looked in both directions. Dunn had turned left, so Haskins turned right. He turned and watched Dunn occasionally, then turned back, satisfied that Dunn was actually looking and not just walking out. Haskins found a few niches that he explored briefly. Finding nothing each time, he came back to the main canyon and continued.

After half an hour, Haskins stared ahead of him. There seemed to be few gullies or draws branching out up ahead. He doubted the kid could have come this far. He turned and stared in the other direction, looking for Dunn. He was nowhere to be seen now. Haskins swore under his breath and turned to retrace his steps. First, he had to find the kid. If Dunn had run out, Haskins would track him down and make him pay.

He reached the arroyo where they had hidden, then walked past it, covering the same ground Dunn had supposedly covered. From time to time, he crossed over to check the opposite walls of the canyon, though his gut told him the kid would have stayed on this side, pulling over into cover at the first place he could find it.

After a few minutes, Haskins's irritation grew as he felt a sharp discomfort in his right foot every time he stepped. He ignored it and pushed on, intent on catching and disposing of the kid. Finally, he'd had enough. He stopped, sat down, took off his boot and shook the pebble out. He put the boot back on, leaning against the canyon wall for support.

Haskins started to move on, then stopped and stared at a spot just beyond where he had leaned up against the wall. He moved forward and looked around a tall, jagged boulder. His face broke into a grin. There was a niche in the canyon wall, and a path opened up beyond it. Haskins slipped into the crevice, moving sideways for a few steps. Then the crevice opened up wider, and things progressed more quickly. His gut told him this was where the kid had hidden.

———

I hesitated as I moved past our horses. I could move a lot faster mounted, but I would have trouble tethering the horse when I dismounted and checked in whatever draws and gullies I could find. We didn't need to lose a horse. I left the horses where they were and climbed out of the Roost. I pulled my watch out of my pocket and checked it. Buck thought he had walked for about thirty minutes after he left the outlaw hideout. I would start checking any likely places leading into the canyon after twenty minutes.

I worried about leaving Sherry back there at the camp, then worried about finding Luke. As I walked, my anger grew. There could be two of them to deal with, I had to remember that. The third one was dead. We had decided the dead one was Burt, who was probably the least dangerous. I had to be careful not to get so angry I made foolish decisions.

I stopped and checked my watch for about the third time. Now I had been walking for twenty minutes. I moved a little closer to the edge of the canyon, stopping at any place there appeared to be a break in the steep, rocky walls. When I saw a few scrawny trees peeking out above the rim and a small depression in the rock nearby, I edged over and looked.

It was promising. The edge gave way to a narrow gorge leading down into the canyon. The path I could see twisted out of sight after about a hundred yards, but I definitely wanted to check this one out. I lowered myself carefully down into the crevasse, taking careful steps until the path widened out and leveled a little. I picked up the pace as much as I could, wondering if I would see my son down there. If I saw him, would he be dead or alive?

CHAPTER 19

HASKINS

The morning light crept in through the small opening cut into the side of the lean-to. Luke hadn't been able to sleep. He had simply waited for enough light to move. He went outside and laid down on the bare rock in front of the lean-to while he waited for a little more light. When he could see well enough to walk, he scrambled down the rock face to the bottom of the crevasse. He had already decided to travel away from the Robber's Roost canyon, so he turned left and picked his way, hoping there was a path up to the rim and out.

Luke felt certain now that Burt was dead. The other two wouldn't let Burt walk free after helping Luke to escape. Burt would have come to him by now if he were able. Progress was slow. He had to pick his way around rocks and splash through areas that had puddles of water. Footing was treacherous. Pausing to look and listen as he came around a bend, Luke froze and retreated against the wall of the crevasse. He thought he could hear someone coming.

Staying absolutely still and straining to hear, Luke knew with a sinking feeling he was right. Someone was moving down the trail toward him. He turned and started the other way, twisting his ankle a bit when he stepped on the side of a rock and lost his footing. In his worst-case situation,

Haskins would come from below and Dunn from above. The faster he moved, the more noise he made. Someone up there must have heard him by now.

He heard a voice behind him and froze for an instant, not quite believing what he'd heard. The voice came again: "Luke?"

In a split second, his little inner voice told him to keep moving. He hadn't exactly recognized the voice, but the only people who knew he was here were Dunn and Haskins. He hurried down the creek bed, having a slight advantage because he had traveled it in the other direction just a few minutes ago. He imagined that the pursuit was falling behind, and he didn't hear the voice again.

Luke felt a slight bit of hope for the first time this morning as he scrambled down the crevasse. If he could beat this guy to the canyon floor, it would put him back in the middle of Robber's Roost, but he would have just a little time to hide again. It wasn't much, but it was something. It was all he had.

As fast as his hopes were lifted, they were dashed again. Now he could hear noise from in front—someone was coming up from the canyon floor. It was his worst nightmare. Dunn was in front and Haskins in the back, or vice versa. Luke had reached the lean-to now, and the guy in front of him was awfully close. With nowhere else to turn, he scrambled back up the slope and ducked down in front of the lean-to.

There was a sarcastic laugh from the one in front. He knew that laugh. It was Haskins. "Nice try, kid, but I seen you go up there. You come on down, and we can talk about this. I ain't mad, but I'm tired of chasin'."

Luke believed not a word of it. Haskins would kill him as soon as he showed his face, he was sure of that. He looked in both directions, and there was absolutely nowhere to run. He laid down on the rock face and waited for the inevitable.

"Come on, kid," Haskins called. "You're gettin' on my

nerves, now. If I come up there, I'll be mad. You don't want me mad."

Luke said absolutely nothing. He was completely out of choices, so he simply waited. There was noise from the other end of the draw now. It was the one he'd heard first, the one chasing him down the crevasse. He looked over as the man came into view. It wasn't Dunn.

Luke stared at the new arrival. He was tall, wearing a buckskin shirt and black hat and black pants. Luke hadn't seen him before. The light wasn't that good, but he somehow looked familiar. The man edged out from the side of the rock wall and stepped out to face Haskins. Luke kept staring, then his jaw dropped.

———————

Haskins had spotted the kid running up the slope, and he knew he had Luke trapped up there. Haskins hadn't slept since the night before, his head was throbbing from all the whiskey he'd put down, and he was tired of chasing the kid around. After he shot the kid, he would have to go and find Dunn. He felt his temper boiling over. He stood in the middle of the creek bed, hands on hips, cursing and yelling at the kid.

Something moved, and he looked straight ahead to see a man step out into the middle of the creek bed in front of him, maybe thirty yards away. Haskins stared, his anger triggering yet another round of cursing. One more fool he would have to shoot this morning. "What are you looking at?" he snarled. "Turn around and go back where you came from. This is none of your business."

The man didn't budge. He stared at Haskins, unblinking, and a little alarm went off in Haskins's brain. This one could be trouble.

"Actually," the man said conversationally, "this is my business. You can turn around and go. I'd head on back down to the Roost if I were you. If you stick around here, you'll die."

Haskins was stunned. He couldn't remember anybody talking to him like that. Questions poured through his brain. Who was this guy? Where had he come from? Finally, he settled on the question he most wanted to ask. "What makes you think it's your business?"

The man shifted his weight slightly and dropped his hands down to his sides. "That's my son you have up there," he said.

Something inside of Haskins snapped. His sarcastic laugh echoed in the draw. "Well, then," he growled. "First, I'll kill Daddy and then I'll kill the boy." His hand swept down for his gun.

――――――

I moved down the draw, following a few twists and turns along the way. Sharp descent gave way to a leveling off of the terrain, and I made better speed. The light was improving. I decided to follow this draw all the way to the canyon floor. I knew it was a race against time to find Luke.

After several minutes on the path, I heard noises in front of me, farther down the wash. I stopped and listened, drawing my gun as I moved. A short while later, the noises became fainter. Whoever it was, they had heard me and turned around. I didn't think the outlaws would retreat—it must be Luke.

I holstered my gun and pushed forward, but whoever it was, they were faster than me. I pushed harder and tried calling out Luke's name, just one time. I didn't know if he'd heard me or not, and for that matter, I didn't know if it was Luke. The noises receded and became quieter. I heaved a sigh of frustration and kept pushing forward.

Suddenly, I saw movement ahead. Someone was climbing up the side of the wash. They disappeared from view when they reached the top. Then I heard a voice.

Somebody was in the draw in front of me, talking. The voice grew louder with anger, and I heard him talking to somebody he called *kid*. I knew then that I had found Luke and one of the outlaws, probably intent on killing Luke.

I stepped around the bend and into the middle of the rocky path. He was clearly stunned to see me, but he regrouped in a hurry. I'll have to give him that. He ordered me out. I had no intention of leaving, and he would have probably shot me in the back, anyway. I kept talking to him, but I was watching those eyes. He had a wild, crazy look in his eyes, and I knew they would give him away when he went for his gun.

I told him Luke was my son, and he broke out in a maniacal laugh. Then I saw something flash in those eyes, and he went for his gun. I had mine out and level, but he lunged and my first shot caught him in the shoulder. He spun as he staggered across the gully, then fired. I felt a sharp sting across my neck, then I fired again. The second shot caught him full in the chest. He stumbled backward and sank to his knees. He clawed for his left-hand gun. I didn't know if he would get that second gun out or not, but I didn't intend to give him a chance.

My third shot caught him in the middle of his left shirt-front pocket, driving right through his heart. I was suddenly aware of the loud ringing noise from the shots in the gully, and things seemed to move in slow motion. He pitched over backward when the third shot hit him. His head bounced off a rock and fell back onto the ground, but he was past feeling it.

I holstered my gun and turned to look up the slope where I had seen Luke go. He burst out at the top and scrambled down to the gorge. He skidded to a stop several feet away from me. We looked at each other, neither of us knowing what to say.

Finally, I just extended my hand. "It's good to meet you, Luke," I told him. It seemed like a completely inadequate thing to say, but I didn't seem to have any other words.

He stared at me for a moment, then brushed my hand aside and rushed in to wrap his arms around me. He collapsed against me and sobbed. I put my arms around him, patted his shoulder, and let him vent what had been building up for more than a week.

He stood back and stared at me. "I knew when I saw you...Mom gave me a locket with your picture. I couldn't believe it was you." He took another step back and stared at the side of my neck. "You're bleeding!" He turned and started climbing the embankment. "I've got a rag," he said. He came back a minute later with a bedroll and duffel bag. He reached in the bag, took out an old shirt and ripped it in pieces, tying one rag around my neck.

"Thanks, son," I said. I looked over at the outlaw. He lay stretched out on the rocks, staring upward. I put my arm around Luke's shoulder. "Let's get out of here," I told him. We started up toward the top of the Roost.

————

Sherry stood with the Winchester in her hands, staring at the spot where Dunn had been standing. Buck walked over and looked down into the ravine.

"Good job," he said grimly. He walked over to his Spencer rifle, picked it up and stepped to the edge of the ravine. He looked back at Sherry, who was still standing there and stopped. He couldn't leave her there alone. No telling what would happen if they found a woman in Robber's Roost.

Buck walked back over to stand beside her, taking the Winchester rifle from her hands. "You did what you had to do," he said. "I would be dead right now."

Sherry nodded, tearing her gaze away from the place where Dunn had stood. "I know," she said. "I can deal with this."

Buck nodded and stood in silence for a minute or two. "What do you want to do now?" he asked.

Sherry drew a deep breath and turned, looking more animated and purposeful again. "I want to follow Spence," she said, pointing to the upper rim of the canyon. "He might need our help. There's another outlaw, and he might have Luke."

Buck handed the Winchester back to her. "Let's go," he said simply.

They walked to the mesa, saddled the horses and led them up out of the canyon. They turned left and began following the path Spence had said he would take, looking down into any draws and gorges they passed.

Sherry paused at an overlook, staring down into the canyon, looking for any sign of movement. A chuckle from Buck interrupted her concentration.

"I don't guess he needed no help at all," he drawled. He pointed ahead.

Sherry whirled and saw Spence and Luke walking toward them. She booted her horse in the ribs, and he leaped forward. As the distance closed, Luke ran toward her. She reined in her horse, jumped off, and enveloped Luke in a hug. Spence walked in and joined them. They stood with their arms clasped around each other, rocking back and forth slightly.

Sherry pulled back to look at Luke. "You're safe!" she exclaimed. "We were so worried about you."

"I'm fine now," Luke assured her. "Haskins almost had me, though. He...Dad...got there just in time."

Sherry turned and saw the rag around Spence's neck. "You're hurt!" She pulled the rag gently aside and looked at the wound. "This is dirty," she announced, throwing the rag aside. She pulled the scarf from around her neck and wrapped the wound. "We'll find a doctor," she said. She took Spence's face in both her hands and pulled him down for a kiss. Luke stared in astonishment, then a grin spread slowly across his face.

Buck stood to the side and began making a harumphing noise after several seconds. "If'n you folks are done huggin' and admirin' one another, we might should get outta here," he observed. "Although I'm assumin' Haskins ain't feeling well right now."

I grinned and gave Sherry a hand mounting, then swung aboard my horse. "I'm thinking you're right, Buck."

I pointed at the spare horse, the mouse-colored mustang. "That's your horse now," I told Luke. "We'll get a saddle as soon as we can." Luke climbed up on the mustang, and the four of us rode out of Robber's Roost together.

CHAPTER 20

HEADING HOME

We had been back in Denver for two weeks now, and we just about had things wrapped up here. The trial for Len Blount had already concluded by the time we got back. The jury of western frontiersmen had little use for a man who beat and threatened to kill a woman, as I'd expected. They were pulling down the gallows just as we rode in.

Tom Anderson had been glad to see us. Our new cows were doing fine, though it was time for us to move them off Tom's pastures. We would do that tomorrow. Buck was already half-crazy from being cooped up in town. He spent most of his days out at the Anderson ranch. Luke wanted to come to live with me in Montana, and I couldn't have been happier about that. He would help Buck and me drive the cows we had left at Anderson's ranch up to our ranch.

I walked toward the bakery, making my usual morning stop to have breakfast with Sherry. Bess had been excited at the prospect of buying the bakery, and Sherry had talked enthusiastically about coming to Montana and starting a bakery in Livingston. We had nothing like that at present in our little town. We had made tentative plans for Sherry to go to Montana by train and stagecoach, allowing Buck, Luke and me a two- or three-week head start with the cattle. Lately, though, she had lost a little sparkle when she talked about it, and I felt pretty sure I knew why. I should have never let it go this long without doing something about it.

I opened the door and went to my seat at our usual table. Sherry came to join me, gave me a kiss and sat down next to me. "Everything set for the drive?" she asked.

"All set," I told her. "Buck and Luke can't wait to get going."

"And you?" she asked.

"I want to get back to Montana," I agreed. "It will be a lot more fun when you get there."

She nodded, her smile a little strained. "I've worked out how to get there," she told me. "I will take the train to Cheyenne, then catch the transcontinental to Ogden, Utah. From there, I can take a stagecoach on the Montana Trail. I'll meet you in Livingston."

I reached out and took her hand in both of mine, reproaching myself again for not having done this before. "I need to do something," I told her. "Can you give me about thirty minutes, then I'll come back and we'll finish this conversation?"

She looked confused, but said okay. "Thirty minutes," I promised her.

I crossed the street outside the bakery and hustled down to the general store. I had seen what I wanted when I was in there the other day. The bell sounded when I went in, and the owner came over. I was the only customer in the store this early.

"What can I do for you?" he asked.

"I need a wedding ring," I told him.

He glanced down the street toward the bakery and broke into a smile. "I was thinking you might come by," he said.

In the end, I took his suggestions on style, size, everything. He put it in a box, wished me luck, and I hurried out of there.

By the time I got back, I found Sherry had done some thinking and was ready for a serious talk about things.

She walked me around to the storeroom in the back when I came in. "I need to tell you something," she said.

I opened my mouth, but I didn't get very far. "No," she said, heading me off. "Me first. I want to come to Montana with you," she started out, "and I'm not one to worry much about what people think of me, and I want to be with you more than anything. But, I'm giving up everything I have here, selling my bakery, and moving off to someplace where I'll only know the three of you. I want to do that, but I want to know...I want to know..." Her voice trailed off, so I finished for her.

"You want to know this is for the long haul. You want to know you'll be Mrs. Clay Spencer."

"Yes!" She stopped and waited. I had all of her attention.

I reached into my pocket for the box with the ring I had bought just a few minutes ago. "I can do something about this," I told her.

I had planned on seeing a sky pilot at home just as soon as she got in up there, but Sherry is a strong-minded, persuasive woman. We delayed the cattle drive for a day, and I got married, for the second and final time, in Colorado.

KLONDIKE GAMBLE

THE SIREN CALL

A special thank-you goes to my granddaughters Audrey and Charlotte, who gave me the idea for writing about the Klondike gold rush and did research on conditions in the city of Dawson during the gold rush boom days of 1897 and 1898.

CHAPTER 1

WINTER BLAST

The only thing worse than the bitter cold was the wind. It cut through my sheepskin jacket and left me hunched over the saddle, peering through the driving snow and trying to find any of our cows that might still be alive. It wasn't likely I'd find any.

The northern pasture of our ranch butted up against the Yellowstone River, which had long since frozen over. Yesterday's temperature had been minus fifty degrees, so it had probably been a fool's errand for me to come out here. Folks were saying it was shaping up to be the worst winter in Montana history, and I believed them. I had been here for almost ten years, and I'd seen nothing like it.

My name is Luke Spencer, and I had moved to Montana with my dad, Clay, and his wife Sherry, after they pulled me out of a deep hole back in Colorado. My dad, known as Spence to everybody, found me after a man called Soapy Smith had captured me. I'd gone looking for my dad in Colorado after my mother died. He hadn't even known he had a son. Sherry had kind of taken me in at her bakery in Denver. She met Dad, figured out the connection, and they saved my bacon after Soapy's gang took me to the Robber's Roost in Utah.

I reached the banks of the Yellowstone River, staring at

the icy formations in the frozen water. The cattle obviously couldn't drink from the river, but they could get enough moisture from the snow. Food was long-gone, though, and the cold was deadly. This storm had struck so suddenly we'd been caught a little flat-footed. We'd started moving them into the corrals and barn from the nearest pastures first.

We had lost quite a few already during this deadly winter. It was now January 1887, and we were lucky that we'd lost only about a third of our herd before this latest storm struck. Now, though, we had lost a lot more during the last few days. Several had strayed off when we began pushing them in closer. I had seen at least a dozen carcasses since I'd ridden out here a few hours ago.

I turned my horse and began plodding home. To be caught out here after dark would be a death sentence. My buckskin and I slogged through the driving snow, and I pulled my hat down farther to keep the flakes out of my eyes. Every square inch of skin was covered, but I needed to get home soon. I sat straight up when I heard a bawling noise. Swinging around in the saddle, I saw a little steer, maybe a year old, struggling through the snow in our direction. I shook out a loop and tossed it over his head, then tied the rope to my saddle. He fell in happily enough behind us.

I took my bearings and turned my horse for the barn. The Crazy Mountains were to my right, and the Absaroka Peaks were to my left. I struck a course right between them and moved out. I glanced over my shoulder at the steer from time to time. He had a little star-shaped blaze on his forehead.

"I'm going to call you Lucky," I told him. He looked like a survivor. I could relate to that.

My mom had left Colorado before I was born without even telling my dad I was on the way. I had bounced around the west with my mom, going from one boom town to another, never getting our feet on the ground. She had passed away when I was still a kid.

A fresh gust of wind blew down from the north, and I

could hear my teeth chattering. We pressed on, but I could feel my horse struggling in the drifts. If he went down, it wouldn't look too good for me. I was bundled well with scarves, two pairs of gloves and several pairs of socks, but I didn't kid myself. I needed to get back in a hurry. A half hour passed, and I kept scanning the horizon anxiously. The barn and house should have been visible by now.

I heaved a sigh of relief when the ranch buildings came into view. The driving snow had kept them hidden until now. I took one more look back at Lucky. His head was down, but he was plodding along back there. We had plenty of hay in the barn to feed the remaining stock we had, so this little guy would make it.

As I opened the corral gate, I saw the back door of the house open and close. Buck moved down the back steps, shrugging into a heavy coat as he came. Buck was a partner and family friend, having been with my dad for twenty years or more. I knew Buck had moved past the seventy-year mark a couple years ago, but he was tough as old shoe leather. Dad claimed Buck might outlive us all.

Buck grabbed Lucky's rope and turned him in with the rest of the herd. He opened the barn door and led my horse inside, stopping to close the door behind him while I dismounted. Buck shook his head and grinned. "I can't believe you found a cow out there," he told me. "Thought you was just wastin' your time."

Buck had forgotten more about ranching and cattle than I would likely ever know, but I never missed a chance at giving him a bad time. "Well," I drawled, "somebody's got to show you old-timers how it's done."

Buck rolled his eyes and tossed a pitchfork in my direction. "Help me put some more hay out," he said. "It'll give you somethin' to do besides sassing me."

We tossed hay for a few minutes, looked after my horse, then headed into the house. The warmth from the wall-to-wall fireplace felt wonderful when I stepped inside. I shed the coat, scarves, and gloves, then reached out my hands to the fire. Sherry brought me a cup of coffee and I sunk into a deep chair next to my dad. My brother Adam, born to my dad and Sherry six years ago, settled on the floor beside my chair. I reached out and ruffled his hair affectionately.

Dad glanced at me quizzically. "Found one steer," I told him. "Looks like he'll make it. Nothing else out there, though."

Dad nodded quietly and stared into the fire. "Half our herd, you think?" I asked.

He nodded. "Yep, probably half. We'll make it, though. We'll be fine."

Sherry settled onto the sofa across the room. She owned a bakery in town—town being Livingston, and the bakery was very much like the one she'd had in Denver when I met her. I knew that between the bakery and the ranch, they would come through this without a problem, as Dad had said.

I stared into the fire, wondering about my own future. They would have no trouble keeping up with the remaining herd without me here at the ranch. Besides, the free range was disappearing these days and they would need to grow hay on more of the land to feed the cows in the winter. I was thinking, more and more, about moving on to start a new life for myself.

I realized Sherry was watching me from across the room. She had always been great at reading my thoughts, and I had a feeling she was doing it again. She knew my life had never really been the same after Clare had died.

———

I shifted uncomfortably in my chair when I thought about Clare. She had been among the last of the families coming west on the Oregon Trail. Her family had stopped short of Oregon, and had come a little north to settle in the Livingston area, here in Montana. They had been among the lucky, all five of them surviving the cholera and dysentery that took so many lives on the trail. They had arrived just six years ago. Clare had been thirteen when they had come here from Missouri.

Clare had started helping Sherry in the bakery when she turned seventeen, doing dishes, serving customers, and learning about baking. I took notice of her around that time, and we became...well, we became sweethearts. After a year, we were thinking about getting married.

Unfortunately, although the entire family survived the trip on the trail west, Clare had never done very well in the Montana winters. Missouri winters could be cold, but Montana winters could be downright harsh. In the early part of the winter last year, Clare had come down with pneumonia. She went downhill in a hurry. The doctors seemed unable to help, and we had buried her just about one year ago.

I got up from the chair abruptly and headed for my bedroom. I could feel Sherry's eyes following me out of the room. I closed the door quietly and stared out through my window. I could see the spot where I'd started breaking ground for a cabin for Clare and me. I'd done no further work on it since the day she died.

I sat down on the edge of my bunk and sorted through the thoughts I'd been having since this harsh winter had set in, and we had lost so many cattle. I wouldn't really be needed here once the winter was over. Dad and Buck could handle things. And down the road, Adam showed a lot more interest in being a rancher than I ever had. Maybe, I thought, it was time for me to move on and find what was out there for me. It was something to think about.

———

LIVINGSTON, MONTANA—MAY 1887

The harsh winter had finally passed, with the last bitter cold stretch coming at the end of March. As we'd guessed, about half our herd was left. I had spent the afternoon repairing some of the fence line, and as I rode in, I could see Sherry and Dad sitting on the back porch. My half brother Adam was sitting on the edge of the porch, swinging his feet over the side. I put my buckskin in the corral and walked over, knowing how difficult this conversation was going to be. The thing is, I think we were all expecting it. Out of the corner of my eye, I could see Buck step out of the barn, take one look in our direction, then duck back into the barn.

I mounted the steps slowly and took a seat in the empty chair next to Dad. He rocked back and forth slowly, and we tossed a few comments at each other about the pasture and stock. Finally, I took a deep breath and waded in.

"I think," I began slowly, "it's time for me to move on." I waited a long time for an answer. I heard Sherry take a deep breath, and then Dad finally spoke.

"Where will you go? What do you plan to do?"

I shifted uncomfortably in my rocking chair. I knew my answer wouldn't make him happy. He'd spent some of his early years chasing the gold strikes and hadn't ever hit pay dirt. I cleared my throat and rushed the words: "Maybe some mining. Mom and I were around some boom towns in California. I guess I've always wanted to try my hand."

Dad nodded and chose his words carefully. "Where? I mean, what strike...mining operation...do you have in mind?"

"Maybe silver. Colorado area, Silverton, Leadville. The government is buying silver. Word is, they're doing pretty good down there. If that doesn't work out, they're still working the Black Hills for gold in South Dakota. Beaver Creek, that area."

He nodded and gazed out across our land. "I'd always thought, maybe...maybe you'd join me runnin' this ranch." He spread his hands and stared at them, then fell silent.

I pointed at Adam, listening quietly now at the edge of the porch. "I think that's your rancher, there," I said.

Dad chuckled and leaned forward. "I expect you're right

about that," he said. After a minute or two of silence, he offered some advice. "Sometimes," he said, "the folks that do the best at a boom town are the folks that go into business, selling stuff to the miners. The miners just come and go. Some get rich, most don't. It's something to think about."

I knew he was right. "I'll bear it in mind," I promised.

Dad sat back and started rocking again. "Rough places, those boom towns," he said quietly. "I know you know how to shoot. Taught you myself. Taught you how to use your fists, too. You're better'n I ever was, I think. Just remember to use your head if it ever comes to gunfights. A bullet is a mighty final thing."

He stood slowly and walked into the house. A few minutes later, he came back out and laid a new rifle and revolver at my feet. I stared at them. I was looking at a Winchester Model 1887 rifle. It was the first one I'd ever seen. Next to it was a new Colt 1873 single-action revolver. The Peacemaker.

I turned and stared at him. "We been expectin' it," he said. "Don't want you to go out there without bein' prepared. Make sure you practice with 'em both before you go." With that, he stood, squeezed my shoulder, and went inside.

————

Three weeks later, with my duffel bag packed and laying on the porch, I stood behind the barn and drew the Colt, firing at some cans on the fence. The gun jumped into my hand smoothly and I knocked down all four cans, one after the other. I holstered the gun, untied my buckskin, and led him out of the corral.

I tied my bag onto the saddle, and Dad slid the Winchester into the scabbard. He and Sherry, in turn, gave me a long hug. I mounted, waved at Buck and Adam, then turned my horse out of the yard. There was a lump that stayed in my throat for a long way down the road.

CHAPTER 2

ROAMING THE WEST

CRIPPLE CREEK, COLORADO—1894

I stepped outside my boarding house room in the early morning chill and stared up at Pike's Peak, pushing up into the sky directly in front of me. I had developed a daily routine of doing a little panning in the creeks near the Independence Strike in the morning, then opening my saloon, such as it was, at around noon for the mining crowd. The saloon was a ramshackle structure of boards and nails, with a bar running down one end of it. If you wanted a seat in there, you'd better bring your own.

I slept in the back room of the saloon, and when I told folks I'd learned to sleep with one eye open, I was only half joking. Whenever a drunken miner decided to break in and help himself to the whiskey or beer, he met my new double-barreled shotgun. That discouraged most folks set on robbing me. Once in a while one of 'em wanted a knuckle-and-skull fistfight, and I obliged 'em. Amazing, the skills a guy can pick up here and there.

I went back inside and splashed some cold water on my face, then stared at myself in the cracked mirror I'd hung above the washtub in the back room. I wasn't a youngster anymore at age thirty-four—that's what the mirror was telling me more and more these days. I still had my dad's black, wavy, full head of hair and firm chin. I'd stayed in shape at six feet one, one hundred ninety pounds. That part was all good. But when I stared hard in the mirror, I saw a disturbing number of gray whiskers on that chin. Sherry had told me I was good-lookin' sometimes, but when she did, old Buck usually snorted, and my little brother Adam always took to rolling around on the floor.

I sighed, patted my face dry, picked up my pan and a shovel, then went outside to saddle up the old buckskin. Some things you couldn't do much about. I didn't really feel older, just looked older sometimes. I'd seen some country, learned a lot, and picked up a small stake for the future, but there were still a lot of things I hadn't gotten done since leaving Montana.

As I saddled, I cast a wary eye over my shoulder at the end of the log I used to tether my buckskin out behind the saloon. There wasn't a bank in town, so I had buried the gold I collected underneath the end of that log. Every couple weeks, I loaded up what I had and rode to my bank in Colorado Springs. I had a few nuggets I found when I was panning Gold Run stream, and I took payment in gold from the miners. And then there was the gold I swept up from the floor in the saloon.

Folks had made fun of me when I had laid down actual board floors in the saloon. They made jokes about what kind of a highfalutin place I was runnin', and asked if I was servin' tea in the afternoons. Fact is, miners can drop an astonishing amount of gold dust and even a few little nuggets out of their pockets. If I saw somebody drop a big nugget, I'd give it back, but a few little pebbles and some dust...well, those things added up and who even knew which pocket they came out of?

There was an old miner who didn't do any mining anymore that slept in the corner of the saloon after everybody else went home at night. He didn't have any place else to go, so I let him stay there. Plus, he made a good watchdog for the place when I was gone. A glass or two of beer at night and a floor to sleep on made him happy. I went back inside, nudged him awake, and rode out of town.

I glanced back at the town as I left. There wasn't a lot to see. I was told Cripple Creek got its name when somebody's calf jumped over a fence, landed in a gully, and broke his leg. I didn't know if that was true or not, but when I looked back, I thought for about the fiftieth time that a fire could wipe that place out in no time.

I turned my eyes forward again and picked up the buckskin's pace a little. I glanced to my right, where the Stratton Independence Mine was in operation on the slope of Battle Mountain. They'd sunk a shaft into the side of the mountain, and folks were pretty hush-hush, but I had a feeling they had found a lot of gold down below.

I could see a few people descending into the shaft, and I just shook my head. Going down below ground to swing a pick and maybe find some gold for somebody else sounded like my idea of going to prison. I'd rather be out in the open air, swishing my pan any day. Besides, I was getting most of my money from the saloon.

I rode on for about two miles and dismounted at the bend in the creek where I'd been coming every morning for a few months now. There was nobody else here, which was the way I liked it. I got my gold pan and walked down into the stream, scooped up a panful of gravel and water, and began sifting. Here and there, I saw a little color and saved it before dipping again.

The work didn't take a lot of thinking. I moved to a new spot from time to time, but there was a lot of time for thinking out here. My mind wandered back to my dad and Sherry back in Montana. I got a letter from them now and then. My brother Adam had grown a lot, and it sounded like he would carry on the ranch for the family. Buck was getting older and a little feebler, but still complaining and doing his share of the work, it sounded like.

Sherry would ask once in a while if I'd found myself a

girl, and I always had to disappoint her on that score. Fact is, I was disappointed myself, but there weren't a lot of women in the towns and places where I'd been. I had to admit that it might be time to take my stake I'd built up here and move on to something else.

I bent down to lift another panful and felt a familiar tug and a bit of pain in my side. I had a man who called himself Black Jack Adams to thank for that. I don't know what his real name was. Maybe the Adams part was true enough. He had left me with the scar along my ribcage, and I'd killed one of his partners back in the Black Hills. I knew I had a lifelong enemy if I ever ran into him again.

I climbed out of the stream and sat down on the bank to give myself a break. Another thing about doing some panning for myself was the fact that I could work and take a break as I chose. I leaned back on my elbows, remembering the huge break in life that almost happened in those Black Hills of South Dakota. The problem was, the memory of how I lost it was just as strong and recent in my mind.

———

Black Hills, South Dakota—1891

I came to Deadwood, South Dakota, in the spring of 1891. Most folks would have said the gold rush in the Black Hills was over by then, and I would have agreed with them if I hadn't learned about using mercury to process the gold.

Until then, I had drifted around, usually showing up at a gold rush boom town after the rush was over and the money was gone. Elizabethtown, New Mexico, was one of those places. I had come to Elizabethtown after a couple years of visiting some places I had lived with my mother, remembering them as exciting places where a man could make some money. By the time I came to San Francisco and the Comstock Lode, though, the real thing didn't seem as good as the memories.

I drifted on down to Elizabethtown, knowing that the gold rush had mostly ended twenty years before, but they were still working on some claims and producing some gold. An old frontiersman and gold chaser in a bar in San Francisco told me that my best bet might be to go to some place where the rush was gone. He said there was usually still some gold to be found in those places, and there weren't so many highwaymen ready to rob you all the time.

I found he was only right about the last part after I'd spent a couple years in the area. I'd done some placer mining in a few spots and had come up with a little color. There was enough to keep a roof over my head and some food on my plate, but not a lot else.

I'd been ready to move on when I met a man from Scotland. He introduced himself as a chemist when we'd shared a table at a crowded café one morning over breakfast. This man, Alex, said he'd learned how to process gold. He called it extracting—extracting the gold from the ore and said that was how I could still make money finding gold. The key was to find some ore with some gold in it, but not enough to have been heavily mined already. Then, he told me, he had a process to pull the gold out, and bind it together.

It sounded like a tall tale to me at first, but we became friends over the next few weeks, and I finally bought him enough beer at the saloon one night to convince him to show me what he was talking about. The key, he told me in a hushed whisper, was to break up the rock thoroughly, then put the crumbled ore in a pan and wash mercury over it. He said the mercury would bind with the gold fragments in the crushed ore.

The next day, we rode out to a place where I'd been working a rock face with a pick for a few days. He showed me how to crush the ore, then wash it with the mercury. It didn't take me long to see he was on to something. A couple of weeks later, I convinced him to sell me a good supply of mercury. I parted ways with him at Elizabethtown, where he was doing pretty well for himself, and I came to Deadwood.

I didn't think there was room for both of us in Elizabethtown.

Deadwood didn't look like much when I arrived and looked around. I guess that part wasn't a big surprise. The major strike and the rush that came with it had ended about fifteen years before. They had found gold around the Deadwood and Wildwood creeks. It was placer gold, which means they'd found loose gold deposits among the soil and rocks around the streams.

It hadn't taken folks very long to claim all the land around the creeks, and after they'd dug up the soil around those claims, there wasn't much left. The one exception was a big outcropping of rock near a place called Lead, South Dakota. Folks figured out that the gold around the creeks had washed away from this spot. There was a big operation called Homestake going on around there. I had no intention of joining them.

I bought myself a good pickaxe and stepped out of the hardware store in Deadwood, laying the pickaxe down beside my bag and staring up and down the street. I led my horse down the main street until I found a boarding house, tethered my horse to the rail in front, and walked toward the front door.

A guy in buckskins with a sunburned, leathery face was sitting on the front porch. He watched me walk up with a small smile at the corners of his mouth. He looked at my pack, noted the Colt at my waist and the Winchester I was carrying, then looked past me to my buckskin. He took in the pickaxe tied to the saddle.

I started to step past him when he spoke to me. "Looks like yore wantin' to do some mining. Lotsa pilgrims show up around here with that idea. You don't look like no pilgrim, though. Mebbe you know how to get some gold outta them rocks."

I stopped and stared at him, mostly suspicious. I searched my head for something to say and came up empty.

He grinned and waved a hand in the air. "That's okay,

you don't know me. You don't have to say nuthin'." He stopped and looked at the saloon across the street. "I'm thinkin', though," he said, "that you just come into town and might want a beer. On me," he added.

I shrugged and agreed. "Let me see if I can get a room," I told him. "Then a beer sounds pretty good."

He extended a hand and shook. "Ezra Hughes. I'll be over there," he said, jerking a thumb toward the saloon.

I found him sitting at a table by the window, with a pitcher of beer on the table. There was a glass in front of an empty seat, and he appeared to be finishing off a glass in another chair. He waved at the empty seat and shoved the pitcher at me.

"Whatcher name?" he asked abruptly. "What brung you to a place like Deadwood?"

I stared at him across the top of my glass. "Luke Spencer," I said. I took a sip and wiped the back of my hand across my mouth. "As for what I'm doing, you saw the pick-axe. I expect you already know."

He chuckled and slapped his hand absent-mindedly on the table. "Yeah, Luke Spencer, I expect I do know. Fair 'nuff." He took a long pull at his glass and leaned back. "I'll tell you what I'm doin' here. You can tell me more about you if'n you want to."

The doors swung open and shut. I glanced up to see a tall man in a dark shirt and vest, wearing two tied-down guns and walking like he owned the place. Two more guys followed him, also wearing two guns apiece. At first look, the second two guys were trying to look tougher than they were. The first guy, I had to admit, might be pretty salty.

Ezra mumbled under his breath and shifted his chair slightly to put his back to the guy in the dark shirt and vest. "Black Jack Adams," he muttered. "Pay him no mind. He's trouble." He waited for the new guys to arrange themselves around the bar, then began telling me about himself.

"I done chased half a dozen gold strikes," he admitted. "Never struck it rich yet. Don't think I'll get rich here, but I can make some money. Mebbe you can too. Right now, I'm just playin' poker at night in this place. I'm pretty good, too, but I don't soak 'em too bad. I always leave some money on the table when I leave. That's 'cause I like myself the way I am, with no bullet holes in me."

He drained half a glass and looked up at me. "That keeps me eating, but I think a man could make a decent stake here if he didn't mind swingin' an axe on an outcropping or two, assumin' he knew somebody could pull the gold outta those chunks he chopped from the rocks."

I still didn't feel like tipping my hand. "Okay, I said, it sounds like you've got a plan. Why are you telling me?"

Ezra snorted a little and leaned back in his chair. "It don't take no Pinkerton detective," he said. "You show up with a pickaxe and a pretty fair-sized bag. You could've come here to traipse down in one of those holes they dug in the mountain and work for somebody else, but I don't think so. Just my hunch, I'll admit. If you was gonna' do some panning in a river, you'd have brought a pan. I think you wanna chop down some rocks that look pretty good and pull the gold out with somethin' in that bag o' yours."

I dropped my eyes to the table, then shook my head and laughed. "You might have that figgered out," I agreed. "Why would I trust you and what could you do for me?"

A small gleam appeared in his eye. "I knowed it." He chortled. "Okay, here's what I can do. I been scoutin' around, and I've seen two or three outcroppings that look pretty good. Nobody's watchin' me or tailing me around. They think I'm just a second-rate poker player." Here, he stopped and glanced over his shoulder at Black Jack Adams. "I've got me a little shanty, several miles out of town. Ain't much, but it keeps the rain off an' there'd be room for you. Got a little draw in the hills behind me where we could break up the rocks and you could do what you do, pullin' out the gold. I can take trips into town to buy whatever we need. Nobody would even know you're still around here."

He stopped and slugged down more beer. I had a feeling he hadn't made a speech that long in months.

I spread my hands on the table in front of me. "What about filing a claim?" I asked. "I guess these two or three outcroppings you're talking about are still open for a claim?"

Ezra frowned and reached for the pitcher again. "They're open and we could file a claim," he said. "But filin' a claim would just give people like Adams, over there, and those goons with him a reason to foller us around. My idea is we knock down the ore in a big hurry—mebbe in just three or four days, working early in the morning. We haul it over to my shanty, process it and take some gold that's partly refined, after yore done with it, and get out of here with a decent stake. Nobody robs us, not too much to haul outta here, and we move on."

He stopped and stared out the window, looking at nothing in particular. "One of these days," he told me, "I'm gonna be just about the first one to a gold strike. Then I'm gonna file a claim, get rich, and get out before all these buzzards show up to pick everybody's bones."

Ezra waved for another pitcher while I thought it over. We were halfway down that pitcher when Adams and his thugs wandered out. Adams shot a glance in my direction, but I just looked down and kept drinking.

By the time the third pitcher arrived, some guys were wandering in and starting up a couple poker games. Ezra shifted and looked over his shoulder at them. "Gotta play some cards," he said, pushing his chair back. "You can finish the pitcher and think it over. You can always find me around here."

I half-stood and held out my hand. "I've thought," I told him. "I like your plan. I'm gonna get some rest over at the boarding house. Maybe we can talk some more tomorrow. I'm in."

Ezra grinned and shook my hand with gusto. "This'll work," he drawled. "You'll see. This'll work."

CHAPTER 3

WIPED OUT

It started out pretty much like Ezra had pictured it. After just one night at the boarding house, I had checked out and moved on. Nobody seemed to pay me any mind. If they pegged me as another drifter, so much the better. Ezra's place wasn't any more than a shack, but there was plenty of room and I'd done worse.

There were three outcroppings of rock over at the spot Ezra had described, and they had enough gold laced in them to make them interesting to me. They didn't have enough that anybody else seemed much interested, and that was important. It helped that none of the outcroppings were near the Homestake operation. Still, we were careful. My dad had always told me a man has a better chance of hanging on to his money if nobody else knows he has it.

Ezra's guess that we could knock down the ore in three or four days turned out to be too optimistic. We worked all three outcroppings for two weeks before we'd hauled enough ore back to Ezra's hideout to be satisfied. We had done everything possible to keep it secret—we arrived at daybreak and worked for a few hours each morning. We left the ore when we were done swinging the picks in the morning and came back at dusk to haul it home. If darkness took over before we got back, Ezra knew the land well enough to guide us home in the dark.

When we worked, I stopped often to listen and look around me. I'd seen nobody watching us out there, but once in a while I got a bad feeling I was being watched, anyway. Since my days in Deadwood, I've learned to pay more attention to those bad feelings when I get 'em. Some lessons you just learn the hard way.

At the end of two weeks, we had decided we had enough ore hauled away to process the gold and get out. We had done our usual—we finished swinging the pickaxes and knocking down the ore at mid-morning, then went home. When we came back that evening, though, I saw a set of tracks leading over from a stand of cottonwood trees about one hundred yards to the north. The tracks made it pretty clear that somebody had ridden up and looked the place over.

I swung around and looked at Ezra, and we both headed out of there, leading the pack mule and not bothering to bring home the day's ore. We doubled back several times and took a roundabout trail home. We kept a watch that night and all the next day, but saw no sign that anybody had followed us back to the shack.

Work proceeded pretty quickly after that. We used sledgehammers to break up the ore a little more, then spread it out in trays. I washed the mercury over it to bind the gold and formed it into small bars. Ezra made the ride into town when we needed supplies, but it was usually just food that we needed, or maybe another pair of gloves. He watched his back trail on every trip, but said he didn't see anyone. He played poker at the saloon a couple nights a week, so it would look like nothing had changed with his routines.

After another couple of weeks, we were done. I had formed the partly processed gold into thirteen small bars. I wasn't sure how much they weighed, but my guess was that we might have fifteen hundred dollars apiece. Maybe two thousand. Ezra's eyes bugged out when I told him my guess. It was more money than either of us had ever seen.

After weeks of being holed up at Ezra's shack and eating whatever we could manage to cook—usually beef and beans —I talked Ezra into riding into town to eat at the café. I knew that nobody had seen me in town for a while, but I didn't see how it could cause any problems to have a decent meal, then disappear for good. Ezra was reluctant, but I talked him into it.

We ate at the café, and I gave the meal my full attention for about ten minutes. Finally, I sat back with a satisfied sigh and took a pull at my beer. Ezra shook his head and looked at me sourly across the table.

"Didn't know for a while if'n you was gonna breathe," he announced after a pause. "I seen a couple of prize sows take longer'n that over dinner."

I ignored him while I finished my beer, then waved for another. "A man gets a little crazy when the only mug he sees for four weeks is yours," I informed him. I took a pull on the new beer, set it down, and leaned onto my elbows.

"Tomorrow," I said, glancing around the café and talking in a lowered voice. "How do you see it going down tomorrow?"

Ezra shrugged, fished a toothpick out of his pocket and put it to work. "We get everything packed up tonight, have it all laid out. We're up before dawn, get the horses loaded up and we're gone at first light. Sooner we get shut of this place, the better off we'll be." He looked around him, then back at me.

"We're headed straight east outta here, we agreed on that. Where d'you plan on going? Californy?"

I shook my head and settled back into my chair. "Denver, for a while," I said. "I'll stay there a couple weeks and decide what to do after that. Maybe California." I shrugged. "Not sure."

The doors to the café opened, and Black Jack walked in with his two thugs. He took a long, hard look in my direction, but I didn't look his way. He mumbled something to one of his thugs, then they all walked over to a table across the room and sat down.

I finished my beer, and we got up and left. For the first time, I started thinking maybe I shouldn't have come into town for dinner. Then I decided I was worried about nothing. We would be out of this town by this time tomorrow, I told myself.

————

We struck the trail at first light, planning to work our way through the ponderosa pines, heading south through the grasslands, then following the Cheyenne River to the west and south. We were worried about this first part the most. Just putting a little distance between ourselves and Deadwood was the first thing, then a little distance from the Black Hills after that. I was still worried about showing myself the night before at the café in town.

I scanned both sides of the trail as I rode, feeling slightly annoyed at the constant sound of a couple of woodpeckers hammering at the pines. I noticed that the packhorse had drifted off to my left, shying away from the trees on my right. I reached out to unwind the rope from the saddle horn, raising my arm to lift the rope over my head and relief the pressure on my side. As I reached out to re-tie the rope, I realized the woodpeckers had stopped. Two of them burst out from the trees and flew toward me.

I turned to shout a warning to Ezra, and the movement might have saved me. A shot burned across my ribcage, and I tumbled from the saddle. I looked over to see Ezra's horse rear up at the sudden gunshot, then the shot intended for Ezra struck his horse in the neck. The horse went down. Ezra jumped free and ducked behind his mount, which thrashed only for a moment, then lay still.

My buckskin ran a few steps, then stopped, but the packhorse bolted down the trail. More shots whined past me, and

I ran in a zig-zag pattern before diving down next to Ezra, behind his dead horse. Ezra's rifle was still in the scabbard, laying now on top of the dead animal. I fired three shots from my pistol toward the trees, where the woodpeckers had been, then reached out and pulled the rifle from the scabbard.

Down the trail, the packhorse, carrying all of our gold, had slowed to a canter. I saw movement in the trees, and the pack horse shied away. I laid the rifle across Ezra's horse and sighted down the barrel. Two men stepped out from the woods. One lifted his arms to stop the horse, while the other grabbed the reins and led the horse toward the woods. I had the clearest shot at the first man—the one who had moved out to stop the horse.

I let my breath out slowly and squeezed off the shot. The man fell over backward onto the trail and lay there without moving. I swung the barrel back to my right, but had no shot at the second man. He had led the horse back into the trees. I didn't dare raise my head for a better look.

A sudden volley of shots from the trees startled me. The shots were coming from a place to the right of where I'd been shooting at. I hunkered down to wait it out. I could hear several of the shots strike Ezra's horse—the poor animal was beyond feeling anything. I crawled to my left to look cautiously around the horse's head, but couldn't see well enough through the trees. Whoever was doing the shooting was well hidden.

My gut told me it was Black Jack Adams firing at us. Black Jack wasn't one of the men who'd been out there on the trail, but the man I'd shot was one of the two thugs I'd seen trailing around with him. Black Jack, or whoever it was, he had us pinned behind the horse, and there was nothing to do but wait it out.

I pulled off my shirt, then wrapped it around my ribs where the bullet had grazed me. Ezra inspected the wound, then tied the knot for me. He grunted and rolled back over to where he'd been, behind the horse.

"You ain't bleedin' like a stuck pig or nothin'," he observed. "I'd say yore likely to make it outta here. Just don't raise yore head or do somethin' stupid."

"Not planning on it," I said. "Not even to get the gold back."

Ezra moaned. "Almost forgot about the gold," he croaked. "It were all on the packhorse, weren't it?"

I didn't answer. I had a tiny bit of good news for him, but we had to get out of this scrape. We laid there on the trail behind Ezra's horse while the sun gradually rose higher and brought warmth to the morning. I was feeling light-headed and really wanted a drink of water. I risked a quick glance over the horse and saw Ezra's canteen laying in the road, several feet away from me.

I rose up quickly and levered a shot into the trees, over where Adams had been shooting at us. There was no answering shot. I ducked down, reached over the horse with the rifle, and dragged the canteen within reach. I grabbed it and dove back down, wincing when I landed on my side. I belted down some water and passed the canteen to Ezra.

I lifted my head again, this time to look for my buckskin. He was cropping prairie grass at the left side of the trail, maybe one hundred yards away. I slumped back down and thought things over, then raised up and fired another shot into the trees. There was still no answer.

I passed the rifle over to Ezra and pulled my Colt from the holster. "I think they've taken the gold and lit a shuck," I told him. "I'm gonna get my horse. Keep 'em on their heels over there if they show their heads."

Ezra grunted, rolled over, and sighted along the barrel. "I'll do better than that if'n they show their heads," he promised grimly. "This here was the best horse I ever had."

I came off the ground in a rush and ran toward my horse. There were no shots, no sounds at all from the trees. I slowed to a walk, covered the ground to my horse and checked him over. He was unhurt. I gathered the reins and led him back to Ezra. We gathered some ammunition and

Ezra's bag from his horse, then walked down to inspect the area where they had laid in wait for us.

The man I had shot was dead, but we already knew that. He hadn't moved since he'd gone down. There was a small pool of blood on a rock, back among the pine trees at the side of the road. It looked like one of the shots I'd pumped into there had found a target.

We scouted farther down the trail and found the tracks of four horses. Two horses had left deeper prints. We figured two men on horseback had led the dead man's horse and our packhorse away with them. Whoever they were, they had probably a two-hour head start on us, and we knew they weren't above dry-gulching us again. Neither us had much appetite for following them right now.

I looked at Ezra, spread my hands and shrugged. "I expect we should go on back to Deadwood, maybe get you another horse."

Ezra stared down the trail, shook his head, took my hand and swung aboard my horse. "I expect I've got enough to get me another horse and mebbe go see Denver with you."

I started my buckskin toward town, then reined in and spoke over my shoulder.

"There's one thing you don't know," I said. "Look in my saddlebag."

Ezra looked in the saddlebag and pulled out the one bar of gold I had put in there. He stared for a moment, then chuckled. "You're right," he said, "I didn't know about this. Mebbe there's a little somethin' there to make another try somewhere. Assumin' yore planning to share."

"I'll share," I told him. "Let's go get you a horse."

———

CRIPPLE CREEK, COLORADO—1894

A trout leaped from the stream and splashed loudly in front of me, bringing me back to the present in an instant. I shook my head and waded back out to the stream to pan for a little while longer. The mining I'd done in the Black Hills hadn't given me what I'd wanted, but half that gold bar had given me a start, and I had saved a decent stake for whatever it was I wanted to do next. The biggest problem was, I didn't have a good plan for what that next thing might be.

After a half hour, I splashed out of the stream, looking at the bit of color I'd found today. I set the tiny pieces of gold aside and shook my head. I did better with what I found on the floor of the saloon. I thought of Ezra and a tiny grin crossed my face. I wondered what he was doing these days. Probably, I thought, still chasing that big gold strike somewhere. It got into a man's blood.

As I rode the old buckskin around Battle Mountain, he began to fidget and toss his head, and I saw and smelled smoke in the air. The closer I got to Cripple Creek, the more obvious it became there was a huge fire in the town. I dismounted, wrapped my jacket around the buckskin's head, and led him as close to town as I could get.

I could see people rushing out of the buildings and fleeing up the hillsides behind the town. Flames were leaping from the buildings, and I could easily see that my saloon would not escape the fire. I watched helplessly for a while, then led the buckskin a safe distance away, tethered him, and walked back to the edge of town to see if I could do anything to help.

There was a line of men, dipping buckets in Cripple Creek, then passing the buckets up the line to throw water on the fire. I joined a line and passed the buckets, but it was pretty clearly a losing cause. A few of the buildings on the edge of the fire could probably be saved, but the center of the town, including my saloon, was gone.

When the fire was finally out, it wasn't really from the water we'd been able to pass up and throw on the buildings. It stopped when there was nothing much left to burn. I pawed at my eyes for about the hundredth time, trying to stop the burning from the smoke. I sat down on a rock, exhausted, and looked at the smoldering ruins of Cripple Creek. At least, I thought, I had my answer about whether it was time to move on. There was nothing left here.

I slept under the trees near the creek that night, along with most of the rest of the people of the town. A small bit of food was passed around in the morning, and the charred buildings had cooled down enough that we could kick around in the ashes, looking for anything that might have escaped the fire. I found nothing at the saloon site. It was all gone.

After another day, when activity had settled down a little, I went out behind the remains of the saloon and pushed aside the log where I had buried my gold. Much to my relief, it was all still there. I packed it up, along with the few other possessions I had, and loaded it on the buckskin. I mounted and rode down along the main street of Cripple Creek, saying goodbye to the people who had been my friends and neighbors.

There was a bucket with money for those who could afford to chip in a little to help people start over somewhere. I tossed some money in the pail and rode out of town, heading north and west. It was time to go back to Montana for a while. Time to spend a little time with my family and decide what's next.

The smoking remains of Cripple Creek fell away behind me, and I picked up the buckskin's pace without looking back. Moving on had become a way of life for me.

CHAPTER 4

ANGIE

WALLA WALLA, WASHINGTON

The plow chattered along behind the powerful draft horse. The plow seemed tiny compared to the animal pulling it. Angie struggled to hold the plow in a steady, straight line. She called to her horse, Clyde, to stop for a moment. She removed her hat and fanned herself with it, then picked up her waterskin and took a long drink. She poured most of the rest of the water into her hat, walked forward, and let Clyde drink.

Angie stroked Clyde's neck and glanced toward her makeshift barn, housing Dale, her other draft horse. The two horses were her pride and joy. Her glance strayed to the two graves located on a small hill just east of the barn. Her parents, Bud and Shirley Parker, had made the hard and dangerous journey west when Angie was just a small child. They had put their hearts and souls into this small farm. It was everything they had ever wanted.

Angie sighed and asked herself for about the fiftieth time why she was still here, working this little patch of land by herself. Her parents had died within two weeks of each other, five years ago, during the long winter of '89. She had stayed on here, determined to make a go of it in honor of her parents. She had wanted to carry out their wishes for this farm and for her.

Lately, though, as she grew ever closer to her thirtieth birthday, she found herself wondering more and more often if her parents would have really wanted this for her. She loved her two horses, but cared little for farming. The country here was beautiful, and the land was good, but farming wasn't what she wanted. She wanted to see more of the world. She wanted to get on a steamship and travel up the coast. She wanted to live in a town, not out here by herself.

Angie pushed herself off the log where she'd settled down and began trudging up and down the field behind the plow again. The trouble with her dreams, she realized, was that the dreams weren't really a plan. If she were to sell the farm and use the money to travel on a steamship, she would run out of money pretty quickly. What would she do when the money ran out? What would she do with Clyde and Dale? She couldn't bear the thought of selling them.

The sun was dipping down behind the Palouse Hills in the west when she finally called a halt to the plowing. The planting could come in another day or two. Thirty acres wasn't really that big a piece of land, but it kept her busy, and provided enough to keep her going. She turned Clyde into the barn and brushed him down, then fed both horses and walked the short distance to her small house. It had seemed crowded when she lived there with her parents. Now it felt empty. Her nearest neighbor was about three miles down the road.

Sometimes, she stopped in at the neighbor's house, and they had made it clear she was welcome. Tonight, she felt like she wanted company, but didn't want to drop in on her neighbors—the Crowders—again. That left the café, about five miles in the other direction, on the edge of Walla Walla. Angie opened the door to her pantry and inspected the contents without enthusiasm. Maybe it was time for a trip to town.

She took a good-natured ribbing when she rode one of the draft horses to town, but it beat walking the five miles, and it was a simple trip for the horses. Angie walked out to the barn, saddled up Dale, and turned him toward Walla Walla. A buggy and two single riders passed her on the way in. She heard laughter from the buggy.

"Showoffs," she mumbled to herself.

After another ten minutes, she had dismounted and tethered Dale to the railing outside Lou's Café. She pushed through the door and braced herself for the comments she would hear from Lou, the good-natured proprietor who bustled over to greet her. She already knew what the first question would be.

"I'm just going to feed you, not the horse, right?" asked Lou.

"Har-har," she answered. "I've heard that one several times." She allowed herself to be steered over to a table near the window. There was no point in a menu. The meals never changed and Angie always ordered the same thing, anyway.

Lou patted her shoulder. "I'll have it in ten minutes," she promised. With that, she bustled away to insult another customer.

The food came as promised, and Angie busied herself with her beef stew. She had to admit it was pretty good, though she would never admit that to Lou. The woman was insufferable as it was. Compliments would only make things worse, she was sure.

A few minutes later, she became aware of a conversation near the front door. There was an older couple standing there, talking to Lou. Angie realized they were glancing over in her direction as Lou talked. Finally, they came to her table, and Lou made some introductions.

"Angie Parker," she said, gesturing, "these are the Willoughbys—Stan and Sue. They are new to the area and are interested in buying a small farm. I thought maybe you would want to talk to them." With that, she hurried away to the kitchen.

Angie stared after Lou, aware only after several seconds that the new couple was still standing awkwardly near her table. Recovering from her surprise, she asked them to take a seat.

Small talk followed for several minutes. The couple had arrived only two days ago, moving west from Chicago. It had always been their dream to move out here, and they had no ties to Chicago or anywhere else, it seemed. They had cash and intended to farm.

Lou came and departed after getting their order. Finally, they talked about the farm. Angie explained she owned thirty acres inherited from her parents. She raised mainly wheat. When pressed for whether or not she would be interested in selling, she hesitated, then gave a long, rambling answer to this couple she found herself drawn to. She was reluctant to give a definite answer.

After several minutes, she paused and gazed at the table. "I'd like to take a trip," she told them. "Maybe on a steamship. But I'd run out of money soon and what would I do then?"

Stan and Sue had been listening patiently and sympathetically for several minutes. When Angie lapsed into silence after her question, Stan pondered for a moment, then offered a suggestion.

"Maybe you could work for the steamship," he ventured. "Is there anything you can do that they might need?"

Angie paused in the act of shaking her head, then sat up excitedly. "I can cook," she blurted. "I'm a wonderful cook. I just don't like to cook for myself."

"Nobody does." Sue chuckled. "I'll bet you can find a ship that needs a cook. Then you could travel and you won't wind up broke."

Angie stared out the window, feeling excitement at the new possibilities. Then her gaze traveled to Dale, hitched outside. "It's just..." She paused and shook her head. "It's my two horses. I don't want to sell them, and I can't take them with me."

Stan's eyes followed her gaze, and they widened when he took in the size of Dale. "Is that one of them?" he asked, pointing.

Angie nodded. "That's Dale. Clyde is the other one. Looks just like Dale."

The Willoughbys chuckled at the names and glanced at each other. "We could feed your horses and care for them," he offered. "It's just that we would need enough money to pay for the feed. I'm guessing those boys can settle in at the trough."

"They're good at that," she admitted, her hopes rising again. They settled down to a discussion of what Angie thought the farm was worth and what the cost of keeping the horses would be. To her surprise, it was dark when she next looked outside. They parted outside the café with an agreement the Willoughbys would come to look at the place tomorrow.

Years later, Angie would shake her head at the memory of how her life changed that night after an unplanned trip to town.

Three Months Later

Angie stood on the deck of the *Juneau*, the newest vessel of the Alaska Steamship Company. She was bound for Skagway, Alaska, and she could hardly believe the events of the last three months.

She had left Walla Walla and traveled by boat down the Columbia River to Portland, Oregon. From there, she had taken a steamship north to Seattle. After spending a week in Seattle, talking to travelers at the docks and doing some negotiating with several boat captains, she had secured herself a job as an assistant cook on this ship. The job would pay for her passage as long as she worked for the entire trip.

Unfortunately, it wouldn't pay for much more than that. She had exactly fifty dollars left in her pocket.

Angie wasn't sure what she would do after this trip. The steamship would take the inside passage when they reached Alaska—she had consulted a map to trace the journey they would make. The first stop would be in Juneau and the second in Skagway. Whether she stayed in Alaska depended on what she found there.

As the days passed, she found herself peeling a lot of potatoes. She had imagined more in her job as a cook's assistant, but potatoes were on the menu at least twice a day. They came at lunch or dinner as either boiled or mashed potatoes, and sometimes, they showed up at breakfast as fried potatoes. In any case, peeling was required.

The food was better than she had expected. There was a lot of salmon being served, which wasn't a surprise, given where they were. The cook, Henri, was a French Canadian man. He was gruff and had little to say, but she had to admit he could cook. There was beef every few days, and once they even had prime rib. Angie avoided the boiled ox tongue when that was served and stuck mainly with the salmon and beef.

After several days, she approached Henri when he seemed to be in a good mood. She had learned to define good mood as it applied to Henri. He had actually said hello when he came in that morning, and he had just broken the sweat that would glisten on his forehead all day long. She watched him as he boiled eggs for breakfast and walked over to him, stopping a couple of feet away.

Henri noticed her standing there and eventually looked up from the eggs. "Huh?" he asked.

Angie gathered her breath and waded in. "I was thinking," she began nervously. "That I could help you with a little baking. I'm pretty good at it, and I bet the passengers would like a few more desserts."

"Mmmphh?" came the reply.

It sounded like a question, so she took the plunge. "I

know we have quite of bit of flour and sugar, and I've seen many baskets full of apples in the pantry. I could make apple pie for a dessert." She lapsed into silence as Henri put down a pan and stared at her. Silence prevailed.

Angie scuffed her toe nervously across the floor of the kitchen. "I could do it for tomorrow night's dinner," she concluded lamely.

Henri picked up the pan he'd set down and began filling it with water. "Make one for me today," he said gruffly. "If I like eet, you make the pie for dinnerre tomorrow."

It took a moment for the victory to sink in. Angie stared at him as he began boiling the eggs. He stared impatiently at her over his shoulder, and she beat a hasty retreat to the potatoes. Time to start peeling.

———

It turned out that her baking was quite a hit with the passengers, and it opened some doors for her. The day after the pie was served for dinner, the captain showed up in the kitchen. He was a tall, slightly stooped man, and he had to bend down to avoid banging his head on the pots hanging on hooks from the ceiling. He approached Henri slowly. Even the captain didn't get too friendly with Henri.

"Great apple pie last night, Henri," he announced. "I didn't know you could bake like that."

Henri shook his head. "I deedn't," he said gruffly. He pointed at Angie, who was holding a half-peeled potato and staring at the captain.

The captain, whose last name was Buckley, stared at Angie, his eyes registering slight recognition. He crossed to where she stood at a bucket of potatoes. "I remember you," he said after a moment. "I hired you, back in Seattle. Assistant cook. Well done, young lady. We could use some more desserts like that."

Angie found her tongue at last. "Thank you, sir," she said

haltingly. "I'm Angie," she added, not sure if he remembered her name.

Captain Buckley smiled and turned to go. A thought seemed to strike him, and he turned back. "Tonight," he informed her, "I'm having dinner with some passengers in the dining room. I do that a few nights a week. Tonight, there's a family named Moore. Why don't you join us? Around seven."

Angie darted a glance in Henri's direction and hesitated.

"Oh, of course, I should check," Buckley said. He swung around and addressed the cook. "That okay with you, Henri?" he boomed.

"Eeef she finish her work, eet is okay with me," Henri responded.

Buckley chuckled and walked out of the kitchen. "Finish your work, Angie," he called over his shoulder.

———

The dining room was slightly intimidating. Angie had grown up in that small house in Walla Walla, eating with just her parents. Her mom made a little conversation with her at dinner, but her father had mainly concentrated on tucking into his dinner every night. Keeping both feet on the floor while eating was considered to be good manners in her house.

There were six or seven tables in the room, and they covered each table with a white tablecloth, which made her a little nervous. She noticed that some plates were chipped, and the tableware was mismatched, which helped her feel a little more at home. She resolved in her mind to learn how to serve dinners like this and become comfortable with it.

Captain Buckley beckoned her over to his table and pointed at a man, his wife, and two young men. "Captain William Moore," Buckley announced. "Steamship captain, miner, explorer, and probably a couple other things. His wife, Hendrika. Sons Bernard and Henry."

Moore bent over her hand and kissed it, which startled Angie considerably. She recovered and greeted Hendrika. The sons seemed rough-hewn and awkward compared to their father. Also, she thought, they were surprisingly young. The father appeared to be at least seventy, and the sons close to her own age. She felt uncomfortable near the sons and took a seat between Captain Buckley and Hendrika.

There was a moment of silence. Angie leaned over to look at William Moore. "Are you really all those things he said?" she asked. "I mean miner, explorer, steamship captain?"

Moore nodded and grinned with satisfaction. "I've done 'em all," he agreed. "I even look over Buckley's shoulder now and then to make sure he's running this ship right."

Buckley snorted and rolled his eyes.

"Mainly, though," Moore continued, "I've been to the gold strikes. Been to all the big ones in Canada, I have. Fraser River gold rush, Cariboo gold rush, Big Bend gold rush, made some good money on a couple of 'em. I got gold rush in my blood."

Moore was expanding on his gold rush tales when Hendrika, obviously tired of the subject, steered the conversation in a different direction. Angie had been interested, but didn't want to interrupt the dinner talk. She decided she would ask Captain Moore about it at a later time.

Angie's reputation as a baker took a leap up when dessert was served. The ship had bought several pounds of cherries when they docked at Vancouver, and Angie had turned them into a cherry cobbler. Moore was smacking his lips as he ate, which earned him a slap on the wrist from his wife. Buckley moaned a few times as he shoveled his down. He pointed at Angie.

"She's my discovery," he bragged, pointing at her. "Found her peeling potatoes, down there in the galley. Now she's makin' these pies."

Moore set his fork down and looked over at Angie. "Delicious, young lady," he barked. "You could go to work for me in Skagway and make a lot of money baking."

Buckley looked injured. "Don't go stealing my baker," he said. "I plan to eat like this all the time now."

Angie smiled at the compliment, but was very interested in what Moore had said. "You're staying and settling in Skagway?" she asked. A second thought struck her. "There aren't enough people there to make money baking, are there?"

Moore leaned back and cupped his hands behind his head. "I bought some land there in '87," he explained. "Right after I got back from exploring White Pass, going through there to the Yukon. Explored with a man named Skookum Jim. Saw the formations up there, came back and bought the land. I'm going to settle down and get ready for the gold rush."

Angie's mouth dropped open, and she stared at Moore. Captain Buckley was doing the same. "Gold rush?" he finally asked.

Moore nodded his head up and down, vigorously. "I saw the formations in the rocks up there," he repeated. "Most promising looking area I've ever seen, and I've seen lots of 'em. Mark my words, there's going to be a gold strike up there. A big one. And I'm going to get ready for it when all those miners come to Skagway."

In the silence that followed, Moore leaned forward and pointed a finger at Angie. "And you, young lady, could make a lot of money doing your baking when the rush starts. I'll help you get started if you want."

CHAPTER 5

PLANTING AN IDEA

The landmarks got more and more familiar as I neared Livingston, Montana. I had passed through Denver and had run into Ezra along the way. The last I'd seen him, he had hitched himself to a table at a café in town, telling tall tales and trying to impress the ladies. I knew he'd get the travel itch and move on after a while, but I was ready to go now. We parted ways after a few days in Denver. I didn't know if I would ever see him again.

I thought about stopping off in town and finding Sherry at her bakery and café, but I elected to head on out to the ranch first. I heard my little brother Adam yelling, "Luke!" as I rode into the yard. I hopped down and braced myself for his running bear hug. My dad came from the barn and joined in the general group greeting. They hadn't known I was coming. I'd meant to send a letter, but somehow hadn't gotten it done.

We moved to the porch and sat down. It was a pleasant afternoon in May. Dad even abandoned his favorite rocking chair to let me have a turn in it. I hadn't come home in many years and was struck the most by how much bigger Adam was these days. He was a young teenager now, and had really filled out. I kept glancing at him sideways in surprise.

Dad chuckled as he watched me. "Yep, he's gotten big. Prob'ly 'cause he eats so much of our food. He's a rancher, though. We've got another rancher in the family." I knew how much that meant to him.

I started to tell them about all the things I had done since I'd last written, and all the things I hadn't covered in the letters, but Dad held up a hand.

"Wait until Sherry gets home," he said. "She'll want to hear about it as much as we do. She'll be here in another hour. She closes the bakery in the early afternoon."

I nodded and looked around the ranch yard, almost afraid to ask about Buck. He would be well past seventy-five by now. Dad guessed what I was wondering and pointed out at the barn. "Other side of the barn," he said. "He insists on splitting wood back there, just to prove he can, I expect. Keeps him in shape, anyway. He doesn't hear as well as he used to, so he probably doesn't know you're here."

I walked toward the barn and could hear the axe as I rounded the corner. I slipped up behind him and watched him take a couple swings, then cleared my throat so I wouldn't startle him.

"You sure you should be swingin' that axe, old timer?" I teased. "You could hurt yourself with that thing."

He buried the axe in a log and straightened up without turning around. "Still pretty sassy, I see," he said.

He turned around, and I stepped forward to give him a hug. He pushed me away after a couple of seconds. "No need to get all mushy on me," he huffed. I noticed he pawed at his eyes a couple times, though.

He pointed at the axe. "You could take a turn or two, seein' as how you're so worried about me getting' hurt," he said.

I grabbed the axe and hefted it for about a half hour, making a nice little pile of firewood and trading wisecracks with Buck. I didn't know what any of us would do when Buck passed on. He'd been with the family for many years.

We wrapped it up when I heard Sherry ride into the yard. We all followed her into the house.

Talk around the dinner table brought back a lot of memories. I told them about my adventures in New Mexico, Colorado, and South Dakota, and they filled me in on local developments. Once in a while, I stole a glance out the window at the place where I'd planned to build a house with Clare. Sherry followed my glance, but said nothing.

After several hours around the table, I took a lantern and went down the hall to bed down in my old room. Nothing had been said or asked about what I planned to do now. I hadn't wanted to bring up the subject, because I didn't know. I had some money in my pocket this time, but I didn't know what I wanted to do with it. I still knew, though, that I wouldn't be a rancher.

———

Several weeks went by, and I was glad to pitch in on some chores and work they hadn't been able to get done around the ranch. At the end of those weeks, though, I had to admit I wasn't any closer to knowing what I wanted to do with myself.

One evening, shortly after everyone had eaten dinner, I walked out and sat on the porch, looking out at the land, admiring how my dad and Sherry had made a pleasant life for themselves here. The door squeaked slightly, and Sherry came out to sit beside me.

"You don't really know what you want to do with yourself, do you?" She glanced at me sideways as she asked the question.

I had to admit, she'd always been able to figure out what I was thinking. I smiled briefly and shook my head. "I've run through a few plans in my head," I admitted, "but I'm not thrilled with any of them."

Sherry nodded and rocked back and forth for a minute or two. "Why don't you come to the café for breakfast in the morning?" she suggested. "There's a man who has been in there for the last few mornings, and we've done some talking. He'll head out of town pretty soon, but I think you might find him interesting."

I was curious to know a little more, but she didn't want to tell me. "I don't want you to be disappointed," she explained. "Just come in and meet him, let him tell you where he's going and what he's doing. If it helps you figure out what you want to do, great. If not, you still get a good breakfast out of it. I promise that much."

She patted my hand and stood to go. At the door, she stopped and looked back at me. "His name is John Moore," she said. Then she disappeared inside.

Sherry's café was pretty empty when I arrived at 7:30 the next morning. I'd expected I would be there before this man Moore arrived. I figured I could help around the café and chat with Sherry before he got there, but she pointed at a man sitting by the window as soon as I walked in.

I got a quick impression of a man maybe ten years older than me, with thinning black hair and a firm chin. He was sipping coffee and gazing out the window. As I approached the table, he stood and held out his hand. Sherry walked over with a cup of coffee for me and made the introductions.

After Sherry went back to the kitchen, I gave him a bit of a puzzled look. I wasn't sure what she expected me to talk to him about. Moore picked up a spoon and stirred his coffee, glancing at me over the top of the cup before setting it down.

"Sherry tells me you've done quite a bit of mining," he said.

I agreed. "I've been in Elizabethtown, Cripple Creek, Black Hills," I said briefly. "Just came back from Cripple Creek a few weeks ago. Lost my saloon in a fire there."

Moore looked up in surprise when I mentioned the saloon. "Didn't know you ran a business too," he said. "Find much color when you were mining?"

I shook my head. "Everyplace I went," I admitted, "the big strikes had played out. I learned a little about working the deposits that weren't so rich. Made more money from the saloon at the last stop," I admitted.

Moore nodded his head energetically. "You can make more money from running a business in a gold strike sometimes than you can from panning or mining. The trick for either plan is to get there ahead of the big crowd."

I sighed and blew on my coffee to cool it off. "I know that's right," I agreed. "Easier said than done, though. How do you know the gold's there before somebody sets off the rush? You have to be a little lucky, I think."

Moore looked at me shrewdly, then paused while Sherry set a heaping platter of eggs and potatoes on the table. "You guys doing okay here?" she asked, resting a hand on my shoulder.

"We're good," I assured her. I was getting pretty curious about where Moore was going with this conversation. He seemed to know a lot more than he was saying. Or maybe, I corrected myself—he just thought he knew more.

Moore passed the platter to me and waited while I spooned some food onto my plate. I waited while he did the same. He stared out the window again, and I thought he was trying to decide how much he wanted to tell me.

"My father is Captain William Moore," he said abruptly. "Ever heard the name?"

I shook my head and waited.

Moore shrugged. "He's been a steamboat captain, miner, businessman. He's been there at most of the gold strikes up in Canada. British Columbia, mainly." He went on to name a few strikes up north of us. I had heard of a couple of them. Queen Charlotte Islands and Fraser Canyon were the ones that sounded familiar.

"Back in 1887, Dad went on a trip, starting from the Alaska panhandle. Where an arm of land comes down, forms a little inlet on the ocean," he explained, after seeing my puzzled look. "Started at the mouth of the Skagway River, went up through White Pass into Yukon, to an area called the Klondike."

He stopped to see if any of those names meant anything to me. "I've heard of the Yukon," I said. "Canadian territory. Haven't heard of the rest of them."

He smiled briefly. "Fair enough," he said. "Most folks haven't, around here. Here's the thing, Dad's been around a lot of strikes in his time—he's about seventy-five now—and he's pretty sure he knows a prime formation for a gold strike when he sees one. He made the trip from the Skagway River up north through something called White Pass into this Klondike area in the Yukon. He's so sure there is a huge gold strike waiting to be found that he bought up a lot of land at the mouth of that Skagway River. He plans to have a wharf and a couple businesses going when the rush happens."

He sat back, stuffed a forkful of food in his mouth, and studied my face. I had so many questions going through my head, I didn't know what to ask first. The key thing I wondered about was whether this Captain Moore really knew a gold formation when he saw one. I decided to save that one for later.

"So, are you going up there to mine?" I asked. "Or is your family just going to start businesses up there?"

John Moore shook his head at the mining part. "You can strike it rich mining," he agreed. "But it's pretty chancy, and sometimes the road agents and highwaymen get the gold before you get out with it. Boom town needs things, though. We're going to build a wharf and a lumber mill to start with. People need to dock ships and need lumber to build houses and such. We own enough land there for a whole town."

I circled around the big question in my head. "Have you seen this Klondike area?" I asked finally.

He smiled briefly and shook his head. "Nope. You're wondering how my father can be so sure there's gold up there." He didn't even check my face to see if I agreed. I guess it was pretty obvious I had some doubts.

He shrugged. "That's where you'd be taking a chance to come up there. A gold strike's never for sure until somebody makes the first big strike. But then," he pointed out, "everybody else knows about it too." He picked up a piece of bacon off a fresh platter Sherry brought over. "I've been around my dad at half a dozen strikes. I think he knows it's there, but you would have to put some money upfront and come up to take a look yourself. That's up to you."

I nodded thoughtfully and took my turn, staring out the window. Moore waited me out. "Why are you telling me about this?" I asked finally. "If I went up there, I might compete with your family for some of that money."

Moore chuckled. "Believe me, if there's a strike as big as my dad thinks, there will be lots of money going around." He turned serious. "There are a lot of outlaws, con men, and highwaymen out to steal your money in boom towns. A town—even a gold strike boomtown—needs honest people to look out for each other. Law comes to those places later on."

He paused and traced a pattern on the table with his spoon. "I've been in here just about every morning for a week. Just wanted to stop for a bit before I go on up to Alaska. I've been talking with Sherry most mornings, and met your father, too. He stopped in a time or two. They told me about you. I'm guessing you're one of those guys who could help us run an honest town. Just a hunch I have."

He put down some money on the table and pushed his chair back. "I've got to get over to the blacksmith and get a couple of new shoes on my horse before I go. Just stayed over this morning because Sherry asked me to stay and talk to you."

He extended his hand. "If you decide to come, get to Seattle and take a steamship up to Juneau, then Skagway. My family is already there. We're building a town. I'd be glad to see you in Alaska."

We shook hands, and he left. I sat there for a long time, staring out the window. Sherry came over to refill my coffee, then she took a seat. "Well," she said, "what do you think?"

I stared at her blankly and shrugged. "I don't know," I admitted. "It really all depends on whether there's gold up there in this Klondike area. Depends on whether I want to spend the time and money to go up there and find out."

Sherry nodded, and we sat in silence for a few minutes. She excused herself when a new customer came in. I finished the coffee and went outside. I think best when I walk, and I nearly wore out a pair of boots that day, walking around in Livingston.

———

Another two weeks went by, and I knew I was just dragging my feet. I knew what I wanted to do, but I wasn't sure how good an idea it was. It was hard to get myself moving.

I rose early one morning, knowing I needed to move on. We had about fifteen calves that we needed to brand, so I went out to help. Adam and Buck rounded them up and drove them into the corral. I held them while Dad did the branding. It was hot, dusty work, but it was over soon enough.

When we were done, Adam headed for the house while Buck and Dad put up the horses. I draped my elbows over the top rail of the corral, watching the calves mill around inside. I was pretty much lost in my thoughts, and it took me by surprise when I realized that Dad and Buck had come out of the barn to stand beside me.

"Yer goin', aintcha?" Buck blurted out.

I nodded my head and laughed. "I guess so," I said. "I've got to find out if there's really a big strike up there. I guess I'll go up and find out."

"I knowed it," Buck bellowed. He slapped me on the back and headed for the house.

Dad took his turn at draping elbows over the corral. "You planning to do some mining or to open a saloon or something?" he asked finally.

"I think...well, I really want to give the mining a try if the place isn't crawlin' with guys already. If I don't come up with much, I think I have enough money to buy a lot and open a saloon. I know how to run one."

Dad nodded his head. "You could do both," he agreed. "If you strike color early and get out, you could already have a business going when the rush comes." He stopped and stared at his hands. "You might have to take care of yourself," he cautioned. "A lot of outlaws and no-goods flock to boomtowns." He glanced at a scar on my chin. "I think maybe you've been in a few knuckle-and-skull fights in a couple of those places," he observed.

I grinned ruefully and touched the scar. "Yeah, a few. Didn't get out of the way of a whiskey bottle fast enough."

"How about that?" he asked, tapping the Colt in my holster.

I shook my head. "Haven't been in a gunfight," I said. "I practice with it, though."

He nodded. "Maybe we could practice a little more before you go. A man has to be prepared sometimes."

With that, he went up to the house. I stayed a little longer, staring past the corral and out to the pastures behind it. Practicing might be a pretty good idea.

The practicing didn't turn out to be more than an hour or two for two mornings. The Colt still came to my hand easily and quickly. I didn't miss any of the bottles Dad set up on a log behind the barn. He watched me critically.

"You're fast," he acknowledged. "And you hit what you're aiming at. Don't panic. Look the other guy in the eye. The eyes will usually give it away. Make sure you've cleared the holster before you come level." His voice trailed off.

"You only draw that gun if you have to," he said finally. "I haven't drawn a gun on a man since..."

"I know," I said. "Not since you killed a man to save my life."

He nodded and stared at the ground. "Not since then," he agreed.

The going away was short and quick, thankfully. Sherry cried a little and hung on my neck. There were a few other misty eyes around there, too. Mine might have been a couple of them. I turned, hugged Adam, Buck, and Dad, then mounted up and rode out of the ranch yard.

It was time to try my luck in Alaska.

CHAPTER 6

BLACK JACK

The steamship was already hull down on the horizon, chugging its way back down the inlet, bound for Juneau and Seattle. Angie stood with her few possessions on the shore of the town becoming known as Skagway. A few teams of mules pulled carts through the mud here and there, balking frequently and protesting loudly in what sounded like neither a whinny nor a bray. Some combination of the two, she decided. She had a feeling she was going to have to get used to that noise.

Angie clutched the ten dollars she had in her pocket and looked at the place she had chosen to become her home. She was both excited and a little scared. The mountains lifted snow-capped peaks in the background, but what passed for streets in front of her were nothing but mud. Walla Walla hadn't been much of a town, but at least it had houses, buildings, and a couple of schools. What passed for the town of Skagway consisted of a few tents on the mud streets. She had seen a few other women here, but only a few. There were a lot of bearded, rough-hewn characters here, and she had never heard so much swearing in her life.

Still, William Moore had impressed on her the opportunity that was here. She could picture that, too. If there was, in fact, a gold strike about to happen up there in the Yukon,

Moore had talked about how fast a town could fill up, and how much gold dust a miner might part with for his first taste in the last six months of a fresh-baked pie.

To that end, Angie had succeeded in buying all the flour, sugar, and beef tallow she could from Captain Buckley before the ship had sailed this morning. She had also managed to get a few dried apples and cherries. She had paid for about half the supplies from her earnings on the trip up. William Moore had lent her the rest. Buckley had agreed to bring more supplies on the return trip, though Angie had a feeling he was charging her a little too much. She didn't really have a choice for now. Maybe she could negotiate better prices later.

She stared up at the pass, lifting to the east and north. The voice in her ear caught her by surprise. "That's White Pass. The trail to the gold strike will run through there and up to the Klondike."

Angie jumped slightly and turned to see Moore standing beside her, stroking his long gray beard thoughtfully and staring upward. After a moment, he turned and strode away, barking orders at a group of five or six men he seemed to have recruited while on the ship to work for him. His first order of business, he had told her, was to build a sawmill. He said he had brought all the equipment he needed along with him. Once he had the sawmill built, he planned to build a wharf.

Angie climbed up the slope toward the mud streets. Moore's men had gathered her baking supplies and her two small personal bags in a haphazard pile along a muddy path she assumed was going to be a street. She stood uncertainly next to her belongings and watched as Moore emerged from a small group of men down near the waterline. He beckoned to a short, powerfully built man only a little younger than Moore, and the two of them moved briskly to join her.

Moore gestured at the man next to him. "This is Conway," he barked. "Conway is going to build you an oven. When that's done, we'll put up a little tent around it, and you'll have a bakery. Later on, when the sawmill's going, we'll build you a proper store."

With that, Moore whirled and strode away. Angie watched him go, then looked over at Conway, who was nodding and bobbing his head up and down.

"How are you going to build an oven?" she asked. "There's nothing here..."

Conway chuckled and bobbed his head up and down a few more times. "Got everything I need, ma'am," he assured her. "Got some flat rocks, gonna mix me up some mud and straw to chink in the rocks, build up a little chimney, I will. This is a nice flat spot to build it right here. Cap'n owns this lot, he does." Conway walked away, mumbling the last few words over his shoulder as he left.

Angie decided the best thing she could do was to get out of the way. She dragged a half-full barrel of flour to the side and perched herself on top of it, waiting to see how Conway was going to build the oven. She stared up at White Pass, noting the steep incline. It occurred to her that anyone going over the pass to mine would either have to make the trip on foot, or use powerful horses to make the climb.

As she stared at the pass, a couple of ideas came to her— the first one was about men needing to climb that pass. The second was about how she might expand her bakery into a restaurant someday, if things went well. The thoughts merged when she remembered her horses, Clyde and Dale, and her friend Lou, back at Lou's Café in Walla Walla.

Angie hopped down from the barrel and rummaged through her bag until she found a pencil and some paper. She climbed back up on the barrel and began to write a letter to Lou. She probably wouldn't be able to mail it until the steamship returned on its next trip, but she wanted to get the letter written now.

Black Jack Adams stooped down behind the barricade at Denver City Hall. Things had gone pretty well for him since returning to Colorado from the Black Hills gold strike several years ago. He couldn't really complain, all things concerned. He was a deputy sheriff here in Denver, and he'd made a lot of money, but things kept getting complicated. Black Jack liked his money to come easier than this.

Creede, Colorado, had been his first stop after the Black Hills, and things couldn't have been better for him in Creede. It was another mining boom town—this was from a silver strike. Boom towns were probably his favorite. There was a lot of money around, and it was pretty easy to take the money away from people who weren't used to having any.

He'd bought up several lots along what was fast becoming the main street in the town. He'd rented out the lots for a steep price. When other businesses sprang up, he'd shaken those guys down for money. Before too long, he had a gambling hall, a couple of saloons, and another business or two to go along with them.

The only trouble with boom towns, of course, was that eventually, the strike played out, and the town wound down and folded up. That's what had happened at Creede after just a few years. Now he was back in Denver.

Denver had been his town before this. The reformers kind up came and went here. After Creede, he'd heard that Denver was a likely spot for him again, and he'd done pretty well until Davis Hanson Waite had gotten himself elected governor of Colorado. Waite was one of those reformers that Adams hated so much, and Waite had proved to be more trouble than most.

First, Adams had to close his railroad ticket business. That one had been a pretty sweet deal. He had an office that offered discount railroad tickets. Of course, there weren't any tickets. When a customer showed up and wanted to buy a ticket, they were told the agent was out of the office. While they waited for the agent to come back, they were encouraged to get an even bigger discount on their ticket by playing some rigged poker.

Waite had proceeded to close most of Black Jack's businesses and had fired three city officials who were "business associates" of Black Jack. Then Waite had actually called in the militia. Adams had been holed here up in the city hall tower for several days with the fired officials, his right-hand man Cap Light and a couple other guys Black Jack used to convince people to give him their money.

They had enough dynamite and ammunition up here to hold off an army, but then again, the militia had shown up with cannons. Nobody likes to argue with a cannon. After several days, they had called the militia off and Black Jack Adams was, for the first time in his life, a deputy sheriff. Even Black Jack himself wasn't quite sure how he'd talked his way into the deputy sheriff job.

He emerged slowly from city hall with Cap Light and his other two guys. Nobody seemed to look in his direction as they scurried past him. He walked down to a café to get himself some dinner while he figured out whether it was time to leave Denver. He took his time over the meal, deciding he could make some money with this deputy sheriff job before he had to leave town.

He made some plans with Cap Light over dinner. The governor had closed the gambling halls and saloons, including the ones Black Jack owned. As the deputy sheriff, though, he figured he could keep the businesses running for a while. The plan he made with Cap Light was to get some guys with a lot of money to lose rigged games at his gambling hall. When they complained about their losses, Black Jack would arrest them. After that, they would be pretty happy to get out of town, even without their money, as long as they didn't go to jail.

It was several months later, after leaving Denver and drifting through some towns in California, then moving north to Portland, that Black Jack Adams first heard some whispers about a gold discovery way up north. He had been playing some poker, cheating as usual, of course, and planning to leave town before he had to shoot his way out. He'd made some money, but not enough.

It was in the early morning hours, his eyes burning with the smoke and too many shots of whiskey, and he was getting ready to cash in. A couple of guys might object to him leaving the game, but Cap Light had them covered from the next table, and Jack always had a hideout gun up his sleeve.

He announced it was time for him to go as he collected one last pot from the middle of the table. One of the three other men in the game pushed back his chair and dropped his hand toward his gun belt. Cap Light stood and pulled his Smith & Wesson .44 from the holster, stopping the man in his tracks. He lifted his hands slowly and moved away from the table. The other two did the same.

Adams collected his money from the table, handed a few dollars to Light, then moved over to the bar for one last drink. He glanced at the money in his hand and shook his head. Portland was full of lumberjacks, and they had too little money. It was time to go.

As he tossed off his last whiskey, he heard some excited mumbling farther down the bar about a gold strike in the Yukon. His ears picked up immediately. He heard the names Carmack and Snookum Jim, but those meant nothing to him. He kept listening, finally figuring out the gold had come from somewhere in Canada, near Alaska. The men seemed to become aware he was listening in, and they immediately quieted down.

When the others had left, he motioned to Cap Light and the other man that still worked for him, a huge, heavily bearded man named Burl. Adams just called him Bear, since he had trouble remembering Burl. He huddled with Bear and Cap Light, pointing at the men leaving the bar.

"I want to know what they know about the gold."

Bear's brow furrowed as he tried to follow the words he was hearing. "Gold?"

Adams sighed in frustration and gave Bear a sharp slap across the face. "Gold. They've found gold somewhere in Canada, or Alaska, or somewhere up there. Find out where and how to get there. Go!"

He gave Bear a shove and watched him lumber out of the bar. A little while later, he heard a few howls of pain. Black Jack grinned a little to himself. The man was dumber than a brick, but if he got his hands on you, you were pretty much going to tell him what you knew.

Several weeks later, Black Jack arrived in Seattle. He set about learning what he needed to know about this gold strike in a place called the Yukon.

———

In the end, I decided to just ride my horse to Seattle. I looked at taking the railroad, but there didn't seem to be any kind of direct connection from our part of the country, and it just sounded like a dirty, noisy ride to me. I thought about riding to the Columbia River and then taking a steamer to Seattle, but my horse was going to be faster and less expensive.

Seattle seemed like a logging town to me, but there was a lot of traffic at the port. I was moving along the docks, looking for a place to buy passage on a steamer, when a kid walked past me, selling newspapers. I took one look at the headline on the paper and bought one, fumbling in my pocket for some change. I paid the kid and walked over to a bench to take a seat.

The paper was called the Seattle Post Intelligencer. The title that had caught my attention said: *Gold Strike in Alaska*. I read the article through, then went back and read it a second time. I folded up the paper and stared out past the docks, wondering if this was good news for me or bad news.

The article said that a man named Carmack had made a major gold strike at a place called Rabbit Creek. It was a stream that flowed into the Klondike River, in the Yukon. So, technically, it wasn't in Alaska at all. I guess the paper wasn't too worried about the headline being a little off. I paced up and down along the docks, wondering if I was just a little too late again, showing up after the gold was gone.

My pacing up and down finally landed me in front of a steamship office. I stood and stared at the sign: Alaska Steamship Company. I hesitated only a moment, then shouldered my way inside.

A bored-looking clerk watched me coming toward his window. He said nothing, just stared at me and waited. "I need a ticket to Skagway, Alaska," I told him.

He didn't blink or say anything at first, he just nodded at me. "I got one ticket left on the ship leaving day after tomorrow," he mumbled. "If you don't want that one, we've got another ship leaving next week."

I took the ticket for the day after tomorrow, paid for it, and brushed past a sharp-featured man who looked a bit familiar as I left the offices. Next to him was an enormous, run-down looking man who had a foul odor of smoke and old, dirty clothes. The sharp-featured man stared at me as I pushed past, but I paid him no attention. There was a lot to get done in the next couple of days.

I found a livery stable and sold the buckskin, which hurt me. He was getting old, but had a few good years left in him. I couldn't see taking him to Alaska. For all I knew, the cold would be too much for him at his age. I didn't know how long I would be up there, and the cost of putting him up at the stable was going to be too much.

I took the money from selling my horse and bought myself a good sheepskin jacket and some other things I would need for the winter up north. I still had the basic mining supplies I had used many times over the last several years. I would take those with me.

By the time I had finished getting ready for my trip, there was just enough time left for a good dinner and a night's sleep at my hotel before leaving the next morning. I was staying near the docks and found a good café for dinner. Not long after leaving the café, heading for my hotel, I became aware I was being followed. Not only was the guy so big that I couldn't miss seeing him, I could smell that same foul odor of smoke and old, dirty clothes. It was the guy I'd seen outside the steamship office.

I had no idea why he was following me, but I figured he wasn't looking to make friends.

Black Jack pulled back as somebody burst out through the door at the steamship offices. He recognized the face and instinctively tugged at his hat brim to shield his face. He searched his mind for where he'd seen that face, glancing out from under his hat brim as the man moved off down the street.

After a moment, he knew where he'd seen the guy. There had been two of them. One older and one younger. They'd robbed the two of them as they left Deadwood, South Dakota, a few years ago. This guy had been the younger one. Adams stared up at the sign above him for the Alaska Steamship Company. He looked back at the man moving down the street. If this guy was going to Alaska, Black Jack couldn't afford to be recognized.

Bear was leaning against the building, staring out at the water. Black Jack motioned at the man walking down the street. Bear paid no attention, seemingly focused on a sea gull diving for fish in the ocean. Black Jack swore under his breath and shoved Bear up against the building. Bear staggered, blinked in surprise, and looked resentfully at him.

"Find out where he's going," Black Jack hissed. "Get back here and tell me when you find out."

Bear nodded dully and shambled off after the young man, who was now about a block away. Black Jack pushed on inside the building, still swearing under his breath.

Half an hour later, Black Jack was in an even fouler mood. There were no tickets left for the next trip to Alaska. He had no choice but to wait for another week. He looked up to see Bear returning.

"Well?" Black Jack snapped.

"Hotel," Bear mumbled. He jerked his thumb over his shoulder, vaguely pointing at any of several buildings down the street. "He's staying at the ho-tel." He hiccuped twice and fell into silence, seeming to be very pleased with himself.

"I don't want him leaving town," he hissed. "See to it."

Bear blinked in surprise, nodded, then kept his distance from Black Jack as they walked away.

CHAPTER 7

NORTHBOUND

I had run some errands in the late afternoon and found myself at the café later than expected. I wanted a good meal before taking the steamer to Alaska because I had some doubts about the food on the ship. Also, I had doubts about the food I would eat up there in Alaska. It could be as bad as the food at Ezra's shack had been. I deserved a good meal before I left.

I dragged out the time I spent at the café by having two cups of coffee afterward, but it was getting pretty dark outside, and I needed to get on back to the hotel. I headed left out the door and began walking along the dock. There wasn't much light except for a full moon over the water, but I knew my way.

I was still on the docks as I moved along the waterfront, maybe three blocks from my hotel. My ears told me I was being followed. A glance over my shoulder told me it was the big, heavily bearded guy that smelled like dirty clothes, and like I said, I didn't figure he was trying to make friends.

A couple blocks from the hotel, I came to a street corner and ducked quickly down into the side street, pressing up against the side of a building. I could hear his pace quicken into a trot, and he came lumbering around the corner, swinging his head from side to side, trying to find me.

I stepped out from the shadows and came at him in a rush, which clearly took him by surprise. A guy his size, he was used to people running from him. He skidded to a stop, starting a slow smile at how easy this was going to be, and swung a long, looping overhand left at me. I stepped under it easily and lifted both fists to his belly—first left, then right. The air left him with a loud whooshing noise, and I lifted a right uppercut to his face. He staggered back, blood pouring from his nose.

He swore loudly and came at me, flailing with both huge fists. I ducked the first one and sidestepped the second, backing slowly toward the edge of the docks. I glanced behind me to check the distance to the water. He swung a slow, overhand right at me, and I stepped inside it, smashing a hard left hook to his face.

He let out a bellow, set his feet, then charged me, reaching out to wrap me up in those meaty arms. I side-stepped again and let his momentum take him to the edge of the docks. He tried to stop, teetering on the edge of the water. I stepped around, planted my boot on his backside, and gave him a shove over the edge.

He landed with a tremendous splash and thrashed around in the water for a while. I knew it wasn't more than a couple of feet deep. I watched from the dock while he got to his feet and waded out. He looked in my direction once, then left, wading through the water, going the other way. He seemed to have had enough for one night.

I went on up to my hotel room and stretched out on the bed, my hands locked under my head while I stared at the ceiling. I didn't figure the guy I'd just fought had anything against me. It must be the other guy at the steamship office —the sharp-featured one who'd looked a little familiar. Where had I seen him?

I laid there and went over the last several years in my head, trying to remember where I'd been and where I might have made enemies. When I came to my time in Deadwood, South Dakota, I sat bolt upright, staring at the wall. Of course! The guy I'd thought I recognized had to be Black Jack Adams. I had done nothing to him, but he certainly had reason to think I might want to get even with him. He and his thugs had robbed Ezra and me on the trail that day, headed west with our gold.

Bear ambled toward the docks where the steamship would depart for Alaska today. He reached a hand up and gingerly touched the bandaging on his nose. Even a slight touch caused pain. He didn't much want to cough or sneeze today, either. The pain in his stomach and ribs made him sorry if he did.

Bear spotted Black Jack Adams standing on the dock and staring angrily at the steamship. Bear followed his gaze and saw the guy who'd given him the sore nose and stomach walking up the plank to board the ship. Bear winced a little, remembering the fight. That guy could really punch. Still, Bear didn't really have any grudges against him. Bear had jumped the guy and got beat, fair and square.

Black Jack was a different matter, though. Bear had done a lot of dirty work for that guy, mostly getting the job done. Adams didn't thank him for any of it, but that was okay if he got paid and didn't get slapped around. Bear knew he wasn't going to get paid for this one. He was prepared for that. He just didn't intend to let Adams slap him around again.

Bear looked left and right. Cap Light, Adams's gun hand, didn't seem to be around. That was good. For that matter, Black Jack himself was said to be mighty good with a gun, but he usually wasn't wearing one. Not around town, anyway. Bear knew about the hideout gun up Black Jack's sleeve, though.

Bear lumbered up to Black Jack, still glancing warily around for Cap Light, but not seeing him. Adams's face was a thundercloud. He was carrying a gold-headed cane and seemed to consider hitting Bear with the cane. Then he changed his mind and drew back his hand to give Bear a vicious slap. He never got the chance.

Bear closed the last two steps with a lunge, then reached out and lifted Adams by his coat lapels, pinning his arms against his chest. Black Jack's legs kicked futilely as Bear lifted him overhead, then took four steps to the edge of the dock. He shoved upward mightily, launching Black Jack out into the ocean. He landed with a loud splash. His hat fell off before he landed, and the cane flew away from his hand. It sunk before he could splash over to retrieve it.

Bear turned away from the dock, then froze when he saw Cap Light stepping toward him, his hand dropping down to draw his gun. Bear leaped forward with surprising speed, and Cap cleared leather but wasn't able to lift the gun. Bear's fist landed on the point of his jaw. It sounded like the butt end of an axe striking a log, and Cap was out cold before his head hit the dock.

Bear turned and looked at the man on the steamship, watching him from the rail. Bear nodded to him, turned, and ambled away.

———

I had climbed the plank onto the steamship, walked down a few yards, then stopped to look over the rail. I was looking for Black Jack mainly, but I was also a little leery about running into the guy that had jumped me last night. I wasn't eager to get into another fight with him.

I saw them both at about the same time. I watched and grinned a little to myself as the big guy grabbed Black Jack, lifted him, and tossed him into the water. The ridiculous top hat landed about five feet away from him and floated there until Black Jack splashed over, retrieved it, and jammed it back on his head.

My eyes swung back to the dock in time to see the big guy swing from the heels and lay out another man with a solid right to the jaw. I could hear the punch from up here, and I winced, knowing how much power that guy packed. The big man massaged his knuckles for a second, then he looked up my way and nodded. I tipped my hat to him. He smiled and walked away.

I looked back out at the bay. Black Jack wasn't much of a swimmer, but he seemed to splash his way back to the shore. I could hear some laughing as he reached a wooden ladder nailed to one post under the dock. He climbed up slowly, water pouring off his top hat and fancy suit. He stepped up onto the dock, glaring in all directions.

He turned his head and looked at me. I was probably fifty yards away, but I could see the pure venom in those eyes. He turned and moved away. I looked up and saw the big guy reaching the end of the dock and climbing up to the street above. I picked up my bag and went looking for my cabin. It looked like I had an unexpected friend and a dangerous enemy. I wondered if either of them would come to Alaska.

———

The oven had been put together faster than Angie would have believed possible. In part, it was the skill of Conway, William Moore's man, who had been assigned to build the oven. In part, though, it was all the volunteer help. When word got out it was a bakery going up, five or six guys showed up from nowhere, scouring the country for flat rocks and hauling them in. They had followed that up with buckets of mud and straw, which Conway used to fill in around the rocks.

The oven was up and working in three days, and in another day, a crude but effective tent had been raised around the oven. Angie left the flap open, and it was a bit hot during these early summer days, but she knew the oven would keep the place warm in the winter. Moore had promised her a more permanent place, built with boards from his lumber mill, by then.

She had given out a few free pies when the oven was done to thank the men who had volunteered their time. It had been a nice thank-you gesture, plus she had several faithful customers now. News of a strike in the Klondike had come through just a few weeks ago. William Moore had redoubled his efforts to finish the lumber mill, and Angie just needed the steamship to come in again with more supplies.

She already had plans in her head to expand her current business, and to maybe start another one besides. She had written to Lou, back in Walla Walla, offering to split the business and become partners in a bakery and restaurant here in Skagway. Besides that, she asked if Lou could bring Clyde and Dale with her on a steamship. She could start another business, using the horses to take the miners and their supplies up White Pass on the way to the Klondike. It was too soon to hear from Lou on her proposal, but Angie hoped the letter had reached her by now.

She was a little disappointed that no one had come back through here from the Klondike gold fields. She had hoped that George Carmack and Skookum Jim Mason would come to Skagway. Word of that could bring the rush of miners that she and Moore were hoping for. She didn't know if they were still up there, or if they might have taken the Yukon River north to come home, bypassing Skagway altogether.

A white-haired man in buckskins and heavy handmade boots came in just then, carrying a rifle like he'd been born with it. He tipped his battered beaver skin hat at her and stood just inside the tent flap, sniffing the smells coming from the oven. He moved toward her, and his eyes lit up when he saw a few loaves of fresh-baked bread lying on a tabletop, along with several pies.

He fumbled in his pockets and came up with a five-dollar gold piece, which he dropped on the tabletop. "I'll have two loaves of that there bread and however many pies that gold piece will buy," he announced loudly. His eyes never left the baked goods while he spoke.

Angie chuckled and handed him two loaves of bread and three pies. He carried them over to a chair at the edge of the tent, then produced a long knife and a sack of what appeared to be beef jerky from his bag. He proceeded to consume an entire loaf of bread and a pie, along with the jerky.

She waited until he sighed loudly and leaned back in his chair, then walked over and took a seat near him. She watched him settle himself down in the chair and chuckled when he sighed again.

"Has it been a while since you've had anything besides beef and beans, Mr...." Her voice trailed off.

"Ye can call me Ezra," he announced. "Yep, been up there in them gold fields for several weeks, now. Didn't have no bread or pies or baked stuff for quite a while afore then."

Angie leaned forward with excitement. "You were up in the gold fields?" she asked quickly. "What's happening up there?"

Ezra snorted loudly. "They shore enuff found gold," he declared. "That country up there is gonna fill up faster'n you can imagine. They've already claimed most of the spots on Rabbit Creek, or Bonanza Creek, or whatever they're gonna call it."

Angie felt the excitement drain out of her. "It's not over already, is it?" she asked anxiously.

Ezra chuckled. "Nah, it's not over. They found some good color, there'll be more. Don't know if they'll find more on Rabbit Creek, though. Man has to be smart, maybe look elsewhere. Got me some ideas, I do. Just got to get me a few supplies afore I go back up."

Angie leaned forward, excited to ask more questions when she heard a loud whistle coming from the bay. She jumped to her feet and whirled. "Steamship," she shouted, dashing out of the tent and running toward the bay.

She watched while the ship dropped anchor, then waited while they ferried passengers to the shore. She waited while they began unloading the cargo, then wandered among the barrels that had been deposited on the bank. She bent to read the labels on a few of them, then jumped when a familiar voice sounded at her elbow.

"Your stuff is over here," Captain Buckley told her. She gave him a quick hug and followed him along the shoreline until he pointed out three barrels of flour and a smaller barrel of sugar, along with some dried fruits of various kinds and a few other items she had ordered.

Angie looked at the heavy barrels and glanced around, hoping to see Conway or one of Moore's helpers. She saw no one. Captain Buckley, following her glance, spread his hands apologetically.

"My men are going to be tied up for a while, ferrying things to shore," he explained. "I can get a couple of them to help you in a few hours, or maybe one of the passengers..." He looked around, then took off his cap and waved it in the air.

"Spencer," he shouted suddenly. "Give us a hand over here?"

Angie turned to see a tall, handsome, dark-haired man moving toward them. She smiled nervously and lifted her hand to smooth her hair. She guessed he was just a little older than her twenty-nine years. He stopped in front of her, smiling and removing his hat.

"Ma'am," he said smoothly.

Captain Buckley glanced back and forth between them, chuckled, and put his hat back on his head. "Angie Parker, this is Luke Spencer. Luke, Angie." He clapped Luke on the shoulder. "Be nice to her, Spencer," he advised. "She bakes the best pies you've ever had."

———

I stood on the rail of the *Juneau*, watching as we steamed into Skagway. This was a nervous moment for me. I had taken out a chunk of my time and money to come up here, and I wasn't sure what I might find. I watched as a few people gathered on the shore, waving at the ship as it came in. The town, if that's what you could call it, spread out behind. There was quite a bit of activity, but I could only see a few tents here and there.

I waited my turn and came ashore in one of the boats when it came around for me. I splashed ashore and stood on the bank, watching people bustle around, trying to decide which way to go. I heard my name called and saw Captain Buckley waving his hat at me.

I walked over, and as I drew closer, I saw a beautiful young woman, tall and blond-haired. She wore an apron and seemed to know the captain. He introduced us and I offered my hand. She gave me a firm handshake, and the captain said she needed a little help, bringing the barrels of flour and a few other things to her bakery. I took another look at her and she gave me a winning smile. I decided hauling barrels was an excellent idea.

I put my hat back on my head and turned to tilt the first barrel so I could roll it. Then I heard my name shouted again. I straightened, but before I could turn, I was grabbed from behind in a bear hug, and my feet were lifted off the ground. Whoever it was, they then proceeded to bounce me up and down.

I was deposited on the ground, then a familiar voice boomed in my ear. "Luke Spencer, you old scalawag, what are you doin' in Alaska?"

I didn't even need to turn around. "Ezra," I said, "didn't you ever wise up and stop chasin' gold from one end of this earth to the other?"

CHAPTER 8

MAKING A START

Barrels of flour weighed more than I'd thought they would. It didn't help when they bogged down in the mud, in what passed for streets in Skagway. I had to admit, though, I didn't seem to mind. It only partly had to do with the promise of a cherry pie when I was done. Angie was a pretty lady, and I admired what she had done, coming to this outpost and starting her business. It reminded me a lot of Sherry, and all the things she had done for me.

Ezra helped out only a little. He carried some of the lighter stuff and gave the barrels a push now and then when they really got stuck. I rolled the last barrel into Angie's tent/shop, wiped a sleeve across my brow, and started at Ezra.

"I ain't givin' you any of my pie," I announced. "I don't think you even broke a sweat."

Ezra cackled loudly. "A lot you know, pilgrim," he crowed. "I got two whole pies and a loaf of bread in my bag over there. Maybe I won't share with you, neither."

I grinned, shook my head, and finished catching my breath. "How come I'm a pilgrim?" I asked. "You've been here maybe, what, three weeks?"

"That makes me a native and you a pilgrim." Ezra chortled. "For as long as I feel like callin' you a pilgrim."

"Now, boys," Angie chided, placing my cherry pie on a table and setting down a couple of glasses of water. "Here's your pie, Luke. I guess you can share if you want to." She set a knife down next to the pie and accepted the chair I pulled over for her.

I cut a piece of pie for me, and grudgingly, one for Ezra. Angie shook her head when I offered one to her. Ezra gulped his down while I was picking up a fork.

"How do you guys know each other, anyway?" she asked. I couldn't help but notice she had pulled her chair a little closer to mine, and I liked it.

Ezra entertained her with a couple stories from our days in the Black Hills while I ate my piece of pie. Captain Buckley was just about right, I concluded. I'd have to call it a tossup between Sherry's pies and this one. I waited for Ezra to finish, or at least come up for air.

Finally, I saw my opening. "What have you been doing while you've been here these last several weeks?" I asked. "Besides sucking down as much pie as you can?"

Ezra put on a hurt look, but it didn't last for long. "Got to talk to you about that," he said excitedly. "I been up to the Klondike strike. They found some good color along Rabbit Creek. I think they've taken to callin' it Bonanza Creek now. Lots of claims filed there. Big crowd. I think, though," he said, pausing for dramatic effect, "I know a better place to file a claim now 'cause Rabbit Creek's gonna play out. There's more up there along another creek, I'm sure of it."

Ezra stopped and stared at my cherry pie. I pulled it in and put my arms over it. "Get your own pie," I growled.

He grinned, got up, and went over to his bag. He pulled out an apple pie and cut two pieces. I noticed that his piece was twice as big as mine, but I wasn't going to complain. I never thought I'd get even one.

Angie laughed and shook her head while we fought over the pies, but I could tell she was interested in the Klondike strike. I waited while Ezra inhaled his piece of the apple pie and gulped down some water. When he was done, he glanced around to be sure we were alone in the shop, then he leaned forward.

"Too many folks fighting it out on Bonanza Creek now," he mumbled. "Smart play is to stake a claim a little ways off from there, and strike it on some new ground. I think I know where to go. Ran out of supplies and had to come back. Goin' back up to stake a claim before the cold weather comes. Got to come back after that, but I wanna be up there again first thing when the thaw comes next year. Get the gold and get out afore winter comes again."

That might have been the longest speech I'd ever heard from Ezra, other than his rambles about whiskey and food. Believe me, I'd heard more speeches from him than I ever wanted to, but this one had my attention. I stared at him, not sure what to say. Angie had leaned forward, too, locked in on what he was saying.

"You come with me, Luke," he said in very soft tones. "Two's better'n one, and I can trust you. We get up there now, get a claim staked, have everything ready to go. Got to be quiet about it, though. There's another creek, not too far over from the Bonanza. Don't know if it has a name. I'm gonna call it El Dorado." He sat back and grinned, clearly pleased with himself. "It'll be at least as good as Bonanza, you wait and see."

I sat back and thought it over. "Okay," I said slowly. "I'll go up there with you. I just need a couple of days. Got to store some of my stuff somewhere, and I want to talk to somebody about buying a lot on one of these streets. I wouldn't mind starting a saloon in this town, when it gets going around here."

Ezra nodded, then got up and put what he had left of the pie back in his bag, which he hefted over his shoulder. "Okay," he agreed. "Don't take too long and make sure you don't say nuthin' to anybody around here."

Angie placed her hand on my arm as she rose from the

table. "I can help you if you want to buy a building lot around here," she said. "William Moore owns most of this. I'll introduce you after I close here. How about in an hour? You can come back, or just stay here if you want to."

I decided maybe staying there could be a good idea.

———

I spent the hour at Angie's bakery and found ways to make myself useful. I cleared a spot at the back for the barrels of flour and moved some boxes around for her. She gave me a loaf of bread for my troubles. I told her she needed to be careful about feeding strays like me. Her laugh, I thought, was something I needed to hear more of.

After she had closed the store for the day, we walked back down in the direction of the bay. She took me a little farther to the south, and I could hear hammers and saws. We rounded the corner, and it looked like Moore was getting a good start on the lumber mill Angie told me he was building.

The first one I recognized was John Moore, who I had talked to at Sherry's place in Livingston. He dropped his hammer and walked over to give me a slap on the back and a handshake. He seemed genuinely pleased that I had come. He turned and waved to a stocky, gray-haired man who was pointing and giving directions to a couple of workmen. When he came over, John introduced me to his father, William Moore.

He took me over to a corner, away from some of the noise. Angie waited with John Moore. William looked me over with keen gray eyes. "John said he met you in Montana," he said abruptly. "Glad you're here. What is it you plan to do in Skagway?"

I answered as briefly as possible, telling him my primary plan was to build a saloon. He glanced away briefly, so I hurried to explain that I'd run one in Colorado, and I tolerated no crooks, thieves, or anybody else who didn't abide by my rules. He smiled briefly at that.

I went on to say I'd met an old friend and planned to go up to the Klondike strike soon, but emphasized that my main plan for the future was to be a business owner in town.

Moore shrugged. "Can't blame you for wanting to go see the Klondike." He grinned. "I've chased more gold strikes than you can count on the fingers of both hands. Love 'em. I'm just getting a little older and don't want to get frozen out up there. I'll sell you a lot and we'll hold it for you."

He named a price. I agreed, and we shook hands. I reached into my pocket to get my money, but he waved it off. "Come see me tomorrow and I'll have a paper drawn up and signed. Not that I don't trust you, and I can see you're ready to pay on the spot. Sometimes, it just helps, later on, to have things on paper."

With that, we shook hands again, and he walked off to supervise the men building his lumber mill. When I returned to John Moore and Angie, John told me they had a small storage building just behind the mill where they kept some things. I was welcome to put my bags in there when I went up the Klondike.

We left the lumber mill site, and I turned to Angie. "Can I walk you to...where you live?" It occurred to me I had no idea where she might have found to live in this place.

She chuckled. "I'm living at the bakery," she said. "It might be a while before there's anyplace else for me to stay."

We stopped part-way back, and I stared up at White Pass. Even though it was summer, I could see patches of snow up toward the top. I wondered how long it would be until the pass would be unpassable until next year.

Angie followed my gaze. "You'll have to go through there to get to the Klondike," she said, guessing my thoughts. "From what I know, you can walk up there, but horses are faster, of course. You descend on the other side and take a boat up the Yukon River the rest of the way."

My face probably showed the confusion I was feeling.

"What boat?" I asked. "Do they have any boats at the river you can use? And what do you do with the horse if you take a boat to the gold fields?"

She shook her head. "I don't think there are any boats up there to use," she said. "I think maybe you have to build a small boat or maybe a raft when you get to the river. Ezra would know more about that. There are people offering horses to take you up through the pass. They go up with you as a guide and take their horses back with them."

I stared back up at the pass. "If you were going up there with supplies to build a boat and then do some mining, you might need a couple of horses. Or else a really powerful horse."

She leaned in a little to get my attention. "I have a couple of draft horses," she said. "I hope they'll be coming up here with a friend of mine. Maybe you could use them if you make a second trip later on."

It wasn't the first time she had surprised me. She was, I thought, quite a resourceful and determined woman.

"They're almost like pets, but I think I could put them to good use up here," she said. "Clyde and Dale—those are their names."

I chuckled at the names, then she surprised me again. "I might want to go with you if you take a second trip," she blurted. "Not just up White Pass, but all the way to the gold fields. I would like to do that."

My mind sorted through several questions. Did she know how harsh the conditions might be? Did she really trust a couple guys she'd just met enough to go out to the middle of nowhere with us? Something told me the answer to both of those questions was yes. What about her bakery? Who would run that while she was gone? I had a feeling she had the answer to that one, too. In the end, my mouth just worked open and shut a couple times, with no words coming out.

She laughed and put her hand on my arm. "I've shocked you," she said.

"Not shocked," I protested. She looked at me and said nothing. "Well, okay, maybe a little shocked," I admitted. I pieced together my thoughts. "Well," I said, "something tells me you could do most things you set your mind to. Maybe we can talk about it after Ezra and I make the first trip and have a better idea of what we're going to do."

She agreed to that, and we strolled back to the bakery. She invited me in and made an excellent dinner, which I insisted on paying for. She protested for a while, but finally took the money.

After I left the bakery, I went down to look at the lot I had agreed to buy from William Moore. I made a couple of trips into the trees and collected some pine needles and spread them out in a dry spot at the back of the lot. I put down my bedroll over the pine needles and immediately fell into a deep sleep.

———

Black Jack paced outside the doctor's office in short, choppy, angry steps. He had found Cap Light, his henchman—and brother-in-law—lying on the dock with blood trickling from the corner of his mouth. He had paid two men standing on the docks to carry Light to the nearest doctor's office while he, Black Jack, had gone to put on a dry suit. He had a feeling the one that had just gone into the bay would never be the same. He had already, with much swearing, jammed his top hat into the trash can in back of the hotel.

A couple of efforts to push his way into the office had resulted in the doctor ordering him back outside. Finally, he had settled down on a bench outside the office, resigned to waiting. He had work for Light to do, plus he had three tickets to sail to Alaska next week. He and Light would go, of course, and he would find some idiot to do the things Bear had been doing for him.

The door to the office opened, and the doctor waved him inside. Adams crossed to the bed and leaned over Cap Light.

There was a bandage winding under his jaw and around his head. The entire right side of his face had swollen up, and there was an ugly purplish color settling in. Adams drew back for an instant and touched his own jaw with a wince. This was worse than he had expected.

"His jaw's broke," the doctor informed him. "He can't talk."

Black Jack leaned back over Cap Light. "Who did this?" he demanded.

Light looked at him and rolled his eyes. The doctor stepped back in. "I just told you, he can't talk," the doctor repeated.

Black Jack lifted his arm to shove the doctor away, then heard the scrape of boots behind him. Another man, apparently a patient, had risen from a chair and was moving toward the doctor, doubling up his fist and glaring at Black Jack. He looked like a logger, Black Jack thought, and he was a huge man.

Adams pasted a weak smile on his face and managed a weak apology. "Sorry, doc," he mumbled. "Can he just nod his head?"

"Okay," the doctor said grudgingly. "But only two or three questions."

Black Jack turned back around to look at Light. "Did Bear do this?"

Cap Light nodded his head up and down slowly, his face contorted with pain as he did so.

The doctor looked at Light's face and stepped back in. "No more questions," he decided. "He won't be leaving here for a week or two. I doubt he'll be eating anything but applesauce and scrambled eggs for longer'n that."

"Impossible!" Black Jack blurted. "We have tickets on the steamship to Alaska next week. He'll have to go!"

The doctor's face took on an astonished look. "You expect that man to bounce up and down on a steamship in one week? That's not happening. He won't even be leaving here before a week, I promise you!"

"He's going," Black Jack snarled. He heard the scrape of boots again and saw the logger headed his way, looking menacing this time. Black Jack raised his hands in the air, pasting the weak grin back on his face as he did so.

"Sorry, sorry," he mumbled. "Whatever you say, doc." He edged his way carefully past the logger and stepped out to the street, where he let loose with a fresh round of cursing. When he finally ran out of words, he reached to settle his top hat on his head, cursed one more time because the hat wasn't there, and set out for the steamship office.

Moving up to the clerk in the office, he waved three tickets in the air. "I need to change two of these tickets from next week to the week after," he announced. "And I need a refund for the third one."

The clerk looked him over carefully, then reached out and took two of the tickets. "I can exchange these two for the week after," he said. "But we don't give refunds. Can't give you your money back for the third one." He put the two tickets in the drawer and pushed two new ones under the window.

Black Jack grabbed the two new tickets, then pushed the remaining older ticket under the window. "Refund!" he demanded. "You'll give me a refund for this one." He heard the door open and close and was vaguely aware that a large man had entered the office.

The clerk stared at him, then drew his words out slowly. "Sorry, no refund. No refund."

It wasn't lost on Black Jack that the clerk's right hand crept under the table top and out of sight. It looked like the clerk had room for a shotgun under there. He took the third ticket and jammed it into his pocket, turning with such haste that he ran into a gigantic man who had moved up behind him.

Bear reached out, pinning Black Jack's right arm along with the hideout gun he carried up his sleeve. Bear reached out and plucked the ticket from his pocket.

"I think that 'un's my ticket, anyway," he drawled. "I'll

just take that." His hand crushed Black Jack's right arm painfully.

Black Jack worked his mouth open and closed a few times, and a pronounced tic appeared in his right eyelid. He reached one more time for the hat that wasn't there, then stepped carefully around Bear and left the office.

CHAPTER 9

GOLD IN THOSE HILLS

Bear stepped off the steamer and glanced around him with curiosity. There wasn't much of a town here, but there was a lot of activity. Men were hustling down to the steamship with pushcarts, some had wagons and horses, others just had their sleeves rolled up and looked like they were ready to unload the boat by hand. Bear grinned. A big powerful man like himself ought to be able to find work up here.

He climbed up the bank and trudged through the mud to what looked like the main street. He looked down at the mud oozing up over the tops of his boots, then moved across to the far side of the street. It was a little drier on this side. Bear ignored the men hauling crates and other goods off the boat. He stood staring out at the inlet. There was one problem he needed to think about.

He'd broken Cap Light's jaw—that news had been going around the saloon before he left Seattle. He had also thrown Black Jack Adams into the bay and had taken the ticket for this boat trip from him. He didn't regret any of those things. Black Jack had treated him like scum from the first day they'd met, and Cap Light was the one who made sure Black Jack got what he wanted. Neither of them would dare to come after Bear in a fistfight or any kind of rough-and-tumble brawl. That wasn't what worried him.

Bear had only gone to school through the third grade, but he didn't need any more book-learnin' than that to figure out these guys wouldn't come after him with their fists. Cap Light might call him out and shoot him, or Black Jack might shoot him in the back when nobody was looking. For that matter, they said Black Jack was lightning fast with a gun himself. Bear needed a friend, or maybe somebody he could work for. That somebody needed to be smarter than Bear. It wouldn't hurt if he was good with a gun and a tough man in his own right.

He dug his hand down into his pants pocket and came out with twenty-five cents. Bear sighed and looked around. He saw a stocky man with gray hair pointing and giving orders to some other men as they came off the steamship, carrying some heavy crates. Bear moved in his direction.

The gray-haired man stopped giving orders for a moment, looking at Bear as he lumbered up the slope. He took in Bear's height and broad shoulders. "You lookin' for work?" he barked.

Bear only nodded, and the man extended his hand. "William Moore," he announced. "I'll pay you two dollars to work for as long as it takes, helping these men haul some crates and supplies off the steamer. They go up to my warehouse." He pointed down the road. "Just follow these guys."

Bear nodded, rolled up his sleeves, and followed a man down onto the steamship. Six hours later, exhausted and pouring sweat, he had two dollars and twenty-five cents in his pocket. He flopped at the side of the street, wondering where he might find something to eat. Looking across the muddy street, he saw a man moving toward a small crowd of people standing outside a tent. The man looked familiar, and in an instant, Bear knew who it was. Bear's face wasn't sore anymore, but this was the guy who'd punched him in the face and knocked him into the bay back in Seattle.

Bear pushed himself up to his feet. Not only did he not

hold any grudges, he also respected a man who could beat Bear in a stand-up fight. Besides, the man must be an enemy of Black Jack Adams, since Bear was just following Black Jack's orders when he started the fight. This might just be the man Bear was looking for. He lumbered slowly toward the tent.

———

I worked for a while that morning, making a little home for myself on the property I'd bought from William Moore. I got some canvas from the Moores and created a little lean-to by running the canvas down from a tree at the back of the property. I staked the canvas down at the other side of the pine-needle bed. Finished, I stepped back and surveyed the lean-to. It would keep the rain off and shelter me from some of the wind. It would do for a while.

Satisfied, I walked down the street and settled down at a table outside the bakery, sipping coffee and waiting for Ezra to show up. Angie came outside with a fresh cup of coffee and sat down next to me. She pushed another cup toward the empty place where Ezra would sit. I think she was just about as interested in our plans to claim a stake in the Klondike as I was. I had a few questions in my head and would no doubt think of a few more while Ezra and I talked. At long last, I saw Ezra trudging down the street toward us.

He nodded when he saw us, walked over to the table and took a slurp of coffee. He wiped his mouth with his sleeve, stopping halfway through the motion.

"Sorry, ma'am," he mumbled. "My table manners are shockin'." He stopped, sniffing the air, and turned toward the tent flap of the bakery. I waited, half expecting him to point like a bird dog. Angie laughed and led the way toward the bakery.

"Just tell me what you want," she told him over her shoulder.

"I expect that'll be most everything, ma'am," I heard him say as the tent flap closed behind him.

When Ezra was settled back in his seat with some rolls and bacon, he fished a worn-looking map out of his pocket and spread it out on the table. He chewed and pointed at the same time, mixing in a little talking. I tried to stay out of the spray area.

"This here's the White Pass," he started out, pointing at the mountains in front of us. We got to climb up over that pass, bringin' our stuff with us. Mebbe we can get us a pack horse. After we've done clumb the pass, we come down t'other side until we can get to the river." He screwed up his forehead in concentration. "Yukon River, that's it. Then we take a raft down the river to the gold."

He sat back in satisfaction and belted down the rest of his breakfast. I stared at the map and tried to figure out which question to ask first.

"You said we could take a raft down the river," I said skeptically. "Where do we get that raft?"

"We have to build it," Ezra said, nodding his head emphatically. "We'll need a couple good axes an' some rope or twine. We can build a good raft in a couple days. I done it the last time I went up there. It's downstream to where we're goin'. We can take a boat the other direction to come back, if'n you want to. Lot more work, though, comin' back on a raft against the stream, I can tell you."

I soaked up that information, nodding my head slowly. "How long does it take to raft to the gold fields?" I asked next.

"'Bout two weeks, if you don't do no lollygaggin' around."

"You said you know a place to stake a claim, besides Rabbit Creek," that's what you said. "You think Rabbit Creek is all staked out by now?"

"I expect it is," Ezra agreed. "There's another little stream, feeds Rabbit Creek and the Yukon River. I think it might be even better'n Rabbit Creek. We need to get up there, check it out an' stake it out. When folks get back to Seattle and San Francisco with gold, there's gonna be a passel of people stompin' around them gold fields."

I knew he was right about the crowds coming up there, and I was willing to take his word about where we could stake a claim. I had a couple more questions for him.

"How do they stake a claim in the Klondike?" I asked. "How big a claim do you think we can stake and hold on to?" Claim jumpers were always a problem at a gold strike.

Ezra leaned back in his chair and mulled that one over. "Mebbe five hunnerd feet by one thousand feet," he said. "Most of 'em on Rabbit Creek were about that size. Any more'n that, an' we'll spend all our time fighting the claim jumpers. We just drive stakes in the ground mebbe every several yards where we're claimin'. I like to carve my initial in 'em. We can clear out the brush between the stakes so folks can see the lines of stakes."

"Are we panning?" I asked. "Digging?"

Ezra fished in his pocket for a toothpick. "Both," he said. "Ground's pretty cold up there, so you have to leave a fire burning all night where you want to dig. Thaws it down maybe a foot. Dig there and see what you've got. If it looks good, do it again the next night. Got something we can use to make panning a little easier, though. Come and take a gander at this."

He led the way around to the back of the bakery. Angie came and took a quick look, then disappeared inside to help some customers. I stared at a small wooden box, maybe two feet square and about as high. There was wire mesh across the top, with a layer of canvas under the mesh. The floor sloped down to the ground, and the box was mounted on rockers.

"A rocker box," I said, nodding approvingly. I knew you poured the gravel, sludge, and water into the top. The wire mesh was the first level, separating the larger chunks of gravel, and hopefully, gold ore. The canvas further strained out the finer gold, and the rest washed out the bottom.

"Looks good," I said, slapping Ezra on the back. He beamed.

"Got to leave soon, Pilgrim," he reminded me, leading the way back around the bakery tent. "We don't wanna be up there when it starts getting' cold. Don't spend too much time moonin' around and making big eyes at Angie. Can you be ready in three days?"

I nodded and watched him trudge away, heading back down the street. I returned to the table we'd been using and took a seat again, musing over the things he'd told me. Everything really depended on whether Ezra knew where to stake a claim.

Angie served customers in a steady stream for the next hour, bringing me breakfast and sitting down next to me again when the morning crowd had let up. I knew she wouldn't take any money for the food, so I spent a few hours each day building her some shelving and doing chores. It was a pleasant way to spend the day.

"So," she said, "you're doing to go pretty soon, right?"

I agreed. "In the next three days, that's what Ezra plans. Yes, I'm going to go up with him and stake the claim. We should have enough time to do a little mining and maybe find some gold."

She waited while I finished eating. "I need to ask him a little more about getting back by taking the river in the other direction. I'm not sure what that's about."

"You can take a riverboat from the town of Dawson over and up to St. Michael on the Yukon River," she answered. "That's the town north of here at the mouth of the river, where it empties out into the ocean. People say that's the rich man's way to the gold. I'm not sure how much it costs, but if you're there long enough to find some gold, you could probably make enough to pay for it."

I looked at her, surprised once again. She shrugged.

"People like to sit here and talk. Sometimes, they tell me about the gold fields." She put her hand on my arm and leaned forward. "I really do want to go with you when you go back. A couple of women have gone up there already."

I nodded slowly. "Do you really want to go into that cold?" I searched her face. "What about going out there with a couple of guys you've only known for a few days?"

She tightened her grip on my arm and smiled. Those eyes were enchanting, I thought. A man could get lost in those eyes.

"I think I know a good man when I see one," she said abruptly. "I think I'm looking at one now. Ezra too. He could use a little polishing up here and there." She chuckled. "But he's honest, and he's respectful. Just like you. Yes, I mean it. I want to go with you."

I nodded my head up and down slowly. I could argue with her about this for several days, but I knew I would lose. Besides, I liked the idea of her being with me.

Angie sat up suddenly, turned her head slightly and whispered in my ear. "Don't look suddenly," she breathed, "but there's a huge man standing over there in the road who's been watching us for a few minutes. Over to your right. Do you know him?"

I picked up my coffee cup and sipped, glancing casually in both directions. There he was, and I did know him. He was the man I had knocked off the pier in Seattle. He looked even bigger now than he had then. He began walking slowly toward us, stopping about ten feet away. He shifted his hat from one hand to the other, then nodded at Angie.

"Ma'am," he rumbled. His voice seemed to come from the bottom of a well. He looked at me. "Can I talk to you for a minute?" he asked, shifting his gaze to me.

I pointed at the chair where Ezra had been sitting, then waited while he took a seat. Angie went back into the bakery. I was very relieved to see he wanted to talk, not pick up where we'd left off back in Seattle. I had my doubts I could come out on top in another fight. I'd had the advantage of surprise that first time.

"I'm Bear," he told me.

"Luke," I said, pointing at my chest.

He nodded. "I'm finding some work here an' there," he rumbled. "Loadin' and unloadin' things. I kinda like it here." He stared at the table. "Black Jack Adams, he's the one what told me to jump you back there in Seattle. I was doin' his bidding, workin' for him at the time. Not no more."

I laughed. "Yeah, I saw you throw him into the ocean," I said. "I guess he fired you after that, all right. Nice throw, though. Must have chucked him a good fifteen feet."

A smile spread slowly across his face, then a deep, rumbling laugh spilled out of him. "Had me some fun, doin' that," he admitted. "He had it comin'. So did Cap Light. I think I busted his jaw. Shoulda done it a long time ago."

I waited, wondering what he wanted with me. He rubbed his hand across his face a few times, then got to the point.

"Black Jack's probly comin' here, after Cap Light can travel. He'll likely be lookin' for you, and for sure he'll be lookin' for me. I don't know why he don't like you, but he sure enough wanted me to get rid of you." He glanced at me sideways.

"Black Jack tried to rob me and kill me a few years back," I told him. "He sure enough robbed me and a friend of mine. Didn't kill us, though. Maybe he's afraid I'm out to get even."

Bear rubbed a massive fist on his jaw. "Yeah, I figgered it was something like that," he said. "Well, I ain't afraid of no man in a fistfight. Black Jack, though, he's poison mean—he's evil. Good with a gun, folks say. Cap Light, too. I got no friends up here, but I like...I thought mebbe..." He stopped and lifted his eyes to look at me. "I thought mebbe I could look out for you an' you could look out for me."

A smile spread slowly across my face, and I held out my hand. He grabbed it with that huge paw of his. "Deal," I said.

"Deal," he agreed. He gave my hand a quick pump, stood

and moved down the street. Angie came out from the bakery and watched him walk away.

"What was that about?" she asked.

"It looks like I have a new friend," I told her.

———

The three days passed quickly. I salted the deer I had shot and smoked for a couple days when we had first arrived. I knew we would need the meat and some other food for the trip. Angie baked some bread for us and tucked a few pies into the backpack. I would have to fight Ezra for those. I hired a pack horse for us. We agreed that one of William Moore's sons would come with us up White Pass and return with the horse.

We met up at the bakery just before leaving. We loaded up our supplies on the horse. I carried my Winchester with me. There were a couple of surprises for me before leaving. Ezra proudly displayed two canoe paddles he had been making for the last few days. He tied those onto the horse.

Angie came out from behind the bakery with a beautiful pair of knee-length leather boots, lined with fur. "These are for you," she told me. "You'll need them up there. I traded a man five pies for these. He was headed back for Seattle, so they were cheap."

I reached into my pocket, but she clasped her hand over mine. "Don't you dare try to pay me, Luke Spencer. These are a gift." She stood on her tip-toes and planted a lingering kiss on my cheek. "Just come back safe."

Bear came along just as we were leaving. I took him aside. "Where have you been sleeping?" I asked.

He shrugged and waved his hand at the woods. "Here and there," he told me.

I took him down the street to the lot I had bought and pointed out the lean-to with the pine-needle bed I had made at the back of the lot. "You can use this while I'm gone," I told him." I just have one favor to ask."

His face turned serious. "What is it?" he rumbled.

I turned around and walked back to the bakery with him. "Just make sure nobody gives Angie any trouble at the bakery," I said.

That slow smile spread across his face again. "You got it. Glad to."

Ezra and I finished loading up the packhorse, said our goodbyes and moved off down the muddy street of Skagway. White Pass lay directly in front of us.

CHAPTER 10

EL DORADO

The trip up to the summit of White Pass was easier than the trip down on the other side. Of course, we had most of our stuff loaded on a horse on the way up. We paid off John Moore at the top. He wished us luck and headed back down the mountain with the horse. I looked down the other side of the summit, seeing a ribbon of water out, but there would be a few peaks between here and there. The trail looked very narrow.

I pointed down the mountain and looked around at Ezra, who was busy loading the heavier pack on my back. "Yukon River?" I asked.

"Yup." Ezra shoved the canoe paddles under my arm and started down the hill.

"What good are canoe paddles on a raft?" I asked as I trudged down after him.

"Them paddles will hep us a little on the raft," he answered over his shoulder. "We only need the raft for the first hunnerd miles. I plan to have somethin' better after we get to a place called Canyon City."

I needed all my breath to hump that heavy pack down the mountain, so I followed on in silence after that. There were a couple more mountain passes first, getting even more narrow in spots than what I'd thought when I looked down from White Pass. Three days later, we reached a place Ezra told me was called Bennett Lake. The Yukon River fed into that lake, so we camped and began building a raft. We felled a dozen large white spruce trees, trimmed the trunks, and lashed them together to make a narrow raft. We kept an additional trimmed trunk, a narrow one, to help pole the raft along. And, as Ezra was quick to point out, we were moving with the current.

We pushed off the following morning. I had brought along some of the deer meat, along with some bread and dried fruit Angie had given us. We put fishing lines into the water as we moved along and caught some salmon to stretch our food supply. I pushed us forward with the pole where I could, and Ezra and I both did some paddling to keep us moving. We figured, with some help from the current, we were making about twenty miles per day.

At the pace we were moving, Ezra said we would come to a place folks called Canyon City after about five days. Ezra was pretty closed-mouth about what we were doing when we got there. He seemed to think we could do better than rafting. After a couple days, the silence was getting to me. I asked him about Canyon City.

"Canyon City," I said, knowing I didn't need to explain the question.

Ezra grunted and leaned back on the raft to take a break from paddling.

"What's there?" I prompted. "Is it a town?"

He scratched himself thoughtfully and leaned over to spit in the river. He shook his head slowly. "Nope, not a town," he mumbled. "More like a few fishing camps. That, and there's a few local tribes what pass through there time to time. Tinglits and a couple of others. Some of 'em say the foam on the rapids near there looks like a white horse."

That thing about rapids caught my attention. "Rapids?" I blurted. "We're going through rapids on this raft we just got done tying together?"

Ezra grinned and stretched out on his back. "Naw, we can get out and go around the rapids."

That only made me feel a little better. "We're gonna carry this raft that weighs about a ton?" I whined. "How far are we carrying it?"

Ezra chortled and leaned over to spit again. "Nope, I don't expect we'll be carryin' the raft. Trust me, pilgrim. I got this figgered out."

With that, he fell asleep and started snoring. I shook my head and kept pushing us down the river. Day after tomorrow, I would see for myself what this was all about. Too bad, I thought, that I didn't have a big canvas. I might try to rig it up for a sail.

————

The term fishing camps pretty much said it all, so far as I could see. The smell of fish was everywhere, and you could see men kneeling and cleaning fish along both sides of the river. I tied the raft off to a tree by the river, noting it needed a little repair where the ropes were coming loose. Ezra waved me off when I started to make repairs. I shrugged and stood with my hands on my hips, looking around me.

"What'dya expect? A rest-too-rant for a sit-down dinner? I told ya it was just fishing camps." Ezra was watching me, shaking his head.

"Okay, you told me that's all there is here. What are we gonna do here, anyway? Just fix up the raft and push on?" I watched as a dead salmon floated past me.

"We're goin' to a Tinglit camp," Ezra informed me. He kneeled beside his bag, fishing around in it until he pulled out an axe and a knife. I hadn't seen either of those until now. He put the knife into a sheath on his belt, wrapped a rag around the axe and climbed up the slope.

I trailed behind him as he took a path away from the fishing camps. We had gone maybe two miles when he left the path abruptly and followed a much fainter trail through the brush. We left the brush abruptly and walked into what appeared to be an Indian camp. A half-circle of teepees was grouped alongside a stream. Two or three dogs ran over to sniff us. Ezra waved at a circle of men around a fire and walked over.

I stayed behind him, feeling wary as he joined the circle of men. I sat slightly behind him and off to one side. Much to my surprise, he began talking in their native language. His words were halting and seemed awkward on his tongue, but after the repetition of several sentences, he seemed to make himself understood.

Ezra stood abruptly and walked over to a birchbark canoe in the stream. He pointed and spoke a few words, and I began to understand. He wanted to trade for the canoe. After more pointing and a few words exchanged, he unwrapped the axe and laid on the ground. Two braves picked it up, felt the weight of it, and tested the sharpness. They mumbled back and forth among themselves for a while, then laid the axe down and shook their heads.

Ezra spoke a few more sentences, pointing and gesturing. They continued to shake their heads. Finally, with a heavy sigh, he pulled the knife out of the sheath and laid it beside the axe. They inspected the knife, then several heads nodded up and down. They pulled out two crude canoe paddles and handed them to Ezra.

"C'mon, pilgrim," Ezra said, keeping the excitement out of his voice. "We got us a nice birchbark canoe to take us to the gold fields. Plus, we've already got better paddles than these." He waded into the stream and climbed in the canoe. I wasted no time following him. I had to admit, it was a whole lot better than that raft we had made back at White Pass.

———————

Up to her elbows in bread dough, Angie kept kneading and ignored the pounding going on around her. She glanced over to see Bear and another of William Moore's men nailing four-by-fours together to make the frame for the bakery building. A small extension on the back side was going to be her home here in Skagway. She smiled briefly and went back to kneading. Bringing those pies to the Moores and doing some cooking for them was paying off.

More hammering noises drifted up from the mouth of the inlet. Moore had finished building his lumber mill and established a flow of logs coming in for lumber. He had moved quickly to construct a wharf down at the inlet. Angie knew how valuable the wharf would be—not just to Moore, but to the coming town of Skagway. Ship traffic in and out of that harbor would be the lifeblood of the town. If there was, in fact, a major gold strike to be found in the Klondike, Skagway would need a wharf to handle the flood of miners to follow.

Thinking about the mining, Angie's thoughts turned to Luke. He and Ezra had been gone for about three weeks now. Not long enough to reach the Klondike, probably. It all depended on how fast they could make that trip down the Yukon River. Ezra had seemed to think he knew a good way to do that.

She washed her hands and began forming the bread dough into loaves. The crowd would come to the bakery soon. It surprised her how much she missed Luke. She had come to Skagway to build a business and make a life for herself better than the one she would have had, living in that lonely little farmhouse in Walla Walla. Finding Luke and spending so much time with him for the last few weeks had unexpectedly filled a huge void in her life. She was already worrying a little about how long it would be before he returned.

A long blast from a ship's horn interrupted her thoughts. She had almost forgotten: today was the day the *Juneau* was scheduled to arrive from Seattle. She washed her hands and dried them, then removed the apron she was wearing. Captain Buckley had been a valuable business partner, and she had given him five percent of the bakery in return for finding the best fruit from Seattle, along with the flour, sugar, and other baking ingredients she needed. He was her lifeline.

She waved at Bear, who had already dropped his hammer and started down to the shore. He knew the routine now, and could be depended on to bring the goods back to the bakery. She was amazed at his strength. A one-hundred-pound barrel seemed like nothing to him.

She saw Captain Buckley and waved as he walked down the plank. She was so intent on reaching him that she didn't hear her name the first two times somebody called it out.

"Angie! Angie!"

She turned, and her mouth dropped in astonishment. "Lou!" she called. She hadn't really believed her friend from the café in Walla Walla would come at all, let alone so soon. They exchanged a hug, and Angie struggled to find the first question to ask.

"So soon!" she exclaimed. "How did you manage it so soon?" Another thought struck her, and she gazed back at the ship.

"No." Lou laughed. "I didn't manage to bring Clyde and Dale on this trip. I have them in a barn outside of Seattle. It was too expensive, and I wasn't sure you were ready for them yet." She looked behind Angie at what there was of the town of Skagway. "Well, it ain't the big city." She chuckled.

Angie put an arm around her shoulders and started them up the bank toward the bakery. "Not yet," she agreed. "It's not much to look at yet, but there's opportunity here. Opportunity and money. Let me tell you about it."

An hour later, Lou leaned back from the table at the bakery and looked around her. "So," she said, "if I understand this, I add a café to this bakery, an' you give me half of the ninety-five percent you have after you pay Captain Buckley."

"Forty-seven and a half percent," Angie threw in.

Lou waved a hand in the air. "Hated math in school, still

do," she explained. "We don't know how much money that amounts to, but if there's a gold rush, it could be a lot." She stared into space as if thinking deeply. "Deal." She laughed, extending her hand. They shook.

Angie grinned and settled back into her chair. Another thought struck her. "How did you get here so soon?" she asked. "What about the café back home?"

Lou nodded. "That's the funny part," she answered. "You remember the Willoughbys? The folks you sold the farm to?" She continued without waiting for an answer. "Well, it turns out she's quite a cook herself and they had more money than we'd have thought. They had just made an offer for the café when I got your letter. I grabbed their money and took off."

Angie nodded and marveled at the timing. "What about Clyde and Dale?" she asked. "You said it would be expensive."

Lou nodded. "To go back and get them and bring them up here would cost about five hundred dollars," she warned. "You sure you want to do that? I could get them sold for a good price down there, what with the logging going on."

"I want them," Angie blurted. She glanced at the mountains behind Lou, then nodded. "I want them," she repeated. "I can make it pay if we bring them up here."

Lou looked at her in confusion, then turned and followed Angie's gaze up White Pass. She turned back, a look of understanding growing in her eyes. "You're quite the business lady now, ain'tcha?"

"I'm working on it," Angie answered. "I'm working on it."

Black Jack Adams glanced over the top of his cards, studying the man across the table. The guy was a pretty easy mark to start with, but the little tic in the left eye when the man was bluffing made this easy. Adams didn't even need the cards he had up his sleeve, or the hideaway gun in his vest pocket.

It had upset him at first when Cap Light wasn't able to travel, even after two weeks had gone by. By that time, Black Jack had decided maybe he would stay in Seattle until the springtime. There was a lot of easy money to be made in this town, and he didn't really need to risk his neck to get it. He could stay here and let all that uproar back in Colorado settle down. Plus, he'd heard how cold it could get in Alaska in the wintertime. He could just stay here and make some money this winter. Spencer and Bear could wait until then. And there should be some good money up in Alaska next summer.

Adams threw in another five bucks and called the guy. The mark threw his cards on the table in disgust and pushed the money in the middle over to Black Jack. He stood up, cursing under his breath, and left the saloon. Black Jack grinned and raked in the money. He didn't even need to cheat much to beat these guys.

Another chump took the seat just vacated and put his money on the table. Black Jack shuffled and offered the cards to the guy next to him for a cut. He took the cards back and dealt a few off the bottom. This was just too easy. Alaska could wait for a while.

———

I suppose you could say that the Yukon River between Canyon City and Dawson City is a pretty stretch of water, but I don't remember it that way. Mornings were frosty and downright cold. The solution for the cold, Ezra kept telling me, was to get in the canoe and paddle. I mostly remember the rapids here and there that we somehow survived, and the really sore muscles I had for the first week.

We carried the canoe—Ezra didn't hold with any fancy names like portaging—around the rapids near Canyon City that looked like the heads of white horses. So they say. If I looked just right, maybe I could see them. I was thankful for the very light birchbark canoe instead of that heavy hand-made raft. At least, I was thankful for it until Ezra reminded me for about the fifteenth time that morning. After that, I just wanted to get it over with.

We had eaten the last of the bread, fruit, and venison long ago, so we were living off salmon and berries. I had to trust Ezra's judgment on the berries, so I made him eat them first. When he didn't keel over right away, I helped myself. So it went for fifteen days until we at last reached the Klondike and Rabbit Creek.

We beached the canoe, then carried it into the woods and hid it. Ezra didn't trust anybody, and I can't say I blamed him. That was a pretty rough-looking crew hanging around the creek. We walked up and down Rabbit Creek for a while, seeing quite a few stakes and a lot of guys panning and digging. And, like Angie had told me, there were one or two women. I still wasn't too sure how safe it would be for her, but I had a feeling she wouldn't take no for an answer.

We walked along the creek for a long way, from where it fed into the Yukon River, past one or two small streams feeding into the creek itself. We passed a couple of guys who seemed like they were mostly watching us. One was a very big man. I'm guessing a couple inches taller than my six foot one and probably a good two hundred thirty pounds. He stood with hands on hips, watching us. The other one had a pearl-handled Colt strapped on. Neither seemed to do much digging.

We walked past them, with Ezra pointing the way a little farther down Rabbit Creek. We started to turn around a bend when we were stopped by the muscle man.

"Hey!" he shouted. "Where you goin'?"

I stopped and turned back to look at him. He advanced on us, and I think it surprised him when I didn't back up.

"Lookin' around," I answered. "Why?"

His face took on an ugly sneer, and he rolled up his sleeves. "Need some manners, do ya?" he snarled.

"I don't expect you're the guy that can teach me," I told him. I doubled up my fists and circled around him. It seemed to me we could fight it out now, or let him boss us around and probably take our gold from now on.

"Jed, back off!" It was the pearl-handled pistol man speaking. He took a couple of steps closer, looking us up and down for weapons. I had left my guns in my pack, which I had just dropped on the ground.

"Let 'em go," he repeated. He took a hard look at me. "You been warned," he said. "You get past him with your fists, you better be wearin' something on your waist besides your belt next time."

We turned and walked slowly around the bend. I looked one last time. Jed, the muscle man, was staring after us. The other guy was leaning back against a couple of rocks. There was still no mining activity to be seen.

"Who are those guys?" I demanded when we were out of eyesight and earshot.

Ezra shrugged and glanced back. "Couple of tough guys, or they at least think so. One is Jed Harmon, while the pistol guy calls hisself Major Howland. Don't think either of 'em are real names, though. I expect they mostly plan to rob guys and go home rich. You better be wearin' that Colt from now on, like they said."

We wound around for about a mile along the creek bed. I gotta say, it was looking pretty promising. I've been around some gold deposits after they've played out, but it didn't look like anybody had beat me to this. For once.

"I'm callin' this creek El Dorado," Ezra crowed. He took me around one last bend and pointed. "There!" he said proudly.

The creek was about twenty feet wide and maybe three or four feet deep in the middle. The bank ran out for about thirty or forty feet before it ended at the base of a cliff. I could see some quartz in the cliff, but I was more interested in the gravel and sand along the bank. I kneeled down to look at it. It was too cold to scoop—mostly frozen ground, here where there was no sun getting through.

I turned and waded out into the stream. The water was freezing cold, and I was mighty glad for the boots Angie had given me. When I was about two feet out, I stopped, bent over, and stared through the clear water at the rocks and gravel on the bottom. I was pretty sure I could see some color.

I stood and waded out, my face covered in a huge grin. "I think you're right," I told Ezra. "This is the place. Now, let's get us a fire started. That's some ice-cold water out there."

CHAPTER 11

QUICK STRIKE

W e made a small fire, away from the river by a couple hundred yards. Our instincts were to be friendly to the other miners, but not trustful. The meeting with Jed Harmon and Major Howland, or whatever their names were, hadn't done anything to change my mind on that score.

We had some decisions to make. Supplies were running pretty low after the three weeks of traveling to get here. Also, we needed to decide how much mining we were going to do, how long it was safe to stay here before we needed to beat the winter weather, and how we planned to get home.

Ezra wasn't much of a planner. He more tended to start doing something and worry later about how things were going to turn out. I gave us both a refill of coffee at the fire and started talking about things.

"Where is there to get some supplies?" I started. "We could use some coffee, maybe some jerky, beans, a little flour."

Ezra jerked his thumb in a northerly direction. "Dawson City, up north a little," he suggested. "They got a general store and maybe a saloon where we could blow off a little steam, get a bottle o' whiskey to warm me up at night."

Well, that was a start. "How far?" I asked. "Can we get there and back in a day?"

Ezra squinted at the fire and laughed. "It ain't but a stone's throw from here," he declared. "They built the town right where the gold is. Mebbe twenty or thirty minutes in that canoe. We could get to Dawson, get our supplies, and get home by nightfall."

"Let's start tomorrow afternoon," I suggested. Ezra agreed.

"Now," I continued, "about the mining. How much do we do and how long do we stay?"

Ezra grabbed a chunk of wood, pulled out a knife, and began whittling. "Been thinkin' about that," he said. "It's August—we don't want to stay too long. My old bones get cold up here. And, mebbe we don't dig on the bank this first time. No sense givin' away where we're mining when we won't be around to protect the claim. How about we just work the river an' use the rocker box? We stake our claim before we leave. If'n somebody's jumped it when we come back next summer, we'll have to deal with it then."

I thought about that one and nodded my head slowly. "You think we'll have to fight claim jumpers when we come back?"

Ezra shrugged. "Could be. Maybe it won't be too crowded yet out there on El Dorado. I 'spect Rabbit Creek will be all filled up by then, though. After these next couple weeks, we oughtta have a better idea if it's worth fightin' for."

"Agreed," I said. "What about getting home? We take the canoe back up the Yukon River?" I made a face. "Against the current?"

He shrugged again. "There's river boats can take us up from Dawson City to the mouth of the Yukon River. Place called St. Michael. Ain't much there, but we can catch us a steamboat from there back to Skagway. Might cost a hunnerd apiece, though. We'll have to see if we can find that much gold."

Ezra got up, walked over, and rolled up in his bedroll. Clearly, he'd done all the talking and planning he could deal with for one night. I reflected on what he'd said for a while, then banked the fire and rolled up in the blankets myself. It seemed like a good plan, all things considered.

———

We were up and paddling on the Yukon River not much past daybreak. We were guessing that if we were up and on the river at first light, we could make Dawson City by early morning, so we started early. Dawson was a ramshackle collection of wood buildings, pretty much begging for a fire to take the place down, it looked like to me. The experience with my saloon burning in Cripple Creek was still pretty fresh in my head.

Still, it was the most civilization we had seen in a few weeks. There were a few businesses around, with some sloppy, hand-carved signs hanging out front. There was a general store, a riverboat office, something calling itself a trading post and a couple other places. The saloon had most of Ezra's attention, but I made him promise to leave that till last.

We stopped in the general store first and picked up basically all the supplies we needed. We moved to the riverboat office and found out that tickets to St. Michael would cost forty dollars. Passage on to Skagway, the guy told us, would be another fifty or sixty dollars. Pretty much what we had figured. The riverboats would run for another five weeks, then shut down for winter. Couldn't take a chance on bein' out there when things froze up.

The guy at the general store had tipped us off that we might be able to sell gold ore at the trading post. We had enough cash between us to buy tickets back right now, but we didn't feel like parting with all our money. Plus, if we could sell the ore we had mined at a decent price, it would save us trying to bring it all back to Skagway. We decided on a trip to the trading post.

We heard a booming "Howdy, boys" as soon as we went in. I looked over to see a guy with about four teeth in his head, holding out his hand to me. I shook it, but I was still looking the place over.

"I'm Elmer," he shouted. He jerked a thumb toward the back of the store. "That there's my wife Mable, my boy Buck is out back. What kin I do fer ya?"

"We're wondering about selling gold ore," I said doubtfully.

"I kin buy it," Elmer hollered. "We got us a brick forge out back. Buck runs the forge. I pay eighteen dollars an ounce for gold. How much your ore is worth depends on how much gold I can get out of the forge. You wanna sell some now?"

I explained how we were just ready to begin some mining, but hoped to have something in a couple weeks. Elmer boomed that we should come and see him then. I looked around one more time.

"Don't you worry," Elmer yelled. "We'll have the cash money an' give you a fair price. Ain't nobody gonna steal from us, neither. We'll be here to do business. Mabel over there has a shotgun, an' I got one behind the counter. Not scared to use it, neither. Then there's Buck." He raised his voice even louder. "Hey, Buck! Get in here!"

The back door slammed and a giant of a young man came in. He looked a lot like Elmer, except he still had all his teeth. He grinned at us and crushed my hand with one shake. I had to admit, I wouldn't want to mess with this bunch. We promised to come back when we had some ore to sell.

Ezra and I huddled outside the trading post. Panned gold, we knew, was pretty rich ore—much richer than ore dug or blasted out of a mountainside. Time to get busy and earn that money to get us home. Hopefully, we agreed, with something extra for our trouble. Then, we would see about next summer.

Before leaving, I dashed back into the general store and bought two canvas travel bags. We needed them, I hoped, to carry the gold. I let Ezra get in the saloon for a bottle of whiskey, then listened to him whining about me dragging him out of there all the way home.

———

We had a new problem to deal with as soon as we got back to Rabbit Creek. We couldn't get to El Dorado Creek, as Ezra had called it, without taking the canoe past the miners' working claims on Rabbit Creek. We didn't mind about most of them—they seemed pretty busy panning the creek, and a few of them seemed to have had some luck.

It was Jed Harmon and Major Howland that worried us. We didn't want them following us around and finding out where we were panning. They were trouble, and they already didn't like us. We came up Rabbit Creek as it was getting dark, and Jed's head came up as we went past. Instead of taking the left fork to El Dorado Creek, we followed a branch of Rabbit Creek leading north. Jed started to follow along the bank.

We beached the canoe while we were still in eyesight and carried the bag of supplies into the woods near the shore. I turned around to look at Ezra.

"You said a while ago that you had an idea for dealing with these boys," I told him. "What do you want to do now?"

Ezra bent down and picked up a thick tree branch laying on the ground. He stepped into some cover behind a thick stand of brush. "Keep going," he hissed. "Make a lot of noise, too."

I could pretty much see where this was going, but I can't say I had any objections. I continued on into the woods, stepping on dry twigs and shoving the brush aside as I went. After a couple of minutes, I heard a solid *thunk* behind me, then silence. I retraced my steps and saw Jed lying on the ground. There was a sizable knot forming on his forehead.

"You just hauled off and slugged him on the head, huh?" I asked, examining the laid-out form of Jed on the ground.

"Yup, shore did." Ezra grunted in satisfaction. "Let's get the gear loaded back on the canoe. It's getting dark. We can slip away when Major comes looking for his buddy."

We loaded up and waited in the gathering darkness. After a while, we could see a dark shape moving cautiously along the bank. We could hear low calls of "Jed?" from time to time. Finally, he got an answering moan from the woods. When Major left the shore and moved into the woods, we pushed off and took the canoe down to our spot on El Dorado Creek.

We started at daybreak the next morning, and we took turns. One man waded into that freezing cold creek and started panning, carrying loads to the shore, where the other man was working the rocker, tending a small fire, and generally keeping an eye out. Neither of us could stay in the water too long, no matter that we had the warm boots. The fire was a powerful comfort. Not to mention it stopped my teeth from chattering.

The nuggets and flakes we pulled out of that creek were rich, we could see that from the start. The gold color shone a little in the bottom of that pan when I carried the first one to the shore. After a couple days, we started talking about how much we were gonna carry out of there. If we carried too much weight in the bottom of the canoe, it was going to be a problem, weighting us down. Plus, we didn't figure we'd heard the last of those two thugs that liked to spy on us. They'd left us alone mostly since Jed got that knot of his head, but every once in a while, we had the feeling of being watched.

About three nights in, we looked at the pile of flakes and nuggets we'd collected. They were pretty close to filling up one of the canvas bags. I hefted it in my hand and looked over at Ezra.

"What'd ya figger?" he mumbled around a mouthful of beans. "How many pounds kin we carry in the canoe?"

I lifted the bag one more time, shook it around, and dropped it back on the ground. "If we fill both of 'em up, they might weigh fifty, sixty pounds," I guessed. "That's probly all we can take in one trip." I looked up Eldorado Creek toward Rabbit Creek. "What do you think about getting past those boys down there?"

Ezra looked down in that direction. "Ya mean the one with the knot on his head and his pal?" He shrugged. "I say we bait 'em in and settle their hash before we leave. I ain't in favor of tryin' to sneak past 'em and lookin' over my shoulder all the way home." He picked up a stick and whittled on it. "I'll think on it some," he promised.

I looked back into the canvas bag. "I got an idea," I said. "Let's sort out the richest, purest-looking stuff we get and only take that on this trip." I peered back into the bag. "Let's pan another ten days or so, save off the best stuff, mark a spot and bury the rest for next summer. We take the best nuggets up to Elmer in Dawson, cash it in, and head home."

Ezra stopped whittling long enough to reach out for a refill from the coffeepot. "I like it," he agreed. "How much do you think we'll get?"

I shrugged. "Maybe several hundred," I said. "Enough for me to get a saloon started and for you to...do whatever you want."

Ezra grunted in satisfaction and turned onto his bedroll. "Don't forget next summer," he reminded. "That's when we can make us some big money."

It didn't take ten days. Only eight, and we had the two canvas bags filled with the best stuff we'd pulled out of that creek. The rest we had pushed back into a niche in the cliff face. We just rolled a big rock under the niche. Marking an X or some fool thing like that would have brought all the poachers and claim jumpers from miles around. I stood back from it and got my bearings, and after a minute, I felt sure I will be able to find it when we came back.

I had gotten in the canoe by myself and paddled it down to Rabbit Creek a time or two in the last several days. Both times, only the one that fancied himself a gun hand was there on the claim, and you could no way say that claim was being worked. No sign of that, and both times, he was just a-settin' there, leaned up against a rock and sunning himself like a big lizard.

If Howland, the gun hand, was staying on the claim, that probly meant that Harmon, the tough guy, was spying on us from the woods. When we had the gold dust and nuggets ready in the canvas bags, we made a show of packing up the canoe and leaving the claim early one morning. We'd already scouted El Dorado in the other direction—there was no way to get to Dawson without going back to Rabbit Creek.

There was a nip in the air meaning cold weather was coming. We weren't getting out any too soon. I loaded up the canoe while Ezra grabbed his shotgun and took the long way around through the woods toward Rabbit Creek.

I dropped the second canvas bag into the canoe, then I heard a whisper of sound at the edge of the woods. Howland stepped out, covering me with his pistol. His eyes roved around, looking for Ezra.

"Where's your pal?" I asked. He over his headache?"

Howland's lips curled back—I wasn't sure if it was a laugh or a sneer. He looked around one more time. "Where's your'n? Where's the old man?"

I took my time, hoping Ezra had done his job. I studied Howland. His black shirt was stained, and he had the yellowest teeth I'd ever seen. He was nervous, and his eyes darted back and forth. The gun hand was steady, though. Whatever else he'd been doing, he hadn't nipped at the bottle today.

Finally, I heard another rustle and Ezra prodded

Harmon out of the trees, giving him a shove and stepping around to cover Howland with the shotgun.

"Ain't this fun?" Ezra announced. "This here is what we like to call a standoff. Assumin' you like your chances against old Betsy here." He patted the shotgun. "I got one barrel for you and the other for Muscles over here. Do what you like. If'n you want a fair fight against Luke, just drop that smokewagon back into yer holster and I'll give it to you. The fair fight, I mean." There was a loud click as he eased back both hammers.

Howland shook his head and slowly dropped the pistol back into the holster. "Don't like them odds," he mumbled.

Ezra stepped back and lowered the shotgun. Howland started to turn away, but there was a crazy light in his eyes that had me nervous. My eyes dropped down. I knew my Colt was in the holster, but I checked it anyway.

Howland took a step toward, and his hand flashed down to his gun. He had it half-drawn, but mine was already in my hand. My first shot struck him dead-center in his chest. I didn't need another shot. His gun clattered onto the rocks, and he pitched over backward, splashing into the shallow water of the creek.

The sound of my shot seemed to echo and hang in the air. It dawned on me that he hadn't gotten a shot off. I swung to look at Harmon. He raised both hands in the air and stepped back, staring at Howland's body. "Ain't got no gun," he mumbled.

"Take yore pal," Ezra told him. "Take him and give him a decent burial. Wouldn't do no harm to say a few words over him."

Harmon looked around him. "Where? No shovel." He rubbed his hands over his eyes.

"Take him back and bury him at your claim," Ezra growled. "We don't want him around here. Go on."

Harmon splashed into the creek, pulled Howland's body from the water and tossed it over his shoulder. He disappeared into the woods. I stared after him, as that last minute burned into my brain. I looked down and saw I was still holding the Colt. I put it back in my holster on the second try, then sat down on a rock.

Ezra walked over and stood over me. "Take yore time, pard. You done what you had to do. Can't believe he was stupid enough to draw." He walked over, pulled out some stakes and began carving our initials on them.

After about fifteen minutes, I started to steady down. I got up and helped Ezra drive the stakes for our claim. When we were done, we got into the canoe, pushed it off, and headed for Rabbit Creek and the Yukon River. We could make Dawson City in no time if we kept moving.

When we reached Rabbit Creek, there wasn't any sign of Jed Harmon yet. Maybe, I thought, he'd stopped and buried Howland in the woods.

CHAPTER 12

STEAMING HOME

E lmer wasn't talking any quieter than before when we got to Dawson Lake. He bellowed at us when we came through the door.

"Hey, fellers! You struck color too, did ya?"

We carried the canvas bags across and laid them down on a table Elmer pointed at. We stared at him.

"We found some," I agreed, pointing at the bags. "Want to cash it in if the price is good." I paused while Buck the giant came in, grabbed both bags like they were pillows, and hauled them out back to the brick forge.

I turned around to look at Elmer again. "What do you mean, struck color too," I asked. "Did somebody else come through here?"

Elmer chuckled and herded us out of the trading post, headed for one of the saloons. "C'mon, I'll tell you about it while I buy you a beer. Guys named Skookum Jim and George Carmack come through here about two days ago, it was. Got them some good color."

I drained my beer, waved for another, and looked at Ezra. I don't know how much he'd played cards, but he had him a poker face, I got to admit.

Since Ezra wasn't talking, I looked back over at Elmer.

"Did you buy from Carmack and Skookum Jim?" I wanted to know. It seemed to me there was a big rush headed this way if they'd hit a lot of gold.

Elmer shrugged and picked up a fresh beer. "Only a little," he said. "Them boys had more'n I could buy, but I bought some of it to give 'em a little pocket money. Paid 'em eighteen dollars an ounce, same as I'll pay you. They can get twenny in Seattle or San Francisco, so they kept most of it an' that's where they'll go. You boys could get twenny too, but you don't have enough to make it pay, sailin' all the way to Seattle or Frisco. I'll go down there to sell mine, though."

I was trying to figure out how to ask my next question when Elmer saved me the trouble. "They'll be lots of folks flocking into this place once word gets out. I heard they done renamed Rabbit Creek to Bonanza Creek. Won't be no open claims left in another two weeks, just from folks around here." Elmer lowered his beer and looked at each of us. "Taint gonna be no rush till next summer, though. Takes a while to get to Frisco or Seattle."

He waved a hand in the air and belched. "Oh, there'll be a few coming in on dog sleds and such. There's gonna be some of 'em freeze up here, too. You don't want to be around here after another month, not unless you're prepared right. Mable and Buck and me, we could make it, but Mabel's got her heart set on San Francisco. We'll be back next year."

Elmer stared off into the corner and seemed to lose track of what he was talking about. I had to prod him a bit to bring him back. "So...you're saying that by the time word reaches Seattle and San Francisco, it's gonna be too late to come up here? Until next year, I mean."

Elmer belched again and nodded his head up and down. "Yep, maybe May sometime, that's when you boys need to come back."

Elmer didn't even stop and wait to hear if we were coming back. "Hit the minin' as soon as you can. Probly want to take yore stuff to Seattle or Frisco when you've got more, next time, I mean. I give it maybe middle of the summer afore the hordes get here." He waved out toward the town. "Got us about five hunnerd here this summer. This time next year, there'll be thousands and thousands. That's some rich ore you boys found out there."

Elmer left off talking and started humming. It wasn't too easy on the ear, neither. Ezra had left off the beer and started on the whiskey. I decided it was a good time to get up and walk around. There wasn't much to see. I found a place where Ezra and I could each get a bed. Elmer thought he would know how much he could pay us by tomorrow.

———

Ezra's poker face was gone. I don't know where it went, but his jaw was hanging open. I gave him a poke with my elbow and he snapped it shut. I think maybe it heard it click. I got to admit, I was staring as much as he was.

"How much did you say?" I finally asked.

Elmer grinned. "One thousand dollars, cash on the barrelhead. You boys just about cleaned me out. Well, not quite. I got some money left. Buck pulled fifty-five ounces of gold out o' those panning nuggets you boys brought in. Richest stuff I ever saw. It actually come to nine hunnerd ninety dollars, but you bought me a couple beers an' I like you boys."

Elmer bent down, and I heard some clicking going on. I was guessing he had a safe down there. There was some chatter still coming while he dialed. "Don't know where you boys was pannin'...don't want to know, neither. Twixt what old Skookum Jim brought in, an' you boys, an' the Trading Post, we've had us a good season here, Mable and me."

He stood up and thumped a pile of gold coins on the counter, then counted out fifty of them. "You boys want a sack? Mebbe two sacks?"

We both nodded, unable to find our tongues. Elmer counted twenty-five coins into each sack and drew up the drawstrings while Mable fussed around, giving us biscuits and jerky. "You boys take this food. You probably ain't et right since you left Skagway," she scolded us. Buck stood in the corner and grinned at us.

We escaped out of the trading post and stood outside, grinning like a couple of fools at each other. I lifted my sack in my hand and started looking around.

"Good idea," Ezra said, reading my mind. "Let's find that riverboat office and get outta here."

The riverboat for St. Michael was leaving the next day, and we got tickets with no trouble. I wondered how easy it would be next year if the things Elmer talked about came true. For sure, I knew if a boat came into either Seattle or San Francisco with gold on it, and word got out, it would bring a crowd. Something about the idea of finding gold gets folks lathered up.

I liked to stand on the deck of the riverboat as we traveled downstream to St. Michael. There were mountains on both sides, peaks covered in snow, and the air was getting colder every day. There were glaciers running right down to the water's edge. I had some trouble sleeping because it stayed light so late every day. Ezra, though, didn't seem to have any trouble sleeping and said seeing mountains just made him think about having to climb them.

There was one day Ezra perked up. That was the day we stopped at a place called Circle City to take on some supplies and wood. The captain came around and told me they'd found some gold around that place about a year ago, and a town had sprung up. He told me some more about the town, and I went looking for Ezra. I knew he wouldn't want to miss this.

I found him in the cabin. He wasn't asleep, which took me by surprise. I told him we'd docked at a place called Circle City and said he needed to come and see the town.

He eyed me like I'd just crossed paths with a skunk. "Why do I wanna do that?" he growled. Boat trips make him crabby.

"Cap'n says they have two theaters, eight dance halls, and twenty-eight saloons," I informed him.

He stared at me. "That ain't funny," he said.

"I didn't mean it to be," I protested. "Cap'n says it's true. He says they stop here every trip. We'll be here for seven or eight hours."

Ezra got to his feet and reached for his hat. "I'm in," he told me.

When I stopped for a second outside a theater, Ezra just snorted and kept going. I caught up to him at the first saloon he came to and followed him inside. We stayed about an hour, and I was hearing my stomach growling at me.

I looked over at Ezra. "Let's go to one of the dance halls and get some dinner," I said. "We'll get better food than we've been getting on that boat. Maybe better than on the next boat, too."

Ezra gave me the fisheye over his glass of beer. Finally, he set it down. "They've got women dancin' in there, right? Not just a bunch of loggers and gold-diggers stompin' around?"

I stood up, reached out, and put his hat on his head. "I'm sure they've got women," I told him. "Who ever heard of a dance hall with loggers and miners doing the dancing?"

Ezra shrugged and mumbled something, but followed me to a dance hall. He got happier when there were some women dancing on the stage, and the food was pretty good. I decided it was a good time to talk about the next trip.

"We come back next May and do more mining, but we get out before the big herd of people shows up, right? Maybe get out by the middle of July?"

Ezra kept chewing but nodded and mumbled something that sounded like a yes.

"There's two people I want to come with us next time," I said. "Two people we can trust that'll help us with things."

Ezra put down his fork, still chewing, and waited.

"The first one is Bear, that guy that Black Jack Adams sent after me, but now he's helping at the bakery and such.

Nobody's gonna mess with him, and he can carry his share. Haul stuff, and dig, and the like. Folks aren't likely to start a knuckle-and-skull fight with Bear around."

Ezra took a swallow from his beer and chuckled. "Yeah, he's got some bark on him. He'll be good to bring along. Who else?"

I took a deep breath and waded in. "Angie," I said. "She wants to come. I want her to come with us."

Ezra put his beer down and stared at me. I swear he didn't blink for about half a minute. "You've done gone loco," he announced. "You want to bring a woman to that place?"

"She's already come to Skagway all by herself," I reminded him. "Started a bakery, and she's doing good. She'll take her turn helping out and she's a strong woman. She won't slow us down. There's other women at the Klondike already. You saw some, yourself."

Ezra just kept staring and shaking his head. "You've done gone loco. You've gone all sweet on that woman an' it has addled your head."

"She'll keep up," I insisted. "She'll keep up on the trail, she'll help with the panning and mining. She'll even do some baking for us. You want to eat our cooking for two months up here next time?"

He finally blinked several times, then picked up his beer, gulped down the rest of it, and slammed the glass down. He shook his head, but I could see he was warming up to the idea. I got him with that part about doing some baking. Finally, he picked up his fork and went after the steak again.

"Never heard of such a thing," he mumbled. "I must be as tetched in the head as you are."

I sat and waited.

Finally, he waved his fork in the air and signaled for another beer. "Okay, she comes," he said. "I must be crazy."

We didn't talk about it again for the rest of the trip. We didn't have as much fun after Circle City, but once we got to St. Michael and got tickets for Skagway, we started to relax.

We wouldn't have to worry about getting frozen in for the winter, and it seemed like a decent crowd of people on the steamship. It took us about thirty days to get to Skagway. I was looking forward more and more to seeing Angie again.

———

Angie lowered her shotgun and put it back under the counter, her heart still racing wildly. Lou rushed in carrying a four-by-four left over from building the frame of the café/bakery. She set it down slowly when she saw it wasn't needed any longer. Two men were lying on the ground. One was out cold, and the left side of his jaw was swelling slowly. The other was on his knees, moaning and holding his ribs.

Bear was standing in the middle of the floor, slowly massaging his knuckles and swiveling his head from side to side. When he saw there was nobody else to deal with, he grabbed the unconscious man under the arms and dragged him out of the bakery. The second man lurched slowly to his knees and staggered out. Bear stood aside and let him go.

The two bowls of stew and two apple pies, things the men had been trying to steal, lay on the ground. The stew and one pie were scattered around. Unlikely as it seemed, the second pie seemed undisturbed. Bear picked it up gently, carried it over, and set it carefully on the counter.

He surveyed the two ladies. "Are you okay?" he asked anxiously, his eyes traveling from one to the other.

Angie nodded slowly. "We're fine, thanks to you, Bear." She walked around the counter and pulled a chair over to him. "Sit down. Everything's fine now."

The two men had come in this morning, people she had never seen before. They had ordered the food and announced they wouldn't be paying for it. She'd told them to pay or give the food back. One had reached across the counter and grabbed her hair. She had yelled in surprise, and Bear had appeared immediately. The fight had been short-lived and very one-sided.

The tent flap swung open, and William Moore rushed in. Angie gave him a short recap of what had happened. Moore patted Bear on the shoulder and asked if he had seen either man before. Bear nodded his head slowly, looking troubled. Moore waited for Bear to tell him about it.

"That one—the first one that I clocked on the jaw. I seen him before, maybe the other'n too. They was hanging out with a guy named Black Jack Adams, back in Denver where I first met Adams. He's a bad'un, Black Jack is. The other one—the one with the busted ribs, I mighta seen him with Adams before, too." He shook his head. "Adams is bad, all bad."

"Bad how?" Moore asked sharply. "Crooked gambling, robbery, murder, what?"

Bear nodded. "All of that," he said slowly. "He don't like me much neither." He looked over at Angie. "He don't like Luke Spencer none either. It's real bad if he comes up here. Haven't seen him around yet, though." He lapsed into a moody silence.

Angie walked around and bent down to look into Bear's eyes. "Why doesn't he like you or Luke?"

Bear shook his head regretfully. "I used to work for him. Done his bidding roughin' some people up." He shook his head again. "Wish I hadn't done that. Anyway, he told me to rough up Luke Spencer real bad." He grinned and touched his jaw. "That Luke, he can punch pretty good. He got the best of me. Anyway, I decided I liked Luke better, an' I threw Black Jack in the harbor, back there in Seattle."

"What about Luke? Why doesn't he like Luke?" Angie prompted.

The grin faded from Bear's face. "Luke said Black Jack tried to kill him and Ezra, back over Colorado way. Maybe he wanted to finish up the job." He looked over at William Moore. "Real bad if'n he comes up here," he repeated. He got up and left the tent.

Angie and Lou looked at Moore. "What can we do about this?" Lou demanded.

Moore shook his head slowly. "I've seen this before, many times, in gold rush towns. Takes a while to get a law-abiding town. If this guy Adams does come, or somebody like him, we just face up to trouble when it comes, like you ladies and Bear did this morning. If somebody like Adams comes and organizes a gang, that's trouble." He lapsed into silence and sighed. "Then you just hang on as best you can. Probably have to organize the town to fight 'em."

Moore got up and prowled around the bakery. "Me, I'll hang onto what's most important—the lumber mill and the wharf. I've filed on my land, all legal and proper, over in Sitka." He stopped and looked at Angie. "Your lot is legally protected. Luke's, too. I'm building a big house a little way out of town. I'll hang onto that, too. The rest, we'll just have to see. Maybe this Black Jack guy won't come." He turned and ducked abruptly out of the bakery.

Angie stood and scooped up the remains of the stew and the apple pie off the ground, then moved around behind the counter to serve new customers coming in. Bear could keep things quiet around here as long as there weren't guns involved. If there were guns involved...well, she would have to cross that bridge if she came to it.

The customers left, and she walked over to sit next to Lou again. "Clyde and Dale," she started.

Lou grinned. "You love those horses. I was wondering when you were going to ask me about them. You have enough money for me to go down and get them? What about food for the winter? You got enough hay and feed?"

Angie nodded emphatically. "I have the money and the feed. William and his crew will build a little shelter for them out back. I want them here in the spring. I'm going to have another business taking miners up White Pass."

Lou shook her head in admiration. "You're such a busi-nesswoman," she marveled. "What's next?"

Angie had a new idea brewing in the back of her mind, but she decided to keep it to herself. "Nothing, so far," was her only answer.

Lou got up to check on the pot of stew she had going over the fire. "Okay, if you can spare me for a couple of weeks, I'll go back down on the next steamer and get Clyde and Dale." She put down the ladle and carried the four-by-four back outside, where she had found it when the fight broke out.

CHAPTER 13

TOWN MEETING

I had fallen asleep on the bunk in the cabin, so it took me by surprise when the ship slowed, and the bell started clanging. I sat up, rubbed my eyes, and shook my head, trying to figure out what was going on.

The door burst open, and Ezra charged into the room. He picked up my boots and tossed them to me, then wheeled to run back out the door. "We're home, pilgrim," he shouted. "Git yer boots on and get out here. I just might steal yer girl from ya if you dawdle." He disappeared down the passageway.

I hurried up to the deck after a couple of minutes. It was getting on toward dusk. I must have been sawin' logs down there for a couple of hours. We moved down the channel toward town, and it had changed a lot from when we'd left.

There was a wharf running out about fifty feet from the shore. They were still working on it, so I didn't figure we could pull up alongside and dock just yet, but pretty soon, ships this size would be able to. A couple of deckhands lashed a stout rope from the bow of the ship to a log at the end of the pier, and Ezra and I could hop from the ship over to the wharf.

I trotted along the pier with Ezra at my heels. I could see several folks from the town hurrying to the dock. I guess it was still pretty big news around here when a ship docked. I spotted Angie headed down for the ship, waving. I waved, but I checked around behind me, too, thinkin' there might be somebody else she was waving at.

"It's you, ya big lunkhead. She's a-wavin' at you." Ezra snorted a few times just to make his point, so I trotted a little faster to put some distance between us.

I hopped down from the end of the wharf, and Angie dashed up and laid a mighty big hug on me, then finished it up with a kiss on the cheek.

A grin split my face from ear to ear, but my tongue kinda froze up on me right then. "I...uh, I, well, I'm so glad to see you. I've been looking forward to it the whole trip back," I finished. I guess it was good enough. It earned me another kiss on the cheek.

Angie put an arm around me and pointed to a lady coming over toward us. "Luke," she said, "this is Lou. I knew her back home in Walla Walla. She going to join me and make the place into a bakery and a café."

Lou gave me a knowing smile and shook my hand. "Heard about you," she said. She glanced over at Angie. "Heard about you a lot."

Angie turned red, and I started feeling better about my tongue freezin' up on me a minute before. Now we'd both been a mite embarrassed. Ezra came steaming up behind us, and I introduced him to Lou. For a minute, things got quiet and a little awkward, then Lou waved and led us toward the town. "Come on," she said, "dinner's on me."

Lou served up some venison, and I could understand why there was such a crowd piling through the door for dinner. Angie added some vegetables and potatoes from the garden she'd been tending for a few months out back, and finished it off with an apple pie.

I finished up, moaned with satisfaction, leaned back and loosened my belt a notch when nobody was looking. I looked around the café—there were several fresh faces in here, and I'd only been gone less'n two months. I realized then how much this town was going to change in the next year or two. I saw a couple of pretty hard faces with some sharp eyes in the room and started to wonder how much of the change would be for good.

Angie followed my gaze around the room, then looked at a clock behind the counter. She made a small sound that sounded like "Oh!" then stood and took my hand to pull me up with her.

"Town meeting!" she said. "I almost forgot, what with you boys coming home. William Morris has called a town meeting at the lumber mill. I'm sure he would want you there." She looked over at Ezra. "You too, Ezra."

We took a seat in some chairs they'd put out on the floor of the lumber mill. William and John Moore saw me come in. John patted me on the shoulder and kept going, but William leaned down and said something like "counting on you" before he moved back to the front of the room.

I looked at Angie, raising my eyebrows in a big question mark.

She leaned over and murmured in my ear. "We've had some trouble." She stopped and looked around at the town folks filing into the room. "A couple of guys tried to steal some food from the bakery a couple of weeks ago," she explained. "Bear straightened it out. I think Bear's a little worried about guys coming in with guns, though."

I pulled back and stared at her in surprise. I felt the anger rising and blood rushing to my face.

She covered my hand with hers and shook her head. "All taken care of," she assured me. "I wasn't hurt. Moore's men put them on a boat back to Seattle. They haven't come back."

Moore cleared his throat and began to speak. "I've invited all of you personal," he explained. "You're all good folks here to start a business or make some money in this new land. I didn't invite the drinkers, card sharps or crooks to the meeting. We don't want them." He stopped and looked around the room.

"All of you know I've built us a stockade at the end of

the main street." He stopped when he saw the surprise on my face. "Well, most of you know," he corrected himself. "Luke and Ezra just got back today. "The stockade's good and strong," he went on. "We can put the troublemakers in there for a couple days when we need to."

He went on to say he was looking for volunteers for a citizen's patrol. He was hoping for enough volunteers so it would only take up about one day a week for each volunteer. He wanted two men on duty each day. He looked around the room.

"We don't need somebody walkin' around all night," he explained. "If anybody's acting drunk and rowdy come nighttime, we throw 'em in the stockade and let 'em sober up till morning. We hear any commotion and carryin' on at night, we all come running."

He looked me right in the eye. "Now, I need some volunteers," he announced. He kept looking at me without blinking.

Angie squeezed my arm, and William was still looking at me. I raised my hand in the air and dug my elbow into Ezra's ribcage. He moaned for a second, then raised his hand, grumbling to himself. Another dozen hands or so went up, and William nodded with satisfaction.

"Looks like we've got us a patrol," he announced.

I stayed after the meeting to ask William a few questions. "What about sheriffs, judges, people like that?" I asked. "Do we have any traveling judges or marshals or anything?" I hadn't thought about any of this before.

William shrugged. "The Alaska Territory is under the laws of Oregon Territory. We've got a court in Sitka, an' not much else. We have one marshal and ten deputies for the whole territory. They don't get down here much."

We were sitting in the café again, and he stopped for a sip of his coffee. "A couple of Northwest Mounted Police came through for a while last year. Canadians got no authority here, though. They moved on. They're talking about setting up a post just over White Pass and all along the

Yukon River. If there's a rush, they'll probably be kinda overrun for a while, but they'll get it straightened out on the Canadian side. Might take a while longer here in Skagway."

Moore left after that, and I got a few more details from Bear about the fight in the bakery two weeks before.

Bear left, then Ezra and I stood to go. Angie wrapped me up in a tight hug, and I wasn't complaining or struggling. She said goodnight, and Ezra and I left. I could hear Ezra cackling and guffawing five paces behind me.

I didn't bother to turn around. "Oh, shut up," I told him.

I got around to telling Angie the next day about the good luck we'd had at the Klondike. When I said Ezra and I had come back with four hundred dollars free and clear after the boat rides, her eyes got big, and she broke into a smile. "I'm coming next spring!" She stopped and bored in on me with those eyes of hers. "Right?"

I waved my hands in the air. "Right," I agreed. "Even Ezra agreed to it. I've got to talk to Bear yet, but we want him to come, too."

"He'll agree in a heartbeat," she assured me. I was nodding in agreement when there was a whistle and some bells. The *Juneau* was docking!

We ran down to the new wharf. Angie was ready to introduce me to Captain Buckley, but he remembered me. We walked back to the café, and I waited while Angie paid for the shipment of baking goods and placed her new order. Bear had stayed back to get things brought up to the store.

When Angie was done, I talked to Buckley about an order for whiskey and beer. Moore's men were working quickly to get a store set up for me. I had already paid for the saloon to be built, and they were almost done. Ezra sat by while I made the order.

Buckley left and Ezra sat there, shaking his head at me. "You really gonna order proper whiskey?" he asked, his voice on the scornful side. "Why don't you just make up some Tarantula Juice? These boys around here will drink it an' pay for it, too. They won't even complain too much."

I had a good idea of what he was talking about, but I wanted to hear it from him. "Just what would you put in Tarantula Juice whiskey?" I asked.

Ezra shrugged. "I expect you know already. Throw three or four gallons of grain alcohol in a barrel an' pour in a good amount of mo-lasses to give it a little flavor. Shave a plug of tobacco and toss it in there. If that don't give it enough bite, throw in a bar of soap. That should do it. Fill up the rest of the barrel with some good crick water."

I sat there and stared at him, just waiting for him to say something else. He didn't look at me—just looked around the café, humming to himself.

Finally, I had to ask. "Did you ever drink that Tarantula Juice?"

Ezra looked hurt. "Course I did, many a time. I bet you've had a little, too. It was better than some of the nasty crick water I've drunk."

"I have a time or two," I agreed. "Didn't feel none too good the next day, though. How about you? After you got done drinkin' some, I mean."

Ezra quit humming and shrugged. "They tell me I howled at the moon a couple nights. Woke up in the town jail a couple times, but that didn't do me no harm. I still say it's better'n a lot of the crick water I've drunk in some of them towns."

Angie stopped what she was doing behind the counter and stood there, not sure whether to believe what she'd just heard.

I nodded my head slowly. "They do serve that stuff in some of the saloons here and there," I told her. "Not me, though. I'm going to serve the good stuff or nothing. I'll wait for Buckley to bring it to me."

Ezra sniffed loudly a few times and got up to leave.

"You'll make more money doin' it my way," he told me. "I'll even make the Tarantula Juice for ya."

I just let him go. There was no arguing with Ezra about whiskey or gold mining. Everything else, maybe. Whiskey and gold mining, never. And sometimes, there was no arguing about women. I got up and walked down the street to see how the saloon was coming along today.

———

Lou returned with Clyde and Dale after a few more weeks. The cold was setting in pretty good by then, but those draft horses had them a thick coat of fur in no time, and I could see they were powerful animals. They were pets as much as workhorses, but I didn't doubt they could haul our stuff up White Pass without breaking a sweat. Well, maybe a little sweat. We wouldn't take them past White Pass, though. The path got way too narrow after White Pass, and too many horses had died up there already. It was a deadly stretch—just a ribbon of a trail, there between White Pass and the Yukon River.

In another few weeks, the snow started to fly, but I'm a Montana boy by way of Colorado, and the snow doesn't bother me. I got the saloon opened and started to do a pretty decent business. Once word got out about the gold up there in the Klondike, they would jam this place full every night. Plus, there would be about ten more saloons, I expect. Those minin' boys can drink, though. I'd do fine around here. Plus, I was determined to visit the Klondike again.

Another saloon opened down the street, and it was a rough and ready place, but things didn't get too bad. The citizen's patrol kept an eye on them, and there were a few nights when Moore and several of the rest of us shut them down for the night. Or, as Bear said, "We threw 'em in the stockade and they was calmed down considerable come daylight."

It was in January that the bitter cold came. It was as cold

as that terrible winter in Montana and reminded me of that a lot. Fewer folks came to the saloon at night, and we were burning a lot of firewood just to keep me, Ezra and Bear warm in there. After a few nights, Angie suggested we move in and sleep in the café, using the oven fireplace to keep everybody warm. We could combine our firewood. We moved in that night and tossed our bedrolls on the floor when the last customers had left.

Angie and I sat up in front of the fire after the others had fallen asleep. We talked about our new lives and plans in Skagway, and about the trip to the Klondike. At some point, I reached over and took her hand. We continued talking, enjoying the warmth and the occasional popping noises coming from the brick fireplace.

After a while, I noticed the flames dropping while the logs charred away. I got up and grabbed two more logs, put them on the fire, and prodded them a bit to get the flames going again. I got down on a knee and blew gently to get the flames leaping up.

I turned, still on my knee, and reached out to grab the corner of my chair and stand. Angie and I were face-to-face. She leaned forward and smiled. Then we kissed for a lingering moment in front of the fire. That's when I knew Skagway would be my home for a long time.

———

The cold gave way slowly to springtime. We saw more people coming in on the steamers. It wasn't a rush yet, but the four of us knew we needed to get back to the Klondike, and we were planning to go in another week. The new crowd coming in had some solid folks, but there were some rowdies coming in, too. The citizen's patrol and the stockade stayed busier these days. I wasn't too worried about it until William Moore stopped in the saloon one day.

It was late afternoon, and the place hadn't filled up for the evening yet. I joined him for a beer at one table in the corner. He took a few sips and looked around at some of the newer faces in town. After a while, he put his glass down and shook his head.

"I've been selling a few of my lots lately," he mumbled. "Didn't get prices as good as I would in another year, or even six months, but I'm not sure I can hang on to all of it. Seen these boom towns before, and it gets hard to hold your ground." He lapsed into silence for a while. "Going to go up to Sitka and be sure I've got the lots filed proper. I'd rather fight in court than with a gun. Too old for that."

I leaned back and thought about it. "I can help," I offered. "Bear and Ezra, too."

Moore shook his head slowly. "I know you'll come to help if I'm in trouble. I thank you for that. A man's got to fight his own fights, though. Needs to know when to move on if he has to."

He finished his beer and stood up, offering me a couple of coins to pay for it. "I'm building me a big, new house up and out of town a little. You come see it when you get back."

I was back behind the counter serving up a couple of whiskeys when Bear came in a couple hours later. He stood for a second, looking for me, then hustled over to the bar. "You better come down to the café. Better have your six-shooter on, too. There's trouble."

I reached for my holster and strapped it on as I hurried around the bar. I'd never seen Bear looking worried before, but he did now. I knew he wasn't any hand with a gun, so maybe that was it.

"Couple guys down there starting to get pretty rough. I kin handle the rough stuff, but one of 'em is wearin' a gun and it looks like he fancies himself with it."

I nodded and picked up the pace toward the café. Bear stopped me when we were near the door.

"There's more," he said. "Cap Light is in there, and I think he's with those first two. He wants me dead, an' maybe you too."

CHAPTER 14

THE KLONDIKE CALLS

It was quiet when we stepped into the bakery. That's the first thing I noticed. Then I saw one of William Moore's workers was pushed up against a wall. A big man with long, stringy hair had his forearm shoved under the worker's chin, and he was making a choking noise, his face white. A tall, thin blond with a beard hanging down to his chest stood in the center of the room. He wore double tied-down guns, one of them drawn and pointed down at the floor.

When I stepped into the room, the one with the guns swung slightly to face me, his gun half-raised now. I glanced at him, then around the room. I recognized Cap Light. He was standing against a side wall, his arms folded. He wore a holster with a single Colt. The Colt was staying right there in the holster for now. A flicker of recognition crossed his face when I looked at him, but he didn't move.

Angie was behind the counter. Her cash box lay on top, and she was pleading with the blond man. Her face was paler than I'd seen it before. She pushed the cash box a little farther over.

"Just take the money and leave my customers alone. This is all I have."

I stepped a little more toward the middle of the room. I caught Angie's eye and nodded slightly toward Cap Light.

She caught my meaning and reached slowly under the counter, where I knew she kept a shotgun. While all eyes in the room were on the gunman and me, she slowly laid the shotgun across the counter and pointed at Cap Light.

Cap Light didn't bat an eye, but he still didn't move, either. The blond with the half-drawn gun, distracted by the movement, swung his head to look at Angie. This was my chance. I stepped to the side to get out of his line of fire, palmed my Colt and fired in one move. His eyes showed shock at the sound of my gun, and he started to lift and swing his own pistol, but he was too late.

His gun fired, but the shot went past me and into the wall. He staggered back, fell to his knees, then collapsed. The big guy released his hold on Moore's worker and turned to face Bear, who covered the ground in two steps. Bear's punch connected with the man's jaw and lifted him from the ground and into the side wall. He collapsed to the floor without a sound.

I swung to look at Cap Light. He had turned to face me. His hands dropped slowly to his sides. A little voice inside me said that if I didn't face him now, I would probably have to do it later. I dropped my gun slowly back into the holster and locked eyes with him across the room.

"Up to you," I said. "I'll give you a fair fight here and now if you want it. If you don't, you need to unbuckle that gun and let it drop. You can spend the night in the stockade with your pal over there". I nodded back toward the man Bear had dropped. "You can have your gun back in the morning. No bullets, but I'll give you your gun back and you can get out of town."

Cap Light stood there and studied my face. He was a cool one, I'll give him that. He looked over at Angie. She still had the shotgun out, but it wasn't pointed in his direction anymore. He looked back at me and shook his head slowly.

"No, I don't believe I'll try you this time," he said softly. He unbuckled his holster and dropped it to the ground. I pointed at the door, and he moved in that direction. Bear stopped, threw the man he'd just punched over his shoulder, and followed us to the stockade.

Bear dumped his man inside the stockade and Light followed him in. He sat down in the corner and watched me while I closed the door and locked it. I hadn't been able to read his expression at all. He was a dangerous man. That much I knew.

When we got back to the café, they were hauling the dead man out of there. I stopped them to take one more look at his face. I didn't know him. I stood back while they carted him down the street, then went back inside to check on Angie.

———

Just one week later, we were on the White Pass Trail. It was the first week in May, and we were gambling a little on having warm enough weather to do what we wanted. But, after talking it over a lot, we thought there was a bigger gamble if we waited longer. A couple of steamers had come in with miners already. We couldn't afford to let the lots fill up on the Klondike before we could get there.

It troubled me some that people were saying Cap Light and the thug from the café might have gone up to the Klondike already. He hadn't left on a ship back to Seattle and he for sure wasn't around Skagway anymore. That didn't leave many places he could go. We might have one enemy from last summer hanging around up there already, and I didn't want to be stacking up too many of those guys while we were mining.

There was some snow still on the ground as we climbed to the peak of White Pass, but there had already been some traffic to pack it and melt it down some. Besides Angie, Ezra, Bear and me, we had Lou with us for this first part of the trip. She was there to take Clyde and Dale back down to Skagway after we reached the summit of White Pass. She would keep the café going while Angie came with us to the Klondike.

Those were a couple of powerful horses, I must say. They were pulling our bags up the pass like we'd put a couple of feathers on their backs. Good-natured animals, too. Always nuzzling my pockets for a treat or two. Angie was scolding me for spoiling the horses, but I noticed her giving 'em a little treat every now and then herself.

We had us a little disagreement right before we left, and again before we got close to the top, about how far we would take those horses. Folks were calling the trail between White Pass summit and Bennett Lake the Dead Horse Trail, on account of the number of animals that had died on that narrow road.

We finally reached a deal after a lot of bargaining back and forth. We took Clyde and Dale with us for another day and a half after we'd topped off the White Pass summit. Ezra and I figured we were about halfway to Bennett Lake. When the trail started to rise and really get narrow, Lou turned around with the horses and went back. After that, we divided up the gear, with Angie getting a smaller load and Bear making up the difference. We made it to Bennett Lake the next afternoon in good shape.

Building the raft went mostly better this time around. Ezra and I had some tricks up our sleeves to make it go faster, and we brought plenty of rope this time so we didn't have to be so careful with tying things off all snug and proper. We had to make a bigger, wider raft, though. We had two extra people this time. Angie didn't take up much space, but ol' Bear was a different story. We had to allow for his weight and his width.

Once we'd pushed off and commenced to paddling, though, we didn't mind the extra weight. Maybe they'd named Bear after the wrong animal. He was strong as a bull. We did all the poling of the raft between the two of us. Angie took a turn with the paddles, along with Ezra, and when we tied it off at night, she made us some fine food.

Ezra and I decided we couldn't have picked better shipmates.

The water in the Yukon River was even colder than last July. I didn't think that was possible, but it was. When it washed over the deck and splashed on me, I sucked in some air, I can tell you. Ezra was the worst, though, whining about the cold water.

Third day out, we hit some small rapids, and Ezra hollered like a little girl when it splashed on him. I told him so, and he dug that paddle in the water and sent a shower in my direction. After that, nobody talked about the icy river water.

———

We came around a bend and spotted Canyon City six days after we put the raft into the water, just like on the first trip. We ran the raft aground, and I held out a hand for Angie. We stood on the shore and looked around. It wasn't much, just like before, but I was looking forward to switching over to canoes. Things were so much easier that way.

Ezra climbed up an embankment, strolled about fifty feet down the trail and ducked into a tent. Angie turned and looked at me, hopefully.

"Is he looking for canoes?" she asked. I had explained to her before how we wanted to get two canoes while we were here.

"Nope, he's looking for whiskey," I explained. "We'll need to give him an hour or two. We can stretch and walk around, though," I said a little doubtfully. I hadn't seen much to look at in Canyon City the last time. Bear shrugged and followed Ezra to the saloon tent.

We strolled down what passed for a street, and to my surprise, I saw a new building there, a short way along the path. The final boards looked like they were going in on the roof, but the doors were open and there were a few people moving in and out. I stopped to read the hand-painted sign at the door: "Whitehorse General Store."

Angie came to a stop beside me, taking my hand while she read the sign. "I'm confused. I thought this was Canyon City," she said.

"It is. Well, at least it was," I explained. I stopped, then I knew what must have happened. "There are rapids just ahead. We'll go around them," I added hastily when I saw the concern on her face. "Some people think the whitecaps on the rapids look like a horse's head. Maybe they changed the town name."

I asked the storekeep, and he nodded. "Some folks still call it Canyon City and t'others likes to call it Whitehorse. I like Whitehorse." He moved off to help somebody who had just come in.

I found Angie picking out an iron skillet and a few other things I could see we might need when we made camp. She stopped and picked up a bag of flour. I hoped I knew what that was for.

"You boys have been eating a lot of biscuits." She chuckled. "I won't be so popular if I let you run out, now, will I?"

I agree that it was a bad idea to run out of biscuits. We took the things we bought back to the raft and sat there until Ezra and Bear came out of the saloon. They moved over to join us.

Angie stood up, looking hopeful again. "Time to get the canoes?"

Ezra looked up at the setting sun and shook his head. "We'll wanna wait till mornin'," he said. "Only a crazy man would go sneakin' up on an Indian village in the dark. Crazy man or a dead'un." He hauled his bedroll off the raft. "Besides," he said, "you can stay here when we go to get the canoes. Mebbe Bear can stay with you."

Angie shook her head vigorously. "No, I'm coming with you." Her tone left little room for arguing. "I can help you with trading for the canoes."

Ezra stared at her. "You can help," he repeated. He turned and stared at me.

I shrugged. "Looks like Angie is coming with us," I said.

Ezra threw his hands in the air. He looked at Bear, who only shrugged. "I give up," he mumbled. "Never thought I'd see the day when I take a woman into an Indian village." He walked up the slope a little farther and spread out his bedroll, still mumbling to himself.

I came awake at sunup, rolling out of my blankets and squinting at the glare of the morning sun off the river. I smelled coffee and bacon, in that order, and when I got to the fire, I could see some of the biscuits Angie had promised. I must have slept later than I thought. I looked over to see Ezra pulling two axes and two large jackknives out of his pack.

He pointed at the ground. "Gave 'em knives last time. Mebbe they'll like these here gadget knives better."

We set out for the village right after breakfast. Angie was carrying a small pack with her. I offered to help, but she shook her head.

"It's not heavy," she said.

I wanted to ask what was in the pack, but she had a downright mysterious air about her, and I didn't think she would tell me.

We reached the camp, and the same bunch of braves came down to the river we'd seen last time, except the chief was with them this time. Ezra parlayed with them for a while, and they pointed at two canoes they had for us. I heaved a sigh of relief. Now, it was just gonna be a matter of how much we had to pay.

Ezra laid out the axes, and they nodded, but kept looking at him. They were wise now to his trick of holding something out to seal the deal. After a while, he brought out the jackknives. They perked up when they saw those, but there was still a lot of jawin' going back and forth, and it didn't look like we had a deal yet.

Ezra waved his arms in the air and carried on, but they

weren't giving in. They crossed their arms, then the chief and a couple others started to walk away.

"I can help," Angie announced. She walked over and pulled a deerskin dress out of her bag. It was decorated with beads around the collar and down the sides, with fringe at the bottom. She laid it over the axes and knives.

Three of the braves commenced to shoving each other back and forth. Then the chief barked something, walked over, and took the dress. He nodded at Angie, then Ezra, then walked away with the dress. The other braves took the axes and knives, pointed at the two canoes, then left.

"Well, that was kinda...helpful," Ezra mumbled.

"He means thank you," I explained.

Angie gave him her best smile. "You're welcome," she said. Ezra growled under his breath and walked down to the canoes. That Ezra, he was lacking in what Sherry would have called the social graces.

Angie followed. "We need to balance out the weight, so I think I should share a canoe with Bear," she announced. She pushed out one canoe, climbed into the bow, and picked up a paddle.

"That won't work," I said flatly.

Angie leaned over, put the paddle in the water, and took a practice stroke. "I don't know why not," she announced.

Bear climbed into the stern of the canoe, and the bow came a foot out of the water. Angie's paddle wasn't even in the water anymore. She had to lean over the side just to reach the river.

Ezra was looking the other way and had his hand over his mouth, but I could tell by the way his shoulders shook that he was having himself a belly laugh. Bear, he had a poker face. He said nuthin' and looked straight ahead. Me, I stared at my shoes and did my very best not to laugh. Can't say I was altogether successful, though.

Angie climbed out of the canoe, walked over and planted herself in front of me. She reached out with both hands to tilt my face back and look me in the eye.

"You're enjoying this, aren't you?" She wasn't laughing, but I could see the laughter in those eyes.

"Well...maybe a little bit," I agreed.

"A lot," she corrected. "A whole lot." She walked over and climbed into the bow of the other canoe. I took the stern of that one, and Ezra waded in to take her place at the bow of Bear's canoe. We paddled back to the raft, loaded up the canoes, and started for the Klondike.

————

Routine settled in pretty fast once we got back on the Klondike River. The snow and ice were a lot lower on the peaks the farther north we went, and there were some chunks of ice in the river now and again. Makes a person pretty careful passing through those rapids. The sprays of water coming over the gunwales of the canoes were bad enough. Nobody had a hankerin' to take a bath in that river.

We took to talking over a small fire in the evenings after we had some food and were wrapped up in blankets for the night. One night, braced up against a log on the shore, we asked each other what we wanted to do if we struck it big. I could see right away, some of us had thought about it more than others.

Ezra grinned from ear to ear, put his hands behind his head, and stretched back. "I'll go to Californy," he informed us. "San Fran, that's where I'll go. Buy me a big house with runnin' maids an' runnin' water. Folks will jump to serve me dinner when I walk in a rest-too-rant." His voice trailed off, and he stared at the river.

Bear just shrugged. "Dunno, but I want a nice house and I don't wanna worry about nothing. Not how to get some food or where to sleep. I just want to not have to worry about takin' care of myself. I like helpin' at the café and saloon," he added.

It was my turn. "I want to stay in Skagway, I think. Grow with the town. I'll have my saloon and maybe another one besides that. Help out with things around the town." I realized all of a sudden that maybe I needed to think it out and make some better plans. What I'd said didn't seem like a lot.

Angie patted my knee. "You'll be mayor or something, just watch." I started to protest, but she laid her finger across my lips. "Just wait, Luke. You can do a lot more than you think you can. Just wait and see."

I stopped protesting and asked her what she wanted to do. "I'll have two businesses—the café and the horses packing things up White Pass. The horse business won't last very long. They'll put in trains out here, I'm sure of it. I've got another idea, too, but I want to think about it longer before I say anything."

She lapsed into silence and snuggled up against me. I wasn't complaining. I remembered I'd seen her writing in a little book sometimes at night. I was guessing it was a diary. Maybe she was writing down her plans in the book.

———

After three weeks, we paddled up Rabbit Creek, except now folks called it Bonanza Creek. We went past the claim where we'd had trouble with Jed Harman and Major Howland. Harman was still there, but he was by himself now. It didn't look like he'd gotten himself a new partner. We paddled past, and he saw me, but just looked down at the ground and walked away. Maybe, I thought, he'd had the fight knocked out of him. That suited me just fine.

We turned up El Dorado Creek, and to my relief, our claim stakes were still there in the ground. There were a couple of guys on a claim down the creek a little, but El Dorado hadn't filled up yet and nobody had jumped our claim. That's all we could ask.

We unloaded our gear and built a little lean-to against the wall of the cliff behind us. Just something to shelter us from that cold rain and give us a little comfort at night. After a day of setting up, we were ready to get to it.

CHAPTER 15

FINDING COLOR

Angie, along with the others, settled into a routine pretty quickly once the camp was set up. She took a turn at panning in the creek, hauling up the gravel and nuggets from the ice-cold water and carrying them to the rocker. The weight of the loaded pans and the frigid water told her pretty quickly she would be of more use doing something else. Ezra took an occasional turn at the panning, but they all decided pretty quickly it was best left to Bear and Luke.

They kept one fire, often two fires, burning at all times. The fires served to warm up the ground along the bank, where they could dig up some good color after the ground thawed. They also needed the fire to warm Luke and Bear after they had been in the water for several minutes. Frostbite was a real possibility in this weather after being in the water, so Luke and Bear warmed themselves at the fire often.

Angie's main job became running the panned samples through the rocker and cleaning out the best nuggets afterward. Luke and Ezra had emphasized how good the ore was here, and they didn't want to carry weight that didn't have a good payoff. They had discussed how they were going to get the ore to Dawson City when they were ready to pull out, but hadn't given it a lot of thought. First, they had to get the gold out of the creek and out of the ground. Getting it to Dawson was another problem for another day. It wasn't that far to travel to town.

Besides running the rocker, she helped Ezra dig on the bank from time to time, giving him a rest when he tired. She also tended the fires at night. They had to be kept going if the ground was going to be soft enough to dig. All took turns collecting enough firewood. And, of course, the fire was needed for meals. She had been unanimously elected as the cook. She didn't mind—she was getting to do what she most wanted to do by coming on this trip, and it could help her reach a dream.

The first few days were too busy to add any thoughts to her diary. She kept it to remind herself why she was doing this. She needed it to endure the hardships of this wild land and keep going. After dinner on the third night, she picked up the diary, sat back from the fire a little bit, and began writing.

The trip up was harder than I had imagined. I knew about the distance and the rafting/canoeing. The water and cold were more than I expected. Still worth it, though. This gives me what I've dreamed of since I came to Skagway. William Moore told me the town would grow and give us all opportunities. I just need a stake to make it happen.

Luke has been watching out for me. He is a special man, and I can't let him down. Can't let any of them down. I have to do my share, even when I'm so tired from watching those fires at night. Just a few weeks of this and we can go home, I hope.

I haven't told anyone what I want to do after this trip. Maybe I'll tell Luke in a few more days. I just don't want anyone to think I'm some crazy dreamer. The café is just a start for me. When the town grows, I want to open a hotel. A luxury hotel. I can move the café to make it a restaurant in the hotel. Maybe I can pay William to build the hotel for me if we make enough money on this trip.

I saw something like what I want in Seattle before I came to Alaska. Couldn't afford to stay there at the time, but I liked it. Something like that hotel in Seattle, I think.

The hotel should have a nice bar. Not the rough saloons with all the spittoons and the swearing, or the rough and ready crowd you can always find in those places.

A classy bar in an elegant hotel. I don't want to scare Luke off with my ideas on that. Just need to keep doing my job here and see how this works out.

Got to sleep now. Those fires die out so fast.

It was becoming a habit to come awake every two or three hours now to tend the fires. She was insisting that if somebody else woke up and the fires were down, they should wake her up to do the job. She hoped she could get back to regular sleep when she got home. Three times during the night she built them back up, then she was up for the day to start on breakfast. A mid-day nap every day was starting to make sense here.

———

I already knew to expect colder water when I went panning. The trip up on the Yukon River had taught me that. The thing I had going for me this time—I knew how rich that ore was. Two or three trips out to get a panful of gravel and ore off the bottom was all I could do at one time. I'd been warned by William Moore and some others that if your toes froze out there it was a big worry.

I'd warned Bear about it, and we never made more than three trips out in the creek for panning without coming up on the shore and warming our feet by the fire. Even with the great boots Angie had gotten for me, I wasn't going to push it any farther. Bear had a good pair of boots, too, but I wouldn't let him make more than three trips without warming for about twenty minutes. Even so, we were piling up some fine-looking nuggets.

Ezra was working on the digging at the shore. It suited him better than the water. He like to moan about getting old, and we gave him a hard time, but I know that water was hard on him. It was some hard digging on the bank, too, but he kept at it, digging up the gravel and knocking the mud off with his shovel. He and Angie took turns hauling water up from the creek and pouring it over the gravel when it went in the rocker. The nuggets at the bottom afterward looked every bit as good as the ones from the creek. Maybe even better.

It was a help that not many people had come down this way to stake claims on El Dorado Creek. If we had more neighbors, we might have to spend half our time guarding our diggings. A man and his boy staked out the spot next to us after a few days. The father was named Stan and his boy, maybe eighteen, was Joe. They were good neighbors and hard workers. We started to watch out for each other, especially at night.

The more our pile of nuggets grew, the more nervous I got. There wasn't much place to hide it around the camp. There must be an easier way, I thought, than digging a hole in the ground the way we'd done last summer with our poorer grade ore. I took one afternoon off to scout back along the woods next to the creek and the rock faces on the hills back behind us and toward the north. Finally, I took an axe and ripped out a hole into the rock on the hill at our backs, digging it out about five or six feet high. I found a natural crack in the rock and dug it back about twelve feet altogether.

I came back to the camp and explained what I had done. Then Ezra and I picked up the bags of ore we had, carried them to the hole in the rock face, and rolled a boulder in front of the opening when we were done. We stood back and looked at our hiding spot, and we agreed it was better than piling up nuggets around the camp. That was just an invitation for thieves.

One night, after we had been in camp for about a week, I was sleeping like a dead man when Angie shook me awake. I fought the cobwebs out of my head and focused on her. She leaned down and whispered in my ear.

"Next door," she said. "There's somebody over at Stan and Joe's camp. I think they're being robbed!"

I could hear voices coming from that direction now. They alternated between somebody giving harsh commands, and the pleading sound of Stan's voice. I rolled out and pulled on my boots, then slung my holster around my hips. Angie picked up her double-barreled shotgun and followed behind me.

When we got closer, I could see by the light from the half-moon that Stan and Joe were on their knees, hands over their heads. Two men were in their camp. One was holding a rifle on them while the other was scooping ore and nuggets onto a piece of canvas. There was no raft or canoe in the water, and I couldn't see any horses. They must have sneaked along the creek bank.

I stepped out into the campsite while Angie worked her way around to flank them. I walked closer and they both saw me at the same time. The one scooping the ore stood slowly while the other one swung toward me with the rifle. The sound of Angie cocking both barrels on the shotgun stopped him cold.

"Well now," I said conversationally. "I believe you boys could hear both of those barrels bein' cocked. That's one barrel for each of you, the way I count it. I just aim to clean up around the edges with my Colt. Your choice, boys. You can drop that rifle, walk away and never come back. Otherwise, it's just too hard to do any diggin' around here for your graves. I expect we'll just have to float your bodies down the creek."

The one with the rifle dropped his weapon and raised his

hands in the air. The other one unbuckled his holster and let it fall. They both turned slowly to face me.

"Good choice," I told them. I pointed toward the creek bank behind them. "Just walk on out. If I see you here again, I won't be stopping to talk with you boys. I'll be shooting."

They turned and walked away, but stopped at the edge of the claim. One turned to face me. "What about our guns?" he asked nervously. "We don't have no protection now."

"I'll make sure your guns get a good home," I said. "It seems to me folks need protection from you, not the other way around. Keep walking or I'll take your boots next."

They moved away, cursing as they went, but they kept walking. I went over to pick up the rifle and the pistol, then carried them over to Stan and Joe. I handed them the weapons.

"I can give you some ammunition for both of these," I told Stan. "It's a Winchester and a Colt. I've got both. I'd keep them handy, if I were you."

Stan looked at the guns doubtfully. "I know how to use 'em," he said slowly. "Just never much cared to. The boy..." He looked at Joe, then looked away. "I've taught him how to shoot, but he's never used a gun." He stared off at the creek.

I set them both down at his feet. "Just think about it," I urged him. "Maybe you won't ever have to use them. Maybe just having them around will be enough to move the robbers on down the line."

Stan nodded in agreement and picked up the guns. They thanked us and offered to keep the fires going for the rest of the night. Stan glanced over at Joe. "I don't expect we'll be sleepin' for the rest of the night anyway," he told us.

We walked back to our camp, and I rolled up in my blankets. I heard the noise of something being dragged and looked up to see Angie pulling her blankets up next to mine. She laid down and snuggled up against me. A slow grin spread across my face. We were lying out on hard, half-frozen ground in the middle of nowhere, but this was down-right pleasant.

———

We were restless the next day, looking over our shoulders and checking with the neighbors, wondering if the robbers were coming back. Nobody talked about it much, and we had another good day mining, but I knew it was on every-body's mind how we were going to get home with our gold. We had already decided that Ezra and Bear would take a steamship to Seattle from St. Michael to sell it, but now we were worried about getting it to the ship.

We had a pow-wow after dinner. Nobody felt good about stacking it up in the hideout, and it would take about ten or twelve trips in a canoe to Dawson once we figured to be done with the mining. I poked the fire and looked upstream toward Dawson.

"They're short canoe trips," I told them. "Really short. The problem is, we'd have to divide up and take it up there a little at a time while two of us stayed back with what we've got. And what would we do with the ore we take up there while we come back for more?"

"How far would it be to walk it?" Angie asked.

I looked over at Ezra, who thought it over for a second. "T'aint but mebbe ten or twelve miles 'twixt here and there," he said. "Just through some trees and these round-shoul-dered hills around here. Break yore back carryin' it, though. Unless..."

"Mules," Angie broke in. "Can we get a couple of pack mules in Dawson and just rent them for a day or two? We could stay together and get all of our gold out at once."

We looked at each, and I could tell we all liked the idea.

I looked over at Ezra again. "Did you see any mules when we were there before? Last summer, I mean?"

Ezra shook his head slowly and poked at the fire with a stick. He was rewarded with a shower of sparks and dodged out of the way. "Didn't see no mules, but I weren't lookin' for any, neither. We could go up and have a look-see."

The plan fell into place pretty fast after that. Ezra and I would take a canoe up to Dawson and check with Elmer at the trading post. Maybe he knew where we could get a couple mules for a day or two. We decided to take about as much ore with us as we had sold to Elmer last time. Maybe he could give us a good price again. It would give us more cash and make less we'd have to haul out of here in another couple of weeks. No sense wasting time, we decided. Ezra and I would go tomorrow. Bear and Angie could watch things at camp.

—————

Angie tossed in her blankets after the others had fallen asleep. They had planned and worked so hard to get here and do the mining, and it had gone really well. Funny that now the biggest problem might be in getting home safely with their money. Finally, she tossed off the blankets, picked up her diary and settled down to write.

> *Just another two weeks and we could be on a ship, going up the Yukon River on our way home! We had to help the neighbors in the next camp over last night, though. Robbers came around. Don't know if those guys are gone for good. What if there are more like them, better armed, coming for our money before we leave?*
>
> *Luke and Ezra are going to Dawson tomorrow to sell some of our panned ore and to see about getting mules. I'm a little worried about that. I remember that guy Cap Light when his boys were going to rob the café. Light is dangerous, I think. He wasn't scared of Luke, he just didn't like his chances that night. He might be up here somewhere.*
>
> *They might run into him around here before long.*
>
> *I don't want to get anybody else worried, so I think I won't say anything. I'm really looking forward to getting home.*

First, I want to see Dawson. They say there is quite a little town popping up there. Probably a little rough, but Skagway is a little rough, too.

I'm going to get Luke to take me into one of those dance halls.

I'll bet that will embarrass him. Can't wait.

Sleep had finally come. When she awoke, the other three were all moving around the camp. Angie scrambled out of the blankets and hurried to fry some bacon to go with the coffee she had going and biscuits she baked. She looked up to see Ezra and Luke carrying a load of the ore to the canoe. That was what they hoped to sell today.

They all lingered a little over breakfast. Angie and Bear decided they wouldn't do any digging on the bank today. Bear would pan the river, and Angie would work the rocker. When Luke and Ezra stood to go, she pushed a list of supplies into Luke's hand, hoping he could find them in Dawson. Luke scanned the list, nodded, and put it in his pocket. She walked to the river with him, then reached up to put her hands on his shoulders.

"You'll be careful, right?" She moved her hands to his face and held his gaze. "If there are crooks and robbers around here, there will be more in a boom town like Dawson. There're more and more people coming every day."

"I'll be careful," Luke agreed. "I'll..."

His words were cut off when Angie pulled his face down to hers and gave him a lingering kiss. Luke broke into a grin and re-settled his hat on his head.

"I'll be careful and we'll be back in no time. We're going to line us up some mules and bring this thing home, you'll see." He looked over at Ezra. "You gonna stand around and harrumph all day, or are you ready to go to town?" He winked at Angie and climbed into the canoe. In a minute, they had paddled out of sight around the corner.

CHAPTER 16

TROUBLE ON THE HOME FRONT

William Moore was a veteran of gold strikes and gold rush towns, and Skagway was worrying him. With the warming weather had come a rush of prospectors, giddy about striking it rich in the Klondike. That wasn't unexpected. Moore was ready for them. The wharf was almost built, and the lumber mill was churning out boards for the surge in building demands. There were a lot of fools trying to rush over White Pass, and they weren't prepared, but the Northwest Mounted Police was establishing checkpoints and requirements. That would settle things down soon. Moore really had no plans to go up the Klondike, anyway.

The problem was with a band of young toughs who had showed up and asked for work as dockhands. There was plenty of work available, working on a second wharf and unloading ships. Moore, though, had turned down most of them for jobs and had fired a couple others soon after hiring when it became obvious they knew nothing about working at the docks. Several of them seemed to know each other, and the ringleader was a big redhead named Callaghan. Several fights had broken out at the wharf and along the main road in Skagway, and Callaghan was usually at the center of things.

Moore had several men who worked for him who knew

how to take care of themselves with their fists, and they were loyal to Moore. So far, nobody had tried to take anything from him. His men kept an eye on Angie's café as well, and business seemed to be fine over there. Luke Spencer had closed down this saloon and stored the whiskey and beer in Moore's warehouse while he was away. Somebody had broken into the saloon the other night, but there wasn't anything there to take. Moore himself had boarded the place up afterward.

The name of Black Jack Adams had surfaced the other day. Moore knew of Adam's reputation in the Denver area, and could only hope the man didn't show up here. Adams had a name for taking over towns by setting up crooked gambling, saloons, and pretty much anything else that was illegal and preyed on men's vices. Moore also knew that Adams fancied himself a gunfighter. Moore didn't know how good Adams was with a gun, but that worried him the most.

There wasn't really any law in Skagway, or in most of Alaska, for that matter. The few deputies available to the territory were spread way too thin. So far, the citizens in Skagway had handled things themselves. Black Jack Adams could change that in a hurry. Gun hands were very few and far between up here. Luke Spencer had taken down a would-be gunfighter a few weeks ago. That was the only thing he had seen since arriving in Skagway. Moore wasn't sure how well Spencer would stack up against Adams.

Moore sat down on a bench to think a few things over. He would concentrate his men on protecting the lumber mill and Angie's café. Moore had begun building a house up in the hills and out of town a bit. He would concentrate on protecting that, too. He didn't want to give up any of his properties without a fight, but he knew from experience it was time to decide on priorities. He had to protect what was most important.

It was two days later, while Moore was strolling down Main Street, as they were starting to call it, when he saw a man dressed like a dandy, headed in his direction. Moore stopped and took in the tall black hat and topcoat, along with a gold-headed cane. He knew immediately this must be Black Jack Adams.

Moore stayed where he was, noting that Callaghan and a couple of other thugs were trailing along behind Adams. Glancing back, it relieved him to see a few of his workers moving from the wharf toward them. Moore watched Adams walk up, but he said nothing, waiting for Black Jack to start the conversation.

"I hear," Adams said, "that you're the man to see about getting vacant lots along here." He lifted a hand to point out the empty lots along Main Street. "That right?"

Moore nodded briefly. "That's right. I own most of the lots on Main Street that haven't been built on yet. I can talk to you about prices."

Adams's lips curled in a sneer. "I think your prices are too high."

Moore stared at him. "We haven't even talked about a price. How do you know I'm charging too much?"

Adams laughed. There was no humor in his eyes or his voice. "I didn't say anything about paying, now did I? My boys and I," he said, looking back at Callaghan and his pals, "can make it pleasant or unpleasant for you to do business around here. A few free lots would make us want to make things pleasant for you."

Moore locked eyes with him. "They might be for sale to you, or I might not want to sell. Nothing is for free."

An uncomfortable silence developed. Moore stood his ground while Callaghan and his thugs fanned out and moved forward. His workers were arriving from the wharf now, several of them carrying hammers and other tools. More workers were coming from the lumber mill.

Black Jack watched the workers as they formed up behind Moore. Clearly, Callaghan and his crowd were outnumbered now. Adams shrugged and turned away.

"Maybe we'll talk about this again," he hissed. Callaghan and the others fell in behind him as he walked away.

Moore watched them move off, feeling the adrenaline draining out of him. He turned to thank his workers, then sat back down on the bench. Things were shaping up for a fight, and he wasn't a young man anymore. He wondered when Luke Spencer would be back. He hoped he could hang on until then.

————

My brain was going in a thousand different directions. The miles to Dawson seemed to zip past us in a heartbeat. The kiss from Angie stayed with me all the way. I knew it was time to make some plans about the two of us when we got home. I managed to ignore Ezra's cracks about "that fool grin on my face" most of the way up there. As we pulled ashore at Dawson, I took a minute to remind myself of what we'd come here to do.

Ezra and I grabbed the two bags with the ore we had brought with us for sale. We scrambled up the slope to the edge of town and stopped and stared. The place must have been twice the size it had been last summer. The sound of hammers and saws filled the air, and there were buildings going up everywhere. The blast of a ship's whistle sounded, and we watched a riverboat unloading crates of goods. Miners poured down the gangways.

Ezra nudged me in the ribs and pointed at the muddy trail winding through the center of the town. A man was leading three mules down the street. He turned into the entrance to a new livery stable, and the mules followed, braying and complaining all the way.

We turned back and looked at all the building going on. Every other structure going up had a hand-carved sign in front, promising that either a saloon or a dance hall would open soon. Here and there, we saw a café or boarding house.

Ezra shook his head back and forth slowly. "Can't hardly keep a gold strike a secret," he drawled.

"Not hardly," I agreed. We set off in search of the trading post and our friend Elmer. We heard his booming voice almost as soon as we saw the trading post.

"Get in here, boys!" he shouted at full volume. He stood in front of his store, waving his arms up and down just in case we couldn't hear him bellowing at us.

We turned and moved toward the trading post. Elmer's eyes lit up when he saw the bags we were carrying. He had the good sense to lower his voice to a dull roar as he clapped us on the back. "Got some more color, do ya? I'll bet it's as good as last year's. Get yoreselves on in there and we'll talk."

Mabel made a fuss over us and left, saying something about going to get us some beer. Buck appeared from the back, grinning good-naturedly and taking the bags from us once again like he was lifting a feather. He disappeared as quickly as he'd come, carrying the bags out to the furnace behind the trading post.

Elmer sat us down, telling us he'd pay just like he had last summer. Buck would let us know tomorrow how much we'd brought. We dodged the question a little when Elmer asked about bringing more. I told him we planned on taking the rest to Seattle.

Elmer's smile dropped off a little, but he nodded his head. "Sure. You kin get a bit better price there," he agreed. Mabel appeared with a pitcher of beer and some glasses, and we hoisted the glasses while Elmer filled us in on Dawson and the Klondike. He told us the town has already grown to five thousand people and expected fifteen or twenty thousand by next summer.

We stared at him. Ezra even left off drinking beer for a minute there.

"Twenty thousand?" I couldn't even picture that.

Elmer nodded his head vigorously. "Yup. We've got five thousand right now, what with the folks pitchin' tents out there in the woods and such. They're pourin' in on those riverboats every day. You boys need to git your claim mined and get out before the craziness sets in. Folks gettin' rowdy around here. Word is Wyatt Earp was coming up here, but he done fell and busted his hip, getting' off a streetcar down in Frisco. Mebbe he'll come later. Don't think he'll do no sheriffin', though. He likes the card games, he does."

Now we were staring at Elmer like he'd lost his mind. He kept nodding his head. "It's true," he yelled. "You can ask anybody. You hang around much longer, you'll probly see him yoreself."

We finally got around to the subject of pack mules. "We saw a guy taking some mules into a livery stable back that way," I said, pointing back down the street. "Does anybody rent out a couple of mules for a couple days, or do they just have the mules for themselves?"

Elmer finished off the beer while he thought that one over. "Yup, you probly can, down there to the livery. Cost you, though. Might cost fifteen dollars a day for a mule."

Ezra choked on the last of his beer. "Fifteen dollars! For each mule? I could buy a mule for a hunnerd!"

Elmer shook his head. "Not around here, you couldn't. You'd be lucky to buy one for one fifty. Mebbe two hunnerd. Whaddya want to buy one for, anyhow? You need 'em for mebbe a couple days. Just pay the fifteen dollars and haul yore gold outta her before this place gets even crazier."

Ezra shook his head stubbornly.

"You ain't never heard of Belinda Mulroney have ya?" Elmer leaned in and stared at Ezra. "Callin' herself the Queen of the Klondike, she is. Come in here with some clothes and hot water bottles. Sells the water bottles for twenny dollars apiece." He waved his arm at the town. "Go and find her if you don't believe me."

We left the trading post with the understanding that we would come back tomorrow, maybe around noon, and find out what Elmer would give us for the gold. Then we left to find some dinner. Ezra found a saloon, and we bellied up to the bar in there for a while. It was when we were leaving the saloon that I got a nasty shock. I stopped in my tracks, and Ezra ran into the back of me.

"What's the matter with you?" he spluttered. "You seen a ghost or somethin'?"

"Worse," I said, staring down the street. "I think I saw Cap Light."

They had stopped mining along the bank of the creek, and that suited Angie just fine. With just Bear and herself on the claim, while Luke and Ezra were in Dawson, they stuck to panning the creek, with Bear doing the panning and Angie working the rocker. That meant they didn't have to keep the fires going at night, which was the best part. She was getting more sleep for the first time since they had come to the Klondike.

It was early evening, and they had stopped for the day. Bear had taken the ore he'd panned today to put it in the hideout Luke had dug in the face of the rock wall behind them. Angie kept a shotgun close to her and was glad to see that Stan and Joe, on the claim next door, were keeping a rifle handy now. They watched out for each other, especially since Luke and Ezra had left. There were a lot of keen-eyed, hard faces paddling past on the creek these days, taking long looks on the way past.

Stan and Joe came over to join them for dinner when Bear returned. Angie had been inviting them most nights, and they did their share, bringing food to the fire. Joe had actually shot a deer two days ago, so the fresh meat was welcome. When dinner was over and the neighbors had returned to their claim, Angie grabbed her diary and leaned back against a log while she jotted down her thoughts.

We have been here for more than three weeks now, and I'm ready to go home to Skagway. I'm glad I came, but I won't do this again. The cold and lack of sleep are dragging me down now. I'm not letting on to the others, though. I'm still doing my share.

Luke and Ezra took some ore with them to sell. I don't know how much we have left in the hideout, but it must be hundreds of pounds of nuggets and ore. Do we have ten thousand dollars? I've never seen that much money.

My share of that would be enough, I'm sure, to start a hotel. Maybe Luke would pitch in and be partners with me.

I hope they'll be back by tomorrow or the next day, and I hope they have mules with them to take us to Dawson and the riverboats. There are more men pouring in here every day. Some of them look like miners and the rest look like highwaymen and robbers.

However much we have, I think it's time to go. Maybe tomorrow.

————

We found a boarding house in one of the new buildings that was popping up all over Dawson. I got a decent night's sleep, and we found some breakfast in a café. Ezra kept telling me I was just seeing shadows, but I was pretty sure I had seen Cap Light. The more I thought about it, the more sense it made for him to be here in Dawson. He wasn't going to do any mining. Why not wait in Dawson and take the money here? Most of the money was coming through the town.

We moved down to the livery stable to find out about mules. The owner, a man who looked to be about a hundred years old, looked us up and down pretty sharp when we asked about renting a couple of mules for two days. He leaned over and spit, then rubbed his chin.

"Two days, huh? How much do you wanna carry on 'em? They can't do more than about one hunnerd fifty pounds. I won't have 'em breaking down. You coming from Bonanza Creek?"

"Two days," I said. "If they can carry one hundred fifty pounds, that'll work. They won't have to carry more than that. How much for two days?" I totally ignored the question about coming from the Klondike. Elmer's prediction about the price was exactly right.

"Fifteen dollars a day for each mule," he drawled. None of Ezra's whining and moaning changed his mind. "Fifteen, take it or leave it. You boys don't wanna pay it, somebody else will. Or else I'll sell 'em in another day or two. Don't make me no never mind. Fifteen." He leaned over and spit again, ignoring Ezra's glares.

"Done," I said. "Sixty dollars for two animals for two days." I reached into my pocket for some money. "I'll give you half now, an' the other half when we come back for 'em in a couple hours." He took the money, shoved it in his pocket and walked away.

"Not all of them robbers hold guns on a man," Ezra moaned as we headed for the trading post. "That 'un there just took about sixty dollars from us and didn't never pull a gun." He kept grousing all the way over to the trading post. Me, I just ignored him. I was used to it.

"Hey Elmer," I called as we opened the door and stepped into the trading post. I let my eyes adjust to the gloom inside, and pulled up short, right inside the door. Ezra had stopped behind me to finish cussing before he came inside.

There were two men inside the room with Elmer and his wife. One of them was tying Elmer into a chair. The man's rifle was propped up against a table, just out of his reach. Elmer had a gag stuffed into his mouth. The other man had Mabel on her knees beside the safe they kept in the corner of the room. That second man held a pistol and pointed across the room at Elmer's head.

"Open the safe, old lady, an' we'll all be good. If'n you don't open the safe, I'll put a brand-new tunnel through this old man's head."

When I stepped into the room, he swung the gun to cover me. Just then, the handle to the back door turned, and all eyes swung to the back door.

CHAPTER 17

GETTING OUT

Things were happening all around me now, and I know everything happened in a few seconds, but things were happening in my mind really slowly, like everybody was stuck in sand. The back door started to open, and Buck put his head through door, then pulled it back out. The guy who was tying up Elmer stood and lunged toward his gun. The one with the pistol on me turned his head to look at the back door, and the movement pulled his gun out of line just a little.

I stepped to the side and dropped into a crouch, palming my Colt as I did. I can still remember how big his eyes got when he turned back and saw my gun coming level. He touched off a shot that went wide of me, then my gun roared, and he staggered back. He clutched at this chest with one hand and tried to bring his gun back around with the other. I fired again, and he staggered back against the wall, then slid down slowly.

The other robber had frozen when the shooting started, then went for his rifle again. Buck leaped through the back door faster than I'd have thought a man that big can move. When the robber grabbed his rifle, Buck grabbed the guy's shoulder, spun him around and smashed him on the jaw with one of those giant fists of his. The robber landed on the floor with a loud *thunking* noise when his head hit the boards.

Behind me, Ezra was lying flat on the ground. All the excitement had set off a fresh round of cussin' with him. He stood up slowly and checked himself over. He straightened up with a couple words I don't think I'd ever heard. I stared at him.

"I can't believe your mama let you go around talking like that," I told him. "I might have just learned a couple new words, but I don't expect I'm gonna be using them."

"Just you wait," Ezra growled. "They might come in handy sometime." He dusted himself off and went over to untie Elmer while Buck helped his mother up and into a chair.

I went over to look at the robbers. The one I'd shot wasn't going to be getting up. I'd hit him in the middle of the chest with the first shot, then through the heart with the second one. I moved over to look at the second. Ezra came over to stand beside me.

"Is that'n alive?" he asked.

"I can see his chest moving up and down," I told him. "I expect he's still alive."

Ezra grabbed one arm while I grabbed the other, and we dragged him out of the trading post and dumped him on the ground.

Ezra prodded him with his foot and shook his head. "He's gonna have a powerful headache when he comes to," Ezra observed. "I don't believe I'd want that boy Buck to punch me on the jaw like that."

We went back inside and dragged the corpse out, leaving it beside the unconscious man. When I straightened and turned, Cap Light was standing there, his arms folded across his chest. He walked slowly toward us, not moving his arms. They stayed crossed over his chest. He turned the corpse over and studied the bullet holes.

"I guess it was a fair fight?" he asked.

"It was," I answered.

Cap Light nodded. "I told those boys not to try you," he said. He backed away a bit and studied my face. His arms still hadn't moved.

"There was a man down Colorado way, mebbe twenty years ago," he said, still studying my face. "I guess his name was Spencer, but folks mostly called him Spence. He was lightnin' fast with his pistol."

"Clay Spencer is my father," I said slowly. "Yes, mostly folks called him Spence, and he lived in Colorado back then. He could use his gun when he needed to. I learned from him."

Light walked over to his horse and mounted up. "I'm forty-eight years old," he said to me. "I've lived this long because I know when to reach for my gun and when to leave it in my holster. I'll not be calling you out, Spencer. Maybe Colorado sounds good to me right about now. Creek's too cold to wade around in, anyhow."

He reined his horse around, then turned back. "Black Jack Adams don't like you much. More than that, he's scared of you." He leaned over and spit on the ground. "He's mighty good with his gun, and he's poison mean. I know, because he's married to my sister. That's something to think about, Spencer." He tipped his hat then and rode away.

We walked back inside the trading post and found Mabel already washing down the walls and floor. Elmer hoisted a shotgun onto the counter and checked the barrels.

"I'll be keeping this handier from now on," he said grimly. He looked and waved us in. "You boys come in here and set. I've already sent Buck for some beer. I owe you boys." He sat down next to us, shaking his head.

"Who were those guys?" I asked, pointing out the door.

"Never seen either of 'em before." We could tell Elmer was feeling better because he was almost as loud as usual. "Lots of new crooks and highwaymen washing up into town." He shook his head again and stared out the door. "Is that one Buck hit gonna' live?"

"I expect he will," I answered. "I don't believe he'll be

eatin' anything except scrambled eggs for a while, though. And he'll want to count his teeth. I don't think he's got a full set anymore. You got a dentist in this town?"

Elmer snorted loudly. "We got one, but you don't wanna go see him unless you've got some powerful hurtin' going on in your mouth." He stopped and looked out the door. "Well, maybe he'll want to go," he allowed.

Buck came in the door with a pitcher of beer, and Elmer pulled a chair over for his son. "Tell 'em the good news, boy," he boomed. "That lot you brought in yesterday is almost as good as you brung last year, and there was more of it." Buck nodded his head vigorously.

"Twelve hunnerd dollars," Elmer barked.

I guess Elmer couldn't wait for Buck to give us the news. Buck was a man of few words, anyway. Swung a mean right hand, but had few words.

Ezra let out a holler and downed his glass of beer in two long gulps. He wiped off his chin and reached for the pitcher again. "There's more where that come from," he crowed. He poured another glass, and I took the pitcher away from him. I didn't need to be dealing with Ezra after a whole pitcher of beer plus two mules on the way home.

We finished the beer and Elmer paid us in twenty-dollar gold pieces. I counted out fifteen of them and held them out to Ezra, but he took only two and pushed the rest back at me. "You keep 'em for me," he said. "I'll spend it in saloons in a week's time and won't have nothin' to show. You hang on to it and help me think of what I should do with it."

We had reached the door, on our way to get the mules, when I heard the low rumble of Buck's voice.

"You want some help haulin' that gold, Mr. Spencer? I could come and hep you bring it back as far as Dawson."

I turned around and looked at Buck, then at Elmer. "If your folks can spare you for a couple days, I'd be glad to have you help us, Buck."

"Sure, take Buck," Elmer bellowed. "He's 'most as good

as a mule, all by hisself. You'll have to feed him a couple times, is all. That'll cut into yore profits a little."

Buck packed a couple of things into a bag, grabbed a rifle, and walked over to the livery stable with us. Ezra took one more shot at talking the old man down on the price of mules, then finally gave up, stalking off down the road toward Bonanza Creek, muttering to himself. We were on our way back to the claim, and we would be there just long enough to pack up and come home.

———

We made the trip on foot back to our camp with the mules in a couple hours. The mules brayed and balked all the way, but Buck had brought along some hay, and when they really dug in and stalled us, Buck cut up an apple and bribed them with the apple. We left the animals about a mile away from our claim site. All that honking and braying would give away the fact that we were packing up and leaving.

When we reached our site, Bear was warming his feet and legs by the fire while Angie ran the rocker. We introduced Buck all around, then started packing things up. We gave Buck a good meal as promised, then hauled the ore back to the mules. Guessing at the weight, I put about one hundred fifty pounds on each mule, then split up packs of maybe fifty to sixty pounds for each of us. Well, Bear and Buck got the heaviest packs and Angie got the lightest. I was guessing we were up to more than five hundred pounds of ore.

There was still a question about the ore we'd left behind last summer, after we had taken the highest-grade stuff and left the rest in a niche in the cliff wall. I walked around to the place where we'd stashed it and rolled the boulder back.

I hefted it out of the rock and felt the weight of the bag in my hand. It was more than we could carry. I figured I could distribute no more than half of it to the packs I'd made for us. After what we'd just been through in Dawson, I didn't want to divide up the few people we had just to get a little more ore up the trail. So, I added what we could carry to our packs, then went around to find our neighbors, Stan and Joe. I brought them over and showed them what was left of last summer's ore.

"It's yours if you want it," I told them. "We want to get going and we can't carry it out in this trip. There's probably a few hundred dollars there. You might want to get going yourselves pretty soon. It's likely to get filled up and down-right rowdy around here before long."

Stan and Joe dragged it away in a blanket, then waved at us from their camp as we headed out. I didn't figure we would see them again, but I wished them well.

We set out for Dawson with Bear and Ezra in front, leading one mule, Buck following in the middle with the other mule, and Angie and me in the back. I had given Bear his money when we came into camp. I opened my pack and offered Angie her three hundred now. She only glanced at it and nodded.

"You hold on to it for me," she said. "I have a place to keep it when we get home." We walked in silence for a short way, then she looked back over at me. "What are you going to do with the money?"

I'd done a little thinking of that one. I needed to do some more, but at least I had a few ideas. "I'm gonna help William Moore building the wharf for Skagway," I answered. "It'll help the whole town to do that—not just me. That's the first thing. Then..." My voice trailed off a little. I wasn't so sure about the rest. "I can fix up the saloon however I want it, maybe open another one."

"I'm going to open a nice hotel with my money," Angie announced.

"A hotel?" I didn't think Angie could surprise me anymore, but now she'd done it again. "Where...how..."

She chuckled and linked her arm through mine. "In Skagway. I want to stay there. I'm not sure exactly where. William is building a big house just outside of town. Maybe he'll stick around in Skagway, maybe not. He seems like he's always ready to head for the latest gold strike somewhere. This one will play out one of these days, but I think Skagway will still be around. It's a natural harbor for people wanting to come to Alaska. Anyway, if William leaves, maybe I'll see if he wants to sell that big house. I could use that for a hotel. Or maybe I can pay him to build me a hotel in town."

"Wow," was all I had to say. She already had two businesses, with the café and the horses, and here she was planning another one. She was putting me to shame, no doubt about it. I stared down the trail, thinking about what else I could do with my money.

"Did you ever think about opening a classy bar in a nice hotel?" she asked. The question caught me by surprise, and I took a minute to wrap my head around it.

"In your hotel, you mean?" I asked.

"Right," she agreed. "The saloons are great for the miners and the guys that work on the docks, but the town and the whole territory are going to grow. This would be a nice place for people who are traveling. Someplace a woman could go and feel comfortable, too."

"So that would make us, uh..."

"Right, business partners." She laughed. "Wouldn't you like that?"

That was a simple answer. "I'd like that a lot," I said, surprised by how easy an answer that was. "I'll have to look sharp to keep up with you, though. You're always a couple jumps ahead of me, thinkin' things out."

She gave my arm a squeeze. "You're the best man I know," she said. "I don't want to be out in front of you. I like it a lot right here beside you."

I shook my head a little at my own good luck. The future was looking pretty bright. All we needed to do was to get home with this gold.

Elmer was out front to greet us when we came in. He helped us unload the mules, and we carried all the gold out to a corner of the room out back where the furnace was. "You can leave it here an' we'll help you watch it 'till you get it on the boat. Buck an' me, we'll help."

We returned the mules and checked on the riverboats headed up to St. Michael. We got a couple staterooms on one of them for the next day. We agreed there'd be two of us keeping an eye on that gold until we had it safely on the boat. Ezra volunteered to take the first shift, starting now, and Bear volunteered to stay with him.

"You two, you go get a nice dinner," Ezra urged. "If I go out there, my money will be gone in no time. Costs a dollar a dance in them dance halls," he moaned. He glanced over at Angie and turned a little red around the gills. "That's what they tell me, anyhow..." He stared at his feet and fidgeted for a while.

"A dollar a dance, huh?" Angie teased. "Well, I think you could still afford to go out and have several dances when we get back from dinner."

Ezra turned it up a couple notches on the red color in his face. I grabbed her hand and gave it a tug. "He doesn't need the encouragement," I advised. Ezra growled and mumbled some things I was pretty sure I didn't want to hear. We left, looking for a place to have a sit-down dinner in the booming town of Dawson.

The first order of business was a place for Angie to stay that night. There were actually a couple of new hotels opening for business. Neither of them looked like they were completely finished, but we found one with rooms open. We agreed it was an enormous improvement over the camping she'd done over the last few weeks.

Angie linked her arm through mine, and we walked down the street, not believing the businesses that had sprung up. There was a tent with Madam Riva inside. She promised to use a crystal ball to help us find gold deposits.

We stopped outside another tent with the name Trans-

Alaskan Gopher Company in big letters on a sign outside. There were cages filled with gophers near the tent flap at the front. A man hustled out to greet us.

"We can hep you get yore gold with no diggin' required!" he barked. He pointed at the gophers in the cages. "These here gophers are trained to dig through the gravel and mud an' such and dig up the gold nuggets!"

Angie and I looked at each other, burst out laughing, and kept walking down the street. "Imagine," she said. "We didn't need to break our backs digging through that frozen gravel and clay and mud after all. We could have bought a couple gophers to do the job!"

There were new restaurants in the town, too. We found one with checkered tablecloths on the tables. The owner, a guy named Al, greeted us at the door and took us to a table. I looked around in curiosity. The people in there were as mixed a group as you'd ever want to see. Some looked like miners, a couple looked like cowboys, and several of them looked like clerks or schoolteachers.

Al told us there were some of all the groups I'd mentioned, plus several others. "Not everybody is here to go mining," he told us. "Myself, I ran a restaurant in St. Louis. I got word of the strike up here and came up just a couple months ago. There're folks runnin' around this place with pockets full of nuggets and gold dust just looking for a place to spend it all."

He pointed to a set of scales in the corner. "I weigh the nuggets or gold dust they give me, and they can pay me by the number of ounces on the scale. They have to take my guess on the quality of the nuggets, though. Nobody argues much."

"What else are they spending their money on?" I asked.

Al shrugged. "Well, I don't throw away the newspapers they use to wrap the fish and bacon I buy," he told us.

I couldn't believe it. "You're not saying you can sell the newspapers, are you?"

Al nodded. "Some folks are so hungry for something to

read they buy the old newspapers, even if they have bacon grease on 'em or they smell fishy. If I've got a whole newspaper, I can sell it for ten dollars sometimes."

Angie and I exchanged looks and shook our heads. She reached across the table to take my hand. I looked around the room again. "How many of these people are here to mine the Klondike, do you think?"

Al looked around and shrugged. "Maybe half. The ones who know a trade or business can't miss for the next couple years around here. The folks who know nothing about mining and are out there looking for color aren't doing so good. I've seen a lot of them pack it up and head home already. Me, I'll stick around for a couple years, if I can stand the cold, come winter."

Al kept the food coming, and a guy came around to play the violin for us while we ate. I looked in his violin case, sitting at his feet while he played. There were various nuggets and coins in the case. I tossed in a couple of coins, and he played a couple songs for us while we had the great dinner Al served up for us. I wouldn't have expected any of this in a gold rush town like Dawson. I'd not seen anything like it, and I'd seen my share of gold rush towns.

We got to the riverboat early the next morning to get the two best rooms. We had some money in our pockets, and we all hankered to get spoiled a little on our way home. This boat did what the Mississippi riverboats had been doing for several years. The nicest rooms were all named after one of the states. Angie was in the Indiana room and Ezra, Bear, and I shared a big room named the Texas room. Folks called them staterooms.

Elmer and Buck helped us make a few trips to get the ore into the rooms. Buck toted a shotgun and he and Bear were a powerful discouragement to anybody who wanted to tangle with us. We got the gold locked away in the staterooms, waved goodbye to Elmer, Mable, and Buck, then settled in for a long trip home. The hard part was behind us.

I leaned against the rail as the riverboat pulled away,

watching the town of Dawson disappear into the distance. Angie came and stood beside me. "What do you think we'll find back there in Skagway?" she asked.

I hadn't thought about it. We'd been gone several weeks, but there were hundreds of new people going through Skagway every week before we'd left. It could have changed a lot while we were gone. It was something to think about.

CHAPTER 18

CALLAGHAN'S CHALLENGE

Black Jack Adams made it a point to stroll down the main street in Skagway every morning. He wore his tied-down Smith and Wesson every day now, even though he didn't like to advertise himself as a gunman. Skagway was still a raggedy-looking tent city, but word was getting out about the gold strike in the Yukon and there were more men showing up wearing pistols every day. He didn't like to do the dirty work himself, but Cap Light hadn't come back from the Klondike yet, and Black Jack had to establish himself as the boss around here.

The citizen's patrol still managed to throw a couple drunks in the stockade every night, but they were afraid of the gun hands, and Adams needed to establish himself as the king in that department. The rest would fall into line. There was talk about electing a mayor and maybe getting a sheriff, but he could usually bribe those people. Black Jack was an old hand at that.

Gunfire broke out—the noise was coming from a tent up ahead of him. Adams stopped to see what was happening. It was one of those saloons that seemed to be opening up every week or so. A man staggered out of the tent, one hand over his belly, a pistol in the other. He lifted the pistol slowly, then another shot from inside the tent drove him to the ground. Black Jack kept walking. He would have to get this sort of thing organized. He needed more people coming to the town—he didn't want them driven away by shootings in the street.

The next thing he needed to do, though, was to start leaning on the business owners to pay him for keeping things under control. He would do it like he had in Denver. For a weekly payoff, the leg breakers and gun hands would stay away from the businesses that paid him off. He would start with that woman's café and the saloon owned by Spencer. He had a score to settle there. Maybe, though, Cap Light had already taken care of Spencer up at the goldfields. He should know about that in a few more weeks.

The old man Moore was already caving in a little on all these lots he owned around this place. Adams had just moved in on a few of them and set up tents, running gambling operations and saloons. When Moore complained, Black Jack had made a point of pulling his coat back to show Moore the Smith and Wesson. Then he'd sent Callaghan to rough up a few of Moore's dock workers. The old man didn't have that kind of fight in him anymore, Adams was sure of that.

Finishing up his walk at the café, Black Jack strolled inside and ordered breakfast from the woman who was running the place while the owner was gone. The owner was Spencer's girlfriend, according to folks around the town. Black Jack's lips curled in a mirthless grin. He could make use of that information.

The woman running the place now called herself Lou. She was a tough old bird, but Adams could handle that. He would just wait to make his move until Spencer was back. For now, he just returned the icy look he got from Lou, ordered his coffee and rolls, and took a seat outside. He would keep this as a café, he decided. This place seemed to do a lot of business.

———

William Moore mostly stayed around the lumber mill now. It was the one place where he still felt safe. The wharf area wasn't too bad—he still had a lot of workers down there who were loyal to him. He had a bad feeling about the rest of it. He'd had to give up several lots to Black Jack, even though he legally owned them. He would still fight that in court, but it would be a while before this territory had laws that were enforced.

He'd seen these boom towns before. He stopped and corrected himself. He'd lived in a lot of these boom towns before. He'd started a few of them, including this one. This was what happened. Folks heard about a gold strike and came storming in. Most of 'em weren't prepared at all. Some made money, and they spent that money like crazy. When the highwaymen and crooks took over, it was time for the next boom, somewhere down the road.

Skagway was a little special to him, though. He'd seen the potential up there in the Yukon and had been here first, with money to buy up lots and start the town. He hated to give it up, but he had to think about his family's safety and his age. He sighed and moved outside the lumber mill, staring down at the bay. There was another steamer alongside the dock, with another hundred or two would-be miners pouring out.

He heard footsteps and looked over to see his son, John, moving up beside him. They'd had some sharp discussions lately, and he sensed John was unhappy with him for not putting up more of a fight against Black Jack Adams. He understood John's frustrations, but he'd seen what people like Black Jack could do, and he knew that neither he nor John could stand up to Adams or his thug Callaghan.

William waited for his son to start the conversation. John looked at the people getting off the steamer. He shifted from one foot to the other, searching for what he wanted to say.

"Are you going to just move away and leave this place?" he asked abruptly.

William, surprised by the directness of the question,

weighed his answer carefully. "I might," he answered slowly. "I might sell what I can sell for a good price, then fight the rest later in court." He paused to let that sink in. "What do you want me to do? If you brace Adams with a pistol, he'll kill you. If you fight Callaghan, he might kill you with his fists. A man has to think about those things."

John Moore blew out a long, miserable breath and walked around for a few minutes. He came back with a proposal. "Leave half the lumber mill to me," he began. "You can think of it as my inheritance. Sell the other half to somebody who will partner with me to stand up against Black Jack Adams."

The idea made some sense, William had to admit. He turned to look at his son. It all hinged on one obvious question.

"Who would you get to partner with you?" he asked. He glanced away at the bay, waiting for the answer.

"Luke Spencer," came the prompt answer. "If Luke comes back from the Klondike with enough money to buy out half the lumber mill, and he is willing to partner with me and fight against Adams and Callaghan and the rest, with my help, will you do that?"

William looked back at his son in surprise. He turned the idea over in his head a few times. He had to admit it—it just might work. He hated the danger involved for his son, but John deserved the chance to stand on his own two feet. He nodded slowly.

"Agreed," he said. They both stood in silence then and watched the activity on the dock.

By the time we got to St. Michael, we knew we were halfway home. There were some card sharps and hucksters trying to sell everything from maps of the gold strikes to miracle potions for whatever ails you. We had no problem ignoring those guys. St. Michael was a really quiet town otherwise. We relaxed for the first time in a while.

There were enough passengers wanting to get directly to Seattle that we had a choice. We could split up, with Ezra and Bear taking the gold directly to Seattle, or we could all go together to Skagway, and Ezra and Bear could take it on to Seattle from there. We decided to get the gold cashed in as fast as we could. The stampede for the gold fields was headed this way, we could tell. For instance, one of the steamboats that had just pulled in was owned by the ex-mayor of Seattle. He'd quit and bought himself a boat to get rich.

There were a few others loading their ore on the boat with Ezra and Bear. We had enough bags to handle most of ours, but the last load of it we had wrapped up in a blanket. We didn't feel too bad when we saw others going by with blankets, bedsheets, tin cans, and anything else they could think of to carry gold.

We saw Ezra and Bear off, then took another steamer directly to Skagway. Prices for the trip were going sky high, but we had the money and wanted to get home, so we just paid for it and took the trip. We had no idea of the things that were waiting for us in Skagway.

———————

William and John Moore were waiting for us at the Skagway wharf when we came off the ship. One look at their faces told me we had some bad news waiting for us. We exchanged greetings, but William put out a hand to stop Angie when she turned to go to the café.

"Maybe you could both come with us to the lumber mill," he said somberly. "There're some things we need to catch you up on."

We filed into the lumber mill behind the Moores. Angie and I exchanged worried looks as we walked. The excitement over our success in the Klondike fields was fading into the background. If we didn't have a safe, happy place to come home to, we would have to use that money to start over, which was something neither of us wanted.

William led us into his office and showed us two chairs we could use. John closed the door behind us and leaned back against the door as William took a seat behind his battered old desk. He looked from one of us to the other, as if undecided about how he could break the news he had for us.

"Do either of you know Black Jack Adams?" he asked abruptly.

My head came up so fast they were all staring at me. "Yeah, I've come across him a couple of times," I growled. "Runnin' into Black Jack is about the same as coming around the corner and finding a rattlesnake in your path. You'd rather not have to deal with him, but you don't dare ignore him or turn your back on him. Is he in Skagway now?"

William nodded his head unhappily. "He is, along with a bunch of ne'er-do-wells, crooks and hucksters that weren't here a few weeks ago. Some of 'em will probably move along to the Klondike, but I'm afraid a lot of 'em are here to stay."

William stood up and began pacing back and forth behind his desk. "There's not too much gun play, though there's some shooting at street corners and at the saloons every now and then. Adams wears a six-shooter and seems to keep most of those guys in line. Adams, along with a big galoot named Corrigan...Calderson..." He heaved a sigh of frustration and looked across the room at John. "What's that guy's name?" he asked.

"Callaghan," John corrected.

"Right, Callaghan. He threatens to knock your teeth out if you don't give him what he wants, and folks are scared to take him on. Black Jack has been demanding money from people to keep Callaghan and his boys away from them. Those that don't pay get a visit that ain't been good for their health."

He stopped and drummed his fingers on the back of his chair. "They've taken over a few of my vacant lots. I don't have enough men to stop them. I have divided the men I have—those who are willing to fight—between guarding the lumber mill and guarding Angie's café. So far, those places are still running without paying Black Jack Adams his extortion money."

William stopped talking abruptly and dropped back into his chair. Angie looked at me, then back at William.

"What about Luke's saloon?" she inquired. "What's happened to the saloon?"

William looked up at me apologetically. "Callaghan's taken it over. They're not really using it as a saloon, though they do a powerful amount of drinking in there. It's more like their headquarters. I think Callaghan's just waiting for you to come back and try to take it back from him. I'm sorry —I didn't have enough men to guard the place. All your whiskey and beer supplies are still here at the lumber mill, though."

I waved off his apology and stood. It was my turn to pace around. "How big is this Callaghan guy?" I asked.

William glanced over at John, who thought it over carefully. "About your height, maybe six foot one or two. Heavier, though. I bet he goes two-fifty or two-sixty."

I nodded and kept pacing. "Is he in good shape?" I asked next. "Does he do a lot of lifting or running, or anything?"

John shrugged. "No, he mostly hangs around your saloon, or goes around and threatens people. Likes his whiskey and beer, I'd say."

"Uh-huh," I said absently. "Have you seen him fight? Does he just come in uncorking big swings and try to finish it fast, or does he take his time and try to soften guys up first?"

John looked over at me, and I could see he'd caught on to what I was thinking. "He tries to knock guys out right away. He might tire out pretty fast in a fight if he can't take you out right away. Do you think you can keep him off you long enough to wear him down?"

"I can," I said. "Do you have any guys who can show up if I challenge Callaghan to a knuckle-and-skull fight? Guys who can keep it a fair fight?"

John broke into a grin. "We have some guys," he said. "I'll bring some guys. Just tell me when and where. After we get this settled, I want to make you a business offer." He looked over at William. "Dad and I want to make you a business offer."

———

Angie and I approached the café, and I spotted Callaghan right away. He was a big galoot, alright, every bit as big as William had said. He wore denim trousers, a checkered shirt, and a brown, dirty vest. His stomach hung out over his belt a bit, and his cheeks and nose were red, like he'd spent a lot of time lifting a bottle. He looked strong, though. I had to give him that.

As we approached the door of the café, he stood and walked over to block my path. Angie went around him and went inside, but he moved to cut me off. There were a few guys I had never seen hanging around that seemed to close in on us, but I could also see several of Moore's men circling us, too.

Callaghan held out one of his meaty paws to stop me. "You ain't welcome inside," he said flatly. "You'll have to stay out here and skip yore pies and cakes and such today."

A few snickers sounded from the crowd. I looked around. There were a few crates and boxes behind Callaghan, and behind that, several muddy spots where the ground hadn't dried from recent rains.

"There's something I need to explain about that," I said, holding up my hands and taking a step closer.

Callaghan's face relaxed, and a sneer spread across his

face. He looked around, enjoying the snickers he heard from the crowd.

I took one more step and hooked my left foot around behind his boots. I shoved him backward with all my strength, and he stumbled back into a couple of crates behind him. He tripped over the crates, turned and fell face down into mud behind the crates.

"What I'm trying to tell you is, I'll go into the café unless the lady says I'm not welcome." I spoke over my shoulder as I moved to the café door.

Callaghan came flying out of the mud and charged toward me, but Moore's men stepped in front of him.

I turned around and looked at him. "If you want to fight, we can do that. Not here at the café, though. I'll fight you in front of my saloon. Noon tomorrow?"

Callaghan was caught by surprise. He stared at me, then a laugh bubbled up from deep inside him. "Your funeral. I'll see you tomorrow," he said. Then he turned and stalked away.

———

Noon the next day came a lot faster than I wanted it to. I spent the night at the lumber mill, on the floor in William's office. I arranged with John to have some of the dock workers come to the saloon at noon. John told me they would be carrying a few hammers and tools just to keep things fair.

I climbed the street toward my saloon at exactly noon. Callaghan was there already, and he had a wicked smile for me when he saw me coming. I stopped several feet from the saloon, and a circle of men formed around us immediately. Callaghan stripped off his shirt. He had some fat on that belly, but he had some muscles on him, too. From where I stood, he looked immense standing over there.

I rolled up my sleeves, and we circled around each other slowly.

CHAPTER 19

TAMING THE TOWN

I circled cautiously, holding my fists high, wary of that one huge punch he wanted to land. I didn't doubt the power behind those fists. At the same time, though, I felt pretty sure he had won too often by charging in like a bull and swinging from his heels. I needed to keep him away from me for a little while and let him tire out.

I saw John Moore and Angie standing at the back of the crowd and a little at the side. Both of them were holding shotguns behind their backs. I couldn't suppress just a brief flicker of a grin. That was one way to keep the fight fair.

Callaghan saw that shadow of a grin and stopped prancing for just a second while his brain processed that one. Whatever he thought it was about, it got him all fired up. He bellowed and charged at me, swinging that right hand in a wide, looping circle. I sidestepped it easily and let loose a short, powerful punch with my left. It caught him on the right eye and snapped his head back.

His eye started to swell immediately. He stopped and shook his head back and forth to clear things up. He stared at me in surprise, but I guess he didn't learn anything from that first try. He loaded up the right hand and charged me again with the same punch.

I did the same thing I did before, sidestepping him and

throwing an even more powerful punch to the same eye. The skin above his eye split open and started to bleed. His right eye was really swelling up now, and within a few more seconds, it looked to be about halfway closed. There was a buzz coming from the crowd around us.

Callaghan paused for a second now, pawing at his eye and staring across the ring at me. I waited, thinking the only thing he knew about fighting was swinging and launching punches. He proved me right, coming at me again with another bellow. He came a little slower this time, raining in punches with both hands.

I backed away and covered up with my arms, letting him swing several times before I backed up and dodged away. He launched a couple more punches into thin air. I thought he was looking a little confused now. Maybe, I thought, he has no idea what else to do.

I stayed away from him for a couple minutes, letting him charge me, swinging those massive fists. He missed entirely with most of them, landing just a couple on my arms. I would have some bruises tomorrow, but he wasn't hurting me.

He bent over and put his hands on his knees, giving me a look of pure hatred. His chest was heaving, and he was pouring sweat despite the cold air and him not wearing a shirt. He shook his head back and forth a few times. Reminded me of a grizzly looking for some grubs. I was pretty sure he couldn't see out of that right eye anymore, so I moved a little to my left, where he wouldn't be able to get a clear look at me.

He let out another yell and charged me, swinging lefts and rights as he came. This time, I didn't back up or dodge away. I stepped inside and launched a short overhand right, smashing his nose. He let out a loud moan and fell to his knees, pouring blood into the dirt. I could have finished him with a kick to the ribs, but I backed away, giving him a chance to get up. I wanted to take him down with my fists in front of this crowd.

He came to his feet, and I stayed to his right, knowing his vision was probably getting worse by the minute. He charged again, and I moved to his left, delivering two hard shots to the left eye. He staggered and turned around, no doubt knowing he had to finish me now while he could still see me.

He came one more time. I let him swing a few more times, moving off to the right. When he turned to come after me again, I swung a rising left fist to his chin. As he staggered backward, I hit him with another overhand right. He hit the ground like a bag of sand and laid there without moving.

I turned around to look at Callaghan's thugs. They were staring at him on the ground, still not moving. One or two of them looked at me, then glanced away. My hands were both swelling up, and I was feeling a couple of punches he'd thrown, but now was the time to back them down.

"Anybody else wants some of what Callaghan got, now's your chance," I barked. They looked at the ground or shook their heads.

"Good," I announced. "Now pick up this piece of garbage here and carry him away from my saloon. If any of you have any of your stuff in there, you've got ten minutes to get it out. After that, it's my stuff." I turned away, then turned back as they picked up Callaghan. "Tell him if I see him making trouble again, he'd better be wearing a gun next time," I told them.

When they had carried Callaghan away and cleared out the saloon, I went inside and sat down heavily in a chair. My hands were swelling, but other than that, I was in pretty good shape. Angie leaned in anxiously.

"Are you okay?" she whispered. She picked up one of my hands. "I'm going to get some cold water from the creek to bathe those in," she said. "I'll see if there's any ice anywhere." She bent down to give me a kiss, then disappeared.

John Moore took a seat across from me, the delight

pasted all over his face. "Beyond anything I could have hoped for," he barked. "I want to make you a business proposition. Can I tell you about it?"

I nodded, then listened as he told me how we needed to be partners in the lumber mill.

———————

Angie moved through the café quickly, looking for ice, but feeling pretty sure she didn't have any. Sometimes, she bought some from one of the ships when they docked, but it didn't take long to confirm she had none today.

She picked up a bucket to bring more cold water from the stream out back for Luke's hands. There was a stream flowing by the meadow where she had put Clyde and Dale. Angie walked along a path through a stand of quaking aspen trees, happy for the green leaves and shade during the summer in Alaska. She found Clyde and Dale grazing at the edge of the small meadow and moved past them to the stream.

When she reached the horses, she heard a branch snap behind her and wheeled to see two men, guns drawn and leering grins on their faces, moving into the meadow. She moved around casually to stand behind the horses, acting as though she hadn't seen the men.

Derisive shouts came from both men. "Come on, girlie. We know you saw us. You need to come with us. Black Jack is down on the docks, waitin' for yore boyfriend to show up. After he's down with that, mebbe we'll move into the saloon and yore little bakery store."

Angie slowly turned the horses to face the two men, then raised her hands and smacked both Clyde and Dale on the rump. Startled, they plunged toward the men, causing them to scatter out of the way. Angie darted into the trees, then moved swiftly farther into the woods, stopping behind a thick tree trunk. She spotted a large limb on the ground and picked it up.

She peered around the tree. The men were moving more cautiously, looking from side to side, trying to find her in the trees. "Come on girlie, no need to drag things out. You'll come with us, and after ol' Black Jack has taken care of yore boyfriend, you'll have a whole new life. Mebbe you'll like it better."

They laughed sarcastically, then split up as they came forward. One was moving beyond her, no doubt planning to enter the woods from behind and work in this direction. The other was entering the trees in front of her, much closer and moving this way. She moved slightly, trying to shelter behind the tree, waiting for the one in front of her to get within range.

He came forward, still holding the gun in front of him, not even trying to pussyfoot. She forced herself to breathe as he came straight toward her. A glance behind her showed the second man was still a way off, just now entering the trees.

The man in front of her skirted two small trees, moving in a line that would take him directly past her. She slowly raised the tree limb in the air and waited. When he came around the tree trunk, she swung the limb with all her might. It connected solidly with his forehead, and he slumped to the ground, crashing noisily on dead branches and leaves. His gun landed on the ground by his side.

The man behind her yelled and fired a shot that came uncomfortably close. A small tree limb exploded above her. Angie dove and grabbed the gun on the ground. She whirled and fired at the second attacker. He cursed loudly and jumped backward, then ran, dodging behind trees for cover as he went.

Angie fired twice more as he ran. He moved away and deeper into the trees, not wanting to present himself as a target out in the meadow. She held her fire when he disappeared from her view.

The man she'd clubbed with the tree limb was stirring softly and moaning. He was in no shape to pursue for a while, so she took off at a fast trot, weaving through the trees. When she reached the café, she broke out in a run, heading for the Luke's saloon.

———

John and I had just shaken hands, agreeing we would partner on the lumber mill. I would see if I had enough money to pay for my share when Ezra and Bear came back from Seattle. I could have used Bear's help out there today, but everybody seemed to leave pretty quietly after I knocked out Callaghan.

I stood from my chair, walking around and flexing my hands. Angie should be back pretty soon with more cold water. Maybe I could get the swelling down with a little more time.

The front door of the saloon burst open, and Angie rushed in. She was carrying a pistol and seemed breathless. She dropped the gun and pointed out the door. "Black Jack Adam's thugs tried to kidnap me," she blurted.

I grabbed my pistol belt and dashed toward the door, but she held up a hand to stop me. "They're not out there anymore," she said. "I knocked one of them out with a tree branch, took his gun and started firing at the other one. He took off."

I stopped and stared at her in amazement, then buckled on my gun. "There's nobody out there now?" I moved past her and looked out the door.

"They're not there now, but they said Black Jack is waiting for you at the wharf. I think they planned to kidnap me to force you to go out and face Black Jack."

I finished buckling on my Colt, held my hands out in front of me and flexed them a few times. They were still swollen. I practiced drawing the gun a few times. It seemed to come out smoothly, and I could hold it comfortably. Not much more I could ask for right now.

Angie stared, shaking her head from side to side. "You're

not going to go out there and face him? He has others with him, probably. Your hands..."

John stood and put out a hand to stop me. "She's right," he said. "There might be others down there with him, maybe even ready to bushwhack you. Even if you take him down, there might be others you have to face. Maybe a couple others that want to fight you like Callaghan did."

I took out the Colt and checked to be sure it was loaded. "My dad used to have a saying," I told him. "He said if you cut the head off a snake, the body will die." I pushed the Colt back into the holster and looked at John. "Maybe you could take that shotgun down there and keep the others off me," I said.

John picked up the shotgun, and Angie moved to pick up hers.

"Maybe you should stay here," I began.

Her eyes blazed and her chin jutted out. "Try to stop me," she growled.

That was a fight I couldn't win, and I could see that right now. I opened the door and led the way down to the wharf. There was a small crowd near the wharf, but I couldn't see any of Adam's gang. I glanced overhead. It was noon, so I didn't have to worry about him trying to position me so the sun was in my eyes.

Black Jack was standing in the middle of the wharf. His black coat lay on the ground next to him, and he was wearing that ridiculous black top hat. He wore two guns, tied down, and he looked confident as I walked out on the wharf.

I came to a stop about twenty feet away from him and stopped, watching his eyes. That was something else my dad had told me. Watch the eyes. That will give them away when they're ready to draw.

Black Jack watched me, his lips drawn back in a thin sneer. He shifted his eyes to the right for just a moment. "Looks like they got your girlfriend," he hissed.

It was just enough to throw me off for a second. I started

to turn, then knew I'd been tricked. His gun came up and boomed, and I felt a sharp pain in my left shoulder. I drew and fired. His second shot burned across my side, turning me slightly. My shot struck him right in the belly, and he staggered back. He loosed a third shot that whined past my head.

I steadied down and fired a second time, then again. Both shots hit him in the chest. He teetered to the edge of the wharf, dropping his guns and struggling to gain his balance. Then he fell over the edge and landed in the water with a loud splash. His hat floated in the water a couple feet away from him. I took a step closer and saw that he was face down in the bay.

I dropped the Colt back into the holster, feeling some dizziness wash over me now. Angie appeared at my side, pulling off her scarf and opening my shirt. She packed the scarf over the shoulder wound to stop the bleeding, then saw the wound across my side. It burned, but it wasn't deep. She tore off a piece of cloth from the bottom of her dress and pressed it down over the second wound.

John Moore and two of his men walked past me, leaned over and pulled Black Jack out of the water. John was checking for a heartbeat, but I knew there wasn't one. After a moment, he and one of his men picked up Black Jack and carried him off the dock.

Angie finished packing the wounds and then wrapped her arms around me. My left arm wasn't quite up to a hug, but I wrapped my right arm around her, and we stood there for a long time, holding on to each other and rocking from side to side.

CHAPTER 20

THE LAST FRONTIER

JULY 1898

I stepped out on the back porch of our new hotel and took a look around. Well, it's only a partly finished hotel, but the people are coming through on the way to the Klondike by the thousands, and they're pretty happy for a place to stay. Even if it isn't completely painted and fixed up just yet, they don't seem to mind. I sat down and sipped my coffee. When Angie came out and sat down beside me, I thought about how lucky I am.

A year makes a mighty big difference when something as big as the Klondike gold strike is going on. The newspapers say about one hundred thousand folks have at least started on their way up here to look for some gold. A lot of them have turned back or will turn back before they get there. They say Dawson has forty thousand people in town this summer. I wonder sometimes about our old friends Elmer and Mabel, but it's hard just to keep up with all the new people pouring into Skagway these days. We don't really want to deal with all the craziness going on up there in Dawson.

Ezra and Bear came back from Seattle with twelve thousand dollars from our little trip up to the Klondike last summer. That was more money than any of us had ever seen at one time. We split it four ways, and then, somehow, we all stayed in Skagway. It all started with William Moore deciding to build a new house in a different spot, up higher in the hills. Angie bought the house he'd just finished with her money, plus what she got from selling half the café to Lou. We are busy turning it into a hotel, just like she planned all along.

I bought my half of the lumber mill with my money, then sold my saloon to Ezra and Bear and used that money to go partners in the new hotel with Angie. Well, it was enough to start a nice bar in the new hotel. Since Angie and I got married about six months ago, we're just calling it even. She still has the business packing supplies up White Pass with Clyde and Dale, and the lumber mill is doing great for me.

I proposed not long after that day last summer when I fought Callaghan and killed Black Jack Adams. I came out of that knowing that a man's life can be pretty short, and got right down to the things most important to me. Angie came in number one on the list.

Dad and Sherry will be here in a couple of weeks to see Alaska. We'll never pull them away from Montana, but they'll have fun visiting. The ranch recovered from that terrible winter ten years ago, and they'll always be at home there. Still, it's only a ride on the railroad plus a ride on the ship to get here. I'll show Angie the place in Montana next year, maybe.

William Moore has made and lost three fortunes that I know of, but that doesn't seem to stop him. He didn't get a proper filing on a lot of that land he bought, and some squatters pushed him off some of it. He says he'll get it back in court. There's more sheriffs and courthouses going up in Juneau, so maybe he will one of these days. He has an itch in him that might never get scratched, though. I see that look in his eyes sometimes that tells me he's looking for the next gold strike. I wish him the best.

Ezra and Bear made a funny pair to own a saloon, but they seem to do alright. Bear throws out the rowdies and makes sure Ezra doesn't drink up all the profits. Ezra makes sure they don't ever run out of liquor and loves to argue with the boat captains about how much he's paying for whiskey and beer. I go over and give them a pointer or two every now and then.

As for Angie and me, we know that Skagway will be our home forever. I know the rush will die down at the Klondike in another year or two. It's always like that at a gold strike. There will still be gold up there, though. It'll just be companies with machines digging into the hills and creek beds that get the gold. I've seen it happen before in South Dakota, Colorado, and New Mexico. Still, gold is money, and it will bring people through Skagway.

Angie went inside to make some breakfast and I stayed on the porch just a little longer. The country is growing up, and there aren't many people who've had the chance to know the west. Not the way my dad did in Colorado and Montana. Not the way Angie and I did, finding a home and a life in the frontier land of Alaska. I count myself a lucky man.

APPENDIX

Captain William Moore was a founder of Skagway, as described in the book. He lived an extraordinary life, much of it centered on gold strikes in Canada. While traveling through White Pass, Alaska, into the Yukon Valley in 1877, Moore became convinced that the area would be the site of a major gold strike! He bought one hundred and sixty acres at the mouth of a river on the present-day site of Skagway, Alaska. He began constructing a lumber mill and wharf in anticipation of the gold rush he was sure would come. He lost much of his property when the rush hit Skagway, though, as described in the book.

Moore left Skagway for one more try in the gold fields when there was news of a strike in Nome, Alaska. Afterward, he retired to a house he built in Skagway Bay.

The character of Black Jack Adams is based on real-life Western villain **Jefferson Randolph "Soapy" Smith II**. Smith was responsible for organized criminal operations in Colorado, and in Skagway, Alaska. He was best known for hiding prize money in bars of soaps and auctioning off the soap. Of course, only his associates "won" soap with money enclosed.

He arrived in Skagway in 1897 but was forced to leave town after setting up illegal gambling operations. Returning in 1898, he put the deputy marshal on his payroll, set up a fake telegraph office, and forced payoffs from local businesses, among other activities. He was killed in a three-way shootout on the pier in Skagway in July 1898.

The character of Angie Parker is based on real-life business owner and adventurer **Harriet Pullen**. Pullen, a single mother of three, arrived in Skagway in the fall of 1897 with only seven dollars in her pocket. She cooked for William Moore and sold apple pies to supplement her income. She sent for her horses in Washington State and used them to haul supplies for the miners over the White Pass Trail, as described in the book. She capped off her business successes by buying William Moore's home and converting it into a luxury hotel.

Wyatt Earp did, in fact, come to Dawson in the fall of 1897, but not to mine or to be a peace officer. He organized a faro game but wound up staying in Dawson for only a month. He moved north to Wrangell, taking a job as a peace officer for ten days, then spent the winter there. The river was frozen when they tried to return to Dawson in the fall of 1898. Earp then moved to Nome for a year before returning to the southwest.

The **Klondike** gold strike on Rabbit Creek came in 1896. It was later renamed to **Bonanza Creek**. The tributary **El Dorado Creek** did, in fact, produce a strike even richer than the original one on Bonanza Creek. Adjusting to today's dollars to account for inflation, it is estimated that over one billion dollars' worth of gold was discovered in the Klondike!

The population of **Dawson** reached around forty thousand people in the summer of 1898, when the flood of gold seekers reached its peak. Two thousand and eight hundred people came from Seattle in one week alone during that summer, but the good spots had already been claimed by then. Most went home with nothing, but a few got rich. Most of those who founded businesses serving prospectors did very well.

The businesses operating in Dawson really did involve all manner of card sharps, hucksters, and con men. There was a record of a newcomer, desperate for something to read, who bought a month-old Seattle newspaper soaked in bacon grease for fifteen dollars. There were clairvoyants offering to disclose the best sites for mining, and there really was a Trans-Alaskan Gopher Company offering rodents to claw through the frozen ground to uncover gold nuggets.

Readers will be relieved to know that no gophers were harmed during the writing of this book.

A Look At:

Latigo's Choice

In the heart of the American West, Latigo Smith stands at a crossroads that will define his destiny.

A deputy sheriff in Texas hill country, Latigo is beckoned by the call of his Colorado roots—a land now pulsating with the fervent excitement of railroads carving through the wilderness and the glint of gold and silver discoveries.

Upon his return, Colorado greets Latigo with more than the promise of adventure and fortune. Mysterious fragments of his family's history begin to surface, intertwined with the enigmatic presence of Joanna, a young woman whose path he was destined to cross. And when highwaymen try to rob him, he routs the robbers, making an enemy he'll have to fight to the finish.

As Latigo delves deeper, he stumbles upon an extraordinary tale: whispers of black gold, unlike any other gold or silver, heard by only a few in the lore of the West. This discovery propels him on a journey that blurs the lines between past and present, as he navigates a land filled with opportunities and secrets. What unfolds is a captivating story of life, love, and gun-blazing action across the American frontier.

AVAILABLE SEPTEMBER 2024

ABOUT THE AUTHOR

Patrick Lindsay came to Texas by way of Missouri, Canada, and California and has been proud to call the Lone Star State his home for more than forty years now. He retired in 2017 from "another life" as a CPA, whereafter he turned his hand to writing.

He has read just about everything by Louis L'Amour and first decided to give Western writing a try on his initial day of retirement. He has been writing ever since and loves the idea that so many people get enjoyment from his work.

Patrick and his wife Michelle live on a cattle ranch near Fort Worth along with cows, horses, chickens, and a very spoiled Great Pyrenees dog. He is an avid fan of the St. Louis Cardinals in baseball and the Kansas City Chiefs in football.